The Gable Faces East

The Gable Faces East

A Novel

ANITA STANSFIELD

Covenant Communications, Inc.

Cover inset photo, © *Lost Images,* Al Thelin
    Taken at The Armstrong Mansion Bed & Breakfast, Salt Lake City
Cover background photo, ® 1999 PhotoDisc, Inc.

Published by Covenant Communications, Inc.
American Fork, Utah

Printed in the United States of America
First Printing: August 1999

06 05 04 03 02 01 00 99   10 9 8 7 6 5 4 3 2 1

ISBN 1-57734-525-8

To Vince, my hero

PROLOGUE

South Queensland, Australia—1879

Jess Davies rode through the night with fury. His brief journey had done nothing but confirm a truth he hadn't wanted to hear. He could feel the stallion's exhaustion. But Jess almost believed the horse understood this need he had to ride fast and hard, as if the speed could somehow drive away his anguish.

Jess thought of his mother. He couldn't talk to her about this. Her fragile mind would never endure it. But the miles passed more easily as he imagined her at the piano. He wanted to just sit and listen to her play, or to breathe the smell of oils while she dabbed paint onto the canvas. He ached to sit across the dinner table from her, and feel the normalcy of life that had always been there, as if it could somehow dispel the horror of what he'd learned earlier today. He knew now what had destroyed her mind, and the thought made bile rise into his throat. He concentrated instead on the moonlit landscape as it became familiar. And he hurried on. He was almost home.

An acrid smell teased the night air. Jess reined the horse in sharply and checked the wind's direction. *Smoke.* He inhaled and coughed while the stallion danced beneath him, eager to run. With little urging the animal broke into a gallop, as if it sensed the panic that made Jess's heart pound into his throat, where it threatened to choke him.

Jess halted at the hilltop, and his little remaining hope crumbled to ashes. Surely it was his imagination! He was tired and distraught. A forefinger and thumb rubbed eyes that ached from sleeplessness and stung from the thickening haze. He blinked away the mist in his eyes and focused on a rosy luster gleaming against the black horizon, illuminating the night like a torch rising from hell.

"No!" Jess cried and pressed the stallion mercilessly. His home was that torch.

Jess expected to find the station in a flurry, all hands attempting to douse the fire. But a deathly stillness greeted him, broken only by the hiss and crackle of the consuming flames. A reddish glow reflected off the somber faces of his hired hands. Hopeless eyes turned toward Jess as he dismounted, posing silent questions that no one dared answer.

"We tried, Jess," Murphy muttered hoarsely, his blackened face streaked with perspiration.

Jess turned his gaze to the rising inferno and heard lumber crash inside the house. Sparks flew into the smoke-darkened sky and he stepped back warily, fearing the entire structure would collapse any minute. Sweat beaded over his face from the intensity of the heat, and he mopped it with the back of his sleeve.

"Where's my mother?" Jess asked, his eyes fixed on the looming fire. When no one responded, he turned loose the fury of his fears. "Where is she?!" he bellowed, taking Murphy by the collar to shake the words out of him.

"Richard tried to get her out," he cried. "We all did our best, but . . . it happened so fast and . . ."

"Where is she?" Jess shook him again.

"She didn't make it, Jess," Murphy croaked.

Jess stared in disbelief until the reality stormed through him and he fell to his knees. "No!" he groaned from deep in his chest, covering his face with his hands. "Please, no!" he howled toward the sky. But it was lost in the din as the roof crashed into the house, and the surrounding flames lapped higher in triumph.

Through the following day, Jess's agony subsided into a numb grief. Everything that mattered to him had gone up in smoke. By evening light he sifted through the barely cool pile of burned rubble, the ashes of his father's dream house. Despite the relief that his father wasn't here to see this, a part of him ached for Benjamin Davies' strength and courage.

Jess couldn't believe the thorough destruction. He found nothing recognizable that he might hold or touch to muster up a good memory. Wanting to be free of the nightmarish surroundings, he closed his eyes. But all he could see were horrifying images of freshly turned graves, and the unsightly burns that now defiled Richard, his closest friend.

"Why?" he groaned, and the answer pounded through his head with perfect clarity. *Chad Byrnehouse.*

Jess dropped a charred plank and strode with vengeance toward the stables. He wiped his sooty hands on his breeches and bridled a spirited gelding. With a racing saddle beneath him, Jess thundered over the miles of Australian terrain to where his land met that of Byrnehouse. The speed drove Chad's heated words through his mind: *I'll see you fail. You will never win another race. Your mother will regret ever bearing you.*

It had been less than two weeks since Chad had uttered his ruthless threats. Already Jess's mother lay dead, and his world smoldered in a mass of charcoal. Coincidence? Gut instinct told him *no.*

Sweat rose over Jess's lip as he waited in the polished entry hall. The evidence of wealth sickened him as he pictured what remained of his own home. Anger tightened his throat when Chad sauntered down the stairs, glaring at Jess with disdain.

"What do *you* want?" Chad sneered.

"You filthy, murderous swine!" Jess muttered as his fist connected with Chad's face.

Blood spewed from Chad's nose, but he recovered quickly and lunged in retaliation. Jess dodged to the right and grabbed Chad by the collar, slamming him against the door.

"Why?" Jess asked through clenched teeth. Chad didn't answer, and Jess slammed him again. "You tell me what I ever did to you to deserve such contempt."

"You were born," Chad growled, wiping at the blood on his face.

Jess pulled back to strike again. Chad blocked it with a forearm and hit Jess across the jaw. Jess fell back briefly, but his motivation urged him on. In his head, he heard his mother screaming as flames engulfed her. Chad doubled over from the fist in his stomach, then reeled backward as Jess struck his lower jaw. Before Chad found his footing, Jess knocked him across the side of the head and threw him to the floor, holding him there with the weight of his body, his hands firmly around Chad's throat. Chad struggled and gasped for breath, but Jess only tightened his grip. "I'm going to kill you," he muttered. "I swear I'll kill you."

Jess ignored the hand on his shoulder and concentrated on the changing color of Chad's skin. He fought against the arms attempting to drag him off, until Tyson Byrnehouse shook him hard and shouted in his ear, "Jess!"

Jess loosened his grip but remained as he was.

"Get him off me!" Chad managed to utter. "He's as crazy as his mother!"

Jess tightened his hold and shook Chad. He *felt* crazy. All he could think of was seeing Chad suffer.

"Jess!" Tyson took Jess by the shoulders. "Stop this madness. Listen to me."

Jess ignored the intrusion. He wanted only one thing.

"Jess," Tyson repeated quietly, "I understand how you must be feeling, but if your father were alive, I don't believe he would be so brash."

Jess met the eyes hovering above him as confusion pressed into his brain. Chad's father wasn't a man Jess liked, but he respected him. "What would you know about that? You hated my father."

"And he hated me, I know," Tyson admitted, a tinge of regret in his voice. "But perhaps he's been gone long enough for me to admit that he was a good man." Tyson spoke quickly, as if he feared Chad might stop breathing. "I knew him, Jess. I know he taught you right, and . . ."

A clear image of Ben Davies appeared in Jess's mind, and he relinquished his grip as if his hands had been burned. Ben's example of strength and discipline was the only thing that gave Jess any peace at all.

"And he loved you," Tyson finished with a breathy sigh. Jess lumbered to his feet as Chad fought to catch his breath.

"So he did," Jess said with a bitter edge. These people didn't know the half of it. In that moment he wished his father hadn't been so adamant about turning the other cheek. But personal experience had made Ben Davies a man who abhorred violence, especially for the sake of vengeance. Despite Jess's fury, how could he blatantly ignore his father's dying admonition to find peace with his enemies? The only enemy Ben ever had was Tyson Byrnehouse. Jess felt as torn as if he were locked in some ancient torture device.

As Tyson helped Chad to his feet, Jess noticed the sooty hand-prints around Chad's throat. He glanced down at himself and was reminded of the blackened mess his life had become. He met the glare in Chad's eyes and felt the urge for vengeance returning. He was almost relieved when Chad lunged toward him, ready to have it out again. But Tyson stepped between them. "You watch yourself, Chad," he admonished, "or you'll have me to deal with."

Chad backed down reluctantly, but Jess kept a wary eye on him. Tyson turned sternly toward Jess, and he felt certain he'd get a lecture. As a youth, he had crossed this man more than once.

"We were sorry to hear," Tyson said with compassion.

"Yeah, sorry," Chad smirked. Jess clenched his fists.

"Might I guess what this is all about?" Tyson asked coolly. Jess said nothing. "Is it possible you believe Chad had something to do with that fire?"

Jess's jaw went tight and his heart beat painfully. How could he tell this man his son was guilty of arson and murder?

"If there is another reason you were trying to kill Chad, just say so." Tyson lifted a terse eyebrow.

"I've reason to believe Chad's responsible," Jess muttered, "if that's what you want to know."

Jess expected him to question this, but Tyson took it at face value and turned to Chad. "Well?"

"Well what?" Chad retorted as if he didn't have a clue what they were talking about.

"If you had something to do with that fire, you'd best speak up now or the trouble will just get deeper."

Chad looked astonished at the accusation, but Jess caught the brief, unmistakable fear that passed through his eyes. "Oh, come now," Chad chuckled as if it were ridiculous. "You can't honestly believe that I would . . . do something so . . . *barbaric.*"

"I would certainly hope not," Tyson said, "but I'm asking anyway."

"Well, I didn't," Chad defended angrily, then he turned prideful eyes on Jess. "And even if I did, you could never prove it."

Jess mustered every bit of self-control he possessed to keep from attacking Chad all over again. Instead he turned to Tyson, knowing full well he'd protect his son.

"I don't think there's anything more we can do," Tyson stated. "We'll just pass this off to the rage of youth, and—"

"Pass it off?" Jess protested. "I'm nineteen years old! I've been running my own station for a year and a half, since my father died. My mother and two servants have been killed and my house burned to the ground. This is not some adolescent fight out behind—"

"Jess." Tyson raised a hand to stop him. "It was an accident. Things like that just happen. It's tragic, but nothing is going to change it."

"That's true," Chad chimed in.

Tyson glared at him. "Get out of here," he ordered.

Chad's eyes filled with defiance, but he only stared hard at Jess and skulked away.

Alone with Tyson Byrnehouse, Jess felt less than adequate. Tyson's stature alone demanded respect, but Jess was surprised to note that he met him eye to eye. Had it been so many years since they'd spoken?

Tyson slowly lifted a finger. "Leave it alone, Jess," he whispered. It nearly sounded like a threat. Was it possible that Tyson also had something to do with this? Jess looked him in the eye and felt sure he didn't. But perhaps he knew why Chad was so bent on destruction.

Tyson was quiet for a moment. He seemed different in Chad's absence. His eyes softened, and he spoke to Jess with grave sincerity. "There is no good to be had in irrational vengeance, Jess. It will always come back to you, and there is no pain so great as living with the truth of your own mistakes." He put a hand on Jess's shoulder, and the wisdom in his words was as real as the despair in his eyes. "No matter how unjustly you've been treated, if you start fighting fire with fire, you'll get burned." Tyson lowered his chin and added firmly, "And in my opinion, you're too much of a man for that."

Tyson patted Jess on the shoulder as if they'd just had a friendly chat at the track. His penetrating gaze pierced Jess once more, then he turned and walked away, leaving Jess stunned. The look in Tyson Byrnehouse's eyes was something he'd never forget. There was nothing he could do now but go home—if what remained of it could be called such.

As Jess turned toward the door, his eyes caught movement. Looking up, he noticed a pair of tiny legs, clad in breeches and riding boots, dangling from the stairs. The face of a child with short-cropped hair peered timidly between the bannister posts. As soon as their eyes made contact, the little girl scampered away, and Jess wondered how much she had witnessed.

The ride home dragged as Jess kept the horse at a gentle walk. While he contemplated the severity of Tyson Byrnehouse's words, thoughts of his parents clouded his mind. He longed for his mother's comfort and his father's sound wisdom. But reality had to be faced: Jess was alone, and he could only try to do what they might have wanted him to.

Jess had no idea of the time as he left the gelding in the stable and went to the bunkhouse. The boys were gathered around the table where they usually played dice or cards. But there were no games, no evidence of anything beyond mourning.

"Blimey!" Murphy noticed Jess first as he closed the door behind him. "What happened to you?"

Jess touched his lip and felt the dried blood. "Oh," he grumbled, "I had a little talk with Byrnehouse."

"Who won?" Jimmy almost smiled.

"I think I won the fight," Jess said gravely, "but I'm afraid I lost the war."

"Do you think he did it?" Murphy asked.

"I *know* he did it, but there's not one thing I can do about it."

Silence confirmed this as common knowledge. The Byrnehouses were wealthy and powerful, one being a result of the other.

"How is he?" Jess glanced toward the other room where Richard lay.

"'Bout the same," Murphy reported. "That stuff the doc gave him keeps him out most o' the time."

"Just as well," Jess mumbled and stepped quietly to Richard's bedside. Though Richard slept, it was evident that pain still plagued him by the way he moaned and writhed. Jess sat carefully on the edge of the bed and put a comforting hand on his shoulder. Gingerly he lifted the edge of the bandage that covered the left side of Richard's face. What he'd hoped would look better was worse. Jess grimaced at the thought of what Richard's life would be like as a result of this tragedy. It was one more reason to hate Chad Byrnehouse, and to wonder if he could live with letting it go.

"I don't know if you can hear me, my friend," Jess said in the most positive tone he could manage, "but we're going to start over. We're going to rebuild. And somehow we're going to make it work."

Richard made no response, and Jess leaned his face into his hands. He didn't feel convinced. The same gut instinct that told him Chad Byrnehouse was responsible nagged him to believe this was not the last of it.

One
THE TRAINER

1888

Alexa knocked at the imposing door and swallowed the fear rising in her throat. Turning to survey the scene from the porch, she grudgingly admitted it was beautiful. But the distraction wasn't enough to ease her anxiety.

Pounding again, Alexa wished they would hurry. She wanted to be done with this. As footsteps approached, she straightened her back and smoothed sweating palms over the front of her dark skirt. A grim-faced native maid answered and eyed her suspiciously. But Alexa had anticipated such a reaction. They were expecting a man.

"I have an appointment with Mr. Davies," she informed the gaping servant after an awkward moment of silence.

"Come in, then," the maid said in too-perfect English.

Alexa stepped inside and paused to admire the abundant staircase that rose from a polished entry floor. The house was fine and elegant, and she wondered about the man who owned it.

For a moment, Alexa was tempted to turn back. But this was her only choice. Silently she followed the maid to Jess Davies' office and stepped through the door, feeling as if she was facing her doom.

The most prominent feature of the man seated behind the desk was a pair of boots. Classic black and well worn, they were crossed at the ankles and planted directly in the middle of the polished blackwood desktop. Alexa watched one foot rotate lazily, then her eyes moved over long legs clad in dark riding breeches, hooked at the waist to leather braces. The sleeves of an old-fashioned, billowy white shirt were rolled up to the elbows. A quick glance at his face told her he was younger than she'd expected. Momentarily hoping to avoid any eye contact, her gaze was drawn back to those boots. They well represented Jess Davies as he leaned back in his chair, twirling a riding crop between his fingers.

As Alexa closed the door behind her, his boots came abruptly to the floor. "Whatever you need," he said firmly, "my housekeeper will see to it."

"I have an appointment with *you,* Mr. Davies," Alexa stated, relieved that her voice was steady.

"The only appointment I have," he retorted, thoroughly bored with this obvious mistake, "is to interview a trainer for my horses."

His tone dismissed her, but Alexa didn't waver. "Yes, I know. I sent you an application and you agreed to see me."

He looked dubious, but rummaged through the papers on his desk and declared, "This says Alex Byrne. If that is who you are pretending to be, then you have misunderstood this position altogether." His eyes turned hard, and Alexa stiffened. "I am looking for a *man,*" he enunciated with an arrogant tilt of his head, "to train my horses."

Alexa's courage began to falter, but she took a step forward, determined not to let this man intimidate her. There was too much at stake to back down now.

"Your advertisement didn't specify that stipulation, sir."

"Because it was obvious," he retorted, his voice beginning to show irritation.

Alexa leaned forward. "You need a trainer. I am qualified for the job. Surely you could at least talk to me."

"About what? The latest fashion?" He pushed an impatient hand through his rumpled brown hair. "I haven't time for this." His mocking gaze raked over her. "I need a man." He spoke it with finality and fixed his eyes on the papers in front of him.

Alexa resisted the urge to turn and run. Jess Davies was the only man within hundreds of miles offering any respectable work that she was qualified for. It didn't matter who he was or how her family regarded him. Without his cooperation, she would be homeless by tomorrow.

She placed her hands flat on the desk and leaned over, challenging him at eye level. He grunted in disgust and his green eyes narrowed. "I need a man," he repeated, so near that she could feel his breath.

Alexa stood her ground. "You need the best trainer in the area. That's me."

Jess Davies laughed and leaned back in his chair to put distance between them. "A trainer in skirts?" he scoffed. "What would people say?"

"I was under the impression, Mr. Davies, that you've never cared one way or the other what anyone thought." Alexa leaned closer. "Surely this wouldn't make your reputation any more questionable than it already is."

A nerve in his cheek twitched, and one eyebrow went up as he sat forward abruptly. "What on earth would you know about my reputation?"

"Enough to know that if I didn't desperately need this job, I wouldn't be here."

Jess sighed and wearily lifted his legs back to the top of the desk, contemplating briefly what this woman knew about him. For the first time in his life he regarded himself as a man with a reputation. But a reputation for what? If he'd been alone, he might have laughed. Could a social recluse, with no time to do anything but stay alive, possibly acquire a reputation?

Alexa could see him appraising her and wished he wasn't so blatantly attractive. With all the horror stories she'd heard, she had nearly expected a monster. In truth, he was everything she *hadn't* expected.

"All right." He waved his hand through the air impatiently. "I'm listening."

Alexa stood up straight and let out a deep breath. At least she had his attention. "I was raised with race horses. It's my life—my love."

"You can't possibly train a horse in skirts," he stated with a demeaning tone, as if it fully represented the problem.

"I don't intend to," she retorted, and again his left eyebrow went up. "If you had any sense, Mr. Davies, you would concentrate more on my abilities than my apparel."

Jess wondered what he'd done to deserve this. After all he'd been through, he had no desire to be confronted by this woman who was certain she knew exactly what *he* needed. And if that weren't bad enough, now she was insulting him. But he had to admit that something about her was intriguing. By her simple attire and desperate plea for work, he might have assumed she was a common woman. But there was an air of refinement about her. He couldn't fathom any woman having the expertise to save him, but he was curious enough to press this a little further.

"Just what makes you so desperate for this job? You don't look so bad off, nor do you look like the type."

"That question is impertinent," she insisted.

"Not if you want the job."

"If I tell you my reasons, what guarantee do I have that you'll hire me?"

"A lot more of a guarantee than if you don't."

Alexa felt cornered and knew he sensed it.

"Now you listen to me." He pulled his boots to the floor and stood. "So far I've seen little more than a self-righteous point of view. My first requirement of all my employees is honesty, and you failed that immediately. I don't know who you are or what makes you so certain I will die if I don't have you in my employ, but if you're not willing to be honest with me, you may leave."

Alexa drew a long breath. She had hoped to avoid this, but he was sure to find out sooner or later. "My name is Alexandra Byrnehouse."

Jess Davies sat down. His eyes narrowed and the muscles in his jaw went tight. The name affirmed her credentials, but it also brought some prominent questions—and emotions—to mind. He couldn't think of one logical reason to trust this woman. Except perhaps instinct. If she even had a clue what the name Byrnehouse meant to him, he doubted that she would have the nerve to set foot in his house. If she had come as one of her brother's pawns, she wouldn't be standing there looking as if her world was about to end. But still, he had to ask, "Why on earth would a Byrnehouse be asking *me* for a job?"

Alexa hesitated. She had no desire to tell this man things that were too painful to even think about.

"Well?" Jess abruptly leaned a forearm on the desk. "I'm assuming you are a sister to the esteemed Chad Byrnehouse." The name pressed through his lips with a bitter taste. "If I am wrong, Miss Byrnehouse, feel free to straighten me out."

"You assume correctly," Alexa stated, her hope dwindling.

"Then you'd better talk fast," he said with contempt.

Alexa cleared her throat and pushed her hands behind her back. She had no idea whether or not her situation would be to her advantage. "My father's will left me with no provision."

He laughed. "What on earth did you do to deserve that?"

"That is my business, Mr. Davies!"

"For someone who has to beg for a job, you certainly have that Byrnehouse arrogance."

Panic rose within, but Alexa covered it well as she retorted, "I have to fight fire with fire."

The words triggered a memory, and Jess felt sure she'd heard the expression used by her father. He squelched a painful thought and folded his arms. He wondered if taking her on would be worth the risk. The name Byrnehouse had a reputation for racing quality that gave Jess's present circumstances a glimmer of hope. And something about her made him want to consider this. She was so unlike her brother.

His eyes went back to the application she'd sent. He had to admit it was impressive. And if she was as desperate as she claimed, where would one so young—and pretty—end up if he turned her away?

"So what if I do hire you, Miss Byrnehouse? Who's to say I'm not asking for a fresh rekindling of this feud I've been trying to avoid? I'm not certain your brother would take kindly to your working for me."

"I doubt he'd care." She raised her chin defiantly.

"Clarify that, please."

Alexa sucked in her breath. "I've been disowned."

Again he laughed outright. Her fingers curled into a fist, and she fought against the words forming in her mouth. The prospect of working for him was less inviting by the minute. Only thinking of the alternatives kept her in control.

Jess pushed back from the desk and stood up. He turned away from her and stuffed his hands deep in the pockets of his breeches. His mind worked over elements of the situation far beyond the present.

"There is a race the end of next month." He pulled the curtain aside and looked out the window at nothing. "It will be held on my track."

"I'm aware of it."

Jess turned to look at her. "I want to win it."

"Doesn't everybody?"

He continued with a severe tone. "I have a jockey and a horse that are running in the five and a half. I'll take you on as a trial until then. If you win that race for me, you've got a job."

"But it's impossible to guarantee such a thing," she protested, not liking the stipulation at all.

"It's all how you look at it. Winning comes through attitude. If you want the job badly enough, you will believe we can win—and we will. Otherwise, no job."

Alexa guessed it was more an excuse to justify making her task impossible than a deep moral conviction. She looked at him dubiously as her relief was overshadowed by doubt. She knew her family's horses were better than his. Jess Davies hadn't won a race in years.

"I'll do my best," she stated blandly.

"I would think you'd show more enthusiasm than that," he jeered. "I just gave you what you came in here begging for."

"I'm grateful, Mr. Davies," she stated, wondering what she'd gotten herself into. But she needed a job to survive, and this was all she knew. She would just have to make it work.

"You should be aware of the provisions for this job," Jess smirked. "You can have a private room, but you'll have to eat and share bathing facilities with the other workers. I'm not in a position to treat you any differently than the rest of the men, and neither are they."

Alexa swallowed the reality and said firmly, "I would expect nothing more."

They agreed upon a salary with a raise coming if the race was won, then he offered to show her around.

"That would be fine," she said. "I'd like to get started first thing tomorrow."

Jess extended a hand across the desk. "It's settled, then." Her fingers slipped into his, and he wondered if he was crazy to be putting his future into such delicate hands. But he'd be the first to admit he was a gambling man.

Alexa accepted his hearty handshake and felt far from indifferent. He seemed amused by the entire transaction, and she didn't know whether to hate him or like him.

Their eyes met briefly. Jess felt it was the best chance he'd get to say something he'd been wanting to since she told him her name. "I was sorry to hear about your father, Miss Byrnehouse." He saw her eyes go wide and fill with moisture before she turned away. "Despite what you might have heard," he continued gently, "I respected him. It's incredible that he, of all people, would be killed in a riding accident."

Jess walked around the desk and took up a flat-brimmed hat. Alexa blinked back the tears and looked up to find him watching her. Did those empathetic green eyes belong to the same man who had just arrogantly attempted to degrade her?

"It was a tragic shock for all of us." She spoke if only to be rid of his expectant stare.

Jess opened the door and motioned her out, noting the slight bustle that swayed past him as she walked into the hall. He couldn't wait to see this woman take control of a horse.

Alexa stole a glance at Jess as he walked by her side. She wondered if he was really as abominable as he'd been made out to be. Despite her family's land bordering his, she couldn't recall ever seeing him before. And he likely hadn't known she existed. The name Jess Davies had always been spoken with contempt by her brother, and with a grudging respect by her late father. Alexa had no idea why. She only knew that his reputation preceded him. Still, Alexa made up her mind to judge him for herself. Neither her brother nor her father had done anything to warrant her trust of their judgment anyway.

They came out of the house by a door at the rear. Alexa was surprised to find one of the finest private tracks she'd ever seen, flanked by a series of buildings consisting of stables, a bunkhouse, carriage house, and storage barns. With the house situated on a hill, and the drive winding through a thick patch of pines, she had not seen these facilities on her way in.

Alexa followed Jess down stone steps that descended the rolling lawn, then over a well-beaten path toward the stable yard. "This is the main stable," he said as they entered. Alexa was impressed. "I expect it to remain spotless, so if you use something, put it back where you found it." Jess patted the muzzle of a nearly black animal in greeting. "This is the horse we'll be running. Her name is Crazy." He ran his hand down the length of her strong neck. The horse's muscles twitched at his touch. "She's my winner. I can feel it."

Alexa had seen better-looking horses, but she kept her opinion to herself, hoping the animal might at least have a winning spirit that could be honed.

Two men at the other end of the long row of stalls turned curiously toward them. "Come here," Jess shouted, motioning with his arm. Speculative glances were exchanged as they approached.

"This is Jimmy," Jess said, indicating a muscular native. Jimmy gave a polite smile and attempted to ignore the elbow nudging his ribs. "He does upkeep of the stables and gallops. This is Murphy," Jess added, indicating the owner of the nudging elbow, a rough-looking fellow with a sparse beard who grinned wryly. "He oversees the horses. You let them know what you need and they'll comply."

The two were obviously surprised by that last comment. Jess smirked as he motioned toward Alexa. "Boys, I would like you to meet Miss Alexandra Byrnehouse . . . our new trainer."

"Trainer?" Murphy growled skeptically. Alexa stiffened and Jess chuckled, only to be glared at by the woman in question.

"You'd do well to pay some respect," Jess added, putting a silence to their chortling.

Murphy looked dubiously at Jess. "You don't mean one of *the* Byrnehouses?"

"It's not a terribly common name around here," Jess answered nonchalantly.

Murphy looked Alexa over, then commented, "You don't look like a Byrnehouse."

Jess knew Murphy enough to catch his complimentary tone, but Alexandra's eyes reacted much as they had when he'd offered condolences for her father's death. For a moment he nearly expected her to cry, but she only reached out a hand. "It's a pleasure to meet you," she said resolutely.

Jimmy sheepishly shook her hand, and Murphy followed his example.

"Please call me Alexa," she added, and Jess lifted that brow.

"Come along," Jess said on his way out of the stable. He showed her the four-furlong track where two hired hands, introduced as Fiddler and Sam, were working at removing weeds along the perimeter. Sam showed no reaction at all, but Fiddler was actually polite.

Next came the bunkhouse, where Alexa met Edward, a tall man who seemed a bit more refined than the rest of the *boys,* as Jess called them. "Edward does the cooking," Jess said, "and any odd job the boys can coerce him into doing."

Edward laughed and greeted Alexa warmly. "Meals are at seven, noon, and seven."

"Thank you." Alexa smiled at the cook, noting that the bunkhouse was finer than most she'd seen, with a separate kitchen and dining area.

She wondered where the bathing facilities were. As if he'd read her mind, Jess pointed toward the back door. "The bathhouse is out there. Edward can schedule you some private time."

Edward nodded to indicate this was true, then Jess asked him, "Where is Tod?"

"Took Demented out for a run, I think. Should be back soon."

Jess nodded. "Tell him I want to see him. Come on," he added to Alexa. "I'll show you your room."

She followed him to the carriage house, between a variety of wheeled vehicles to an open staircase at the rear. The heels of his boots resonated on the wooden steps as he ascended and threw open a door with a flourish. "It's all yours," Jess said elaborately. She walked in and looked around. The room was small with slanted ceilings and minimal furnishings, but it was clean and she liked it.

"Thank you." She glanced out a window that overlooked the yard between the stables and the bunkhouse, where the drive ended. "It should be fine."

"It'll have to be."

Alexa expected him to say something more or leave, but he only stood looking at her. She felt suddenly uncomfortable as his presence seemed to fill the tiny room. She maneuvered past him with the intention of going back to the stables to get better acquainted.

Walking into the dim hallway, Alexa was met by a face so ghastly that she screamed and stepped back, bumping into Jess, who was right behind her. She was briefly distracted by warm hands lingering at her waist to steady her.

"It's all right." Jess laughed softly near her ear. "It's only Richard."

"I'm sorry," she said quickly, embarrassed by her reaction.

Jess chuckled. "Richard *is* pretty scary looking."

The comment didn't seem to affect Richard. He smiled warmly as Jess introduced him. "Miss Byrnehouse, meet Richard Wilhite. He helps with everything, especially keeping track of my mobs roaming the hills. He also occupies the room across the hall, so I'm certain the two of you will have plenty of opportunities to get acquainted. Richard, this is Alexandra Byrnehouse, our new trainer."

Alexa was surprised to hear a deep, refined voice. "It is a pleasure, Miss Byrnehouse."

Alexa nodded and looked directly at him, pretending not to be disturbed by his appearance. Severe burn scars covered the entire left side of his face to just above his lips. His left eye was useless, and the left side of his head was without hair where the scars covered his ear as well.

"I apologize for frightening you," he said kindly.

"Oh," she smiled, "don't be. I—"

"If you'll excuse me," he interrupted, "Edward's waiting for me."

Jess nodded, and Richard ran lightly down the stairs. Jess's attention followed him for a moment, then he turned to Alexa. "I guess that takes care of everything for now. Do you have any questions?"

"I don't believe so," Alexa replied, wishing she could ask about Richard. It was obvious Jess felt some responsibility for him, more than she'd sensed with the others. "If you would have the jockey meet me first thing in the morning. . ."

Jess nodded and hurried down the stairs. When he stopped abruptly and turned back to look at her, Alexa was embarrassed to realize she'd been watching him. Jess smiled as if he'd caught her at mischief, but Alexa kept a straight face. "Was there something else?" she asked tersely, but his smile only broadened.

"Crazy is very important to me." The sober tone defied his expression. "I trust you will treat her well."

"Of course," she said before he hurried on down the stairs. Alexa didn't turn away until he was long out of sight. She couldn't recall ever finding such an interest in the cut of a man's breeches.

It took little time for Alexa to collect her belongings and settle into the room above the carriage house. But it took great self-control not to fall apart as she turned her back on everything she had ever known and cared for.

At seven sharp, Alexa stepped through the door of the bunkhouse dining room. All eyes turned toward her. Last to arrive, she felt conspicuously out of place as she took a seat at the end of the bench.

"Miss Byrnehouse," Edward greeted as he set a plate before her. Alexa smiled and proceeded to eat, trying to ignore the brash conversations going on around her. She noticed a small man sitting at the other end of the table, eying her warily. By his build, she knew he had to be a jockey. Alexa nodded in greeting, but he turned away and made no acknowledgment.

Silently she tried to put names with the faces, hoping she had them straight. Richard was the only one not participating in the exchange of tasteless jokes. He caught her eye once, gave a slight smile, and turned away.

Alexa ate quickly and told Edward it was truly delicious before she left the bunkhouse, grateful to have it over with. Back in her room, she went to the window and looked out, astounded by the beauty of the view. Beyond the track were rolling green hills stretching into a high, blue range in the distance. Jess Davies likely owned the land as far as she could see, perhaps beyond. It was all so beautiful that she almost envied him.

Alexa's heart ached for Byrnehouse Station, with its vast acreage that was so familiar. It was the only home she had ever known. But Byrnehouse was lost to her now. Davies land had a different feel to it, a uniqueness that intrigued her. Did Jess ever pause to gaze over his land and admire it as she was now?

Alexa forced herself to clear her head. She prepared for bed early so she could get up and make a fresh start at her new job. By habit she knelt to say a prayer, then she extinguished the lamp just as a knock came at the door. Retying her wrapper, Alexa opened the door a crack, then wider when she recognized Richard.

"Excuse me," he said softly, making an effort to keep the left side of his face turned away, "but I. . . well, have you got any ink I could borrow? I ran out in the middle of—"

"Oh, of course." She turned away and left him leaning in the doorframe. "I'll get it."

Alexa returned a moment later and held out the little bottle.

"Thank you." He took it from her slowly, making her aware of the calloused roughness of his hand. "As soon as I get more, I'll—"

"Don't worry about it. I'm glad I could help."

Richard glanced past her. "All settled in, then?"

"Yes." She looked over her shoulder at the tiny room. "There wasn't much to put in place."

"If there's anything I can do to help . . . ," he offered without looking at her.

"Thank you." She smiled.

"Good night, then." He turned away and took hold of the door to his room.

"Good night," she replied and was about to close the door, but he turned back.

"Don't let them bother you," he said with a tone of empathy. "They're really pretty decent guys. They're just cautious. Once they get to know you, they'll ease up."

Alexa wondered if her discomfort at supper had been so obvious. "Thank you. I appreciate that."

Richard smiled again and went into his room.

The following morning, Alexa dressed in a white shirt, well-worn breeches, and riding boots. She stuffed her hair beneath a riding cap to keep it out of the way, and headed to the bunkhouse. With breakfast behind her, she rose from the table, determined to get to business.

"Which one of you is Crazy's strapper?" she asked, and all eyes turned toward her as if she'd demanded the moon. After a ridiculous silence she added, "Surely the great Crazy has someone who will—"

"I think that would be Murphy," Richard said, finally easing the awkwardness slightly.

"Me?" Murphy protested. "But I don't wanna—"

"You're the logical choice, and you know it." Richard rose and slapped Murphy's shoulder on his way toward the door. "Jimmy can help."

Jimmy grunted in dismay. Murphy looked around the room as if something might rescue him from having to work with a woman. He was answered with nothing more than a variety of smirks from his fellow workers.

"All right, Murphy," Alexa said in a tone befitting her position, "would you please get her ready and on the track as soon as you're finished here."

She walked out before any rebuttals could be thrown at her. But half an hour later, Murphy still hadn't appeared at the track. Alexa returned to the stable and found Crazy still unbridled. And Murphy working idly at some odd task. "What seems to be the problem?" she asked.

"I got other things t' do," he retorted. "I'm sure a woman of your know-how should be able t' saddle up a horse."

Alexa thought of a long line of retorts, but she bit them back. "Fine," she said curtly. Behind her, Jimmy sniggered like a naughty schoolboy. She turned toward Crazy's stall, certain her biggest challenge would be getting these people to take her seriously.

"Mount up," she ordered Tod, who was leaning casually against the track rail when she approached, reins in hand. He scrambled awkwardly into the saddle, and Alexa motioned toward the track. As Tod eased the horse forward, depression engulfed her.

Alexa sighed and leaned against the fence. The dread of a hopeless task overwhelmed her. She jumped as a hand grabbed her shoulder and Jess Davies said, "So, Tod my boy, how do you like the new trainer?"

Alexa turned and looked up in amusement, wondering if she looked so bad in these clothes as to be mistaken for the out-of-shape jockey. "Personally," she said as his eyes widened in embarrassment, "I think she could do wonders for this place."

"Uh, excuse me." He retracted his hand. "I thought you were Tod."

"I'm not," she said with an insulted tone. Rubbing her shoulder where the warmth of his grip still lingered, Alexa pulled off the cap, and her hair fell in a disheveled mass to the top of her shoulders. As Jess took notice of it, Alexa glanced away, knowing it was far from attractive.

"Your hair is short for a woman," Jess stated. Alexa took the comment as a polite way of telling her it wasn't becoming.

"I cut it to pass myself off as a jockey," she said, and his brow went up. "It's been slow growing back."

"I take it I'm not the first you've lied to."

Alexa glared at him, apparently not appreciating his attempt at humor. The sun caught subtle reddish highlights in her hair, and he decided that short as it was, he liked her better with it down, rather than in the tight little knot she'd had it rolled into yesterday.

Alexa challenged Jess's stare and noted the curls hanging down the back of his neck. She couldn't resist saying, "Your hair is long for a man."

He made no comment but she held his gaze, absorbing his appearance as she hadn't quite dared the day before. His rich, brown hair was short over the ears and combed off his brow in thick waves. As it grew longer in the back, it tightened into an array of almost feminine curls hanging over his collar; a striking contrast to the masculine cut of his jaw, the slightly cleft chin and hooded green eyes, all richly soaked with the sun. Jess Davies was slender and firm, and his shoulder came above her head. His presence spoke of vigor and gave an impression of tenacity that Alexa couldn't help but admire. Simply put, he was handsome. His hair was near the color of her own, but she wished she had his thickness and natural curl as opposed to her own blunt tresses.

Alexa's brief study was so intense that his brow went up in question. Embarrassed, she looked away. Surely all she'd heard about the contemptuous Jess Davies made her curious.

"Any problems so far?" he asked.

Alexa wanted to tell him that everything was a problem, but she only shook her head.

"Have you got everything you need?" he added.

She nodded and Jess sauntered into the stable, galloping out moments later on a high-spirited stallion. Murphy must have had it saddled and waiting. She watched with interest until he disappeared into the hills, noting his stature and the fine way he sat a horse. Reluctantly she turned her attention to her charge.

Two
ON THE BRINK

The day wore on with absolutely no progress. Alexa's request for help in any matter was disregarded, and the jockey put little effort into his work. She kept waiting for Jess to return so she could talk to him, but he didn't, and she wondered where he might have gone.

By supper, Alexa felt near despair. This would be her fourth meal with these blokes, who wouldn't even do her the justice of treating her like another man. She felt more like an oddity that was less than politely ignored.

Walking alone to the bunkhouse, she looked up to see Richard hurrying her way. "Thank you again for the ink."

"It was my pleasure." She nearly laughed, grateful for a civil word. "Writing letters?"

He looked surprised. "Nah. Everybody I know lives here."

Alexa stole quick glances at him as they walked. She could only see the right side of his face, and when he turned just so, the scars weren't visible, revealing an otherwise handsome man. His shoulders were broad, and he had an aura of virile strength. But when he turned toward her, the scars were gruesome. Alexa wondered what had caused the scars. And the silence he usually observed around the boys made her wonder about the man behind the mask.

It didn't take much to see that Richard was a kind and decent man. She was pleased when he sat beside her at the table. He made her feel less disoriented. But still, she decided that were it not for Edward's cooking, mealtime would be unbearable.

Through the window, Alexa saw Jess Davies ride into the stable. She immediately rose from the table and ran to catch up with him as he started up the path toward the house.

"Excuse me, Mr. Davies."

He grunted but kept walking.

"I think we need to talk."

"So talk. I'm listening."

"Could we perhaps stand still?"

Jess stopped and faced her abruptly, taking her off guard.

"Talk," he insisted when she said nothing. Jess looked intently at the breeches she wore as she leaned her weight onto one leg and put her hands to her hips. Was it the very fact that he'd never seen a woman in breeches before today that made him feel like melting butter when she was anywhere nearby?

"I'm having a few problems, and . . ." The sentence drifted into nothing. She wished he wasn't standing so close. He smelled of leather, and horses, and mountain air. All of it—combined with the way he looked at her—made concentrating difficult.

"Everything was fine this morning," he stated when she faltered.

"Things change." She snapped herself back to her purpose.

"Go on."

"I want to know how you expect me to win a race when I get absolutely no cooperation."

He looked surprised. "Clarify that."

"Your boys treat me like some simpering schoolgirl. My requests for assistance are met with cheeky remarks and sniggering."

Jess bent his head forward, trying not to smile. He didn't doubt that the others were as thrown off as he by having a woman step into their territory. He couldn't help finding the situation amusing.

When he said nothing, Alexa went on. "And this prize horse of yours is not in proper condition. Why don't we race Demented? He's a far better—"

"Crazy has potential that Demented will never reach," Jess argued adamantly.

"That could be. But right now, Demented is better trained and—"

"We're racing Crazy. That's all there is to it. You'll have to do whatever it takes to make her ready."

Alexa suppressed a groan of frustration and went to her next problem. "And this jockey of yours is ten pounds overweight and lazy. It's like you're giving me peaches and telling me to make an apple pie."

Alexa had hoped to give him an analogy he could understand. She neither expected nor wanted him to throw back his head and laugh.

"This is not funny!" she insisted. "I need some cooperation if this is going to succeed, and—"

"Now, Miss Byrnehouse," he continued to chuckle, "there's no need to get riled. I'll have a talk with the boys and set them straight. You keep working with Crazy, and . . . well, I guess you'll have to find a way to get Tod in shape, as well."

"How badly do you want to win this race, Mr. Davies?" she asked intently, and his eyes narrowed. "Let me clarify that," she continued. "How much support are you willing to give me if I give everything I have on your behalf?"

The question struck so deeply that it took Jess a moment to gather his wits. "We have to win," he stated with such conviction that Alexa felt a nervous twitch at the back of her neck.

"Then while you're out there talking to your boys, Mr. Davies, you can sit your jockey down and tell him that he will adhere to everything I say—strictly—or he will be out of a job."

"You're going to fire my jockey?" Again he eyed her quickly from head to toe. The woman had spunk. He had to give her credit for that.

"You're going to fire *me* if I don't win this race," she retorted, "and if I have to, I'll win it myself."

"You will do no such thing." His voice became edged with anger.

"If you don't want a woman to ride your race, Mr. Davies, then get out there and tell Tod where his bread and butter is coming from."

Jess was momentarily stunned. What made this woman—a Byrnehouse, no less—so willing to fight the odds head-on for his sake? His eyes narrowed. "You're really serious about this."

His tone of disbelief caught Alexa by surprise. "Aren't you?"

"Yes," Jess said gravely, "I am quite serious." But he had to admit within himself that until this moment, a part of him had already given up. He had told her that if she believed they could win, they would.

Now he had to wonder if he believed it himself.

After a moment's contemplation beneath the heated gaze of the most intense blue eyes he'd ever seen, Jess turned back down the path with Alexa right behind him. Like a silent pillar of sustenance, she hovered near him as he came through the bunkhouse door to find the whole crew in the middle of supper.

"All right, boys," he nearly shouted, and their attention turned from the food. "I have a word to say, and I expect it to be adhered to. I am not paying Miss Byrnehouse to saunter around and give you fellows a good laugh. She claims she knows her business, and she deserves a fair chance to prove it. There is no point pretending that we don't all know how important this race is. Think of where we'll all be if we lose, then keep that in mind when Miss Byrnehouse requests your assistance. You will heed her word as you would mine."

Alexa realized there was something going on here that she was unaware of. But Jess had been taken seriously, and that's what she wanted.

Jess allowed a moment to let his words be absorbed. "Any questions?" he asked, and got no response. "Tod," he bellowed, and the jockey's head shot up, betraying that he'd expected this. Jess glanced around, and Alexa wished the situation was different. It didn't seem right for Tod to be scolded in front of these men he had to live with. She held her breath, then sighed in relief when Jess stated, "I'll see you in my office as soon as you're finished here."

"I'll hurry," Tod replied, and Jess left at a brisk pace. Alexa wanted to follow and thank him, but she figured she'd pressed it far enough for the moment. She sat down to her cold supper and attempted to eat. No one said a word through the duration of the meal, and Alexa felt like an ogre sent to inflict hardship on these men.

Tod was the first to leave the table; Alexa was the last. She idly rummaged through her food with her fork, trying not to think about what her life had been like only days ago. She didn't so much miss the social life, or even the niceties she'd left behind. She was accustomed to spending as much time in breeches as a lady could get away with, and the track and stables had always been her playground. It was something deeper, less tangible, that made Alexa's heart ache when she stopped to think about the circumstances.

"Is it really so bad?" Edward's voice startled her.

"Oh, no," she apologized. "The food is really quite good. I just . . ."

She trailed off, and he finished for her. "You're just worried about winning the race, wishing these people liked you more, and realizing you hate this job."

"Are you a mind reader?" She managed a smile.

"Nah," he grinned, "just a cook."

Edward picked up a handful of plates and turned toward the kitchen. Alexa did the same.

"Edward," she set her pile of dishes on the counter, "what did Mr. Davies mean when he said to think where we would all be if we lost the race?"

"You don't know?"

Alexa shook her head and began scraping plates.

"Well," Edward wiped his hands on the stained apron about his hips and leaned against the big work table, "it's pretty cut and dried. Most of us are here because Jess needs us. He gives us a roof over our heads, food to eat, and no promises. If he wins this race, the purse money and bets could likely save the station."

"Save it?" she gasped.

"You might as well have it straight out." Edward folded his arms over his chest. "Jess Davies is on the brink of bankruptcy."

Alexa took a moment to digest this, then nodded toward Edward in appreciation for his candor. She walked outside, pausing to absorb what she'd just learned, not quite understanding why it affected her so deeply. It was obvious now why Jess had told her she wouldn't have a job if she didn't win; none of these people would. And Jess Davies would have nothing.

The station was beautiful, and Alexa sensed Jess's pride and belonging. He was a part of his surroundings; it was as simple as that. Her heart went out to him. She couldn't imagine how he must be feeling to have all of this hanging on the thread of a horse race. She didn't know whether to feel complimented by his faith in her or scared to death to realize what rested on her shoulders. Either way, she would give everything she had to win this race.

Feeling a need to speak to him, Alexa walked toward Jess's office. She lifted her hand to knock just as the door opened and Tod stepped out. "I'll see you first thing tomorrow, Miss Byrnehouse." He didn't look terribly miserable as he hurried down the hall, so Alexa assumed Jess had handled it well.

Jess was seated at his desk, lost in thought. He apparently hadn't heard her, and she knocked on the open door to make him aware of her presence.

"Miss Byrnehouse." He pulled his legs from the desktop and rose from his chair. He looked so tall. "Come in."

"Thank you." She closed the door behind her.

"Have a seat." Jess motioned to a chair and sat back down. He wanted to tell her he'd been thinking about her, but it sounded so trite. She'd only been here a day, and he was beginning to feel as if she was the center of his life. In a way, she was.

"I'm not staying long." She declined a chair. Jess felt panicked until she added, "I mean, I need to get some sleep. Tomorrow will be a busy day. I just want to thank you for your cooperation. It should make my job easier."

"We must learn to work together," he stated humbly.

Their eyes made contact, and she felt somehow uncomfortable. "Mr. Davies, I—"

"Why don't you call me Jess," he interrupted. "Everybody calls me Jess. Even my enemies."

"I hope you don't consider me an enemy."

"You're a Byrnehouse," he said, then his lips twitched upward. "But I think I can overlook that."

Alexa glanced down and pushed away the realization that she was no longer a Byrnehouse. She met Jess's eyes. "Edward told me about . . . your circumstances. I hope you don't mind. I—"

"I figured you'd find out sooner or later. Better that you know what we're dealing with."

Silence hovered for several moments, and Jess would have given a great deal to know her thoughts. She *was* a Byrnehouse, for crying out loud. And here he sat, putting his entire future into her hands. Had he gone mad?

"I just want you to know . . . Jess, that I will do everything in my power to win this race for you."

Jess cleared his throat. Her willingness was so evident that he near-ly wondered if she had motives he couldn't see. "Thank you," he said tersely, "but don't win it for me. Win it for you. You need the job, remember."

"Yes," she agreed, "I do."

"Then perhaps we're on the brink of some good luck, eh?" he added dryly, certain it was not something he'd be entitled to.

"Perhaps." She nodded, not deterred by the skepticism in his tone. "Good night, Jess."

He nodded in reply and she left the room, only to come back a moment later. "Excuse me," she said, and he raised a curious brow. "I have a rather bizarre request."

"Go on," he urged when she hesitated.

"Would you happen to have a piano?"

"A piano?" He wondered what benefit that might possibly have to her occupation. She waited silently for him to answer. It took him a minute to recall for certain that he had one. "Yes," he said, "I've got a piano."

"Would it be too much to ask if I might . . . it relaxes me to play, and . . . if you don't mind letting me use it—when you're not around, of course. I wouldn't want to disturb you, but . . ."

"I see no problem with that."

"I believe I could work better if—"

"Come along." He rose and moved around the desk, seeming distracted. "I'll show you where it is. No one else uses it. You might as well."

Alexa followed him down long hallways to the other side of the house. He picked up a lamp from a hall table and entered a room, hesitating slightly.

"There it is," he announced coldly. "You may come and go as you like. I'm rarely in this part of the house."

"Thank you." She glanced around. The room was decorated attractively in pale blues with a feminine appeal. Her eye was drawn to a painting of a young boy running across a field of blue wildflowers. She turned to Jess and found him absorbed in it.

"Thank you again," she said, and he looked startled.

"All for a good cause," he said tersely, and set the lamp back where he'd found it. He walked briskly away to leave Alexa standing alone in the hall, wondering what had caused the change in him. For a moment she was tempted to follow, but impulsively she picked up the lamp and set it on the piano. She lifted the cover and reverently placed her fingers on the keys. The piano was almost new. She wondered if it had ever been used at all.

As Alexa played a quiet Beethoven sonata, the tension of the day filtered away, giving her the hope that perhaps she could face this task and succeed after all.

🌱   🌱   🌱

Early the next morning, Jess found Edward in the cellar with orders from Miss Byrnehouse that the jockey and trainer would be eating high quantities of fruits and vegetables, and very little beef. He found some of the boys giving a fresh oiling to the racing saddles and gear, and the others in the paddock with Crazy, giving her a vigorous workout. But he couldn't find Tod or Miss Byrnehouse. After a worthy search, he asked Murphy where they were.

"Went for a walk," Murphy replied sourly. He hurried back to his chore so quickly that Jess knew Alexandra Byrnehouse had moved in and taken over.

Jess was about to get on a horse and go find this trainer of his. Of all things, to be out taking a walk when there was work to be done. Hearing a woman's voice, he looked toward the hills to see Alexa walking briskly, calling over her shoulder, "Come on, Tod. We're almost home. Just a little farther."

Jess watched in amazement as Tod came into view, looking miserable and exhausted.

"Good morning, Jess," Alexa called out brightly as she passed by with Tod close behind. The jockey gave him a dubious glare, and Jess followed them into the bunkhouse.

"Edward," Alexa called, "is it ready?"

"Right here." Edward emerged from the kitchen and set a pitcher and two glasses on the table.

"Ah," Alexa said while Tod collapsed on the bench, "looks delicious. Why don't you get a glass for yourself and Mr. Davies?"

Edward grinned and returned to the kitchen. Jess leaned his palms on the table and asked with a wrinkle in his nose, "What is *that?*"

"It's lemonade, of course," Alexa smiled. "Tod's very favorite drink. I promised him, with Edward's consent of course, that he could have lemonade every morning after our walk."

"Your walk?" Jess lifted that brow.

"It was delightful. You should join us. In no time we'll be running the distance."

Tod groaned, and Jess chuckled as he sat down and removed his hat. "Thank you, Edward." He took the offered glass. "I do believe I'll try some of that." He poured out a cautious amount. "Might I ask where you got the lemons?"

"You wouldn't believe me if I told you." Edward poured some for himself.

Alexa raised her glass toward Jess, then drank like she'd been in the outback for days. "Well," she started toward the door, "no time to lose."

Jess replaced his hat and followed to see for himself what Alexandra Byrnehouse was capable of. He would have expected a Byrnehouse woman to be accustomed to primping, simpering, and wallowing in wealth. True, she had been disowned, but she didn't seem too out of sorts with getting her hands dirty. In reality, he was amazed at how capable those dainty hands became when holding reins. A vague sensation of affinity tingled over the back of his shoulders as she mounted Crazy for the first time and took her around the gallops. The horse was spirited and eager to run by her own will, but Alexa maintained perfect control. It didn't take much for Jess to realize that she had not made false claims. She knew what she was doing.

The next morning, Jess came across Murphy and Jimmy hard at work on some odd contraption while Tod and Alexa were gone on their walk. Jess could see they weren't terribly fond of the chore, so he didn't ask questions.

Alexa returned with Tod to enjoy their lemonade. She left Tod to rest a few minutes while she went to see how the project was coming. "Oh, it's perfect, boys." She couldn't hide her excitement.

"I'm glad you like it." Jimmy gave an embarrassed shrug.

Murphy removed his hat and scratched his head. "But what is it?"

"It's a horse," Alexa replied.

Everyone squinted at the object, trying to visualize a horse in the structure of boards and nails. Alexa didn't bother to explain. She just retrieved a saddle and threw it over the middle. Those standing about were engulfed with expressions of enlightenment.

"Blimey!" Murphy professed. "It *is* a horse!"

Jimmy grinned. "I thought it was a horse, but I didn't dare say nothin'."

"It's the stupidest lookin' horse I've ever seen." Sam folded his arms stiffly.

"I don't know," Fiddler tipped his head as if contemplating rare art, "I think it's rather . . . intriguing."

Murphy grunted. "A little on the ugly side, but . . . What did you say? Intriguing?"

"It may not be pretty," Alexa stated, "but it works. Mount up." She pointed at Tod, who had emerged from the bunkhouse.

Tod hesitated, looking skeptical. Jess was quick to bark at the boys, "Get back to work and leave Tod to his training."

With a firm coercing from Alexa, and an absence of watchful eyes, Tod climbed aboard and turned his attention to this trainer and her bizarre methods.

Jess was impressed as Alexa got Tod comfortable in the racing saddle, then began intricately going over the details of his skills in a way he'd never done before. They spent hours working with his rein maneuvering, then hours with his legs and body placement. And Jess, who figured he knew quite a bit about this business, was continually learning something.

On a warm afternoon, Richard surprised Jess as he observed the session. "She *is* good."

"Yes, she is," Jess agreed.

"Would that be because she's a Byrnehouse?" Richard watched Jess for a reaction, and wasn't surprised by his glare.

"It could be because she has a lot of experience, and . . ." Jess's eyes went back to Alexa. "And . . . perhaps a gift."

"Whatever it is, she's certainly got Tod on his toes."

"How's that?" Jess asked, curious as to how the others viewed this woman in breeches.

"He hasn't worked that hard since you hired him." Richard gave half a smile. "But the funny thing is, he's enjoying it. That boy's warmed right up, I'd say."

Jess noted the two working closely together. "Yes, it would seem he has."

As they spoke, Murphy and Jimmy sauntered over to Alexa. While Tod relaxed, the group exchanged words out of earshot, then broke into hysterical laughter. Alexa comically kicked Murphy's backside, and Richard laughed too.

"Would seem Tod's not the only one warming up," Richard commented lightly. Jess gave a noise of agreement that made Richard look over in question. "Is something wrong?"

"Why would anything be wrong?" Jess snapped. "I have a wonderful trainer and everybody loves her. Looks like everything is perfect."

Richard ignored his sarcasm and took the comment at face value. "Yeah," he grinned, "it didn't take long for these blokes to see her for what she really is."

"And what's that?" Jess asked sharply.

"A hard-working woman who knows her business." Richard slapped Jess on the shoulder. "You sure know how to pick 'em, Davies. It seems our future is in good hands."

Richard walked away and Jess grunted again. As Murphy and Jimmy went their separate ways to see to Alexa's orders, Jess had to admit they *were* in good hands. But he preferred to keep to himself the fact that he hadn't picked Alexa. She had all but held him at gunpoint to get this job, and he wondered why he should be so lucky. At times she just seemed too good to be true, and it almost made him angry. Or perhaps a little leery.

Alexa watched Jess follow after Richard and wondered, as she often did, what went through Jess Davies' mind while he quietly observed her work. She'd gotten used to his nearly constant presence, but she wasn't sure if he found her methods worthy or not. Jess kept his opinions to himself.

As Alexa observed her employer, she could see nothing distasteful from her point of view. In truth it was quite the opposite, and she wondered why her family held him in such contempt. It was apparent the boys respected and admired him, and slowly she found their respect for her growing. Murphy was outgoing and witty, and almost gallant in his willingness to help. Jimmy was quiet but shadowed Murphy. The two were always together. Fiddler was humble and reposed, with a great deal of insight. And Edward was so enjoyable to talk to that Alexa often helped him clean the dishes just for the conversation. Sam was the only one that Alexa didn't feel comfortable with, perhaps because he was a little cynical. But she made an effort to treat him the same as the others, and there were moments when she was certain he accepted her as well.

Alexa shared a good working relationship with Tod, but it was Richard she liked the best. Though he was reserved and guarded, he casually slipped her an appropriate word of encouragement when she needed it most. Once she grew accustomed to his appearance it didn't disturb her, and gradually he became more at ease and willing to face her when he spoke.

As being with the boys became easier for Alexa, she began to anticipate mealtime rather than dread it. But the conversation around the table didn't compare to the occasional evening when they built a fire in the yard and gathered around it. The boys attempted to outdo each other with tales that got taller each time they were told. And Fiddler would do what he'd been dubbed for—break out the fiddle and play.

Alexa rarely wore a skirt, as there was hardly an appropriate time for one. In many respects she felt like one of the boys—something Jess Davies was not.

She wondered where he went at mealtime, and who he was with, if anyone. Alexa had never seen anyone, except a couple of servants coming and going. Did Jess Davies have anything in his life besides these horses, and the mobs of sheep and cattle out roaming the hills? The question began to obsess Alexa. She wondered about him at times while she lay awake at night, or when she'd pause from her work for a moment to study that big house he lived in, all alone.

Alexa enjoyed having Jess linger about while she worked. But she began to feel uneasy when she realized how much she looked forward to seeing him every morning, though they hardly exchanged a word. Jess was nearly always waiting in the bunkhouse when she and Tod returned from their run, but one morning he appeared before they started. "Hey, Miss Byrnehouse," he called in a particularly jovial tone, "why don't you just tell him to run and let him do it himself?"

"I like to run," she called back, and caught a seldom-seen grin as the sun glanced off his straight, white teeth. A giddy lurch made her miss a step.

When they returned for lemonade, Alexa wiped the sweat from her face and neck with her sleeve, then sat across from Jess to share their daily ritual. "Why don't you just tell me to train and let me do it myself?" she asked as he took a long sip.

Jess glanced up. He was tempted to feel insulted, but her expression was so genuine that he shrugged his shoulders. "I'm learning."

Alexa was surprised by the admission. "What happened to your last trainer? I assume you had one."

"He quit when I couldn't afford to pay him what he thought he was worth. But then, I haven't won a race in years. He couldn't have been worth much."

Alexa smiled and rose from the table. "Why don't you call me Alexa."

Jess watched her walk away, wondering if she ever sat still for more than three minutes. He followed her out, surprised to see Murphy leading both Crazy and Demented toward the track. "Alexa," he called, liking the feel of it on his tongue. She turned, but continued walking backward. "What are you doing?"

"We're having a little race. That *is* the business we're in, you know."

Jess wasn't amused. "What are you doing with Demented?"

Alexa stopped walking and put her hands behind her back. "I've made the decision to train Demented along with Crazy, so we'll have an alternate." Her eyes filled with determination. "We can race the fastest horse."

Jess's first inclination was to get angry. She was outwardly defying him and acted proud of it. Calmly he swallowed his defensiveness. "We will race Crazy, Miss Byrnehouse."

"A moment ago it was Alexa."

"A moment ago you were agreeable."

"Mr. Davies," she leaned forward, "I work according to logic. Crazy will race when Crazy can beat Demented."

She turned to walk away before he could retort, but he wasn't about to let her have the last word. Abruptly he grabbed her arm and forced her to stop.

Alexa looked scornfully to where his fingers bit into her arm, then she wrenched out of his grip. "If you have something to say, Mr. Davies, just say it."

She saw his eyes flicker and knew he was aware of the boys hovering nearby. She was sure he wouldn't allow her to talk him down in front of these men, but neither would she let him belittle her. Their respect was something she'd worked hard to earn, and she would not let it go so easily.

"We will race Crazy," he said with finality. "If you've got a problem with that, go work for somebody else."

"Mr. Davies," she tilted her head slightly, "you hired me on the condition that I win this race. I'm not sure I can win it with Crazy at this point in time. You can't have it both ways."

"Are we discussing apples and peaches again?" She winced from the degradation in his tone.

"We are talking about gambling, Mr. Davies. When a man is putting everything he owns on a single bet, he'd do well to play his cards right."

Alexa saw the anger flash in his eyes, but she would have been disappointed if he hadn't jumped to defend what he was fighting for.

"I will do *anything*," he lifted a fist in front of her and spoke through clenched teeth, "to keep what is mine, Miss Byrnehouse. That is exactly why we will race Crazy. She is the only chance we've got."

"All right," Alexa lifted her chin, "if Crazy is such a wonderful horse, perhaps you wouldn't be opposed to having a little race of our own. Just you and me, Jess." Her voice softened in challenge. "I'll lay my odds on Demented."

Jess studied her determined expression. He felt as if she was challenging him to a duel and inviting him to choose his weapon. Well, if she wanted a challenge, so be it.

"All right, Alexandra. I'll play your game, but we'll play it on my terms. First of all, this will be no track race." He pointed toward the stretch of flat land opposite the stable yard. "We'll ride east. And secondly, it's obvious that I'm at a disadvantage. For one thing, you weigh less."

Alexa took in the width of his shoulders and his muscular frame that stood a head taller. Doing her best to imitate an appraising gaze she'd learned from him during their first interview, she looked him over thoroughly and smirked. "That's true," she agreed and heard a snigger from one of the boys.

"With that in mind," Jess said, ignoring anything but his purpose, "you should be able to discern from your professional expertise which is the better horse. Tomorrow," he lifted a finger, "right after breakfast."

Jess walked away, pausing to glare at the hovering spectators. "If you can't find anything to do," he snarled, "clean out the bunkhouse.

I walked in there this morning and nearly passed out. It smells like somebody died in there."

"Oh, that's just the dirty laundry," Jimmy reported, as if that made it acceptable. His dark face broke into a wide, white grin.

"Then wash it," Jess said tersely. "We're raising horses here, not swine."

Alexa watched Jess walk toward the house and wondered what she'd gotten herself into. She didn't realize how her aura must have changed in his absence until Fiddler startled her.

"You okay, Missy?"

She looked at him in surprise. "Yes, of course. Give the horses a little exercise, then let them rest." She glanced in the direction Jess had gone. "They're going to need it."

Three
RUNNING CRAZY

"I hear we're having a little race in the morning."

Jess looked up to see Richard leaning in the doorway of his office.

"Is betting allowed?" Richard added lightly when Jess only glared at him.

"No!" he snapped.

"That's a relief." Richard sat down and stretched out his legs. "I'd hate to tell you who my money would be riding on."

"Did you come to cheer me up, or what?" Jess asked, resting his chin on a clenched fist.

"I came to offer a little friendly advice . . . unless you don't want any."

"I need all the help I can get." Jess leaned back and lazily stacked his boots on the desk.

While Richard contemplated his words, Jess idly tapped his riding crop against the toe of his boot.

"You'd do well to pay attention to that woman," Richard stated, and the tapping ceased.

"Listen, Wilhite. You know as well as I do why it has to be Crazy."

"Yes, but does she?"

Jess looked away abruptly.

"Maybe if you were honest with her, she'd be more willing to trust your judgment. After all, I do." Richard crossed an ankle over his knee. "But then, I'm not the one with the know-how that could either save or destroy us." Jess looked up, a defensive spark dancing in his eyes. Richard pressed it further. "Face it. You put all of our lives into her hands when you hired her. I'm sure you must have trusted her or you wouldn't have done it. But trust can't go halfway, Jess."

"She works for me, Richard. If she does what I tell her, we might make it through this."

Richard could see his advice had fallen on deaf ears. He knew Jess respected Alexa's abilities because he'd seen it. And when it came down to the bare facts, Jess would likely be humble enough to admit that he needed her. But was it her being a woman, or a Byrnehouse, that held him back? It was tempting to scold Jess for being so prideful, but it had been so long since he'd exhibited any pride at all that Richard couldn't fault him now. Whether Jess realized it or not, Alexa's determination had already begun to change him. There was a long-absent hope in his eyes. And with any luck, Jess's competitive spirit would be stimulated just enough to make him realize that Alexa was fighting on his side.

"Just thought I'd mention it." Richard stood and turned to leave.

"Richard," Jess stopped him, "just between you and me . . . what do you think of her . . . really?"

"I assume you want honesty." Richard smiled wryly.

"No, I want you to lie to me and make me feel better," Jess retorted with sarcasm.

"I won't lie to you," Richard said, "but I *can* make you feel better." He folded his arms and leaned his weight onto one foot. "She's the best thing that's happened to any of us since we lost Emma."

Jess hung his head and sighed. "No one could ever replace my mother, Richard."

Richard laughed. "I don't think Alexa wants to be your mother, Jess. She just wants to win your race."

Jess chuckled dubiously, wondering what this woman did to win such undying approval— especially from a man like Richard, who had once stated that no woman was worth more than a good night and a good time.

"The problem is," Richard added, "you're the only one who hasn't accepted it."

"Accepted what?" Jess laughed. "That she doesn't want to be my mother?"

Richard looked at the ceiling in feigned disgust. He pointed a finger at Jess. "She's the best thing that's ever happened to us."

Once alone, Jess groaned. He turned in his chair and threw his riding crop at the wall in a fit of frustration. How could he admire her so much and be so afraid of her at the same time? Richard was right. She could either save or destroy them—and at the moment he felt powerless to stop it either way.

❦   ❦   ❦

Alexa picked nervously at her breakfast. The boys hurried through it then went to the stable in a mob, joking about the odds on this morning's grand event. Only Tod paused to speak to her. "I sure hope you win, Alexa. I'd rather ride Demented."

"Whether I win or not," Alexa said dryly, "I have a feeling you won't get your way."

Edward chortled as he stacked plates. "She is a smart one." He nodded to Tod, who walked out looking dismayed.

Alexa gave Edward a sidelong glance. "You all think I'm crazy, don't you."

"Crazy?" He laughed. "Nah, we think Jess could use a run for his money." He lifted his brows comically. "But then, you gotta learn who's boss."

Alexa sighed and looked around to find only Richard remaining. "Go ahead. You might as well let me have it, too."

"What?" He laughed as he stood, lifting his legs over the bench then putting one foot onto it. "I admire what you're doing, Alexa. And believe it or not," he pointed at her quickly, "I think Jess does, too."

"I don't know about that." She stood and brushed her hands together. "But I'll guarantee one thing. If nothing else, when this is over he's going to respect me."

Alexa went to the stable and found Crazy and Demented saddled and ready to go. While she greeted the horses with whispered words, she noted the saddle on Crazy was custom-made for racing and looked about right to accommodate Jess Davies. She was just wondering what kind of horseman he might be when a hush fell over the boys. She looked up to see Jess in the doorway, the sun at his back, his stance wide. He tapped a riding crop against his thigh.

"Good morning, boys," he said jovially. Then he nodded toward Alexa, "Miss Byrnehouse."

The boys started up their bantering again as Jess sauntered in. "I thought I told you no bets," he scolded.

"Oh, we wasn't bettin'," Murphy grinned wryly. "We was just speculatin'."

Jess scowled and put his foot in the stirrup.

"Just for the sake of it," Fiddler said as he handed up Crazy's reins, "who would you lay your odds on?"

Jess nearly disregarded the question, but something about Richard's advice compelled him to say, "I'd put my money on Miss Byrnehouse if I were you."

She looked up in surprise as Jess situated himself in the saddle. His eyes briefly delved into hers, and she caught a glimpse of the respect she was seeking.

"As far as horses go," he added, "I suppose that's a matter of opinion."

Alexa nodded slightly in appreciation of the comment, then jumped onto Demented's back. Crazy snorted and danced impatiently while Jess held the reins lax in one hand and kept his eyes on Alexa. She looked so delicate in contrast to the muscular stallion. It was almost unnatural the way her tiny hands controlled him so perfectly. Their eyes met, and he nearly expected someone to call off paces then order them to turn and fire. She smiled deviously, then bent forward to whisper something in Demented's ear.

"Are you ready?" he asked when she had apparently finished.

"Not yet." She sidled up next to Crazy and bent close to her ear. Jess almost believed the horses were paying attention as Crazy snorted and tried to bolt forward. Jess gazed dubiously at Alexa as she made herself comfortable and eased Demented forward.

"Be careful, Jess," Murphy called as they trotted past a cluster of trees to the indicated starting point.

"Yeah," Jimmy added, "don't fall off and break somethin'."

Like his pride, Alexa thought.

"Ah, shut up," Jess called over his shoulder and took the reins into both hands. Alexa looked over to see if he was ready. She was surprised to see him smile.

"All right, Alexandra Byrnehouse, let's see what you've got to offer."

"More than you'll ever be able to handle," she said lightly and leaned into a starting position.

"Ready?" he asked.

"You say when."

Jess took a deep breath. "Go," he muttered, and it began. He hadn't contemplated what to expect, but riding neck and neck with a cloud of Australia flying behind them, Jess looked over at Alexa and felt a thrill unlike anything he'd ever known. She was incredible! With the wind in her hair and fire in her eyes, she became a part of the horse, the two flying as one like the eye of a storm. She looked over at him and smiled as if they were strolling down a garden path. Jess grinned in return, then impulsively tapped her leg with his riding crop and eased ahead a little. He barely heard her laugh amidst the thundering hooves. He could feel Crazy's will battling his, and he knew that what Alexa had said was true. The horse had spirit, but it needed taming and guidance.

Jess glanced over his shoulder to see her sidle up next to him. She smiled with a triumph in her eyes that he didn't understand until she shifted just slightly, leaned forward a little more, and put her entire concentration to the horse beneath her and the ground ahead. A moment later, she disappeared in a cloud of dust.

Jess wanted to be angry, but instead he laughed and let up on the reins. She'd proven her point, though he couldn't say for sure what it was. But when the dust cleared, she was nowhere in sight.

Alexa glanced back only once and laughed, wishing she could see his face. She rode at a full gallop until she realized she was on Byrnehouse land. Feeling uneasy, she slowed Demented and began to circle back when she saw a horseman approaching. For a moment she thought it was Jess, but she knew he couldn't possibly have gained enough to be coming from that direction. Squinting to get a better look, her heart began to thud. *It was Chad.* The odd thing was that he seemed to be waiting for her. But how could he have known she'd be here now?

Alexa attempted to bolt past him. But he lurched in front of her abruptly, and she had to fight to stay in the saddle when Demented reared back.

"What do you want?" she hissed when he grabbed the reins before she had a chance to regain control.

"I'm wondering what you're doing on my land," he sneered, and hauled her down from the horse.

Alexa looked around quickly, wondering where Jess was. "Yes," she said sarcastically, stepping back to put distance between them, "I'll bet you were just terribly concerned that I might chew up a little of *your* dust."

"What are you doing here, Alexa?" he demanded.

"I'm riding," she snapped.

"So I see." He glanced at Demented, his eyes lingering on the brand. "A Davies stallion, of all things."

"What I do is none of your business."

"Alexa," he looked at her in disgust, "how could you be so stupid?"

"What do you care? Just where did you think I would go?"

"I don't know, but not to Jess Davies. Seriously, Alexa, what kind of insanity has gotten into you?"

"I needed a job. He had one to offer."

"Yes," Chad smirked, pushing an arrogant hand into his dark, short-cropped hair, "I'll bet he did. But tell me, Alexa, is he as good as they say?"

"I don't know what you're talking about," she said quite honestly.

Chad stepped forward and looked at her smugly. "You're no better than your mother."

"She was your mother, too," Alexa retaliated, wondering what he was implying.

"Yes, but at least I know who my father is."

Alexa bit back the pain, determined not to let him see it. "You might have his blood, but we both know which of us he trusted. Is that why you were so anxious to be rid of me? Couldn't bear the thought of your father loving me?"

Chad grunted begrudgingly, then gave an almost wicked smile. "Yes, that was evident in his will."

Alexa clenched her fists but said nothing.

"Actually," he added, "there are other more important reasons why you would have gotten in the way. But that's not what I want to talk to you about."

"Then get on with it," she insisted, wondering where Jess was. Crazy couldn't be *that* slow!

"You should have left here, Alexa. You're not doing any of us any good by staying in the area."

"Is that a threat?"

"It's a suggestion. You'd do better with someone else. I don't think Jess Davies is your type. Get on a train and go away."

"Jess Davies is a good man, Chad, despite what you might think. He's giving me a chance, and I'm taking it."

Chad's voice lowered and his eyes turned hard. "You have no idea what Jess is, or you wouldn't have even considered this madness." His chin jutted forward. "Let me repeat myself. He's not your type. The man's a coward and a cheat."

Knowing Chad as she did, Alexa wondered what kind of threat she might be to him as long as she was in Jess's employ. In light of the upcoming race, it wasn't difficult to figure. But she'd always gotten the impression that Chad had little faith in her abilities. More determined than ever not to let her brother do her in, Alexa drew up her chin and retorted in Jess's defense, "He is more of a man than you'll ever be."

"Oh," he smirked, "so that's it, eh? Is it your mother's wanton blood that makes you go to the neighbors in search of a warm bed? Do you—"

Alexa slapped him before he could finish, but she wasn't prepared for his immediate retaliation. Chad backhanded her across the face with such force that she barely clung to consciousness. She didn't know Jess had arrived and dismounted until she fell at his feet.

Jess glared at Chad, who wore an arrogant smirk. Alexa groaned and attempted to find her equilibrium as the ground swam too close to her face. Jess's booted leg was the only thing that kept it from swallowing her.

Appalled at the scene he'd come upon, Jess wished he'd followed his impulse to intervene before the hands started flying. He was itching to let Chad have it, but he knew from experience it would only spur Chad to further violence. Alexa groaned again and Jess bent to help her, keeping a wary eye on Chad. "Are you all right?" he whispered.

"I will be," she muttered. He put his hands beneath her arms and hoisted her up, keeping a supportive arm around her.

"That's just like you, Byrnehouse," Jess said stiffly, "to hit a woman—your own sister, no less."

"Yeah, well," Chad said, disregarding the comment, "it's just like you to need a Byrnehouse to bail you out." He mounted his horse and looked down with disdain. "You're not a very smart man, Jess. Before this is over, you could regret that she ever walked through your door." As he turned away he added, "You'd do well to get rid of her now."

Alexa watched Chad ride away, dilemma pounding through her head with such force that she wanted to die. When Chad was gone from view, she slumped wearily and would have fallen if Jess hadn't caught her.

"Whoa," he said lightly and steadied her against him. She looked up, and he knew her weakness was not entirely physical. He tried for a moment to imagine how she must be feeling, and he wasn't surprised to see moisture rising in her eyes.

Alexa looked down and tried to move away, embarrassed and afraid. But Jess kept his arm firmly around her, and she couldn't deny being grateful.

"Are you all right?" Jess asked again, and she wondered why he sounded so kind. Hadn't he heard what Chad just said?

"Yes, I'm fine," she insisted, though she made no attempt to stand on her own.

"We'd best get you home," he said gently, and she gave a satirical laugh. How could she call anyplace home? "Come along." He lifted her into his arms and carried her to where he'd tethered the horses.

"Put me down," she pleaded. "I am perfectly capable of getting on a horse, Mr. Davies."

"Yes," he hoisted her up, "I'm well aware of your capabilities, Miss Byrnehouse." Jess secured Crazy's reins to Demented's saddle and mounted behind Alexa.

"What are you doing?" She tried to sound insistent while stars swam before her eyes.

Jess pushed one arm around her waist and took the reins into his other hand. "I'm going to make sure you get home without another black eye." He urged the horse into an easy gallop.

Alexa fought with the pain in her head until she had no choice but to lean back against Jess's firm chest.

"You okay?" he asked.

"Just a little dizzy," she admitted. "Jess, we have to talk."

He hesitated, contemplating what she meant. "There's nothing to talk about."

"Didn't you hear what he said?"

"I heard him."

When he said nothing more she added gravely, "I should leave."

"And where would you go?"

"I don't know," she nearly shouted, "but I can't stay!" Alexa hung her head forward. "I'm sorry, Jess. I never dreamed he would . . . threaten you like that. I just didn't think he'd care where I went."

"He probably wouldn't have if you'd gone anywhere else."

"I have to leave, Jess," she repeated, but he ignored her. If he was completely honest, he would tell her that Chad Byrnehouse was not known for making idle threats. He could spend hours reciting details of the scars Chad had left on his life. Their encounters had been rare but volatile. When they were boys, Chad had never missed an opportunity to dig where it hurt. Even now, at moments when he least expected it, childish taunts would surface in his thoughts. And to this day, Jess continued to struggle with it, until he often doubted his own mind. He wondered why he let it affect him so deeply. Could it be that for all his warped ideas and crass behavior, Chad knew the truth? And here was Alexa. Heaven only knew how she fit into all of this. If he really got to the core of it, he could tell her that he was afraid of what Chad might do next. But she was scared, too. He could feel it, hear it in her voice.

Amidst all the wondering and confusion, one fact stood out clearly. She was on his side. There was something about the way she'd defended him to Chad's face that stirred Jess. Instinctively he tightened his arm around her. He would not let Chad win this time.

"Are you listening to me, Jess?"

"I'm listening," he said, "but we're almost there, and I have no desire to argue with you in front of the boys."

They ambled into the yard, and a welcoming committee quickly gathered to investigate their unusual return.

"What's wrong with Crazy?" Jimmy demanded.

"Nothing's wrong with Crazy," Jess reported. "She did beautifully."

"Who won?" Murphy asked as the group followed them into the stable.

"Chad Byrnehouse won," Jess said and dismounted.

"What's he got to do with it?" Fiddler scowled and took Demented's reins.

"It's not worth mentioning." Jess put his hands about Alexa's waist to help her down.

"Then what's . . . ," Murphy began as Alexa leaned into Jess. "Blimey! Where'd she get the shiner?"

Alexa looked to Jess. So far he'd handled it well enough, and she was grateful when he simply said, "It was a little present from her brother. Get back to work. Everything's fine."

"What happened?" Richard pushed through and took hold of Alexa's chin to examine the swollen cheek and darkening eye.

"It's nothing, really," she insisted, then wavered a little. Richard looked skeptical.

"Richard," Jess ordered, "you see that she gets to her room and rests."

Alexa felt a strange sensation as Jess shifted his support of her to Richard. She leaned blindly against him, wishing the pain and lack of balance would cease to torment her.

Jess turned to Fiddler. "Have Edward take her some lunch at noon." Then to Alexa, "I'll come by and see how you're doing a little later." He pointed a stern finger. "You stay put until then."

"What happened?" Murphy demanded when Jess had gone.

"Like Jess said," she replied, "it's not worth mentioning."

Richard didn't prod Alexa with questions as he guided her to her room. She was grateful to feel a bed beneath her, and she immediately relaxed.

"I have to ride out and check the sheep," Richard said. "Is there anything I can get you before I go?"

"No, thank you." She tried to smile. "I just need some rest."

"You're upset," he guessed, and she closed her eyes.

"Yes, I'm upset. I also have a pounding head."

"I'll let you rest," he conceded, then without permission pulled off her boots and stockings. He filled the basin with cold water and wet a rag that he folded and placed against her swollen eye. "There, maybe that will help."

"Richard," Alexa stopped him at the door. "Thank you . . . ," her voice cracked, "for everything."

"My pleasure," he smiled, closing the door behind him.

Once alone, Alexa's thoughts rolled in turmoil. The dilemma raged on long after Edward brought her lunch. She managed to get enough down to ease her hunger. Fiddler came in mid-afternoon to get the tray. He sat to talk, and without hardly realizing it, she told him what had happened. He asked if there was anything he could do, but she kindly sent him away, knowing there was nothing anyone could do. The more she thought about it, the more she knew how unfair it would be to expect Jess to keep her here under the circumstances.

Alexa kept waiting for him to come as he'd said he would. She wanted to talk to him and get it over with. She wondered where she would go—what she would do. But the thought was so unnerving she chose to ignore it for now, and deal instead with getting up the nerve to just leave. In the brief time she'd been here she'd come to feel at home, and leaving these new friends would not be easy.

Jess finally made it to Alexa's room in the early evening. He knocked at the partially opened door and pushed his head inside when there was no response.

Alexa lay on her side with bare feet showing below her breeches. Her head rested against her arm. Her eyes were closed. The room was filled with a dusky pink light from the setting sun that shone through the west window. Jess watched her a moment. Her presence alone gave him confidence in what he'd come to tell her.

Quietly Jess closed the door and leaned against it. At the clicking of the latch, her eyes opened and she leaned up on one elbow. Her wind-tangled hair tumbled over the side of her face until she pushed it back with one of those delicate hands. "Hello," she said.

"How you doing?" He sat on a chair that had been placed close to the bed by a previous visitor.

"I'm fine. It still hurts, but I think I can see straight now."

Jess smiled and glanced away. "Oh," he held up his hand where a folded cloth lay, "Mrs. Brown sent this."

He moved it toward her face and she grimaced. "It smells horrible."

"I know," he laughed, "but she swears it'll do wonders. Close your eye." He urged the poultice to her face.

Alexa winced slightly, then opened one eye to look at him. "Thank you." She pressed her hand over it to replace his. She thought it funny as their fingers touched that she recalled how it had felt to lean against his sturdy frame as they'd ridden home this morning.

Jess leaned his forearms onto his thighs and looked around the room, noting the feminine shape it had taken since he'd last seen it.

"We need to talk," Alexa insisted when he said nothing.

"I told you earlier, there's nothing to talk about."

"But what Chad said—"

"He didn't say anything," Jess interrupted.

"He said you'd regret my coming here; that you should get rid of me now, and—"

"Alexa," he put a hand over her arm, "Chad Byrnehouse is full of wind."

She relaxed slightly. "You mean . . . it's just talk?"

"Most likely," Jess lied.

"I don't know." She shook her head. "Perhaps I should go anyway. I wonder if I should have ever come here. If anything happened because—"

"Listen to me." He stopped her again. "We may not exactly agree on methods, but I'm not such a fool that I can't see you know what you're doing around here." Her one eye widened at the compliment. "Face it: I need you, and you have nowhere else to go. I'm not about to let your brother's bad manners make me lose the best trainer I've ever had." His eyes turned hard. "And I'm not going to allow him to run my life. He's certainly tried, but so far I'm still standing."

Noticing his bitter tone, Alexa wondered what he wasn't telling her. She had the urge to ask, but part of her didn't want to know. She already felt caught in the middle of something she didn't want to be involved in.

Jess shrugged his shoulders, and one corner of his mouth went up wryly. "Besides," he added, perhaps to ease his pride, "Fiddler told me if I let you go, he was going with you. You'd probably have the whole lot of them following after you like a litter of puppies, and I'd be mucking out stables myself. I think I'd rather not."

"So you're trying to convince me that if I left, you'd be on your own." She shook her head. "It was a worthy effort, Jess, but I don't think so."

Jess's heart began to hammer. Was she trying to tell him she was leaving in spite of all he'd said? He tried to convince himself that with the work she'd done so far, they could perhaps manage. But he knew there was more. He couldn't pinpoint it. He didn't understand it. But he knew he wasn't about to let her go—threats or no threats.

"Jess," she spoke when he didn't, feeling it was something he ought to know, "he thinks that . . . well," she looked away, "that you and I are—"

"I know." He spared her the embarrassment of having to say it. "I heard what he said." Seeing the warmth in his eyes, she wondered what else he'd overheard.

"And you don't care?"

"Why should I?" He chuckled carelessly, then on impulse he quoted her, "It shouldn't make my reputation any more questionable than it already is." She smiled. "Besides," he surprised her by taking her hand, "I was thinking perhaps we should become involved and give him something to talk about."

"Jess!" She laughed it off and turned away, but a barely discernible squeeze of his hand drew her gaze back to his. The severity in his eyes made her wonder if he was serious. His lips twitched upward, and she decided he was teasing her.

Jess came to the edge of his chair, feeling suddenly tense. "I'll expect you on the job early tomorrow."

"Are you certain?" she asked gravely.

"Let me put it this way, Alexandra." He pointed a stern finger. "You and I made a deal. I expect you to be in my employ until this race is over. And that is final."

"But what if—"

"And *if* anything happens, well . . . that's a gamble I knowingly took when I hired you." He smiled warmly. "You'd better get some rest."

Impulsively, Alexa scooted to the edge of the bed. Holding the smelly poultice in one hand, she put her arms around his neck with a forceful hug.

"What was that for?" he chuckled, pressing his hands to her back. Briefly holding her against him, something inside sparked to life.

Alexa drew away to look at him, but kept her arms on his shoulders. "Thank you, Jess. I'll work hard for you."

"I don't doubt that." He gingerly touched the ailing cheek. "I believe the swelling is going down a little."

"For all that stink, it ought to do something."

Jess's fingers moved over her face, almost caressing her. Their eyes met, and for a timeless moment goose bumps rippled down Alexa's back. It wasn't until he left and the sensation finally ceased that she felt as if destiny had tapped her on the shoulder. She was glad she didn't have to leave.

The following morning, Jess arrived at the track just as Crazy and Demented were being led toward the starting line. His heart quickened as the horses were put into place. He leaned against the rail and watched with anticipation as the boys hovered around, each doing their part to ensure that all was set. After Tod was in place on Crazy's back, with a few instructions from Alexa, she climbed onto Demented.

Jess felt an odd sensation that had recently become familiar; it happened each time she sat a horse with such finesse. Or sometimes a certain tilt of her head would set it off. Could it be the responsibility he had put on her to save him? Whatever it was, he couldn't deny his fascination.

"Ready, Murphy?" she called.

"Goodo," he shouted.

"Ready, Fiddler?"

"Ready."

"Tod?"

"Yo."

"Let it go!" she called, and the horses bolted forward. Jess sat on the fence to get a better view, but his excitement faltered when Demented ran lengths ahead of Crazy.

This began a daily run that disheartened Jess a little more each time. He could see improvement with both Tod and Crazy. Still, they could not beat Demented.

But this didn't seem to discourage Alexa; in fact, little could. Jess was continually amazed at this woman's determination, as well as how hard she worked. He often caught a glimpse of sweat on her face and neck. Her too-short hair was always pulled back ridiculously in a ribbon to keep it out of her face, or shoved up beneath a riding cap that Jess thought looked atrocious on her. Or maybe he didn't like the hat because it hid her eyes.

"Those eyes," he said aloud, grateful no one was nearby. That deep electric blue made him freeze each time he caught them. He was careful to study her only when she wasn't aware. But he could hardly deny his intrigue with those eyes—and the woman behind them. If she was Chad Byrnehouse's sister, she'd gotten the best of whatever he'd gotten the worst of.

Thoughts of Chad made Jess's stomach churn. Nothing more had been mentioned about his threats, and the work went on as before. Jess did his best not to think about it. And as Alexa's black eye slowly returned to normal, he found it easier to think of her without being reminded of her brother.

Her skill and natural ability astounded him, and he realized she had other talents as well. It became increasingly difficult to avoid eavesdropping when she came in to play the piano. He enjoyed sitting in the next room to listen, absorbing the memories that were gradually becoming mingled with a sense of hope for the future.

Admittedly, Jess liked Alexa. And as time passed, his hopes for winning the race broadened. If Alexa kept her job, she would stay. The thought intrigued him, even though he knew his feelings for her were pointless. She was a Byrnehouse, for heaven's sake. Her grandfather was the second son of an English Lord. The woman was as close to royalty as an Australian could get. Perhaps that was the very reason he found it difficult to comprehend her as his employee. Disowned or not, she was still a Byrnehouse.

Four
TRUST

Jess returned from town wondering how the work had gone in his absence. He found Alexa out by the bathhouse, bent over the water pump, washing her hair. With her eyes squeezed shut and water running over her head, he took advantage of the opportunity to watch her. He wondered if he'd ever get used to seeing a woman in breeches.

Jess smiled when she blindly reached for the little bottle of shampoo and soaped up her head. While she rinsed, he quietly picked up her towel and waited. "Looking for something?" he chortled when she couldn't find it.

Alexa flipped her hair back so quickly that she sprayed water over his face. "Make yourself known." She grabbed the towel abruptly. "You scared me nearly to death."

"That water is cold." Jess laughed and wiped it from his face. He watched her wrap the towel around her head like a turban, then she set her eyes on him and he nearly forgot what he'd come to ask her.

"Did you need something?" Her voice snapped him out of a daze.

"Just wondered how Crazy did today."

"About the same," she said curtly and hurried past him. Alexa had made a point to keep her opinions to herself. She was grateful just to be here, and she didn't want to stir up any tension. But as the race edged closer, she became increasingly nervous.

"What seems to be the problem?" Jess asked, following close behind.

Alexa stopped and turned to look at him in disgust. "There is no reason for me to tell you the problem."

Jess sighed and watched the toe of his boot shuffle back and forth through the dirt. He really hated this.

"Jess," she said, and he looked up to meet those eyes, "is there a reason why you insist that Crazy race now?"

"I want her to, and that's reason enough."

"Haven't I convinced you yet that Demented is the better horse?" She pulled the towel from her head and shook her hair free.

"No," he said coolly, watching her push it back off her face with a dainty hand, "Demented is better trained. Crazy is the better horse. I know what we're up against, and Demented doesn't have what it takes. He's there for a backup. That's it."

"Have you got a backup jockey?" she asked, and he made no response. They both knew he didn't. "Tod's good," she said, "but he's edgy. He holds back. He gets nervous, and the horse can tell. We've got an alternative in case something happens to the horse, but what about the jockey?"

Still Jess gave no answer. Alexa suddenly felt so frustrated that she walked away to avoid getting angry. As hard as she tried to do this the way Jess wanted, it just didn't seem to work.

Jess was at the rail the next morning when the boys put the horses in place for their run. Alexa approached him, and he could see by her eyes that she had a speech. He was both relieved and disappointed when Murphy called, "Ready, Missy."

Alexa gave Jess a hard glance and ducked beneath the rail to run across the track. Jess leaned forward, and a tight knot grew in his stomach. It happened every time he grasped the reality that everything he owned—all his father had worked so hard for—was hanging on a nervous jockey and an insufficiently trained horse. His only hope was Alexandra Byrnehouse. But even she couldn't make apple pie out of peaches, as she had so quaintly put it.

And if that wasn't bad enough, he had begun to feel like Chad Byrnehouse was constantly looking over his shoulder. It wasn't like him to make threats and not show any sign of himself for so long. Jess wondered when he would appear. The closer it got to the race, the more nervous he became.

Jess noticed some commotion and perked his attention. Something tugged at him when he realized Alexa had ordered Tod onto Demented, and she was mounting Crazy herself. What was she trying to prove?

The horses bolted forward, and for the first time since they'd started this, the competition was close. Crazy and Demented remained almost side by side. Jess began to feel a fresh confidence in his instincts. He silently leapt for joy when Crazy nosed ahead on the final stretch and won.

The boys all cheered except Tod, who looked disheartened. Alexa dismounted and sauntered toward Jess. She stopped before him, and he fully expected one of her lectures.

"All right," she said, "we'll race Crazy."

"What made the difference?" he asked soberly.

"I'm a better rider."

"You weigh less."

"Not enough to make that much difference."

Jess stared at her, completely at a loss for words. And to make it worse, she just had to catch him with those eyes.

"Let me ride her, Jess," she asked in a low voice.

"No," he retorted, "absolutely not."

"Why?"

"I'm not having a woman jockey."

"You didn't want a woman trainer, either."

"They'd probably disqualify us."

"I doubt it, but if you prefer, they wouldn't have to know."

"It's dangerous."

"Don't be ridiculous!" she scoffed. "I have been racing since I—"

"It wouldn't be the first time that one of my competitors did something underhanded to make me lose."

"If you mean Chad, I—"

"Yes, I mean Chad, Miss Byrnehouse! *Your* brother has—"

"Why does my being a Byrnehouse come up when you and I disagree on something?"

Jess swallowed and ignored the question. "I won't be responsible for your getting hurt."

"But you will for Tod?"

"It's different."

"How?"

"You're a woman."

"I'm a capable woman, Jess. Is it my welfare or your reputation that concerns you?"

"Miss Byrnehouse," he said gruffly, "you will remember that you work for me. Crazy will run—and Tod will ride her. That's it! You've still got time to make Tod do it right. I'll hear no more about it."

Jess finished with a hard stare to make certain she knew he meant it. Defiance rose in her expression, but she simply said, "Honesty."

"What do you mean?"

"You demand honesty. You should expect to give it. I can accept being content to be your trainer and let Tod ride, but I have a right to know the real reason you're set on Crazy."

"I told you," he stated, "she's a better horse."

"The real reason," she repeated.

"Instinct," he told her and she knew it was true, but not the whole truth.

"And?"

"And what?"

"Odds wouldn't have anything to do with it, would they?" she asked, and he looked at her sharply. "I thought so. Nobody in their right mind would bet on a two-year-old filly that had never run before. You put all your money on Crazy, she wins, and you make a clean sweep."

"You're too perceptive for your own good," he said with an attempt to make it light.

"I'm a Byrnehouse," she said with spite.

Jess sighed. "So you know. Demented has never won, but his record isn't too bad. I want the odds high."

"Isn't that a little risky?"

"My whole life has been risky since . . ."

"What?" she asked when he faltered.

"Never mind," he said tersely. "Let's get back to work."

Alexa met his eyes, wishing she understood him. "Why didn't you just tell me to begin with?"

"You're a Byrnehouse," he answered quickly.

"You don't trust me." She was surprised that it hurt.

"Should I?" he retorted.

Alexa ran toward the track before he could see the tears surfacing in her eyes. "Get Tod on Crazy," she shouted. "We're doing it again." She mounted Demented and rode with fury, wishing it would push Jess Davies out of her head.

❦   ❦   ❦

Jess began making himself scarce, and Alexa wondered why. She also wondered why his absence made her tense. The hours seemed longer and more difficult, and she took frequent advantage of the opportunity to play the piano to relieve her nerves. After finishing late one evening, she moved into the darkened hallway and bumped into Jess. She gasped before she realized it was him.

"Forgive me." He chuckled. "I didn't mean to frighten you. I heard you playing and had to stop and listen. I hope you don't mind."

"I didn't intend to disturb you."

"You didn't disturb me," he insisted. All was silent for a moment, and Alexa nearly excused herself. "You look different." He noted the dark skirt and striped blouse she wore, with her hair pinned up neatly at the back of her head.

"It's dark," she replied.

"Not too dark." Even now, when he could barely see her eyes, they still affected him.

Alexa felt far from indifferent, being alone with him like this. She didn't know if she wanted to stay or run away. "I should get back." She knew staying was preposterous. "It's getting late."

"I'll see you in the morning," he said and she walked past him, aware that he was watching her. Impulsively she turned around, then wished she hadn't. For several moments they stood with darkness shadowing their expressions, silence making their hearts pound.

"Good night, Jess," she finally said and hurried on.

Alexa returned to the carriage house and found Richard waiting for her at the bottom of the stairs. She was grateful for the distraction.

"Hello, Alexa." He came to his feet. "I hope you don't mind that

I waited up for you. I wanted to show you something."

"I don't mind." She smiled. He took her hand and led her up the stairs into his room, where the door had been left open. He motioned her to the only chair, then handed her a piece of paper.

"Tell me what you think." He seemed a trifle nervous.

Alexa looked toward him in question, then began to read. It was a poem, simply written with perfect rhyme, about a woman and a horse. She sensed something personal in it and glanced up at him before she was half through. His expression was guarded, and she turned back to finish.

"I really like it," she said with genuine enthusiasm. "You wrote it?"

"I'm afraid I did." He sat sheepishly on the edge of the bed. "Just something I try my hand at once in a while."

"I must say I'm impressed." She smiled warmly at him. "Surely it's fulfilling to express yourself this way."

"It is," he stated.

Alexa glanced over the piece again, trying to place this man as a poet. She looked up and found him watching her, but it was easy to smile and not feel uncomfortable beneath his gaze. She would never look at him, his work-worn hands and muscular frame, and comprehend the sensitivity and insight expressed in his hand-written words.

After freshly absorbing his presence, she read it again. He quietly watched her. "Is this about me?" she asked timidly.

"I was hoping you'd notice. I don't want you to be embarrassed or anything, but you have added some life to this place." He grinned almost wryly. "You inspired me."

"I must say I'm flattered." Alexa reached her hand out to take his, and he squeezed it.

She handed the page back to him, but he refused it. "No. You keep it—please. It would honor me."

"Thank you," she said, touched by his sentiment.

"I should let you get some sleep," Richard said, but he didn't let go of her hand.

"Actually, Murphy told me the boys are all going into town tomorrow for one thing or another. I guess that gives me the day off. Oh, but . . . ," she came to her feet, "you're probably going with them, and they'll be leaving early and—"

"I'm not going." He put enough pressure on her hand to make her sit back down.

"Why not?" she asked so innocently that his response caught her off guard.

"When people like me go into town, it causes quite a stir."

Alexa glanced away, embarrassed. But instinct drew her eyes back to face him. She wondered if he ever talked to anyone about such feelings.

"It must be very difficult for you," she said gently.

"It can be if I let it." He didn't seem disturbed so far.

"Would I be rude to ask how it happened?"

"Not as rude as you would be to pretend it's not there." He leaned back against the wall to make himself comfortable. Casually he put his hands behind his head and stretched his long legs over the bed, crossing them at the ankles. Alexa leaned forward, putting her elbows on her knees as he clarified, "It might sound funny, but I appreciate the way these blokes I work with don't try to ignore it. I'd rather have Jess tell me I'm scary-looking than try to convince me that I'm Prince Charming, if that makes any sense."

"I think it makes perfect sense," she said. "So how did it happen?"

"I was trying to get out of a burning house," he began, and though his expression hardly changed, Alexa sensed the difficulty of the subject. "I can't tell you what happened exactly. The memories are kind of blurred. Life hasn't been much the same since."

"How long has it been?" she asked like a curious child.

"Ten years; well . . . not quite."

"And how *did* it change your life?" she asked. "I mean . . . aren't you the same Richard? You don't have to answer that if you don't want to. I was just . . . wondering."

"I don't mind," he admitted, "but I'm not sure I could put it into words. I don't recall ever discussing it before."

"Try," she urged with a smile that lit her eyes.

Richard leaned forward and looked down. "I don't know. Perhaps my life wouldn't have changed so much if my priorities had been different." Alexa waited patiently for him to go on. "Before it happened I was . . . well . . ." He gave an embarrassed chuckle. "You might as well know. I was a philandering womanizer. There. That's the truth of it. I was a rogue."

"Really?" Alexa smirked, somehow intrigued.

"I suppose you find that difficult to believe."

"I don't find it surprising at all," she said. "I have no doubt you had to fight the ladies off."

Richard ignored the compliment. "The ironic thing is that I was so blasted cocky about it. I actually found a woman or two worth sticking with, but I was determined to remain a bachelor. I wanted to have it all without commitment." He sighed deeply, but with no trace of self-pity. "Looks like I got what I asked for, but I wouldn't exactly say I've got it all. Still," he leaned back again and crossed his legs the other direction, "I have to say I'm a lucky guy. I have a home, a job, good friends, and . . . it might sound odd, but in a strange way I'm glad it happened."

"Glad? Why?"

"The thought of living out my life as I was is almost terrifying. I'm grateful for the chance to see how wrong I was, and to appreciate what life is really about."

"And what is that?" Alexa asked, mesmerized by his wisdom.

Richard caught her eyes and smiled—a warm, complacent smile that filled her. "It's inner peace, Alexa. That is what I have that makes my life worth living."

"You're an incredible man, Mr. Wilhite. Would it sound trite of me to say that you've been a great boon to me through this adjustment in my life?"

"Words are never trite when they're spoken with sincerity," he said, still holding her eyes. Alexa looked away as his words struck deeply. But he went deeper still. "Would it be rude of me to ask why a Byrnehouse is working for Jess Davies?"

Alexa was surprised. "I would have thought you'd heard by now."

"Why would I?"

"I just assumed that . . . well, surely Jess would—"

"Jess is no gossip," Richard stated with respect in his voice. "Now, if you had told Murphy," he added with a chuckle, "the whole station would know."

"But surely Jess must have given an explanation for my being here. The boys couldn't help but be curious."

"He told them you were fed up with your brother, then said he couldn't blame you."

Alexa smiled, and her thoughts wandered briefly to Jess. What was he doing now? Was he alone or . . .

"Where are you?" Richard startled her.

"I'm sorry. I . . . well, if you must know, it was the other way around." She tightened her lips. "Chad disowned me."

Richard's brow furrowed.

"Actually, my father discredited me in his will, but he left the matter in Chad's hands. Chad told me to . . ." Alexa took a deep breath when she felt emotion rising. "I think I'd rather not talk about that. It's still a little too . . . well, you know."

Richard nodded his understanding, and she sat up straight to stretch her back. "So," she changed the subject, "what exactly do the boys do when they go into town?"

"Besides picking up supplies, you mean?" he said lightly. "You could sum it up by saying they're out to socialize. They don't get much opportunity for that out here."

"No," Alexa smiled, "I suppose they don't." She came to her feet. "I must confess I'm getting sleepy, but I enjoyed *our* socializing."

"So did I." He slid off the bed and walked her to the door.

"Thank you for the poetry. It's lovely."

Richard only smiled and watched her until she stepped into her room and closed the door. She pondered briefly over the things Richard had told her, and felt grateful for finding such a friend. Alexa tacked the poem to the wall and read it once more before she crawled into bed. Perhaps this life wasn't so bad after all.

❦   ❦   ❦

Alexa took advantage of her day off to straighten her room and get rid of the dust. She was appalled at how the cobwebs had taken over, and stood on her chair to dust them away. Where the ceiling slanted it was easy, but at the peak near the door she had trouble reaching, and strained until she nearly toppled. A gasp of fear turned to startled surprise when strong hands caught her about the waist. "Richard," she laughed, "I believe you just saved me."

"Good thing I came along when I did." He smiled and set her on her feet, allowing his hands to linger a moment too long. Alexa looked up at him and smiled so genuinely that it took him off guard. No woman had looked at him like that since his face had been rearranged by fire. "What are you trying to do, anyway?" he asked to distract himself from her eyes.

"I'm trying to get rid of these dreadful cobwebs." She looked up with disgust and slapped her dusty hands on her breeches. "I rarely see spiders, but they certainly leave their trail about as if they own the place."

"Perhaps they do," Richard said. "They were probably here before we were."

"Good point," Alexa chuckled, "but I'm here now, and I'll not have cobwebs overrunning my room."

"Here," Richard took the rag, "let me." He stepped onto the chair and quickly dusted all of the ceiling she couldn't reach.

"You make it look so easy." She laughed softly.

"It doesn't take talent to be six-foot-three." He stepped down, throwing the rag over the back of the chair. "Now you, on the other hand," he straddled the chair and leaned an elbow on the back of it, "are talented."

Alexa gave a dubious noise and sat on the edge of the bed. "Not talented enough for Jess." She glanced about to be certain the cobwebs were all gone.

"What's that supposed to mean?"

"Oh, I don't know," she moaned. "Sometimes I just feel like he disregards my abilities because I'm a woman."

"Has he said that?" Richard asked.

"No, but—"

"Don't attempt to read minds, Alexa," Richard cautioned. "Especially his." He paused, and Alexa looked up curiously. "He's a complicated man."

"Yes," she agreed, "and a touch arrogant as well."

Richard laughed. "Arrogant because he won't let you ride the race?"

"How did you know about that?"

"One ear works just fine." He pointed to the right one. "He just doesn't want you to get hurt."

"I think there's more to it than that."

"Probably. But face it: we work for Jess. He's the boss."

"Yes, you're right," she had to admit.

"Look," Richard shouted, pointing to the floor, "a spider!"

"Where?" Alexa shrieked and pulled her stockinged feet off the floor.

Richard laughed. "There's no spider. They all moved out when you destroyed their homes."

Alexa groaned in mock anger and threw her boot at him. "With any luck, they'll have moved across the hall."

Richard dodged the flying boot and laughed. "If I find any, I'll bring them over to redecorate."

Alexa threw the other boot. Richard ducked and laughed again. "You'd do well to remember who's bigger." He came to his feet, snarling like a great beast.

Alexa giggled and stood on her bed. "You wouldn't dare!"

"Wouldn't I?" He lunged for Alexa, but she jumped past him. She reached for her boots but he was quicker. "You'll get what you deserve," he said, and tossed them out the window.

Alexa gave an astonished laugh. "You rogue!"

"Am I?" he chortled proudly.

"Yes," she attempted to be serious, "now you go out there right now and get my boots!"

"No, I will not," he retorted, "but I'll take you out to get them."

"Like this?" she questioned, pointing to her feet.

"Here," he added more seriously, "I'll carry you."

Alexa only hesitated a moment before she allowed Richard to lift her onto his back where he held her thighs to keep her steady. He ducked to go through the door, then practically jumped down the stairs. Alexa screamed and giggled at the same time.

"It's a good thing these stairs are strong," she said, "or we'd both be goners."

"I built them myself. They could hold a tribe of aborigines."

"Did you bring one in to test them?" she asked behind his ear as he wove between the vehicles in the carriage house.

"No," he laughed, "but I might."

"Let me know so I can lock my—"

"Let you know what?" Jess asked, pulling open the door just as Richard was about to kick it. His eyes went skeptically to Alexa's stockinged feet, then to her legs wrapped around Richard's waist and her arms dangling over his shoulders.

"We were just discussing bringing in a tribe of aborigines to test the stairs," Richard stated as if it were important business. Alexa giggled, then pressed her mouth to Richard's shoulder to suppress it when Jess glared at her.

"I was just coming to find you," Jess said, but they weren't sure if he meant Richard or Alexa. "Might I ask what you're doing, beyond discussing aborigines?"

"We need to get my boots," Alexa informed him.

"Your *boots?*" Jess lifted a brow.

"They're right over there." Richard nodded, and Jess turned to see them lying on the ground.

"I see," Jess said skeptically. "Well, after you get your boots on, could I borrow Richard for a little while, if it's not too inconvenient?"

"I think I could manage," she said, "now that the cobwebs are down."

Jess gave a dubious grunt and turned toward the house. Alexa put on her boots and sent Richard after him. She went to the stable and found it unusually quiet as she saddled Crazy and took her out to the gallops for a good workout. She returned to the bunkhouse kitchen to munch on the cheese, beef, and baked apples that Edward had left for her and Richard. Deciding she'd like a peaceful evening, she took extra portions to her room and later shared them with Richard while they talked late into the night. He was easy to be with, and despite their age difference of fourteen years, Alexa felt as if they'd been friends forever.

She went to bed exhausted but content, and rose determined to push Crazy beyond her limits. The boys were back at work, and she felt a need to get serious about this race. She gave Tod an assignment to work on strengthening his leg muscles, and left Murphy and Jimmy in charge to see that he did it. The evidence of their hangovers made her wonder if they were up to even that.

With Crazy saddled, she headed for the hills. She was gone hours, but felt it was beneficial. Crazy showed progress, and Alexa told her what a good horse she was as she led her to a stall to brush her down.

"Where have you been?" Jess came through the door, obviously upset.

"I took Crazy out for a run. I think it helped. She—"

"I didn't give you permission to take Crazy anywhere."

"I am the horse's trainer," Alexa argued, wondering what had gotten into him. "If I see that it's necessary to—"

"I am the horse's owner," Jess stated sharply, "and your employer. I don't want Crazy taken out where she might possibly get hurt. The race is too close. I won't risk it."

"I wouldn't do anything to put Crazy at risk!" she protested, wondering where his faith in her had gone.

"Miss Byrnehouse," he said in a voice that was low and gruff, "I'm asking you not to take Crazy out again."

Alexa wanted to tell him it didn't make sense, but in his present state of mind she doubted that anything she said would make a difference. In that moment, she felt just plain frustrated with Jess Davies and the stipulations he put on her employment.

"You will be a very lucky man, Mr. Davies," she said coolly, "if you even come close to winning this race."

"You'd best watch your tone, Miss Byrnehouse," he snarled, "or I'll send you back to your brother where you belong."

"What has my brother got to do with this?" she demanded.

"He paid a little visit while you were out."

Alexa's expression turned from anger to fear, but at least she understood his mood. "What did he say?"

"Oh," Jess folded his arms satirically, "first of all he accused me of coercing you into working for me so I could win a race for a change. Then he reminded me of some things I'd rather not be reminded of, which I won't bore you with. And then he told me how much pleasure it would give him to buy my property from the bank as soon as they've taken it from me, and to see you and me in ruin together."

"I'm sorry, Jess. I—"

"And then," Jess shouted, "he called me a bastard, and said you and I were two of a kind."

The last brought visible pain to Alexa's eyes, but Jess ignored it. "I don't know where your brother gets his warped ideas, but I'll tell you something, Alexandra. I am not going to let him *or you* destroy me! If I ever find out that you are here for any reason beyond what you've told me, I will see you—"

"Now, wait a minute!" she interrupted harshly, turning her hurt to anger. "How dare you accuse me of being on the same level as him! You have no right to—"

"Don't tell me what I have a right to do. I will not—"

"What did he tell you?" she cut in with a quiet tone that caught his attention. "He told you something about me, didn't he."

"As a matter of fact, he did," Jess scoffed.

"What?" she demanded, but he hesitated. "I will not allow you to be angry with me without having a chance to defend myself."

"It's quite simple, actually. For once, he almost made sense. He told me I was a fool to believe your being here was what it seemed. He asked me what logic there was in thinking a Byrnehouse would—"

"Oh," she snapped, "so it's my being a Byrnehouse again!"

"He told me I'm a fool, Alexa, and I have to wonder if he's right. If you had a clue what's going on here, I don't think you'd be so blasted arrogant. Your brother has been trying to destroy me for ten years. Little by little, he always manages to keep me under his thumb. If it's not the sheep, it's the horses. Why do you think I'm on the brink of losing it all? I have to do anything—*anything*—Alexa, to protect myself."

Alexa's eyes widened in astonishment, but she intended to make one thing clear. "You must know I had nothing to do with that, or I don't believe you'd have tolerated my presence here this long."

"Still, I have to wonder," he said with hard eyes.

"If you feel that way, why didn't you let me go last month when—"

"You know perfectly well why I—"

"No," she shouted, "I do not! I am not now, nor have I ever been, here to do anything but help you win this race, Jess Davies. You've either got to learn to trust *me* or trust Chad. Take your pick, but I will not stay here if you can't—"

"Enough said!" Jess insisted, pushing his hand through the air abruptly. "I want Crazy kept where we can watch her. That's all."

"Fine," Alexa retorted, certain Jess hated her. It was evident he didn't trust her. His blatant disregard of what she had to say caused her intangible grief, and she wondered why she cared. "I'll ride a different horse," she added curtly, impulsively mounting Crazy's sire without a saddle.

"Where do you think you're going?" he snapped. "I'm not finished with you yet."

"You just told me that enough had been said. Working for you doesn't mean I have to stand here and be degraded because I have the misfortune of bearing the name Byrnehouse."

"Get down here." Jess took her waist and dragged her down from the horse despite her protests. For a moment, Alexa became distracted by the strength in his hands and the heat in his eyes. Her anger began to dissipate into confusion as his nearness somehow warmed her, but he was quick to shatter it with his cold words. "You're a little too uppity, Miss Byrnehouse. You're not a wealthy little snip anymore, and you'd best learn to mind your manners."

Jess could see that his statement hurt her, and for a moment he wished he hadn't said it. Still, he had to let her know where he stood. There was no denying who she was, and right now he felt threatened.

"Let go of me!" Alexa cried. Vulnerable tears pooled in her eyes, magnifying the intensity of the blue. Jess stepped back, letting go abruptly.

She mounted the stallion and galloped out. "Wretched woman," Jess muttered under his breath. He walked outside and watched her disappear into the hills before he looked skyward and his heart quickened. How could she be so stupid, he thought, to ride out of here like that with a storm threatening?

Jess tried to find something to keep him busy in the stable, wishing she'd come back, wondering why he cared. When Jimmy ambled in, Jess was quick to ask, "Has Miss Byrnehouse returned yet?"

"Haven't seen her," he replied.

Jess glanced away, and his cheek twitched.

"Somethin' wrong?" Jimmy asked.

"She rode out toward the hills. If she doesn't get back before that storm worsens, she'll likely end up dead."

"Ah," Jimmy waved a careless hand, "she grew up 'round here. She knows not t' mess with th' land."

"She knows Byrnehouse, but it's not like my land." He moved to stand in the doorway and a brisk wind greeted him. "Those hills all look the same when rain sets in."

"Yeah," Jimmy laughed, and Jess felt irritated by his indifference, "I r'member the time we lost eight cows just 'cause a storm hit, and . . ."

He stopped when Jess grabbed his long coat from a hook and pulled Demented out of his stall. "Where you goin'?" he asked as Jess secured the bridle and mounted bareback.

"Someone's got to find her," he said. Jimmy lifted his brows curiously and Jess added, "She's the only trainer we've got."

Five

THE STORM

Bent low over the horse, Jess rode toward the hills, pushing Demented to his full capacity. He didn't know where to begin looking. But he muttered a quick prayer and stuck to what he thought was the obvious route, considering the direction Alexa had gone. He hoped she wasn't too unpredictable.

The wind worsened considerably. Thunder rumbled threats in the distance, and the sky darkened. At a particularly loud roar, Demented reared back skittishly. Jess urged the stallion on, wondering if this was nothing but a futile search.

He was both grateful and afraid when Alexa's horse galloped past with no rider. Knowing it could go home on its own, Jess trotted up the trail, calling Alexa's name as rain began to fall. Peering through the water that ran off the brim of his hat, Jess's mind filled with images of Alexa lying in the mud, her neck broken. His stomach churned, and the muscles in his back tightened into knots.

"Alexa!" he called over and over until his throat hurt. He prayed inwardly that she would survive this, and was surprised to realize that his thoughts had little to do with the race resting on her shoulders.

"Alexa!" he called again, and his heart beat audibly when he heard her respond.

"I'm here!" she shouted, and her voice guided him to the left, through a cluster of trees, where he found her sitting on the ground.

"I hate to admit it," she yelled to be heard above the storm, "but I'm glad to see you. Stupid horse bucked me when it thundered." She didn't want to admit that she might have been able to stay on if she hadn't been crying.

"Don't call my horse stupid when you have no business riding it up here in a storm." Anger tightened Jess's voice as he dismounted and pulled her abruptly to her feet.

"Careful," she shouted, "it wasn't an easy fall."

"Are you crazy, woman?" he shouted back, holding her forearm firmly. "You could have got yourself killed."

"Don't be ridiculous. I only—"

Thunder and lightning cracked simultaneously. Jess jumped to catch Demented, but he bolted and ran.

"Oh, terrific!" He threw his hands in the air. "Now we get to—"

Another ominous crack broke the air, and the rain turned to sheets. Jess could almost bet they were as good as dead. Alexa went to her knees and tried to shield her head with her arms, but Jess dragged her to her feet and ran toward an overhanging rock, the only possible shelter in sight.

Abruptly he shoved her to the ground against the rock wall and knelt beside her, leaving only his back exposed to the pelting rain. "Wretched woman." He tried to press closer to the rock while she huddled beneath him.

"I'm sorry, Jess," she cried. "I had no idea that—"

"Shut up!" he shouted, and bowed his head over her shoulder. The rain only worsened. "And pray we're not in the path of a flash flood."

Nothing more was said as the storm continued relentlessly. Alexa watched water drip from his hat, and occasionally he took a deep breath to sustain himself. It seemed hours before the rain lessened enough for Jess to relax slightly and sit on the ground beside her. When the rain finally ceased, a heavy mist settled in. Near to losing the emotions she'd been fighting to control, Alexa kept her face turned away. She felt humiliated over the mess she'd gotten them into, and afraid of what might have happened had he not come. Thoughts of the argument that had spurred all of this brought on a fresh rise of emotion. She was reminded of the fear she had of her brother, and the lack of trust from her employer. But overriding all else was an unexplainable sensation rising within her because of Jess's nearness.

Shifting slightly, she became aware of facets of Jess Davies she'd never noticed before. The way he sat nearly encircled her with a masculine protection from the shrouds of mist beyond. The wet smell of his oiled coat provoked a memory so keen that she closed her eyes to more fully absorb it. How old had she been when she'd gotten lost in a spring rain and her father had ridden out to find her? The year eluded her, but she recalled well the perfect security she'd felt encircled in his grasp, wrapped in his wet, oiled coat. It was the first time she had really felt like Tyson Byrnehouse loved her, and from that day their relationship had grown steadily closer. Looking back, she understood now. When Alexa was a child, he had resented her existence because she was not his. But in time he had grown beyond that, and she knew without doubt that he'd cared deeply for her. If only . . .

Alexa opened her eyes to stop the memories before they evoked pain. The present flooded back in the masculine security enveloping her, reminding her so much of Tyson Byrnehouse's fatherly protection. But the resemblance ended there. What she felt for Jess could never be felt for a father or brother. Never had she been so close to a man, so intently aware of what attracted female to male. She had a perfect view of his booted leg and the tan, work-roughened hand that fidgeted over the wrinkles wearing in the leather. Turning her head just slightly, she was confronted with the mostly dry front of his shirt, showing where his coat opened. The fabric clung to his chest, partly revealed by three buttons left undone. Alexa's mouth went dry as she lifted her eyes to study the lines of his face, set in studied thought. As if he sensed her appraisal, Jess turned slowly, catching her eyes in a near-tangible grip. Reality descended, and the emotion surged forward.

Jess noticed Alexa's shoulders tremble as she put her face into her hands. He had to ask, "Are you all right?" Alexa nodded but kept her face covered. Jess took hold of her chin to look at her. "You don't have to cry!" He sounded disgusted.

"Oh, shut up!" She jerked away. "I can cry if I want to."

Tired of painfully holding it back, Alexa turned from him and let the tears flow, not caring what he thought.

"Wretched woman," Jess muttered and pulled her close to him, nearly forcing her face against his chest, where she cried so hard he wondered what kind of pain she'd been holding inside.

Despite Jess's apparent anger, Alexa couldn't deny the instinctive comfort she felt wrapped in his embrace. The tension fell away, and she allowed herself to cry. She cried for her father's death and for the coinciding discovery that he wasn't her father at all. She cried for the fear she'd felt in leaving everything she'd ever known to start a new life with practically nothing. And she cried for the gratitude she felt in knowing that, despite their differences, Jess Davies cared. When the tears finally ceased, Alexa barely had time to appreciate the feel of Jess's chest against her face before she drifted into an exhausted slumber.

Jess's anger dissipated in Alexa's tears, but when he realized she was sleeping in his arms, he was overcome with emotions he hardly recognized. Her petite frame felt vulnerable, almost childlike within his grasp. Instinctively he wanted to protect her. With hesitation he touched her wild hair, still damp from the rain. A sense of wonder accompanied his fingers over her face, and he whispered her name aloud.

Carefully, Jess lay on the ground without disturbing her. She shifted in her sleep and relaxed her head against his chest, seeming as comfortable as if she were in her own bed. She shivered, and he eased her closer in an effort to give her warmth.

The circumstances weren't so uncomfortable that Jess couldn't sleep. But his thoughts were stirred by Alexa's nearness, and he stared into the darkness that had settled around him. He couldn't help wondering why the hole that existed in him suddenly seemed filled, then he scolded himself for thinking that Alexandra Byrnehouse would even consider being anything more in his life than she already was. Certain he was taking something for granted, he simply took advantage of the moment and relished having her in his arms, nearly wishing that morning would never come.

Alexa awakened with a gasp, disoriented by the darkness until a soothing voice whispered near her ear, "It's all right."

She sighed as it all came back to her. "Where are we?" she asked warily.

"Same place," Jess said. "I'm afraid we're stuck here until this mist lifts and we have some daylight to guide us."

Alexa shifted and realized that Jess's arms were securely around her. "What's the matter?" he asked. "Cold?"

"A little."

Carefully Jess eased her on top of him and slipped his arms out of his coat to pull her into it with him. "There. That'll keep you away from the ground, at least." She felt tense, and he chuckled. "You can relax, Alexa. I realize this isn't exactly conventional, but I'm the only warmth within miles, so you'd best take what you can get."

Gradually her tension eased, and he felt her hands soften over his ribs. She rested her head against his shoulder and lay silent for a long while. Unable to deny that he enjoyed her closeness, Jess tightened his arms around her and she trembled.

"Are you still cold?" he whispered.

"No."

Jess paused before adding, "Then why are you trembling, Alexandra?"

"It must have been your imagination," she said curtly, then she resituated herself and relaxed. "Do you suppose they're worried about us?"

"They know I can take care of myself. It's you they'll be worried about." He paused, and she could almost hear him smile. "I think the blokes actually like you."

"Imagine that." She wanted to add that she was glad somebody did. But then she thought of Chad and his threats and lies. If it was as bad as Jess had told her, he had good reason to be upset.

"I'm sorry, Jess." She lifted her head to look at him, wishing she could see more than the vague shadow of his face.

"You told me that already."

"I mean about Chad," she clarified. "I had no idea he—"

"Go to sleep, Alexa," he said sternly. Alexa sighed and rested her head against his shoulder. Trying not to think about how close they were, she willed herself to relax, knowing there was little else to do at the moment.

Jess felt Alexa's breathing fall into a peaceful rhythm. His hand found her hair, and he turned his head to find his face nearly touching hers. He told himself he had no business touching her this way. But she was like water to a thirsting man. No amount of self-discipline could hold him back.

Alexa was barely this side of sleep when she felt Jess's fingers move methodically through her hair and over her shoulder. The sensation was dreamlike, but soft lips against her brow brought her mind to full consciousness. Fearing that he might stop, she remained still, pretending to be asleep. Again his lips brushed over her brow, teasing gingerly along her temple. Alexa's heartbeat quickened, and she feared it would betray her. She wondered what would make him express this secret affection, when earlier he'd not been able to speak a civil word to her. The contradictions in him were confusing, but for the moment she concentrated on his touch, his nearness, the experience of sensations unlike anything she'd ever known.

As Alexa apparently slept, Jess gained confidence in his attentions. He allowed his hand to wander over her back. There was a softness about her that intrigued him. Contemplating the newness of feminine ways to his thinking, Jess wondered how he had reached the age of twenty-eight and never once held a woman so close. It was true that his effort to save himself from Chad Byrnehouse took full concentration at times. But if he'd wanted companionship badly enough, wouldn't he have found a way? Could it be possible that knowing what he did about his parentage made him somehow afraid of becoming involved with a woman? The idea seemed preposterous, and he quickly disregarded it.

Alexa found it increasingly difficult not to respond to Jess's touch. There was an innocence about it she found intriguing. It contradicted the man she knew as her employer. Was this the philandering Jess Davies she'd been hearing her brother talk about all her life? Instinctively she felt something deeper and richer in the man holding her, touching her almost reverently. Her heart quickened further, and she unintentionally gasped aloud.

Jess stiffened before she realized what she'd done. She held her breath and sensed he was doing the same. She wondered if he would continue—or would he pretend that his touch hadn't given a message of tenderness? Now that he knew she was awake, Alexa lifted her head to gaze toward him through the darkness.

Jess felt like a boy caught with his hand in the candy jar. He didn't see any point in pretending that his behavior was appropriate for their relationship. Prudently he moved his hand over her back and into her hair, where he playfully grabbed a handful and chuckled. "Your hair's still wet, Miss Byrnehouse." She didn't move. She didn't react. "And your clothes, too," he added, pressing his other hand over her back.

Alexa would have given a month's wages to see inside his head, but she couldn't even see his face. While his touch filled her with unspeakable longing, what was filling him? Meekly his fingers skittered over her back. She shifted her weight and told herself that pressing her hands over his torso was necessary to remain steady. But she was keenly aware of the lean ribs beneath the fabric of his shirt, and the subtle, almost indiscernible groan that came from his chest.

"You don't feel especially dry," she finally replied, hearing her own voice sound raspy, almost shaky. "I hope you don't get pneumonia and die."

Jess caught her vague humor and chuckled, but he wondered why her voice trembled at the same time her shoulders did. "Are you cold?" he asked, and felt more than saw her shake her head. "If I die," he added lightly, "you'd be out of a job."

"And if *I* die," she retorted, her voice more steady now, "you'd be out of a trainer."

Jess instinctively tightened his arms around her. "You mustn't do that."

He said nothing more, and Alexa relaxed. Moving her head toward his shoulder, she instead met his face and her cheek brushed over the bristle of a day's growth. She shifted quickly, as if the contact singed her, then settled her head against his shoulder. Her mind reiterated what had just taken place. She might have imagined it as affection until she recalled his lips on her brow. The very thought made her flutter inside, and she wondered what was happening to her.

"Are you sure you're not cold?" he asked.

"Maybe a little," she replied, and Jess took advantage of it to tighten his embrace further. She softened in his arms and nuzzled closer like a child seeking warmth. Her display of dependence made it easy to press his lips into her hair. She tilted her face toward him, and he found them against her cheek.

"You know," he said, and Alexa could feel his lips moving as he spoke, "the boys would be worried if they knew the situation you're in right now."

"You mean cold, wet, and lost?" she asked lightly, giving in to the urge to knead her fingers over his shoulder like a contented kitten.

Jess pressed his lips to her cheek in a way that could not be misconstrued as anything but a kiss. "That too," he said, and briefly tightened his embrace before he relaxed.

Alexa awoke to clear daylight in Jess's arms, pinned to the ground by his chest. Carefully she attempted to ease the aching muscles in her back. Jess moved in his sleep, only to leave her completely immobile, but she looked at his face and didn't care.

It was incredible what just the sight of him did to her, and the thought of being close to him through the night only intensified the feeling. As she urged her true feelings to the surface, Alexa had to ask herself how long she had been fighting them. But now she had to admit that what she felt for him was real, which made his misjudgments all the more difficult. Recalling his dreamlike attentions in the night, Alexa wondered if he had reconsidered his harsh opinions—or, more likely, it had just been a natural reaction to holding a woman so close.

The intrigue of being in his arms pushed other thoughts briefly into oblivion. Alexa carefully brought her hand to his face, and a rush of excitement enveloped her. The reality was frightening. There was so much in him that seemed good and admirable, but there was a part of him she didn't understand.

Jess stretched himself awake, then moaned when he realized where he was. He glanced toward Alexa and held her gaze while one eyebrow moved slowly into an arch. She wondered if he would yell at her or make reference to their quiet whisperings in the night. He only said, "Are you all right?"

She nodded and Jess adjusted his weight, which brought her a little closer. She took a sharp breath, and his brow went up further as he scrutinized her expression. Expectancy made Alexa's heart quicken. His eyes were unreadable until he gave a wry smile.

"You look awful, Miss Byrnehouse." He took it upon himself to finger some of the mud out of her hair.

"You don't exactly look your best." She lifted her hand to pull caked dirt from the curls against his neck. Their eyes met and his narrowed, as if to question her motives, or perhaps his own. She quickly averted her gaze and was relieved when he stood abruptly. He took her hand to help her up, then he disappeared and she moved the opposite direction into some brush. She returned to find him leaning against a rock, meticulously brushing dirt from his hat.

"Ready?" he asked without looking at her. He didn't wait for a reply before he situated the hat firmly over his head and started down the mountain. "We'd best start walking," he said. "I think we've already missed breakfast."

Alexa followed him in silence, hoping he couldn't hear her stomach rumbling. Infuriated at having to wonder what he was thinking, she finally said, "Aren't you going to yell at me?"

"I did that yesterday."

"But surely you've got more to say," she prodded. "You should say: Wretched woman!" She lowered her voice to mimic him. "When are you going to learn that these are my horses, and I'll not have you . . ."

He stopped abruptly and turned, which put an end to her speech. She didn't know whether he looked insulted or amused, or if one was attempting to disguise the other.

"Miss Byrnehouse," he said, and she met his eyes stoically, almost wishing he knew how she felt about him.

Jess froze as her eyes seemed to bore right through him. He didn't have a clue what he'd intended to say. He could only remember how it felt to hold her last night, and he wondered what it might be like to love her. But all of that fled in the face of reality. Alexandra was his employee, and he felt certain her regard for him was not of the highest esteem. Her attitude toward him much of the time was enough to make him angry. And if that didn't, the way she made him feel certainly could.

"Did you want to say something?" she asked.

Caught off guard, Jess reacted purely on impulse. "One of these days," he took hold of her shoulders, "you will realize who is in charge."

With that, he kissed her. Alexa didn't even have a chance to anticipate it before it was happening. She pressed her hands against his chest, attempting to move away. But despite his brashness, her mind went back to his holding her in the night, and she began to soften. When he set her free, she stepped back to catch herself. She felt breathless and stunned, but the triumph in his eyes made her angry.

"One of these days, Mr. Davies," she growled, "you will realize that it doesn't matter who is in charge, as long as we learn to respect and trust each other."

Alexa saw his brow go up before he shot an arm around her waist and pulled her against him. He bent to kiss her, and she was surprised at the way she willingly accepted it, going on her tiptoes to accommodate his height. She had to admit it was not his advantage of strength that made her succumb, but she couldn't help wondering if his motivation was a display of affection or an attempt to prove his physical supremacy.

Jess drew back to study her expression. Alexa saw evidence of something affectionate flicker in his eyes before he kissed her again. She felt almost wicked for the way she enjoyed it, but it was evident that Jess enjoyed it as well.

Jess asked himself why he was doing this, and he couldn't come up with an answer. But even more baffling was the ardor in Alexa's response. Was this the same woman who defied him on a regular basis? The intensity of their kiss made him anxious to act on the awakening desire stirring within, but an accompanying fear forced him to reconsider. He stepped back abruptly and let her go, afraid this longing inside him might break into something irrational if he didn't.

Alexa looked up at him in question, feeling her lips quiver and her face tingle. For a moment she saw his eyes soften, as if he might say something tender. "Let's go home," he said tonelessly, and the moment passed. She gave him a hard glare and moved ahead of him on the trail, wondering if all men were so infuriatingly difficult to understand.

Jess occupied himself through the tedious walk by watching Alexa lead the way. It was something she did well, he decided. Of all the women to be feeling this way about, it had to be one with a will as strong as a mule, and a determination that no man could match. But oh, how she wore those breeches! He contemplated the fit of her boots over what he guessed were delicate calves. And though the breeches were a little baggy, when she moved just so there was no questioning that she was built much differently than any man. If he wasn't so hungry, he could almost wish for another cloudburst.

Six
ALEXA'S EYES

It wasn't long before Fiddler and Murphy found them. They'd been searching the mountain since dawn, and a flare was fired to let the others know Jess and Alexa were safe. They returned to the station amid flurries of relief, and by afternoon everything seemed back to normal, as if nothing had happened.

But Alexa felt different. Until last night, she had admitted to being intrigued by Jess Davies. But now her feelings had intensified into something deeper. And it frightened her.

Jess didn't show himself for the remainder of the day, but at supper, Alexa was informed that he wanted to see her. After all that had happened, she had to face the possibility that he would let her go. If her being here was going to make Chad more of a menace to Jess, then it was likely better. But still, the thought left her terrified.

Alexa ate quickly and went to his office, but he wasn't there. The maid came across her in the hall and saved Alexa the trouble of having to search the house and embarrass herself.

"Could you tell me where I might find Mr. Davies?"

"In the dining room," she said curtly.

"And where might that be?"

The maid gave directions, and Alexa wondered how Jess would feel about having his meal interrupted. But surely she wouldn't have been told where to find him if it defied any strict rules.

She knocked lightly at the door and heard him call. As she entered, he stood abruptly at the far end of a huge dining table, where he sat alone.

"You're early," he said. "You must have eaten quickly."

"I'm sorry. If you like, I can wait in your office, or—"

"No," he tossed his napkin on the table, "I'm finished." The same maid came in to clear the table and he said to her, "I'll take my coffee outside, Sarina. Miss Byrnehouse will be joining me."

"Yes, Mr. Davies," she replied with a condescending glance toward Alexa as she exited the room.

Jess motioned Alexa toward some French doors at one side of the room. She stepped onto a veranda just ahead of him and sat down to a breathtaking view of the hills. Jess sat across from her and said nothing for several moments. He stared at her as if attempting to read her thoughts, and she looked away. Her mind wandered to the happenings of last night. Was this the same man who had touched her with affection in the darkness and caused such stirrings within her? She thought of him kissing her this morning, and a violent fluttering seized her. She quickly broke the silence. "You wanted to see me?"

"Yes," he shifted in his chair, "I'm afraid I owe you an apology."

Alexa looked up in surprise. "On the contrary, I—"

"I was upset yesterday, as you could tell."

"With good reason." She flicked a piece of lint off her breeches and smoothed a wrinkle with a trembling hand.

"But with nothing to warrant my saying the things to you that I did. You have done nothing to give me reason not to trust you. I should judge you by your own merits, not by your name, and I apologize for my brashness."

Alexa was stunned. She had expected him to fire her, and he'd just given her a perfectly humble apology.

"I too must apologize." She drew up her chin and folded her hands in her lap. "I fear what might have happened had you not come to find me. Thank you."

Jess nodded slightly, and Alexa felt a mutual memory hover in the air between them. But it was as she'd feared: the moments in his arms were being ignored. She had to accept the reality that it was nothing more than circumstances that had brought on his attention. She turned her eyes away.

"If it's any consolation," she began, then the maid brought out the coffee tray and Alexa waited, not wanting to be overheard. When they were alone again, she took it upon herself to pour the coffee.

"You were saying?" Jess urged while he watched her capable hands maneuvering the china with perfect agility. For the first time, he tried to comprehend her as the lady he knew she'd been raised to be. She handed a cup to him, and their fingers briefly touched. He wanted to kiss her.

"Yes," she said after taking a careful sip, "I was just going to tell you that . . . well, in truth, I share your sentiments toward Chad. He told me that he didn't care if he ever saw my face again, that he hoped I would have to grovel in the streets to survive, and . . ." She glanced down, fighting her emotion. "Well," she bit her lip, "you get the idea."

Jess attempted to lighten the mood. "How did you ever come into that family?"

"Now that," she said too soberly, "is a good question."

Together they laughed. Alexa's eyes were drawn to his, but she quickly turned away.

"May I ask you something?" He set his cup down and leaned forward.

"Of course," she replied calmly, defying the expectancy she felt inside.

Jess's voice lowered melodically. "What are you hiding behind those eyes?" Alexa gave him a blank stare, and he chuckled. "Stupid question, but I had the urge to ask you. It's just that you have the most . . . intriguing eyes."

"My father used to tell me that," she said for lack of anything better to say.

"Do you miss him?" Jess asked.

Alexa looked at Jess quickly, wondering what Tyson Byrnehouse would have thought to see them together this way. She stood and set down her cup, unnerved by the rising tension. "I should be going. Thank you for the coffee."

"But you hardly touched it." He stood also.

"I need to wash out some clothes before bed, and . . . I should get up early and make up for the time we lost this morning." Her eyes darted to his, and she saw him remembering the cause of lost time, just as she was. "Thank you again," she finished and hurried away, wondering if it was Jess or her feelings that made her run down the long hall and across the lawn.

Returning to the carriage house, she lost her ambition and ended up sitting in the trap, trying to make sense of the effect Jess Davies was having on her life. The thought of exploring this attraction left her wary. Was it simply habit? Had all these years, hearing her father and brother speak ill of him, left an impression? Or was it something more?

"Is that you, Alexa?" A voice startled her, and she turned to see Richard leaning against the trap, arms folded across his chest. "May I join you?" he asked.

"Of course." She moved over and motioned for him to sit beside her.

"Where are we going?" he asked, and she laughed.

"I used to hide in the carriages when I was a child. For some reason it seems a comforting place to be when I know they're not going anywhere, and I can just think."

"I can appreciate the theory." Richard crossed an ankle on his knee. Alexa became lost in her thoughts and he asked, "Where is your mind, my friend?"

"Oh," she laughed softly, "just wandering, I suppose."

"You okay?" He looked at her with concern.

"Of course," she insisted.

"You did have quite an ordeal last night."

"Ah," she smiled, "it wasn't so bad." Her eyes turned distant. "Jess kept me warm."

"Did he now?" Richard retorted.

Alexa looked up, surprised at his tone. "Don't jump to any conclusions, Richard. It was a matter of necessity."

Richard frowned, pondering what made her so defensive. His uneasiness deepened when her eyes got that faraway look again. He was about to question it when she asked quietly, "Do you know Jess well?"

Richard hesitated, wondering over her motives, and then he had to wonder over his. Would lying to Alexa now tip the scales in his favor later on? It was tempting, but his integrity was not something he took lightly. "As well as anyone. Of all the boys, I've been here the longest."

"What's your opinion of him?" she prodded. "Generally speaking, of course."

Richard cleared his throat and looked away. "I have a great deal of respect for Jess. He's given me much. I dare say any of the boys would tell you the same. It seems we're all here because we were in need. He's got a soft heart, that boy."

"What do you mean?" Alexa asked, intrigued.

"Well," he leaned back and counted on his fingers, "Mrs. Brown, the housekeeper, needed a job when her husband died and the bank foreclosed on her property. Murphy worked on the tracks in Melbourne, but got fired when he confronted some shady business going on. Jimmy worked with him; he quit and came with Murphy. Fiddler lost his wife and son in a carriage mishap and turned to drink until Jess pulled him out of the gutter, so to speak. And Sam . . . well, I don't know him very well, but I believe he was gambling heavily on the races and got himself into trouble. Tod was left without a job when he lost one too many races, and he hasn't any family. Most of us don't, I guess. Who did I miss?"

"Edward," she provided.

"Ah, yes. Edward was a cook with Her Majesty's Navy, but he came up with a heart disorder and they didn't want him anymore; dismissed him just like that." He snapped his fingers. "He's got no more than five years left to live, the doctor says."

"I don't believe it," Alexa said in astonishment.

"I couldn't either, but it's true. Did I miss anyone? Oh, Sarina."

"Who?"

"The little maid. Surely you've seen her. Native girl." Alexa nodded. "She showed up on the doorstep one day, wanting a job. Turned out she was barely pregnant; apparently she'd been sorely taken advantage of. Jess took her in. She had the baby here, and Jess gave the boy everything a child could want. Sarina occasionally goes to visit her relations in the outback, but she's the most faithful native I've ever seen. Always comes back, works her heart out for Jess."

"I can see why," Alexa said quietly, trying to absorb what all of this meant concerning Jess Davies. It didn't seem that Chad knew him very well after all. "Where is Sarina's boy now?"

"Little Ben? He's with his grandparents. Apparently they think the world of him. They keep him about half the time."

"And what about you?" Alexa asked.

Richard looked down. "My parents worked for Jess's father. We grew up together. My mother died when I was young, and my father was killed about ten years ago. Jess has helped me through . . . ," he cleared his throat and added curtly, "the worst of times." He was silent a moment. "All in all, I'd have to say he's a pretty decent guy. I'd trust him with my life any day."

"I suppose he did the same for me," she said. "I had nowhere else to go when I came here. That pretty much makes me one of the boys."

Richard laughed. "Not entirely."

Alexa's thoughts turned again to Jess, and her heart quickened a little.

"You know," Richard startled her back to the present, "your eyes always seem so . . . full of life."

"Really?" She laughed.

"Really," he answered quietly.

After a long silence, he found the courage to ask, "Alexa, is something . . . happening between you and Jess?"

She gave a tense, almost flippant laugh. "Don't be absurd. All we ever do is yell at each other. Surely you've noticed."

Richard made no comment, but he didn't like what he sensed between her words.

"I should go up to bed." Alexa moved to the edge of the seat. "I need to get up early and wash out some things."

Richard stepped down from the trap and held out his hand to help her. He continued to hold it as they walked up the steps together and he opened her door.

"Good night, then," he said. She only smiled and went into her room.

Alexa closed the door and noticed, even in the dark, a sheet of paper lying on the floor. She bent to pick it up and quickly lit the lamp to see what was written there.

Vivacious eyes, bewitching eyes, eyes that stir my soul.

Losing myself within those eyes could only find me whole.

"Oh, Richard," she said aloud, sensing an affection in the poetry that made her wonder if his feelings for her were becoming more complex. Comfortable as she was with their friendship, she disregarded such a possibility and tacked the poem on the wall with the other. She noticed then that the handwriting was different. The one he'd given her before was written in longhand and signed at the bottom, whereas this was printed in tiny block letters and there was no signature. She wondered briefly if it might not be from Richard, but she couldn't think of anyone else who would possibly write such a thing. Assuring herself that it had to be him, Alexa wondered if he chose to keep his more personal feelings anonymous, and printed rather than writing it out.

Grateful for Richard's friendship, Alexa dressed for bed and said a prayer before she crawled between the cool sheets. By their own will her thoughts drifted to Jess, and with them she fell asleep.

❦ ❦ ❦

As the race drew closer, Alexa found it increasingly difficult to know where she stood with Jess. He often came out to watch their trial races, but he kept his distance and rarely spoke with her. When they did converse, she found him unnaturally kind and considerate. Part of her wanted to believe he was feeling the same attraction. But in the end she convinced herself that she was reading her own desires into it. She blatantly avoided any eye contact, fearing he might read there what she preferred to keep to herself.

By the way Alexa avoided looking at him, Jess felt certain she simply didn't like him. Any personal attention she gave him at all, he credited to patronizing him for the sake of her job.

Five days before the race, Demented was still winning and Jess wondered if his hopes were futile. It was as foolish to believe he could save himself with a horse race as it was to ponder exploring this obsession he had with Alexandra. He knew this was the last time they could push the horses before the race, and he decided he didn't want to go out and see Crazy lose again. He wandered the house idly, then found himself on the side lawn, gazing out across his land, feeling it slip through his fingers like an elusive dream.

A feminine voice startled him from his thoughts, and he turned to see Alexa running up the lawn toward him. "Jess," she said breathlessly, "I'm so glad I found you."

"What's wrong?" he demanded, trying not to sound panicked. Alexa stopped to catch her breath, and he wanted to shake the answer out of her.

"Jess," she said again with an absorbing smile, "Crazy just won by a head."

"With Tod?" he asked, and she nodded exuberantly.

"Aaah!" He laughed and lifted his face skyward. Impulsively he picked Alexa up and turned with her in his arms. "We did it!" he shouted. "I knew Crazy could do it."

"You have good instincts." She tried not to sound disappointed when he set her down and stepped back.

"I have a good trainer."

Alexa felt his eyes probing hers, and she turned away as it quickened her heart further.

"Come on," she said, "let's try it one more time."

The whole crew whooped and hollered when Crazy won again, this time by half a length. They knew it wasn't a fluke.

"Alexa is a miracle worker," Richard professed.

Jess nudged him in the ribs and grinned. "She makes apple pie out of peaches."

Richard glanced at him dubiously, but Jess only laughed.

While Crazy rested for her big day, the boys were hard at work preparing the station for the coming onslaught. This race was by no means a derby, but to those who took it seriously, it was the center of society and sport. Bored and tense, Alexa did what she could to help, concentrating most of her efforts on supervising the cleaning of the bunkhouse.

With only two days to go, Alexa became acutely aware that she hadn't seen Jess. Concerned, she went to the house in search of him, but Sarina insisted he'd gone out.

She found him standing at the highest part of the lawn, his hands deep in his pockets, his eyes distant. Alexa stood quietly beside him to look in the same direction. He turned his head for an instant to acknowledge her presence, then his eyes went back to the view.

When minutes passed and he said nothing, Alexa tried to guess his thoughts. It wasn't difficult to figure what might be going through a man's head at such a point in his life, and compassion filled her. Wanting to be positive she said, "It's beautiful, Jess."

His eyes silently agreed as they focused on the stretch of wooded hills left to him by his father. "I can't even imagine what it would be like to leave here."

Alexa wanted to tell him to have faith, but she sensed this was not the right time for such words. A part of him had to face the possibility of losing. It couldn't be denied. "Where would you go?" she asked quietly.

"Where would any of us go?" He shifted his weight to the other leg and sighed. "I don't know. I can't even begin to think."

"But surely there would be time to prepare and—"

"Not if Chad buys it," he interrupted.

Alexa stared at the ground. "I believe we can win, Jess."

He turned to look at her. "Do you really?" he asked with more sincerity than she'd ever heard from him.

"I've been through a lot of races," she stated in a businesslike tone. "I think we have an extremely good chance."

"I pray you're right." His eyes went back to the view.

"And if I'm not," she smiled brightly, "we'll know we did the very best we could. Something good has got to come out of it somewhere."

Jess looked into those eyes and wished he could begin to tell her what that meant to him. He thought of all he had learned from her these past weeks, and the hope she had instilled into him. He seriously considered kissing her, but decided she'd likely resent it. Instead he just tousled her hair like he would have Tod or Murphy, then he put his arm around her neck with some semblance of a hug. She laughed and looked up with shining eyes.

"Maybe something good already has come out of it," he said with such intensity that Alexa had to turn away and try to recall what had brought her out here in the first place.

"Oh," she said, "it's almost four o'clock. Would you care to join us for tea?"

"Tea?" He laughed dubiously.

"Let's just say I'm bored." Without permission, she took his hand and led him over the lawn. "I've been trying to think what I've really missed since I came here, and I've decided it was having tea. Not that I stuck to it religiously or anything, but once in a while civilized people just need to sit down and have tea."

"Might I ask where you found any civilized people around here?" he chortled.

"If the boys aren't civilized yet, they will be."

Jess felt sure this was some kind of joke until she ushered him through the bunkhouse door. Everyone except Edward sat around the table, tapping fingers and looking bored.

"I told them if they got the bunkhouse clean I'd reward them," Alexa announced.

"We're still waitin'," Murphy growled.

"Did you get it clean?" Jess asked.

"See for yourself." Fiddler leaned back and grinned smugly.

Jess stepped into the other room and they could hear him exclaim, "Mercy! This place *does* have a floor."

"I think Alexa had something to do with that," Richard said. Jess sat across from him while Alexa went into the kitchen.

"Did Alexa find the floor?" Jess asked.

"No," Sam frowned, "she stood over us with a riding crop while *we* found it."

"I like Alexa more all the time," Jess said vehemently.

"We're still waitin'," Murphy shouted toward the kitchen.

"Shut up and mind your manners," Alexa called back.

Edward appeared with a tray of the usual tin cups, and Alexa followed with the good old reliable coffee pot. But instead of the normal strong, dark brew, she poured out a concoction that made their noses wrinkle.

"It's not exactly fine china," she said as all eyes turned toward her in amazement, "but it will do."

"I thought you said you was gonna reward us," Jimmy snarled skeptically.

"Smells like punishment to me," Murphy added with disgust.

Alexa stuck her tongue out at him. "What a bunch of ornery blokes. Just be patient."

"I can assure you she's been baking all afternoon," Edward chimed in on his way back to the kitchen.

"This had better be good," Sam interjected.

"I think having tea is a fine idea," Richard said and received several glares. "I used to have tea occasionally with Emma, and I rather enjoyed it."

Alexa wondered who Emma was. She didn't miss the nostalgic glance that Jess passed to Richard before she returned to the kitchen.

Jess closed his eyes and inhaled the tea. Memories flooded over him so strongly that he nearly expected to hear his mother's voice. Instead, he heard Alexa's.

"Here it is," she announced, and he opened his eyes to see her set a huge platter on the table that brought a hush over the room. She might as well have put a pile of dung there by the way the men stared in horror at the neatly arranged little frosted cakes.

"What are *those?*" Murphy asked, breaking the silence.

"You got enough there to feed a mob," Jimmy added.

"You're a bunch of cowards," Jess snarled, and reached over to take one carefully between his thumb and forefinger. He held it in front of his face and turned it over for a close examination while everyone watched expectantly.

"You'd think it was going to bite you first," Alexa snapped, but Jess flicked a teasing glance toward her and she smiled.

"I just want to appreciate such fineness to its full degree," he said dramatically.

"Get on with it," Edward insisted. "We haven't got all day to be lounging around like a bunch of . . ." He stopped when Fiddler glared at him. It was obvious the word he'd intended to use wouldn't be appropriate for tea with a lady.

Jess closed his eyes and sank his teeth slowly into the little cake while the men held their breath. "This is wonderful," he said with his mouth full, then he swallowed and licked the sweet cream filling from his lips. "How did you manage?" he asked Alexa, then consumed the rest of the cake in one more bite.

"I'll never tell," she grinned.

As Jess picked up another, Richard was quick to follow, then Fiddler. The three began making noises of pleasure, and the others finally mustered the courage to give it a chance. Alexa laughed to see the way Murphy looked at the cake in his hand as if it might break. He nibbled a little corner by barely touching it to his teeth while Jimmy watched him, eyes wide with amazement. A minute later, they were eating so eagerly that all conversation ceased.

Fiddler finally commented, "I'd say it's about time we had some feminine influence out here."

"We have Sarina and Mrs. Brown," Jess said.

"No," Fiddler argued, "*you* have Sarina and Mrs. Brown. We needed someone like Alexa." He looked up at her as she walked around the table to refill cups. "I think tea is a splendid idea."

"Thank you," she beamed. "Perhaps we should make it a habit."

"Who's going to train horses if you're in the kitchen baking crumpets?" Jess protested.

"Well," she shrugged and leaned over him to fill his cup, "perhaps we'll just have tea once in a while."

"Aren't you going to have any?" Richard asked as she came around the table to fill his.

"Looks like I'd better before they're all gone," she said. Murphy, Jimmy, and Sam all looked up at her innocently, their mouths full and a cake in each hand.

While Alexa made certain everyone had enough to drink, Jess watched her and pondered what Fiddler had said. Alexa had touched all of their lives in a way that he couldn't quite define. She sidled onto the bench next to Richard, and he noticed the warm glance they exchanged. There was a time when he'd believed Richard would never look a woman straight in the eye again. Jess met her gaze across the table and felt recently familiar stirrings from those electrifying pools of blue. She turned away abruptly, making him wonder if she preferred to keep a reasonable distance from him. After the way he'd treated her at times, he couldn't really blame her. But a part of him ached to know the Alexandra Byrnehouse behind those eyes.

With the cake devoured and the teapot dry, Jess ordered the men back to work. One by one they filtered out, complimenting Alexa with varying degrees of warmth. Edward cleared off the table except for the cup wrapped in Alexa's hands, and Jess found himself alone with her.

"That was enjoyable," he said. "Thank you."

She smiled and took a long sip of her tea as if it were pure nectar.

"What else do you miss?" he asked. Her eyes moved up while her mouth stayed against the cup.

She straightened her back and cleared her throat. "I'd rather not talk about that," she said coldly and went into the kitchen.

Seven
FEMININE INFLUENCE

Jess returned to the house and wandered idly, contemplating his memories and his fears. After dinner he had coffee on the veranda and watched the distant stable yard. The boys filtered in and out of the bunkhouse to see that everything was done before they went inside for what he guessed was the usual game of cards or dice. He saw Alexa and Richard go into the carriage house together, and he could hear their laughter as they disappeared. Something akin to jealousy crept over him. He wondered what it was about himself that kept Alexa from sharing the kind of friendship she seemed to have with the others. Maybe she just didn't like him, he thought, or perhaps she believed everything Chad had told her about him—whatever that might be.

With the yard now still, Jess glanced around. He hated the quiet. He longed for laughter and conversation. And when he thought of Alexa, he longed for other things as well. He chided himself for even thinking such thoughts. It was crazy to believe she would want a man like him. And for all he knew, they'd all be out on the streets next week and going their separate ways. A man with empty pockets was a fool to believe he could ever offer Alexandra Byrnehouse what she deserved.

Jess heard a door slam across the yard, and looked up to see a petite form in breeches move lithely through the evening dusk toward the stable. With ease he jumped over the veranda rail and trotted across the lawn. He came quietly through the stable doorway and leaned against a post. He could see Alexa silhouetted against the light of a single lamp. She scratched Crazy behind the ears and received a snort of pleasure. Gently she stroked the dark muzzle with a caress that Jess envied. He was about to make himself known when she spoke.

"Only two more days, my love, and we won't have to worry anymore. We're all proud of you, Crazy." She laughed softly. "What a silly name. Maybe you could give me a clue why you earned it. No matter. You've come far these past weeks, but you've got to take us a little farther. All we ask is that you do your best. You run with everything you've got, my love, and maybe Jess will want to keep us both around for a long time."

"I already do," he said. Alexa gasped, absently putting a hand to her heart. Uncertain and embarrassed, she eased carefully to the other side of Crazy.

"You shouldn't eavesdrop," she scolded. "It's not polite."

"You can't expect to civilize us all in one afternoon." He sauntered toward her and eased into the stall, peering behind Crazy's mane to see her blush. Alexa turned and leaned into Crazy's neck. With practiced agility, Jess ducked beneath the horse's belly and stood beside her.

"What are you doing here, anyway?" she asked. "Crazy and I wanted to be alone."

"So I heard," he said in mock anger. "The two of you conspiring against me behind my back."

Alexa looked up to assure herself he was teasing. His eyes were stern, but his lips twitched slightly. "I named her Crazy because she understands me."

"Are you crazy?" she asked.

"Maybe."

"And that's why you call your horses insane names?"

"Crazy likes her name."

"How do you know?"

"How do you know she doesn't?" he retorted, and she nuzzled against Crazy again to hide her face. It was unnerving to have Jess standing so close, watching her skeptically. She was afraid to look at him, fearing what her eyes might betray, certain he would only mock her if he knew the truth.

To distract herself from the growing tension, she spoke quietly to Crazy. "Is it true? Do you like your name?" The horse snorted and Jess chuckled. "Do you understand him, Crazy?" She watched Jess out of the corner of her eye. "Then tell me what he's doing here, invading our private conversations."

"Just lonely and nervous," Jess said. Alexa looked up abruptly, surprised by his honesty.

"I think we're all a little of that." She nonchalantly moved around the front of Crazy to put the horse between them.

Jess wished he could read her mind. There were moments when she seemed to enjoy his company, while others made him certain she could barely tolerate him. He wondered why she was so unwilling to look at him.

"I must say I agree with Fiddler." He deftly maneuvered beneath Crazy again to stand beside her.

"I'm sorry?" She looked bewildered.

"He said it's about time we had some feminine influence around here." His voice lowered provocatively. "He said we needed somebody like you."

"It worked out nicely, then." She kept her eyes fixed on Crazy's ear as she scratched it. "Since I needed a job." She felt more than saw Jess step closer. A quick glance at his expression brought to mind the stories Chad had told her of the womanizing Jess Davies. She wanted to ask him if it was true. Did he freely spread himself over Australia, with no thought to a woman's feelings or reputation? If so, why hadn't he tried before now to have his way with her? He'd certainly had opportunities. Perhaps because she worked for him. Did he fear that any advances would leave him without a trainer? As she realized that her job was essentially finished with respect to this race, Alexa heard pulse beats in her ears. Why did he have to stand so close? Why did he have to look at her like that? And worst of all, why did she have to feel this way about her employer—the philandering Jess Davies, no less?

"I wonder if you would mind telling me," he said in an almost businesslike tone, giving her hope that his purpose was the same until he added, "how many of them have tried to kiss you."

He eased an arm around her waist, and she found herself trapped. Crazy danced uneasily as if she sensed the mounting tension. For a moment Alexa was tempted to make her feelings known, but fear ruled it out. If he was the kind of man Chad said he was, he would likely trample on her heart and leave it to bleed. But oh, how it felt to have him close!

"You didn't answer me," he said indignantly while he drew nearer. Crazy fidgeted, but Jess paid her no mind.

Alexa looked up at him, attempting to mirror his tone. "Only you have been so brash, Mr. Davies. Unlike you, they respect me."

Jess felt momentarily hurt. "What makes you think I don't respect you?"

"There's no need for me to tell you that." She looked down, unable to meet his eyes another second. When he made no response she spoke, if only to ease the quiet. "I have a good working relationship with these men. We're . . . friends."

Jess took hold of her chin and lifted her face. "And if they're your friends, Alexa, what am I?"

When he wouldn't allow her to turn away, she closed her eyes. "I work for you," she said as nonchalantly as possible, considering the way he held her.

"And that's all I mean to you?" he asked, unable to hide his disappointment. Alexa jerked her chin free and turned away. Her silence told him she agreed, but a part of him wouldn't accept it. With a bold exertion of pure male instinct, Jess urged his lips to her throat.

"Jess, please don't," she insisted, defying all she felt inside.

Jess ignored her and set a finger to her chin, bringing her face close to his. Alexa closed her eyes to avoid his gaze, but he took it as an invitation to kiss her.

Alexa felt the world spinning. Any effort to remain uninvolved in the play of his lips was futile. She leaned toward him as her hand went to the back of his neck to brace herself. She drew back to gasp for breath, and his words caressed the corner of her mouth. "You're lying to me, Alexandra."

"You can't blame me for being human." Her voice turned dreamy as she toyed with the curls hanging over his collar.

"Nor can you blame me," he whispered huskily and kissed her again.

Alexa thought she would die from the ecstasy as he held her closer, kissed her harder, left her weak with longing. Their eyes met. She felt embarrassed and intrigued. And scared. She pressed her face to his shoulder and wrapped her fingers around his upper arms. His lips breathed a sigh against her brow.

"Don't do this to me, Jess," she whispered.

"What am I doing?" He feigned innocence.

"You're toying with me, and you know it. We have to consider tomorrow."

"For me there is no tomorrow," he said and kissed her again. Alexa felt her mouth become a part of his, as if they had been born to be together this way, to fill each other with life-giving sustenance. He urged her impossibly closer and spoke against her lips. "At this moment I have no comprehension of life two days from now. What will I be when this is done? Where will I be?" He kissed her again. "Who will I be with?"

"Life will go on, Jess." She opened her eyes, able to look at him now that they were discussing something beyond their attraction.

"Yes, life will go on, Alexa." He kissed her tentatively, teasing her lips with his. "But right now I don't care." His voice lowered to a gruff whisper. "Spend the night with me, Alexa."

She held her breath and looked into his eyes to assure herself that he was serious.

"We'll ride together on a spirited stallion, and fly like the wind with moonlight to guide us. We'll exchange moonlight for candles and share tea from the same cup. Then we can build a fire in the hearth and lie together by the flames. I'll take you into oblivion with me, Alexandra, where nothing matters but you and me."

Alexa became mesmerized by his poetic images. Her heart pounded from the thrill of what he was offering. But she wasn't so foolish that she couldn't see the emptiness in it. Here he stood, rambling on about no tomorrow at the expense of her virtue. As much as she wanted it too, Jess Davies had to know she was not a woman to be trifled with.

"Your offer sounds intriguing, Mr. Davies," she said with a straight voice and hard eyes, "but I must decline."

"Why?" he asked hoarsely.

"Because there is only one thing I really need from you right now, and by morning I wouldn't have it. Whether we win or lose, Jess, I will walk away from that race with your respect."

"What has the race got to do with it?" he asked almost angrily.

"I don't know what motivates you to think I would be had so easily, but you're beginning to sound like the man Chad always told me you were."

Jess stepped back as if she'd slapped him. Only his hands at her shoulders kept her from falling. Crazy sidestepped uneasily and whinnied as if she sensed the hurt that Alexa saw in Jess's eyes. Those same incongruities of his character rose up to haunt her. She had told herself she would judge Jess by her own standards, not by Chad's warped opinions. And here she was, bluntly ignoring her own resolve. She wanted to apologize and somehow make it right, but emotion rose in her throat to be joined by the fear she was trying to swallow. All she could do was try to escape.

Alexa ran to the carriage house as if her feelings for Jess might catch up and smother her. She nearly bumped into Richard on the stairs, and was grateful for the darkness that hid any evidence of the tingling she felt in her lips.

"Where have you been?" he asked in concern. "I was about to come looking for you."

"I'm perfectly capable of taking care of myself," she retorted and pushed past him.

"But you said you would be gone five minutes."

"I ran into Jess." She paused at the doorway, her back to Richard.

"Arguing again?" He sounded amused.

"I guess you could call it that."

"You're not still determined to ride the race, are you?"

"No, of course not. That had nothing to do with it."

"You obviously don't want to talk about it," Richard said, and she appreciated his perception. "I'll let you get some sleep, but I want you to remember one thing."

"And what might that be?" she asked curtly.

"This is not easy for Jess, but if you look past his pride you'll find a decent man."

Alexa looked up at him and nodded as his words struck her deeply. "Good night, Richard," she said gently and went into her room.

Without lighting a lamp, she leaned against the window and peered out at the high moon. Her stomach fluttered violently to recall Jess's overture. The passion in his voice came back to her, and she rubbed the goose bumps from her arms. She was surprised to look down and see him standing in the yard below, gazing up at her. Her heart quickened as she thought how easy it would be to walk out there and accept his precarious offer.

His expression was lost in the shadows, but his affable stance confirmed what she had already begun to conclude. Jess had put it well himself once: Chad was full of wind. Whatever he'd had to say about Jess Davies had no validity as far as Alexa was concerned. The problem was how to let Jess know that, since she'd blatantly told him the opposite. She pressed her fingers to the glass as if she might touch his thoughts with hers. He lifted his chin expectantly, then turned and walked away.

Through a sleepless night, Alexa pondered all that was happening, everything she felt. She found it difficult to separate those feelings into categories of "professional" and "personal." But by dawn, she knew it was the only way to deal with them. She worked for Jess Davies, and they were on the brink of proving whether or not her efforts would be successful. She demanded his respect and knew that he deserved hers. Knowing where to stand on her personal feelings for Jess was not so easy. For the moment, she made up her mind to ignore them.

Too nervous to eat, Alexa skipped breakfast and went into the house. Guessing that Jess took his meals at the same time, she went directly to the dining room. She knocked lightly, then pushed open the door without waiting for a response. Her resolve to disregard her feelings fled quickly as Jess rose from the table but said nothing. His eyes told her he was sharing her memories of the night before. She forced herself to look down and clear her head.

"Forgive me for intruding." She looked back up, her expression all business.

"Why don't you join me?" He motioned toward the chair at his right.

Alexa was tempted, but knew it would only make this more difficult. "Thank you, no," she replied, lifting her chin with determination. "Perhaps another time." Jess nodded, and she cleared her throat. "There is something I need to say."

Jess stepped out from behind the table. "Should we go to the office or—"

"No," she insisted. "It won't take long." He looked disappointed, and Alexa became briefly distracted by the longing in his expression. If she had decided he was not trifling with her, what was she to think of the affection in his eyes? That violent fluttering returned. She glanced down and cleared her throat again. *Business,* she reminded herself.

"I came to apologize," she stated firmly, meeting his eyes with courage. He looked surprised but said nothing. "The first time I walked through your door, I told myself I would not allow anything Chad had said to influence my judgment. I apologize for losing my perspective on that. You have been generous with me, and I am grateful."

Jess watched Alexa put her hands behind her back and set her booted feet close together. Was this the same woman who had melted like snow in the hot December sun when he'd held her in his arms last night? Her aura was all business, while her eyes bordered on something deceptive. Trying to discern the thoughts between her words, he guessed that she was likely as nervous about the race as he was. Jess hoped that was the reason she appeared so cool and withdrawn. How he longed to warm her! He wanted to tell her that he *did* respect her. But if he told her that, he'd be compelled to tell her that he was obsessed with her. With all he wanted to say, he settled for a simple, "Forgive me, Alexa. My intention was not to offend you."

His words brought back the memories, and Jess saw a glimpse of melting snow. "I know," she said with a trace of tenderness. "It's forgotten."

Alexa turned and walked out, knowing she would never forget. If she left here tomorrow and never saw Jess Davies again, she would never be free of the impression he had branded on her. A few straying tears confirmed it, and wiping them away didn't change the hard truth. She loved him.

❧　❧　❧

Knowing the boys were still at breakfast, Alexa ambled into the stable and just stood with her hands in her pockets, watching Crazy. The horse was restless, and Alexa hoped the urge to run would stay with her until tomorrow.

"Come along, little lady," she murmured and bridled Crazy for a walk. She met Richard on her way out of the stable.

"Where have you been?" he asked. "You missed breakfast."

"I'm too nervous to eat," she admitted, and led Crazy toward the paddock.

"Is that all?" Richard asked, strolling idly beside her.

Alexa glanced at him, wondering if he could sense the change in her. She wanted to pour her feelings out to him, and at the same time hold them secretly forever, as if doing so might protect them. Unable to do either, she said nonchalantly, "I'm a little concerned about . . . Jess."

Richard looked surprised, but Murphy interrupted the conversation. "Want me to do that?" He took Crazy's reins. "Why don't you get some breakfast, Missy. Edward's waitin' for you."

"Thank you, Murphy. I suppose I should. Be easy on her now," she added, and Murphy grinned.

Alexa's stomach growled, and Richard took her arm. "What about Jess?" He urged her toward the bunkhouse.

"Oh, I don't know." She felt as if she were lying. "I know so little about him, but I'm concerned that . . ."

They entered the bunkhouse, and he sat across from her as Edward set a plate out. "I thought you'd show up sooner or later," he smiled.

"Thank you," Alexa said. "You're a darling, as always." Edward winked and Alexa began to eat, almost hoping Richard would forget what she'd been talking about.

"Concerned about what?" he prodded, leaning his forearms on the table after Edward returned to the kitchen.

Alexa tried quickly to think of something legitimate to say that expressed her concerns without touching her true sentiments.

"What if we lose, Richard?" she asked quietly. "Does Jess have anything besides this land? Anyone in his life beyond those of us who work for him?"

Richard's expression mirrored her concern. "Not to my knowledge," he reported, "but then, do any of us?"

Alexa looked down. "I suppose not." She pushed her eggs around with her fork, feeling little appetite. "But it's different for him, isn't it? The rest of us are losing a job, but Jess is . . ."

"Yes, I know," Richard said when she didn't finish.

"Does he have any relatives or—"

"Not in this country," Richard said gravely.

"His parents?" she asked, if only to ease her curiosity.

"Long dead."

"Did you know them?" She recalled what he'd told her earlier and added, "But of course you did. You grew up here."

"Why all of this . . . interest?"

Alexa looked away guiltily. "Just . . . curious, I suppose."

Richard sighed and apparently accepted her justification. "They were good people. His father was one of the finest men I've ever known. Jess is a lot like him. And his mother was . . ." Richard hesitated unnaturally and she looked up, wondering what he didn't want to say. "She was kind through and through," he said at her insistent gaze.

"That's not what you were thinking," she guessed with a degree of confidence.

"They're dead, Alexa. This conversation has nothing to do with our present concerns."

"Yes, but . . ." She smiled wryly and he chuckled.

"You want to know anyway." Richard's expression sobered. "She was not whole, Alexa."

"What do you mean?" she asked in a whisper, feeling her heart pound without understanding why.

"Her mind," he answered. "She was a wonderful woman, full of love and generosity. But she didn't live in reality."

Alexa leaned back, recalling bits of conversation just last night in the stable, in reference to Crazy's name. She ached to ask more but feared being intrusive. Richard looked at her expectantly and she posed one more question. "How did she die?"

His expression changed so abruptly it almost frightened her. "Eat your breakfast, Alexa." He came to his feet. "I've got work to do."

Alexa felt stunned, wondering what she'd said to provoke such a reaction. Her thoughts stayed with it through the morning, evoking a deep compassion for Jess, though she couldn't quite decipher its source. Her feelings gravitated toward Richard as she speculated over what the two of them might have shared in years past that seemed to have left hidden scars.

Throughout the afternoon, participants in the race began to arrive. The stables and bunkhouse, which usually seemed so large, gradually became filled to their capacity. Alexa much preferred peace and privacy, but there was an excitement in the air that compensated for the crowds. She couldn't deny that horse racing was in her blood as a familiar anticipation settled into her, and she hoped it would help her put aside thoughts of Jess. But as the day wore on, the reality of what rested on this race combined with her awakening feelings for Jess, and she began to feel a sense of desperation.

She didn't see Jess or Richard through the day, and she wondered if they were both avoiding her for different reasons. Convinced that nerves were getting the better of her, Alexa went to her room after supper, hoping to avoid the crowd gathering around the fire in the yard, drinking and laughing and speculating about tomorrow. Answering a knock at the door, she was glad to see Richard.

"Sorry about earlier," he said with an embarrassed smile, but he didn't offer any further explanation.

"Come in," she said eagerly. "It will be nice to have someone to talk to."

"Actually," he replied, "I came to tell you that Jess wants to see us—all of us—right now."

Alexa went to the house with Richard, hating the tense silence hovering around them. Was it possible that he sensed what was happening?

They found the others already gathered in the office, chatting and laughing; everyone except Edward, who'd been left to watch over Crazy.

"Good, you're here," Jess said when they entered and sat beside each other. Murphy closed the door and leaned against it while Jess sat on the edge of his desk.

"I just wanted to tell you, boys," he caught Alexa's eye and seemed amused to include her in the term, "that I appreciate all your hard work in preparation for this. All I ask now is that you come through with your assignments, and we'll hope for the best."

Jess paused and took a deep breath before adding, "If we win, you'll get the bonuses I promised, and . . . if we don't . . . well, you might as well know, it will probably be less than two weeks before it all goes." A hush fell over the room until Jess finished with a firm, "We'll just have to win."

"I believe we will," Richard said with enthusiasm.

Tod groaned, and Murphy slapped him on the back with a hearty laugh. "Cheer up, boy. By this time tomorrow we'll be sittin' pretty."

Nervous knots twisted in Alexa's stomach, but she felt a kinship with these men that she'd never felt with the hands at Byrnehouse Station.

"And remember," Jess continued, "please—check and recheck everything. I don't want any accidents. Questions?"

"I think we're set," Murphy said.

"Are you ready, Tod?" Jess asked him. Tod glanced toward Alexa, and together they nodded with surety.

"I guess that's all, then," Jess said. "Let's not have any drinking tonight. I want everything under control early. Get a good night's sleep, and I'll see you in the morning."

Murphy opened the door and the men filed into the hall. Alexa went last, pausing to look back at Jess. Their eyes met, and butterflies rushed through her to swarm amidst the nervous knots. She wanted to ask if he was all right, but the others hovered in the hallway waiting for her to join them. She felt sure Jess was not nearly as calm as he appeared to be, but she reminded herself there was nothing she could do about that without crossing boundaries that she simply could not cross. Not yet.

Alexa walked into the hall, and the group moved together outside. She stuffed her hair up beneath her cap and stayed in the midst of them, hating it when strangers looked at her oddly, as if they couldn't figure which gender she belonged to.

Once safely escorted to the carriage house, she prepared for bed but found sleep impossible. Tomorrow she would either be a hero or without a job. The sounds of laughter and commotion filtering from the yard only deepened the reality.

At nearly midnight, a knock at Alexa's door made her grateful for a good excuse not to lie and stare at the ceiling. She rose eagerly to answer it, thinking it would be nice to talk with Richard and ease her nerves. But it was Jess Davies standing in the hall, his hands deep in his pockets, his expression severe.

"I'm sorry," he said quietly. "I hope I didn't wake you, but I—"

"No," she interrupted, "I couldn't sleep. Come in."

Jess stepped inside and closed the door to realize they were in the dark. Quickly she lit a lamp and pulled her wrapper tighter around her as she motioned for him to sit down.

Jess glanced unobtrusively to her bare feet peering from beneath the billowy white fabric that hung loosely over her petite frame, making her look like some kind of angel. Her hair was as mussed as the open bed-linens, and her eyes looked taut with anxiety. How he longed to stay with her, to soothe away that anxiousness, for her as much as for himself.

"No, that's fine," he said. "I won't keep you. I simply want to thank you." He chuckled slightly. "I believe you've made an apple pie out of peaches."

Alexa laughed timidly. Their eyes met and he became briefly dazed. He cleared his throat and glanced away. "If we do lose, it will be no fault of yours. I want you to know that whatever happens tomorrow, I appreciate your efforts, and I wish you the best of luck in whatever you—"

"You make it sound as if we'll lose," she protested.

"There's always that possibility," he replied soberly.

"I need this job," she said lightly. "I believe we'll win."

"I hope you're right." He gave a stilted smile. "Well, I'll let you go back to bed. Thank you again."

Jess went to the door and opened it. He paused to glance back at her, then closed it behind him. Alexa heard his boots descending the stairs. She went to the window and watched him walk toward the big house. For reasons far beyond needing a job, Alexa prayed inwardly that she would not have to leave here.

It surprised her to see Jess turn abruptly and head back to the stable. While she imagined him checking on Crazy, she wished she could even think about sleeping. Her feelings for this man were strong and undeniable, yet for all she knew they were sharing their last hours together. While the thought of becoming involved with him was frightening, the prospect of never seeing him again seemed more so.

Alexa was still gazing out the window when Jess emerged from the stable, riding his favorite stallion without a saddle. With no thought of consequences, she opened the window and called to him. "Where you going?"

Jess reined in and looked up to see Alexa nearly hanging out her window. "Nowhere in particular, but I know I can't sleep."

A moment of tense silence preambled Alexa's impulsive words. "May I come?"

Jess opened his arms with a welcoming shrug while the horse danced, eager to run.

"I'll be down in two minutes," she said and closed the curtain. She hurriedly exchanged her nightgown for a shirt and breeches and pulled on stockings and boots. Bursting breathlessly out the carriage house door, she found Jess waiting and wished she could see his expression through the darkness. She was about to go get a horse from the stable when he reached out a hand. After a moment's hesitation, she took it and was barely seated behind him when he eased the horse into a steady trot.

Jess's heart pounded as Alexa leaned against his back and pressed her hands around his waist to steady herself. He'd had fantasies like this. He guided the horse around the house and broke into a gallop as they cleared the trees. The wind seemed to press Alexa's touch further into him, searing him with an elusive fire. She said nothing, but he was conscious of her every move. If nothing else, Alexa was proving a worthy distraction from the reality of what tomorrow might bring. He wanted her, but he also wanted to be more to her than *just* a friend, or *just* a lover. He could kick himself for behaving so brashly with her at times. But he didn't know how to do this. Women were like a foreign language to him.

Jess stopped at the crest of a hill. He swung one leg over the horse's mane and slid to the ground. While he tethered the horse he looked up at Alexa, wishing the night weren't shadowing her eyes. The moon was bright, but not enough to give him any clue as to what she was thinking.

Alexa held her breath as Jess took hold of her waist to help her down. She wondered what to expect of him now, and asked herself if it was foolish to even be here. Reminding herself not to judge him wrongly, Alexa allowed her hands to hold his shoulders while she found her footing, and his fingers lingered momentarily at her waist.

"You're quite a horseman, Mr. Davies," she said, unable to bear the silence. "It takes skill to maneuver a horse like that without a saddle."

Jess's voice turned nostalgic. "My father rode with me like that nearly every day when I was a child."

Alexa could hear respect in his words. "He must have been a wonderful man."

"He was." Jess looked down at his boot as he pushed it back and forth in the grass. His eyes lifted to the moonlit scene before them. The perfect view of his station brought clearly to mind a memory he'd rather be free of. He wondered if he'd ever forget how it felt to look down from this point and see his home in flames. And now. Now he was on the brink of possibly losing it all.

"What are you thinking?" Alexa nearly startled him. Jess shook his head. "About your father?" she guessed.

"In a way," he admitted. He sighed and stuffed his hands in his pockets. "I doubt he'd be very pleased with me now, gambling everything he left me on a horse race."

"You're a good man, Jess," she said.

He looked at her in surprise, wondering what would make her say such a thing. Recalling his behavior with her last night in the stable, he felt the need to apologize. "Alexa," he began cautiously, "I . . . I've been terribly worried about the race lately, and . . ."

"That's understandable," she stated when he faltered.

"I must confess that I . . ." He shifted his weight to shuffle the other toe over the ground. "I don't think I've been quite myself, and . . ." He cleared his throat and forced himself to get to the point. "I hope you can forgive me for the way I've behaved with you. I suppose I'm just not used to having a woman around. I don't want you to take it personally. I just—"

"I understand," she interrupted with a cold voice, not wanting him to say any more. With great effort she blinked back hot tears. So that was it. Hadn't she suspected such a thing the night they'd been stranded on the mountain? His attention was nothing more than a distraction, a male reaction to a woman—any woman. How grateful she was for the darkness that kept her true feelings concealed. When he said nothing more, Alexa swallowed the knot in her throat and added, "I dare say we're all a little nervous. Desperation can drive people to behave strangely."

Jess wanted to agree, but he couldn't bring himself to tell her that his desperation was for her. Without thinking, he lifted a hand to her face and sensed her surprise.

At Jess's touch, Alexa's heart quickened so drastically she feared she might faint. Unwillingly she leaned into his hand and felt him cup it against her cheek in response, as if he sensed the support she was seeking. In that moment, Alexa almost didn't care what his motives were. She only wanted to be with him. She didn't care whether or not they won the race. She only wished he would hold her. She wanted to get down on her knees and beg him to take her with him, wherever he might go. Her voice was blocked by a fear that kept her from speaking, but desperation forced her to return his touch, her fingers subtly contemplating his stubbled face.

Jess reacted quickly and followed his impulse to kiss her. At the first sign of response he drew her against him, finding an undeniable comfort in her affection, for whatever reason she might be offering it.

Eight
THE BEGINNING OF A DREAM

"Alexa," Jess whispered hoarsely as she leaned her head against his shoulder, "I feel as if my life is in your hands."

Alexa sighed, wishing he could see beyond the race. Confusion assaulted her freshly. How could she be such a fool to be in this position with a man like Jess Davies? Everything logical implied they would only bring difficulties to each other. Tersely she eased away. "It's not. My work with this race is finished, Mr. Davies." Her voice turned harsh. "Right now, your life is in Tod's hands. It's too bad he's a man."

"What's that supposed to mean?" he asked sharply.

"Why don't you take me home?" She evaded him. "We ought to get a little sleep at least, or—"

"What's it supposed to mean?" he repeated, taking hold of her arm.

"It means that I am your trainer, Jess, not your plaything. I understand how difficult this is for you, but if you and I are to continue working together, you're going to have to draw a line somewhere."

"Are you telling me that our relationship should remain purely professional?"

"I think we can have any kind of relationship we choose to have, as long as we learn to trust each other. But I'm not sure that's possible."

"Why not?" he asked gruffly.

"Because," she shouted, "you're a Davies and I'm a Byrnehouse! And as hard as I try, I find myself wondering if what I've heard is true."

"Why don't you just ask me?" he insisted. "If I'm going to have a reputation, I'd at least like to know what I'm being reputed for. Go on," he challenged, "ask me if it's true."

"I'm not sure I want to know."

"Because you know Chad lied to you. Whatever it is, you can almost bet it's not true."

"Is almost good enough?" she demanded, but didn't give him a chance to respond. "Apparently not. You were certainly quick to believe what Chad told *you* about *me*. Don't stand there and tell me how prejudiced I'm being when you know good and well that my being a Byrnehouse has been the source of much anxiety. I didn't ask for the name," she cried as a sensitive chord was struck. "I'm not even entitled to the name, but you can't see me as anything *but* a Byrnehouse."

"Now, you listen to me." He took her wrists into a firm grip. "I don't care who you are, or who I am. I'm a man, and you're a woman, and that's all that matters."

"Which brings us right back to where we started," she said tersely.

"And where is that?"

"I feel like a plaything, Jess, like a distraction. Is that what I am? Just one more woman to—"

"Stop it!" He nearly shook her. "You don't even know what you're talking about."

"Neither do you!" she snapped. "Face it, Jess. I'm the only white woman under fifty out here in the middle of nothing. How do you expect me to feel? It's evident you're attracted to me, but there isn't a lot to pick from. Don't take your frustrations out on me because—"

"And what about you, Alexa?" He pulled her closer, maintaining a firm grip on her wrists. "What makes you react the way you do when I hold you?" She said nothing. Through the silence, Jess contemplated where he stood. Maybe she was right. But he intended to make one point clear. "Perhaps I'm just a wicked man, Alexa," he whispered near her ear, and she held her breath. "Perhaps I'm so deprived, so lonely, so wanton . . ." He pressed his lips to her throat and pushed an arm around her waist. Alexa gasped but didn't protest. "But if I am so wicked, Alexa," he took the back of her head in a firm grip and tilted her face toward his, "you and I are two of a kind."

Alexa didn't realize she was crying until a high-pitched sob rose from her throat. Jess put his mouth over hers to silence it, and no amount of self-control could keep her from responding. She wanted to tell him she wasn't wicked. She loved him. But such confessions became lost in the fear that they would never be reciprocated. Instead, she concentrated on the moment. The world around her dissipated before the reality of Jess's kiss, Jess's touch, Jess's overwhelming presence.

Lack of sleep and the power of her emotions left Alexa weak, and she nearly collapsed in his arms. Jess fell to his knees when he couldn't find the strength to support them both any longer. Together they knelt, while he did his best to devour her with his kiss, as if he could somehow bring her inside himself and keep her there forever.

When Alexa could bear it no longer, she pressed her arms around his shoulders and lifted her throat to his lips, gasping for breath.

"Alexa," he murmured, "I want you so badly." He nibbled at an earlobe. "I've never wanted anything so much in my life."

Alexa wanted to question his motives, but it was apparent now, just as with the race, that however their motives might differ, they both wanted the same thing. Still, one of them had to maintain reason.

"Jess," she murmured against his face, "we mustn't." With a kiss he ignored her. She took his face into her hands. "We can't, Jess," she implored without conviction, and he paid no mind. "We just can't. I fear that . . ." Her words became lost in her own desires, but this time Jess was listening.

"You fear what?" he whispered, but she didn't answer. His heart quickened as passion became replaced by deeper motives. He wanted to know her, and he wanted her to know that he cared.

"You fear what?" he repeated gently, taking her shoulders into his hands.

Alexa looked up at him through the darkness, disoriented and distraught. "I . . . I don't know. I . . ."

Jess sensed a warming from her, and a new insight filtered into him. He rubbed a timid thumb over her cheek. "Alexa," he murmured, "is that what's hiding behind those lovely eyes?"

Alexa didn't know how to respond. She couldn't just tell him outright that her deepest fear was his rejection. Looking up at him, she blessed the darkness for hiding her expression, and cursed it for hiding his.

Jess pondered her lack of response and spoke tentatively, wanting to put them on equal terms. "Are you as afraid of me, Alexa, as I am of you?"

The tenderness in his voice touched Alexa. This was not the cold, arrogant man she was trying to believe him to be. She felt no need to answer him now; instead she relaxed against his shoulder and pressed her hands around his back, holding him tightly. She sensed expectancy from his unanswered question, but she neatly avoided any probing into her feelings with a simple, "I fear that I'm exhausted, Mr. Davies."

Jess chuckled and rummaged his lips through her hair. "Should I take you home?"

"Not yet." She urged him closer. "Just hold me."

They sat together on the ground, silently absorbing the night around them, mutually contemplating what the coming day might bring. Alexa was barely aware of him helping her onto the stallion until he mounted behind her and took the reins. She quickly relaxed again as he eased the horse into a smooth gallop and held her firmly about the waist. "We're home, Alexa," he said, and she stirred from the beginning of a dream.

The yard was quiet as he halted near the carriage house door and helped her down. Alexa thought of a thousand words to say, but exhaustion muddled them into nonsense. She went on her tiptoes to kiss his cheek, then took a step back. "Good night, Jess," she said.

"Do you want me to walk you up to—"

"No," she interrupted, "I'll be fine. Thank you."

Jess watched her open the door, wondering what it might be like by this time tomorrow. She turned back briefly and said with a sleep-tainted voice, "I'm not wicked."

Jess laughed and walked the stallion toward the stable, where Murphy was at his turn keeping watch. Her words echoed through his mind, but it wasn't until the race was over that he began to grasp their full implication.

❦   ❦   ❦

Morning came too soon for Alexa. Her hands shook visibly as she dressed in the only skirt she had and pinned her hair up. Surveying her reflection in the little mirror, she sighed, wishing she had something more suitable for the social gala she would encounter around the track. Her hair looked awful and she attempted to resmooth it, appalled by her nervousness. "It's just another race," she told herself aloud. "You've done this a thousand times, Alexa."

She was almost disappointed to find everything in perfect order. The boys were calm—except Tod, who was shaking as much as she. They urged her off to the track, where she found people gathering to place their bets. She had barely come into the crowd when she turned to see her brother walking beside her. "What do you want?" she snapped, trying not to raise her voice.

"To see you," Chad stated.

"That's just like you," she retorted, "waiting like some kind of vulture."

"Now, Alexandra." He chuckled. "I simply wanted to inquire about your well-being."

"I was under the impression that my well-being was something you were not concerned with in the least. Or perhaps you're concerned that I'm not as miserable as you would like me to be."

"Still a snippety little thing." He laughed. "But I'd wager a lot to say you'll lose that attitude when your dear Mr. Davies doesn't have a job to give you."

"Just how much would you wager?" she asked curtly. "Put your money where your mouth is," she said and moved deliberately away.

❦   ❦   ❦

Jess purposely waited until it was nearly posting time before he left the house. His nerves were as tight as a bowstring, but he took a stiff drink just before he went out, and fought to appear calm on the surface.

He wandered through the crowds as they placed bets and mingled. Several people stopped to chat, ranging from old friends of the family to outright competitors who would smile and shake his hand as if none of this really mattered. He wondered if these people would be congratulating him or giving him pity by the time this was over.

He checked on the present odds for his horse and felt a combination of excitement and fear. If he won he would win big, but if he lost, he'd be ruined.

"Good morning, Mr. Davies." At the sound of a familiar voice, he turned and momentarily lost all fear in Alexa's eyes.

"Good morning." He smiled wryly. He wanted to ask if she was feeling wicked. *He* certainly was.

Alexa blushed slightly and turned away. "So, what is it?"

"What?"

"I know you were checking the odds. I can't help being curious."

Jess laughed slightly.

"Is it funny?"

"That all depends on if we win or lose."

"We'll win, of course," she said with confidence.

Jess smiled warmly, appreciating her optimism. He leaned forward and whispered in her ear, "Eighty to one."

Alexa drew a sharp breath. His voice sent goose bumps down her back. His revelation left her speechless. Their eyes met, and she wondered if he had any idea how she really felt about him. He cleared his throat and looked away. She was certain that either he didn't, or he was content to ignore it.

"The first race is about to begin," Jess said. "Would you care to join me?" He offered his arm and she put her hand over it, nodding graciously as they moved toward the track.

Alexa glanced up at him and her heart quickened. She'd never seen him dressed up before. The black jacket and bow tie gave him a look of refinement that charmed her. If he wasn't so thoroughly rugged, it wouldn't have such an effect.

The first race meant nothing to either of them, but the moment it ended their eyes met with blatant nerves showing. Crazy was scheduled to run in the second.

"I think I'll go check on Tod," Alexa said with an edge to her voice. Jess nodded his understanding and she slipped away.

"We were makin' bets about when you'd show up," Murphy chortled when she found him and Richard waiting with Crazy.

"We didn't figure you could stay away," Richard smiled.

"Everything all right?" she asked tensely.

"As you can see," Richard stated, amused by her nerves, "Crazy is perfectly chipper."

"And where is Tod?" she insisted, looking around to assure herself of his absence.

"He'll be here any minute," Murphy informed her. "Saw him just a bit ago, all dressed and ready to go."

Three silent minutes later, Alexa announced, "I think I'll go find him."

Tod was sitting on his bunk, dressed in a yellow and pink silk jacket and white breeches, holding one arm over his stomach and the other to his head.

"What's the matter?" Alexa asked, panic edging her voice.

"Oh," he looked up, startled, "I'm so nervous I could—"

"Come now." She attempted to hide her own nerves for his sake. She sat beside him and rubbed his shoulders. "There's no reason to be nervous. You just do your best. That's all Jess expects. You'll do beautifully. Look how much you've improved, even in the last week."

"How can you tell me not to be nervous, when everything is riding on this race? I can't do it, Alexa."

"Sure you can," she insisted, trying to suppress the knots forming in her stomach. "We've talked this through a hundred times, Tod. You'll do fine."

Sam appeared with a glass of warm milk and gave it to Tod. "Thought it might help settle your stomach," he said. Tod grinned, obviously surprised by the gesture.

"Thank you, Sam," Alexa said. "That was thoughtful of you."

Sam excused himself, but to Alexa's dismay, Tod's condition only worsened, and he ran into the other room to throw up.

Alexa sighed and put her face into her hands until a spark came to life inside her.

"Take the silks off, Tod. I'm going to ride the race."

Tod's peaked face peered around the corner. "Jess will be furious."

"You're sick," she protested. "Besides, he won't find out."

Tod disappeared and threw his cap out the door, soon followed by the jacket and breeches. "Are you sure you can pull it off?" he called.

"Of course I can," she said, but Tod was throwing up again. Alexa scooped up the clothes and went cautiously back to the carriage house to change.

❧ ❧ ❧

"It's about time ya got here," Murphy growled as Alexa walked into the stable, her head bent forward. She said nothing, wondering how long it would take them to recognize her.

"Get up here and let's go," Murphy added. "We're late. Alexa will—"

"She'll what?" Alexa looked up, amusement in her eyes.

"Alexa!" Richard nearly choked.

"Hush," she insisted.

"Where's Tod?" Murphy demanded.

"He's sick," she said. "This is the only choice we've got. So let's get out there and pretend that nothing is out of the ordinary."

Murphy chuckled and bent to help her mount, but Richard stopped him. "Wait a minute. I don't think this is such a good idea. What if—"

"Richard," Alexa looked at him closely, "it probably isn't a very good idea. But it's the best one we've got."

It was apparent he wanted to argue, but he stepped back and watched in dismay as she situated herself in the saddle. Murphy mounted the guide horse and ushered Crazy out of the stable.

"Be careful," Richard called.

Alexa waved toward him, then bowed her head forward. "How do I look, Murphy?" she asked.

He only chuckled, but Alexa didn't feel nervous anymore. It was in her hands now, and she knew she could do it.

❦ ❦ ❦

As the competing horses for the second race paraded onto the track, Jess panicked. Crazy wasn't among them. He glanced around uneasily, wondering what had gone wrong, then he sighed with relief to see them approaching. Tod bore a stance of confidence, and Murphy saluted Jess casually as they rode past. Crazy showed an eagerness to run that made Jess smile, but he was distracted by a hearty slap on the shoulder.

"How's it going, old pal?" Chad Byrnehouse wore a self-gratified grin. Jess wanted to strangle him.

"Fine, and you?" he replied curtly.

"Couldn't be better." Chad held his hands together behind his back and rocked on his heels. Jess saw a vague resemblance to Alexa that he found disturbing. There was no question they shared the same blood.

"I was dismayed to hear you'll be moving from the area soon," Chad said with mock concern, and Jess glared at him.

While Chad smiled triumphantly, Jess recalled his more recent threats. Nothing had gone wrong in all the weeks Alexa had been here. A nervous twitch crept up Jess' neck, but he smiled in spite of it. "Don't count your chickens before they hatch, Byrnehouse." With that he moved away to find someplace else to watch the race.

As the horses paraded to the post, Jess glanced around the crowd, wondering where Alexa had gone. He wanted her here, to hold her hand. He imagined himself kissing her if they won, or crumbling in her arms if they lost. He was distracted by the announcement of posting time and his heart rose into his throat, knowing in minutes it would be over.

Jess both wanted it to begin and hoped it could be put off indefinitely. As the jockeys moved their mounts into position, he said a silent prayer that all would go well. He tried not to think about the times Chad had done something underhanded to make him lose races—things that he knew had been intentional, but could never be proven. He pushed the thought away, knowing he'd given careful instructions to check and recheck everything.

Jess took a deep breath and held it when the horses bolted forward. Crazy held her own, but the competition appeared close and his heart beat painfully. He wished he'd remembered his field glasses so he could get a better look.

"Come on, Crazy," he whispered, clenching his fists inside his pockets. The first furlong went well, and the second. Then Jess felt himself turn pale as something snapped and Tod nearly slid off the horse, while Crazy went briefly out of control.

"Please, no!" Jess cried. His fingernails bit into the palms of his hands. The crowd gasped in unison, then became still as Crazy lost speed drastically, and Jess wondered what had happened. Watching closely, he saw Tod pull his feet from the stirrups and grip the horse with his thighs. Moving nearly onto Crazy's neck, he put one arm behind him and flung the saddle off the horse. Tod reseated himself bareback and leaned forward, then miraculously gained speed.

But Jess felt sick. He knew they would never make up the time. It was as good as lost, and he thought he'd die inside to realize what it meant. He saw Fiddler run onto the track and pick up the saddle. Jess itched to find out what had gone wrong with it, but for the moment all he could feel was despair. Oblivious to the crowd's growing enthusiasm, he tried to imagine how it would feel to sign his life over to the bank.

He was surprised to hear Murphy's voice rise above the din, but he chose to ignore it and turned away with the intention of finding someplace to be alone. Jess stopped, and his heart went mad before Murphy's words fully registered when he shouted again. "Come on, Crazy! You can do it! Go, lady, go!"

Jess turned back and gripped the rail. His eyes frantically attempted to focus on the galloping mass of horses and colored silk sprinting toward the finish line. His heart leapt into his throat as Crazy nosed into the leading three. He held his breath and clenched his fists as if he could make the horse go faster by his own will. His heart beat painfully as Crazy eased ahead. He couldn't believe it. For the first time in ten years, he felt real hope. He only wished Alexa was here to share it. Before he had a chance to wonder where she might be, he realized Crazy had won by a head. Jess laughed toward the sky and used careful discipline not to make an utter fool of himself.

He had barely absorbed the joy when he glanced toward the track and saw Tod slip down and run toward the stable yard. Jess wondered if he was all right, then he caught it. Even from the distance, the stride was too feminine.

"Alexa," he muttered and pushed through the crowd.

Alexa feared the whole scheme would be blown when she realized Jess was following her. If she could only get to her room and lock the door, he couldn't prove anything. She tripped in the carriage house but recovered quickly and made it to the stairs. But Jess caught her ankle and she fell to her knees.

"Wretched woman!" he snarled, grabbing her around the waist. He pulled the cap from her head and threw it down. "What on earth do you think you're doing?" he shouted. "You could have been killed!"

"Don't be absurd," she protested.

"Where is Tod?" he demanded.

"He's sick." She attempted to squirm away. "Let go of me." After a breathless struggle, she ended up sitting on the step. Jess knelt in front of her, holding both her wrists in his hands.

"You listen to me, Miss Byrnehouse." His eyes burned with fury. "I made it clear that I didn't want you to ride."

"No one saw me."

"How do you know?"

"Your jockey's in the bunkhouse throwing up!" she shouted. "What was I supposed to do? I need this job!"

"Do you have any idea what—"

"I just won your race!" she screamed, wrenching her arms from his grasp.

Alexa saw his eyes soften as he came to his feet and backed down a step. She had imagined many reactions to the results of the race, but not this.

Reality came down around Jess with an enveloping weakness. Moisture burned into his eyes, and he turned away before Alexa could see it. He sat on the step for fear he might collapse, and pushed both hands into his hair. So many weeks of fear and anxiety, so many years of fighting to stay on top of it all. But he had made it one more step. They had won. No, Alexa had won.

"Alexa," he breathed and blinked back the tears to turn and face her. There she sat, her face smudged with the sweat of exertion and the dust of the track, her eyes reflecting all he felt. "I'm sorry." He came to his feet. "I should be thanking you."

"There's nothing to thank me for." She stood and brushed off her breeches. "I did it for me."

"Thanks anyway," he said, and Alexa looked up to meet his gaze. Like so many times before, she felt her eyes betraying her and turned away.

As the anxiety of the race rushed away, Jess grasped something entirely foreign to him. Like a splash of cold water, a new perspective left him stunned. Abruptly he caught her chin with his hand, and Alexa looked at him reluctantly. The color fled from his face and stopped in his throat as what he read in her eyes mirrored something he'd been fighting within himself. He nearly froze as those eyes burned through him, compelling him to face something he was inwardly longing for, but hadn't dared hope to have reciprocated.

"Don't look at me like that," she insisted and turned away, unnerved by his expression. Not knowing what to say or do, she hurried to her room, leaving Jess alone on the stairs.

He chuckled and shook his head. Had he finally grasped what Alexa's eyes had been trying to tell him? He was about to go after her when he heard someone shout his name from outside. Getting a grip on his senses, Jess hurried into the yard. He stopped to glance briefly back toward the carriage house and found Alexa watching him from the window. Their eyes met for only a moment before she closed the curtain and Fiddler grabbed his arm.

"Good, I found you," he said with an edge of panic.

"What's wrong?" Jess demanded.

"It's not over yet, I'm afraid. Byrnehouse is down there giving the officials hell. You'd best come quick."

"I should have known it was too good to be true," Jess muttered as he ran with Fiddler close on his heels.

Jess found Chad pointing a harsh finger at the officials, spouting off a long list of his credentials, most of which were related to money.

"Is there a problem?" Jess coolly ignored the fear pounding in his chest.

"A problem?" Chad shouted, turning to find Jess right behind him. "The horse finished without a saddle. Don't you find that slightly . . . unfair, Davies?"

Jess swallowed hard and nodded toward the officials. "And what do you have to say on that?"

"I don't care what they have to—" Chad began.

"Now you listen to me, Byrnehouse," Jess said firmly. "When you agreed to be a participant in this race, you agreed to leave all disputes in the hands of the officials."

"How do I know you didn't pay them off?" Chad scoffed.

"Because I can't afford to. How do I know *you* didn't pay them off?" Jess retorted.

"I can assure you that no one has paid us off," one of the solicitors said indignantly. "If you calm down, Mr. Byrnehouse, we can discuss this rationally."

"Fine," Chad snarled, albeit quietly, "the horse finished without a saddle. I call for another run."

"Mr. Davies?" the official asked.

"I haven't had a chance to check it out, but I believe the saddle was tampered with."

"You can't possibly prove such a thing," Chad blurted, as if the very notion was preposterous.

"That's what you always say," Jess muttered for Chad's ears alone, earning him a barely detectable triumphant glare.

"Mr. Garfield and I have already discussed this," the official report-ed, and Jess's heart nearly stopped. "It's true that a horse finishing with-out a saddle is not exactly conventional, but on the other hand, it lost a great deal of time getting rid of the blasted thing. It's our opinion that if a horse can recover like that and win, it deserves to win."

Jess let out a deep breath. "Thank you, God," he muttered under his breath.

"Ooooh." Chad swung a fist through the air that hurled him around with the momentum. He turned back quickly and pointed a finger at Jess as the officials moved away. "You'll pay for this, Davies."

"I always do," Jess stated. "Is there a particular reason you can't tol-erate my winning a race? That is where all this started, isn't it? When I won my first—"

"Don't waste your breath, Jess," he interrupted and walked away. Jess closed his eyes and sighed. He forced himself not to think of what Chad might throw into his future. Crazy had won. Today, life was worth living.

🌿 🌿 🌿

Alexa peered out the window again when she heard Jess and Fiddler talking in the yard. By the way they took off, she knew something was wrong. She hurried to change back into her skirt, smooth her hair, and wash the grime from her face. Running toward the track, she could see Chad and Jess exchanging strong words and knew exactly what the problem was. She hurried to intervene, but Chad walked away before she got there. Jess caught her eye just as Chad grabbed her arm.

"You just can't leave well enough alone, can you," she snapped quietly.

"Oh, don't worry, sis. Your dear Jess will get what he deserves, and you might too, for that matter. If you wallow with the swine long enough, Alexa, you'll start to smell like one."

"Actually, I'm just beginning to get rid of that foul Byrnehouse odor," she retorted.

"If you only knew." He shook his head with a dry chuckle.

"Go stuff your mouth with wool, Chad. We'd all have more peace if you did."

"One of these days," he lifted a finger and smiled slyly, "you're going to wish you'd listened to your big brother."

"Threats?" She tilted her head to glare at him. From the corner of her eye she saw Jess amble slowly toward them, alert but keeping a distance.

Chad leaned toward her and spoke softly. "Just between you and me, Alexa." He turned to look at Jess with contempt. "You can't seriously intend to stay here. I mean, you've won his race. You've proven a point, I suppose. Now, don't you think you'd be better off to—"

"Mind your own business, Chad, and I'll mind mine."

"You do mind it well," he chuckled. "I'll give you credit for that." He leaned a little closer and Jess moved toward them. "It was you," Chad whispered, "wasn't it."

"I don't know what you're talking about."

"Oh, you handled it well, I'll admit, but I have no doubt it was you out there. No one else could have done it."

Caught off guard, Alexa was relieved when Jess came close enough to intervene with a terse, "You'll never prove it."

Chad shot a defiant glare in Jess's direction. "You've only won a single race, Jess. I wouldn't be getting cocky just yet. You've got a long way to go before you're free and clear."

"Thanks to you." Jess gave a mocking smile before he added firmly, "Now get off my land."

"I'd be happy to." Chad nodded toward Alexa. "And one of these days when you're not so busy bailing Jess out of the muck, come and get your things."

"What things?" she asked. "You told me I couldn't take anything with me."

"But you managed to get away with something, didn't you." Chad smirked unpleasantly, and Jess wondered what they were talking about. "I have no use for all those silly clothes. You might as well come and get them."

"Fine, I will."

"Let us know when you'll be out of the country and we'll make a day of it," Jess added, and Alexa fought to keep a straight face.

Chad gave a stilted grin and walked away.

"I wonder how much money he just lost," Jess said, and Alexa laughed.

Nine
MORE THAN HIS RACE

Alexa felt Jess's eyes on her and glanced up warily. "Is everything all right?" she asked, not looking at him for long.

"The officials called it good," he reported, wanting to see her eyes. He took hold of her chin and forced her to face him. "Are *you* all right?"

"I'm fine." She smiled and tried to turn away, but he wouldn't let her.

For a long moment Jess searched those incredible eyes. What he read confirmed his earlier assumptions, and he smiled.

Alexa felt unnerved by his expression and walked away. Jess wanted to follow her, but a slap on the shoulder startled him into a hearty round of congratulations from Jimmy and Edward.

"Looks like you're not going to get rid of us after all," Edward chortled.

"Too bad," Jess grinned.

"Tod really pulled it off, eh," Jimmy added.

"Yes," Jess chuckled, "he really did."

Alexa peeked into the bunkhouse to check on Tod. He sat up in bed when she walked in.

"How are you feeling?" she asked.

"Better, I think," he said, his eyes wide with expectancy. "Well?" he demanded when she said nothing more.

"We won, of course," she stated as if it were nothing.

"I knew we could do it if you were riding."

"Nonsense. You've improved magnificently. Of course there will be more races. Crazy will be challenged. So you'd best get back on your feet."

"We've still got a job." He laughed as if he couldn't believe it.

"You do indeed." Jess startled them both.

Tod shot a panicked look toward Alexa. She picked up on his concern and quickly put him at ease. "It's all right, Tod. He knows."

"I'm sorry, Jess." Tod tried to sit up until he was afflicted with a stomach cramp. "I don't know what happened."

"It's okay, Tod," Jess assured him while Alexa avoided Jess's eyes.

"At first I was just nervous. I thought the milk would help," he said more to Alexa, "but it just got worse after I drank it."

Jess's expression turned hard. "What do you mean by that?"

"I was feeling upset, and Sam gave me a glass of warm milk to soothe my nerves," Tod reported.

"Are you sure it was Sam?" Jess asked, and Alexa grasped the implication.

"Jess, you don't think that—"

"Take care of yourself, Tod." Jess left abruptly. Alexa smiled at Tod and followed Jess into the yard.

"What's wrong?" she asked.

"You tell me," he said. "What happened out there, Alexa?"

She knew now that what Jess had told her of such things occurring was not idle talk, but she didn't know what to say.

"Come now," Jess said. "It's a miracle you didn't fall off and break something—or kill yourself. I want to know what happened."

"The girth broke," she said.

A muscle in his cheek twitched, and his lips tightened. "Why?" he asked gruffly.

"I don't know!"

"Who was supposed to check it?" he asked, and Alexa's eyes widened.

"Murphy checked everything, but he told Sam to recheck it."

Jess cursed and turned away, his breath quickened with anger.

"But, Jess, I checked everything just before I mounted."

"And it was intact?"

"It certainly appeared to be."

"But it must not have been what it appeared," Jess said. "The strap was probably weakened from the belly side. I've seen such things before. And I have to admit that of all the boys, I know Sam the least. It's hard to know what to think."

"Do you believe Chad had something to do with it?"

"I *know* Chad had everything to do with it. But somebody's got to do his dirty work."

Alexa met his eyes, biting her lip with concern. She could see his thoughts change, and she turned away as his gaze seemed to penetrate to the core of her.

"I can't believe the way you recovered out there," Jess said. The anger softened into a respect she had craved. "I admire your skill, Alexa. Tod couldn't have done it."

"I know." She laughed meekly. "But don't tell him that. You'll hurt his feelings."

"Alexa," he whispered, and she sensed something tangible pass through the air between them. She wanted to just take him in her arms and confess everything she felt. The look in his eyes nearly convinced her that he would accept her heart and not break it. But she pushed such thoughts away, crediting them to the emotion of victory.

"We did it, Jess." She attempted to lighten the tension.

"*You* did it," he corrected, and the thrill of winning came rushing freshly over him. "Aah!" he laughed and pulled her into his arms, turning with her until she giggled from dizziness.

"You're feeling better today," she said as he set her feet on the ground but held her against him a moment longer.

His eyes probed into her, searching for something that left her weak. He smiled when he apparently found it. "Oh, yes," he said, "much better."

Alexa stepped back and cleared her throat. "I think I'll go check on Crazy. Would you like to join me, or . . ."

"I should probably get down to the track and look important, since I do own the place."

"I'll see you later then," she said and he nodded, though his eyes seemed hesitant to let her go.

Alexa turned and walked toward the stable, almost relieved to be free from the tension she felt in his presence. She didn't see any more of Jess as commotion filled the remainder of the day. She stayed close to her room, avoiding the crowds and contemplating the future. She'd won the right to stay here permanently if she chose, and admittedly she had no desire to go elsewhere.

Alexa slept heavily through the night and rose late. Her growling stomach told her she'd likely missed breakfast, but as always, Edward had something waiting for her.

"Where is everybody?" she asked as he sat across from her to chat.

"The boys are getting things back to normal. Richard's out checking on the mobs, and Jess went into town."

"Yes, I suppose he would." She smiled to hide her disappointment at missing him.

"I'm certain he's enjoying it," Edward chuckled.

Alexa thought of the pride Jess would feel to pay the bank their demands, then she thought how it felt to have him kiss her, and turned warm.

"You all right?" Edward asked and startled her.

"Fine, why?"

"I guess it's all the excitement yesterday."

"Most likely," she agreed, and finished her breakfast.

When it became apparent there was little for Alexa to do, and she couldn't take any more of the boys teasing her about the race, she mounted a sturdy mare and rode into the hills. She returned late in the day to find Richard sleeping and Jess still gone. After supper she enjoyed a long bath, contemplating the gratification she felt from this race that she'd not experienced before. Never had she been a part of anything so worthwhile. She felt a kinship with these men as they expressed their gratitude for being able to stay and see Jess keep his land. Only Sam didn't share their enthusiasm, but she tried to ignore him, wondering if Jess had done anything about that yet.

Alexa dressed and combed through her wet hair, then she decided to relax at the piano. As she played, her mind wandered to her now-permanent employer. She wondered how she was going to deal with these feelings. Her heart quickened to remind her she'd become obsessed with thoughts of Jess Davies. Her music grasped her mood as it became wistful, and she closed her eyes in an effort to become lost in it. She opened them to see Jess standing at the other end of the piano.

"I'm sorry," she said. "I didn't mean to disturb you."

"How many times do I have to tell you that your playing doesn't disturb me?" He smiled at her, but she looked away quickly and began another piece. Jess absorbed the aura that flowed from her, from her music, filling the room with a warmth and peace that was the perfect end to a gratifying day.

Alexa played until his presence began to unnerve her and she stood abruptly. "I should be going. It's getting late, and—"

"Please sit down," he said, and she did.

"Did you talk to Sam?" she asked.

"I did," he stated, disinterested in the topic.

"What happened? If you don't mind my asking, of course."

"He pleaded innocence; swore he had nothing to do with it. I'm not sure I believe him, but what could I say?"

"It couldn't possibly be anyone else, could it?"

"It's none of my boys," Jess said easily, "but there were a million people here yesterday. We'll have to let it go. But if I ever find Sam has been dishonest with me, he'll be sorry I ever gave him a job. That's no concern of yours."

Alexa smiled at him then glanced away abruptly. Jess sauntered toward her, and a wave of goose bumps rushed over her shoulders. She sensed something different in him since the race and wondered how to react, being alone with him now.

"It really is getting late." She stood again. "I—"

"Sit down," he said, and again she did.

An intense silence enveloped them. Alexa could hear herself breathing. Jess sat beside her on the bench, his back to the piano. He looked directly at her, and she could feel her eyes betraying the truth.

"You know that I expect honesty from my employees, first and foremost."

"Yes, I know," she replied, certain they were still talking about Sam.

"And since I can still afford to have employees," he smiled, "I have a right to expect it, don't you think?"

"Of course," she said. "I agree that honesty is very important in working relationships." Jess watched her fidget with the pleats in her skirt. This was not turning out to be as easy as he'd hoped, but another brief glimpse of her eyes confirmed his deepest hopes. He wasn't about to back down now.

"Alexa," his voice lowered, "tell me why your eyes do that when they meet mine."

She looked away abruptly, and he could see her shoulders move with each breath.

"Tell me, Alexa," he whispered. She attempted to stand, but he caught her arm. "Look at me," he said, but she hesitated. He touched her chin with his finger and brought her face close to his. "I was so preoccupied with thoughts of you that I didn't stop to realize you were thinking of me, too."

Alexa closed her eyes, held her breath. What was he saying? Could it be possible he shared her feelings? She hardly dared look at him, hardly dared hope.

When Alexa made no response, Jess added cautiously, "If I am taking something for granted, Miss Byrnehouse, just say so. I'm not about to impose my heart upon any woman—especially you."

Alexa opened her eyes, searching for sincerity. She was surprised to find it so easily. At her continued silence, vulnerability crept in to shadow the green of his eyes.

"Are my feelings so invisible?" she asked.

He drew a long breath. "I almost didn't see them."

"Jess," she said, "I . . ." The intensity between them got the better of her, and she attempted to stand. Jess stopped her, and she ended up closer to him than before.

"You what?" he insisted.

"I . . ." She faltered again, and he lifted that brow.

"Honesty," he whispered. "I want honesty."

"I'm glad that I get to stay."

"I know. You need the job."

"I need more than that," she admitted.

His gaze intensified. "All these weeks I was so afraid we'd lose— and I would lose everything. Then I began to realize it was *you* I didn't want to lose. Why do you suppose?"

"Because I keep the bunkmates laughing?"

He smiled and shook his head.

"Because I run with the jockey?"

He shook his head again.

"Perhaps it was the tea and little cakes," she teased.

"No, though they were enjoyable."

"Because I can beat you by a furlong? No. Then it must be because you like the way I look in breeches."

"You're getting closer."

"Perhaps it's because the stables are cleaner than they've ever been, or—"

"Shut up, Alexa," he said and pushed an arm around her waist. He put a hand to the back of her head, fingering her damp hair, inhaling the freshly bathed scent of her. Slowly he brought her face close to his. Alexa held her breath as he bent to kiss her. His lips were warm and tasted of the sun. She tipped her head back and moved unwillingly toward him as he kissed her in a way that she'd never known. Defenses slid away and true emotion seeped into it. They parted a moment and gasped for breath until he pressed his mouth over hers again with urgency.

"Alexa," he whispered, his lips skittering over her face, "you must be crazy."

"I'm not crazy. I'm in love with you."

"One and the same."

Alexa realized what she had just said, and fear took hold of her freshly. "I should go, Jess. It's getting late, and—"

"Do you really mean that?" he asked, his brow furrowed.

"Of course. It's very late."

"Not that."

"What?" She feigned innocence, almost hoping he hadn't heard her.

"You just said that you're in love with me."

Alexa turned away. "You said you wanted honesty." She set her eyes firmly on him. "Do you give what you expect?"

"How honest do you want me to be?" he whispered against her face.

"I want to know everything." She kissed his eyes.

"I want you, Alexa." He urged her closer. "Not just now, not for a week or a month. I want you forever. I think about you constantly. I'm obsessed with you. I ache for you." He kissed her mouth tentatively and looked into her eyes to see them turning moist. "I love you, Alexandra Byrnehouse, and I will love you long after this life is over."

Alexa sighed and pressed her face to his throat. "I never dreamed you would say such things to me."

Jess chuckled and buried his face in her hair. "I never dreamed you would want to hear them."

A recently familiar passion took hold of Jess as Alexa nuzzled close to him. But his desires had offended her in the past and he eased away, attempting to put them in check.

"It's late," he muttered. "I'll walk you home."

Jess rose and took her hand. They left the house in silence. "It's a beautiful night," she said as they moved slowly down the path.

Jess put his arm around her shoulders and kissed the top of her head. "If it was raining, it would still be a beautiful night."

Alexa embraced him in silent agreement. Once inside the carriage house, they stopped at the foot of the stairs and he turned toward her. Silently his lips found hers in the darkness. "Jess," she looked up at him, "what if . . . ," she drew a deep breath, "what if Chad—"

"What about him?" Jess demanded, not appreciating the subject at this moment.

"I fear he will cause more trouble for you if we become involved."

"We're already involved." Jess pulled her closer. "And Chad can eat dust, for all I care." He said it lightly but with determination. "It's his sister I'm going to marry."

Alexa drew back in surprise. "You are?"

"Unless you don't want to, or—"

"You haven't asked me."

Jess chuckled. "One of these days I'll have to do that."

Alexa sighed and leaned against him.

"You'd best go to bed, my love." He urged her away before the passion had a chance to take control.

"Good night, Jess," she whispered and reluctantly went to her room.

Alexa rose feeling as though the world was in her hands. Never had she known such peace and contentment. Never had she felt such joy. Knowing that Jess Davies loved her seemed to compensate for everything rotten that had ever happened in her life—even the dreadful circumstances surrounding her father's death. With Jess, she could surely take on the world and win.

Realizing there was no need to get up, she relaxed and gave in to speculations over her feelings and what the future might bring for her and Jess. The prospect of spending the rest of her life here with him sent chills of excitement through her.

At last she got up and decided a ride would be nice. She had to stop and chat with the boys on her way to the stable. They were still laughing it up over the glorious win, but to Alexa that now seemed insignificant. The victory of the race was suddenly overshadowed by the winning of Jess Davies' heart.

"Good morning, Alexa." Richard took over bridling the horse she intended to ride.

"I haven't seen much of you lately." Alexa turned to retrieve a saddle.

"No," he smiled and took it from her, "but I've certainly been hearing a lot about you."

"Oh, you're not going to gush about the race like the rest of them, are you?"

"You did save us," he smirked, "and you got your own way to boot."

Alexa didn't find that funny. "I did what I had to do, Richard." She glared at him as he tightened the girth beneath the horse's belly. "I was not trying to get away with something just for the sake of it."

"Whatever you did," he straightened up and leaned an elbow onto the saddle, "it worked."

"It certainly did," Jess said from the doorway. Alexa turned to him and smiled, oblivious to anything but the love blossoming between them. She could see it in his eyes.

"Hello, Jess." Richard's voice startled her. She saw him glance between her and Jess, and wondered if he knew. But the look in his eyes bordered on disapproval, and she found herself hoping he'd never find out.

"Mrs. Brown is looking for you." Jess pointed at Richard as if he were a naughty boy.

"I suspected she would be." At Alexa's questioning glance he added, "I promised to help her with some heavy work. She's rearranging furniture again. I could be there all week."

"That's likely true," Jess agreed lightly and sauntered toward Alexa. Neither of them noticed Richard quietly leaving.

"Good morning, Jess." Alexa met his eyes with nothing to fear.

"Did I dream it?" He set his fingertips meekly to her face.

"I don't know. Tell me what you dreamt."

"A beautiful woman walked into my life, won my race single-handedly, then told me that she loves me."

Alexa coyly turned her attention to the horse. Jess pushed a stray wisp of her hair back with his thumb. Her eyes returned to his by some invisible, magnetic force. Jess wanted to kiss her, to hold her, to love her. But he reminded himself to tread carefully.

"Going riding?" He nodded toward the saddled gelding.

"Want to come?" She squeezed his hand hopefully.

"Are you sure?" He smirked. "I've got a reputation, you know."

"And where did you hear that?"

"From you." He lifted her into the saddle and mounted behind her. "I didn't realize I had a reputation until the day you walked into my office."

"Come now," she laughed, leaning into his chest as he eased the gelding into an easy gallop, "I've heard you have quite a way with the ladies."

Jess wondered if that's what she'd been implying he was guilty of all these weeks. "You must have heard that from your brother."

"I suppose I did." When he said nothing more she asked, "Where are we going?"

"Crazy," he retorted impishly. In response to her dumbfounded silence he added, "I'm going crazy, aren't you?"

"It seems to be a favorite word of yours."

"My favorite horse."

Jess tightened an arm around her waist and slowed the gelding as it climbed into the hills.

"Alexa," he spoke behind her ear. She set a hand on his leg and he tightened his embrace. "I want to put Crazy in the derby."

"I assumed you would, but I want Tod to ride her."

"Whatever you think is best," he stated with a tone of respect that didn't go unnoticed. "You're the trainer, but that's not why I want to take you to Melbourne."

"Melbourne?" she gasped. "Really, Jess. Crazy is good, but I don't think she's ready for—"

"I didn't say I was taking Crazy." He chuckled and kissed the side of her neck. "At least not this year. I want to take *you* to Melbourne. It's been years since I attended the Cup. I thought it would be a good excuse for a vacation. Would you like that?"

"I would love it."

"I hoped you would say that."

Jess halted the horse in a clearing where a wide stream of clear water ran over smooth stones. Clusters of trees rose toward a blue sky as if they'd been there forever.

"This is beautiful." Alexa's eyes echoed her words as Jess helped her dismount.

"Favorite place of mine." He held her arm to help her over some rocks to a grassy spot near the water's edge. "I come here often."

"Is this where you go when you ride off into the hills and don't come back for hours?"

Jess nodded, appreciating that she'd taken notice of his habits. It added reality to these feelings that still seemed so fragile.

Alexa impulsively sat on the ground and pulled off her boots and stockings.

"What are you doing?" An amused smile teased the corners of his mouth.

"There's nothing like an invigorating wade in mountain water to stir the spirit."

"Who told you that?"

"I made it up just now."

Jess laughed as she rolled up her breeches and carefully put a dainty foot into the water.

"Cold?" he asked when she grimaced.

"Quite," she said, but put the other foot in and walked gingerly over the stones to the opposite side. "Come on, Jess. Try it."

"You must be crazy," he laughed. "That water's too cold for my feet. It's barely thawed snow. But then, you wash your hair in cold water. You must thrive on it."

"Only when I don't have time to heat it." Alexa bent down to scoop water in her hands and throw it at him. He skillfully dodged it and laughed, but she did it again and got his shirt wet.

"Wretched woman." He laughed again and sat down to remove his boots and stockings, his eyes gleaming with mischief. Alexa grinned triumphantly until he ran into the water, picked her up, and sat her down in it.

She gasped from the cold and feigned defeat. "All right. You've proven you're stronger. Now help me up."

She reached out a hand and couldn't believe he fell for it. With a strong grip she pulled just hard enough to make him lose his balance, and he laughed as he went to his knees. Attempting an angry growl, he grabbed her around the waist. Alexa tried to squirm away, but ended up falling as she turned on the slippery stones. With the harm already done, she jumped on Jess and rolled him backward into the water. He laughed and struggled to his knees, wiping the water out of his eyes while Alexa dragged herself onto the bank and lay face down. Jess followed and lay on the grass beside her, where spots of sunshine filtered down through the trees to warm them.

"I should know better than to mess with a woman in breeches."

"There are some things that you just can't do in a skirt."

Jess leaned onto one elbow, his eyes absorbing her. "You are so beautiful." He pushed her damp hair away from her face. He wondered if anything might have changed between them as he brought his lips close to hers where they lingered almost timidly, then he pulled away to study her eyes.

Alexa had no reason to doubt that Jess's affection was genuine. But the intensity of the situation drew her to reality, and a new fear seeped in to taunt her. He kissed her warmly, and she clutched his shoulders as if she might drown in these desires.

"Jess," she whispered in a tone of protest that was hardly convincing. As much as she wanted it to go on, Alexa willed herself to blow in his ear, none too softly. Amidst the distraction she eased away and giggled. Abruptly she jumped to her feet, regretting his stunned expression. Not knowing what to say, she turned and walked through the water to the other side of the stream. Jess was quick to follow.

"Is something wrong?" he asked, severity lingering in his voice.

"No," she laughed flippantly, "of course not."

Jess wanted to ask a thousand questions. Despite their confessions of love, did she still believe he was toying with her? Didn't she trust him? Or perhaps she didn't want him the way he wanted her. She turned to smile at him and he found the latter difficult to believe, but he couldn't bring himself to ask. He ignored the tension between them and tossed water at her. They played like children until Alexa's stomach began to growl and they reluctantly returned to the station.

Riding in silence, Jess felt the tension between them. It was as if she wanted to be close to him, and yet she didn't. Their eyes met as he helped her dismount in the stable, but her gaze dropped quickly, much like it had when she'd been trying to hide her feelings. A nervous fear crept through Jess that he couldn't voice.

"I'd best hurry in for supper," she said, and left him removing the saddle.

Alexa entered the bunkhouse to find everyone eating. She ignored their speculative glances as she sat down, realizing she must look a mess. She was as surprised as the rest of them when Jess appeared in the doorway and announced he was eating with them.

"That is, if you have enough," he added to Edward, who only grinned and went to the kitchen to get another plate. "You *are* a better cook than Mrs. Brown," Jess muttered while the boys attempted to grasp the change in him. "Of course, don't tell her that. It'll hurt her feelings." Still they remained silent. "That dining room of mine is so big. I hate it. I think I far prefer the decor here."

"If you're trying to get an open invitation to eat with us," Edward finally said with a smirk, "I think it could be arranged."

"Good." Jess grinned toward Alexa.

"We do work for you," Murphy chortled. "We'd probably do just about anything as long as you pay us."

"Even sit with you through supper." Fiddler almost sounded serious.

"I'll bear that in mind," Jess said, then his eyes met Alexa's and his surroundings froze. He hated the subtle tension between them, and made up his mind to confront it head-on at the first opportunity.

The conversation gradually picked up, but Alexa was content to watch Jess until she realized someone was missing. "Where's Richard?"

"Still helpin' Mrs. Brown," Murphy reported.

"Good," Jess inserted. "He can eat my supper."

The boys chuckled, but Alexa sensed they were a little baffled by Jess, and not certain how to react.

"Miss Byrnehouse." Jess rose from the table before anyone else. She looked up abruptly, a question in her eyes. "I would like to see you in my office as soon as you're finished here."

She nodded with her mouth full and he left, pausing only to say, "Thank you, Edward. It tasted great."

"What's gotten into him?" Jimmy asked the moment the door closed.

Murphy laughed boisterously. "Isn't it obvious, boy?"

"I'd say Alexa won more than his race, eh?" Fiddler winked at her and she blushed slightly, wishing they'd have waited to bring this up until she'd gone as well.

"Yeah," Murphy laughed, "the bloke's lost his heart."

"Oh, stop it," she gushed, rising from the table. "You boys are worse than a bunch of old gossips."

Her comment brought on a variety of chuckles to accompany her out the door. "Give him a kiss for me," Murphy called and she slammed it shut, though she could hear his loud laughter halfway to the carriage house.

Ten
GOING HOME

Alexa quickly poured water into the basin and splashed it on her face. She changed into a clean shirt and brushed through her hair, then she hurried into the house to find Jess seated at his desk. He wore a shirt she'd never seen before, with tiny stripes in cream-colored fabric.

"Miss Byrnehouse." He motioned toward a chair.

"My, aren't we formal," she teased and sat down.

"This is business."

Alexa elaborately sobered her expression and straightened her back, but it only made Jess laugh and she quickly lost the facade.

Relieved by the absence of tension, Jess stood and removed a painting from the wall that concealed a safe. Alexa made no comment as he opened it, pulled out a thick envelope, and closed it again. He rehung the painting, straightened it carefully, then turned and tossed the envelope to Alexa.

"Your wages for the past two weeks," he said, "and a bonus as well. Your salary will increase ten percent now, as I promised. Paydays remain bimonthly as they have been."

"I assume you can afford this." She glanced warily at the envelope in her hands.

Jess laughed as he sat behind the desk and planted his boots in the center of it. "Right now, I can afford just about anything. Six months from now . . . ," he shrugged, "we shall see."

"But of course you paid the bank." He looked briefly alarmed and she added quickly, "I'm sorry. Perhaps it's none of my business."

"No," he shook his head, "it's fine. I forget that you don't already know. Everybody else here does. There is an extended mortgage on the property, with payments due every six months. I've still got a few years left." He picked up a riding crop and twirled it through his fingers. Alexa sensed he felt uneasy. "I wouldn't have had such trouble making this last one, except that I lost my entire wool harvest last year."

"What happened?" She frowned, realizing the severity of such a thing from her father's involvement in the same business.

"It's not worth repeating." Jess wished he hadn't brought this up.

"Did it have something to do with Chad?" she insisted.

Jess said nothing, but she saw the truth in his eyes.

"You told me Chad was full of wind."

"He is."

"This isn't the first time you've said something to indicate it's a lot more than idle threats. So what's the truth of it?"

Jess turned to stare at the wall, but a muscle in his cheek twitched.

"You lied to me." She stood and leaned over the desk. Jess's eyes shot to her in defense. "You told me it was just talk, but it's not, is it."

"And if I hadn't?" he retorted. Alexa hesitated. "If I had given you any indication that Chad Byrnehouse is a man of his word, you'd have walked out and never looked back."

"Perhaps that would have been better." She took her chair again, all too aware of the hurt in Jess's eyes. Still, she persisted with her point. "If my being here is going to make Chad all the more determined to hurt you, then—"

"You're being here is the least of it, Alexa, I can assure you."

"Then . . . why?"

"If only I knew." He gave a satirical chuckle. "He's been breathing down my neck since my father died. I've yet to figure it out." He set harsh eyes on Alexa and held up a clenched fist. "I don't care what his reasons might be. I don't care who he is or what he might do to me. I will not let Chad Byrnehouse come between us."

Alexa closed her eyes and sighed with relief, touched by the ardor of his conviction.

"It's time to look to the future." His countenance brightened. "I have been blessed to keep my home for another six months, and I will do my best to keep it beyond that. Right now, it looks exceptionally good. I can afford to pay up all the back salary I owe the boys, as well as some maintenance that is long overdue. And I have every intention of making an excellent harvest this year."

"I'm glad." Alexa smiled, appreciating his candor concerning things she knew he didn't have to tell her.

Jess rose and held out a hand. "If this keeps up, we'll be partners before you know it."

"Partners in what?" She took the offered hand, wondering if he meant horse racing or something more personal.

Jess ignored her question with a mischievous smirk. "Would you care to join me for coffee, Alexandra?" Alexa stood and walked into the hall with him. "Mrs. Brown scolded me for not coming in to supper, even though she admitted to feeding Richard. But I promised her that even when I dine at the bunkhouse, I would always be delighted to enjoy some of her coffee."

"I dare say you flatter the woman terribly."

"She thrives on it." Jess laughed and put his arm about her waist.

"And what about me?"

"You're far too intelligent to be flattered." He looked down at her with serious eyes. "With you, I have to be completely honest when I tell you that you're beautiful and I enjoy your company." He stopped walking and bent to kiss her. A tingling consumed Alexa, filtering to every nerve. She went on her tiptoes and pushed a hand into his hair. Jess drew her more fully into his arms, resisting the urge to carry her upstairs.

"I love you," he whispered against her face. He saw caution in her eyes and wondered if she still hesitated to trust him.

"And I love you," she replied with conviction.

Jess smiled and pushed open the door to the music room. "I told Mrs. Brown we would have our coffee here. I hope you don't mind."

"Why would I mind?"

"I enjoy hearing you play," he admitted, "but you don't have to if—"

"It's almost my favorite thing to do," she interrupted.

"What comes above it?" he asked, escorting her to the bench where she sat and leaning over the piano to watch her.

"Horse racing, of course," she said, and began a sonata.

"Why do you love it so much?" He was fascinated by everything about her.

"That's easy." She watched her fingers move eloquently over the keys. "There's the joy of feeling such a kinship with a horse that you could swear you know its thoughts. And then there's the fulfillment that comes from seeing an animal turn into a winner. But most of all, it's that thrill of feeling the horse fly beneath you." She finished her brief piece with a strong note and placed her hands in her lap. A vibrancy in her eyes added strength to her words. "It's the glorious uncertainty of the whole thing that's so thoroughly consuming."

"I can appreciate that."

"But it's not at the top of the list for me." She looked up at him, her eyes shining. "Not any more." His eyes narrowed in question, and she gave him a serene smile. "You are at the top of the list, Jess Davies."

"You put me above horse racing and the piano?"

"Bet your life on it."

"I just might do that." He lifted a brow and bent over the piano to reach her with his lips. Alexa pushed her hand over his shoulder as his kiss left her breathless.

The door opened, and together they turned to see an astonished Mrs. Brown holding the coffee tray.

"Thank you." Jess nodded toward the table, but she didn't move. "Come now." He took the tray from her and set it down. "Surely you've seen two people kissing before. It's rather quaint. You should try it sometime."

Mrs. Brown eyed him in disbelief. He bent to place a kiss on her cheek, and she left the room in exasperation.

"You'll have the woman looking for work elsewhere," Alexa scolded as Jess chuckled.

"Ah, she loves it." He poured out a cup of coffee and handed it to Alexa. "She just pretends to be stuffy because she thinks it's expected of a housekeeper. I know her better, you see." He winked and whispered, "She was my nanny."

"But I thought she came here when her husband died and—"

"Oh, she did," he broke in. "She worked here when I was a child, then left when I grew up. It was some years later that she returned as a widow."

"I see." Alexa added cream and sugar to her coffee and took a careful sip before she set it on the piano.

Goose bumps repeatedly engulfed Jess as he watched her fingers bring the ebony and ivory to life. The room became filled with music that reminded him of a wordless description of the mountains on his land, shrouded by a rainy mist. He noticed a touch of sweat on her brow as she finished. Her fingers quickly brushed it away before she reached for her coffee, unaware of the spell she had cast with her music and her presence.

While Alexa sipped her coffee, her eye was drawn to the painting on the wall. She had often taken notice of it and wondered over its origin, but now Jess was here to ask.

"Where did you get the painting?"

Jess's brow furrowed. He didn't know what she was talking about until she nodded toward it and his eyes followed. Though it was subtle, Alexa didn't miss the way his expression hardened. "Read the signature," he suggested dryly.

"I can't see that it has one."

"It's there. Look in that cluster of flowers, almost into the frame."

Alexa stood on the piano bench and peered at it closely. "I see it now. Emma Davies." She dusted the bench with her sleeve, then sat back down. "A relative?" she asked, taking another sip.

"My mother," he replied.

Alexa made a noise of approval that echoed from her cup before she set it down to admire the painting again. "It's really beautiful. Did she do others?"

Jess sighed in an effort to keep emotions from showing. "Yes," he said, then wondered how to tell her this was the only one that hadn't been in the house when it burned. He cleared his throat and attempted to sound toneless. "She did several, but this is the only one available."

Jess was relieved when she didn't question him further, until she asked, "Is that supposed to be you?"

His eye was drawn to the depiction of a young boy running through a field of blue flowers. He'd never done any such thing in his life, but he had to admit, "Most of her paintings were of me, so I suppose it is. Though I don't see the resemblance."

"It's nice," she said and began to play again, gradually distracting Jess with her music. When she finished, Alexa caught his gaze with those incredible eyes, and he forgot about everything but his feelings for her.

"Alexa." He clutched her hand and straddled the bench to sit beside her. Her lips parted with a breathy sigh, and he took the opportunity to kiss her. And kiss her. And kiss her.

"Alexa," he cried against her face, "don't leave me alone. Stay with me tonight. Please, let me . . ."

Alexa pulled back abruptly and the tension returned, falling between them like a rock.

"What?" he demanded, recalling his conviction to face this head-on. Alexa stood and turned her back. "Listen to me, Alexandra. I'm not laying my heart out on the table so we can play guessing games."

"I'm sorry, Jess." She moved to the window and stared into the darkness. "It has nothing to do with you. It's just that . . ." Alexa knew she needed to tell him the reasons, but now wasn't the time. "This is all moving so fast." She turned and smiled. "I love you, Jess." She stepped toward him and put a hand to his face. "What is happening between us is wonderful, and I don't want it to stop. I'm just . . . not ready to take certain steps. Not yet. Not without commitment. Be patient with me." Alexa felt relieved to have that out. Though it wasn't the whole truth, it was the truth.

Jess searched her eyes for sincerity and found it. He pressed his face into the folds of her shirt while she played with his hair.

"I should take you home," he said finally, fearing any other course of action at the moment would bring back that tension.

Alexa nodded, and Jess eased away to retrieve the envelope she'd left on the piano. "Don't forget this." He set it in her hand, and together they walked to the carriage house and up the stairs. "Thank you, Alexa," he whispered close to her face, "for an unforgettable day."

"We will have many more, I think."

Alexa felt Jess smile in the darkness and met his kiss with expectation. Though she feared getting carried away, it was difficult not to give in to this need for affection, strong as it was. Her response was quickly reciprocated, and their kiss became heated.

"Is that you, Alexa? I—" Richard's door came open, and light shone into the hall. The interruption didn't seem to bother Jess much, but Alexa stepped back quickly, upset by Richard's stunned expression as he stood with a piece of paper in his hand.

"It can wait." Richard tersely broke the silence and closed the door as quickly as it had opened.

"Well," Jess said lightly, "it certainly is difficult to kiss a woman in privacy around here."

Alexa opened her door and went on her tiptoes to kiss him quickly. "Good night, Jess."

"Good night," he replied, disappointment evident in his voice. He kissed her again and reluctantly allowed her to slip away.

❦　❦　❦

Richard leaned against his door and tried to breathe. He couldn't believe it. He'd seen it coming, even suspected it, though a part of him was convinced it would never happen. But it had. And by the way they'd been holding each other, it was evident their feelings were not mild by any means.

He wanted to die. An unreasonable pain bubbled up from inside him, and his back slid down the door until he sat helplessly on the floor. He looked at the carefully scribed poem in his hand, then crumpled the paper and threw it across the room.

Groaning in anguish, Richard buried his head in his hands. Of all the men she could have chosen over him, why did it have to be Jess? He cursed the fate that had changed his life with these wretched scars, and he cursed Alexandra Byrnehouse for ever coming here. His life would never be the same.

❦　❦　❦

Alexa watched out her window until Jess disappeared up the path toward the house. She sat on the edge of the bed and reflected on the happenings of the day, rubbing her arms to soothe the chill of excitement. Then she thought of Richard, and a rippling of uneasiness invaded her bliss.

Courageously she stepped into the hall and knocked at his door. Surely it was little more than her imagination that he disapproved of her and Jess. Only silence answered, and she knocked again.

"Richard, are you there?" she called. Still no response.

Alexa sighed. She knew he was in there. Could it be possible that her affection for Jess had hurt him? Was that the reason for this consuming uneasiness?

"Richard," she pounded on the door, "open this door and talk to me."

It came open so quickly it startled her. "Did you need something?" he asked with a straight face. "I was going to bed."

Alexa attempted to read between his words, but his hard stare revealed nothing. "You wanted to see me?" she asked.

"Nothing particular," he stated. "Just wondered how you're doing."

"Fine." She smiled, determined to not feel guilty for her feelings. "Is something bothering you?" she asked outright. "You seem . . . upset."

"I'm just tired, Alexa," he insisted, but she knew he was lying. She was tempted to prod it out of him, but if he was going to be so stubborn, she didn't want to deal with it.

"I'll see you tomorrow, then," she said, and he closed the door. Alexa went to her room, wondering momentarily if she was doing the right thing in regard to Jess. It only took a minute to be certain that she was, and she slept little as her thoughts were consumed with the turn her life was taking. But she was oblivious to the man across the hall, unable to sleep at all for the same reason.

❦   ❦   ❦

A strange disorientation filled Alexa as Jess halted the wagon near the side door of the home she'd grown up in. Her trunks were collected without incident, while the servants regarded her tersely.

"Can we go now?" Jess asked when the wagon was loaded. She nodded, sensing his uneasiness, as if Chad might appear out of nowhere and level a curse on them both.

"Wait," she said before he had a chance to help her onto the seat. "Before we leave, there's something I must see."

Jess saw the emotion in her eyes and nodded easily. "Take as long as you need." He knew this must be more difficult for her than she let on. He wasn't surprised to be led toward the stables. They moved tentatively inside, where an elderly stable-hand turned toward them, first looking baffled, then sentimental.

"Miss Alexandra." He beamed, and she hurried to embrace him.

"It's good to see you, Lowery. How are you?"

"Well enough, Miss. And you?"

"I'm doing wonderfully." She glanced toward Jess, and the old man seemed to know the situation.

"You came to visit?" Lowery questioned.

"I came to get some of my things, but I'd like to . . ." She gazed longingly down the long row of stalls.

Lowery put a fatherly hand to her shoulder. "Feel free. I'll be outside if you need me."

Alexa thanked him and motioned for Jess to follow her.

"Oh, Jess," she exclaimed softly, nuzzling against a gray mare, "she's still here."

An unexpected wave of emotion washed over Jess as he observed a reunion that he knew was difficult for Alexa.

"She's the only thing I really miss." Alexa's eyes filled with tears, and Jess felt too moved to speak. He had seen the relationship she'd developed with Crazy, but he'd never stopped to ponder what she'd left behind in that respect.

"Look at you," she said to the horse. "They've let you get fat and lazy."

"Her name?" Jess questioned, stroking the animal's neck.

"Lady's Maid. Father named her. He said she was mine the minute she came into the world."

"And Chad wouldn't let you take her?"

"Obviously not." Her tone was only a little cynical. "One day," she whispered to Lady's Maid, "I will find a way to get you back. And we'll run again—like we never have before."

Jess met Alexa's hand in the mane and squeezed it.

"Let's go home," she said, and Jess ushered her from the stable.

"Are you all right?" he asked after most of the ride had passed in silence.

"You know," she said thoughtfully, "I don't miss it as much as I expected to." She leaned against his shoulder and sighed. "Home is with you, Jess."

Jess put his arm around her and fought the urge to cry. She couldn't know what that meant to him when keeping his own home was so precarious. With Alexa, he truly believed that wherever they went they could be happy.

Jess and Fiddler carried Alexa's trunks into the carriage house and slid them under the stairs.

"What's in these things, anyway?" Jess asked when the last one was in place.

"Mostly a bunch of useless gowns and such." Alexa trotted up the stairs and Jess followed. She entered her room, then stepped back with a breathy scream. Jess appeared behind her to see the reason, and bile rose in his throat.

"What are you doing here?" Jess demanded.

Chad lazily polished the toe of his boot with a corner of the bedspread, then he looked about the room with a nauseating smirk. "Quaint little place, sister. Did you decorate it yourself?"

"Get out of here," Alexa insisted. "You have no right to—"

"Now, now." He chuckled and stood, stretching as if he'd been there for hours. "No need to get upset. I heard you'd stopped by and I missed you, so I thought I'd return the visit and give you this." He pulled a silk scarf out of his pocket and dangled it in front of her like a carrot for a rabbit. "It somehow missed getting in with the other things."

"It's not mine."

"I know it's not yours," Chad laughed. "It's your mother's. I just thought you'd like to have it."

"How sentimental of you," Alexa retorted, snatching it away from him. "Now get out."

"There's no rush, little sister."

"I'm not welcome in your home. You're not welcome in mine."

"I'm going." Chad sauntered toward the door. Alexa moved aside to let him pass, but Jess stayed as he was, partially blocking the doorway.

"How are you, old pal?" Chad grinned and rocked on his heels.

"I'll be better after you leave," Jess stated tonelessly.

"Going to the derby, I hear." Chad spoke as if they were sharing tea.

"We're looking forward to it," Jess replied.

"I can imagine." Chad gave that cat-swallowing-the-canary grin, and Jess wanted to strangle him.

"Good-bye, Chad." Alexa eased Jess out of his way and motioned her brother toward the door.

Chad glanced at Jess, then at Alexa. He shook his head as if it were pitiful, then said in a quiet voice, "If you only knew."

"Get out!" Jess made it clear he meant it. Chad grinned and sauntered down the stairs.

"I'm sorry, Jess," Alexa said as Jess moved to the window to make certain Chad had left.

"Why should you apologize for his being a jackass?"

Alexa tried to suppress a giggle, but it escaped with an unfeminine snort. Jess turned in surprise, and together they laughed.

Feeling suddenly panicked, she opened her drawers and glanced quickly through them to assure herself that they were undisturbed. She sighed with relief and turned back toward Jess.

"It is pretty." Jess took the scarf and watched it slide over his fingers, the sheer blue fabric shimmering in a way that reminded him of Alexa's eyes. "My mother loved things like this," he added with a vague yearning in his voice, then he returned to the present and touched it to Alexa's face. "Real silk." He smirked. "Expensive, eh?"

Alexa took it from him and tossed it on the bed. "It was a gift," she said as if the topic was annoying. "Chad and I were both there when my mother received it. She pretended she didn't know who had sent it, but I knew she was lying."

Alexa glanced at the scarf. With respect to more recent events, she understood now where it had come from. A lover's gift, no doubt. Her father, perhaps? But why had Chad made such a point of giving it to her now?

"How did you know she was lying?" Jess asked, wondering what she wasn't telling him that put such bitterness in her eyes.

"I've got work to do, Mr. Davies," she stated.

"So you do." He followed her outside. They passed Richard on their way to the stable, and Alexa caught a terse glance.

"How's it going, Rich?" Jess asked jovially.

"Absolutely marvelous. How about you?"

"The same." Jess laughed, apparently not catching the sarcastic undertones. Alexa reminded herself that she was not responsible for Richard's feelings—or Chad's bad manners. But she didn't feel convinced on either count.

Days wore on with business as usual. Jess rarely left Alexa's side, and Richard rarely showed himself beyond mealtime. Jess's frequent declarations of love began to sink in, but as he seemed to purposely hold back his affection, Alexa realized her attempts to keep the situation from getting out of hand had likely communicated a misinterpreted message. She became concerned when his absence was keenly noticed at supper in the bunkhouse one evening. She hurried into the house and found him seated behind his desk, lost in thought. He'd left the door open and Alexa leaned quietly against the jamb, contemplating the evolvement of their relationship as she tried to figure where his head might be. Recalling events prior to the race, she decided a display of trust was in order. He had certainly earned it.

"Does your offer still stand?"

Jess turned abruptly, startled as much by her question as her presence. "My offer?" he asked, wanting a justification for the pounding of his heart.

Alexa put her hands on the desk and leaned toward him. "Before the race you mentioned something about . . . ," she tried to recall his wording, ". . . galloping together in the moonlight on a high-spirited stallion and—"

"I believe we did that." He leaned his elbows on the desk and set his chin on clasped fingers.

"Yes," she smiled, "I suppose we did. But I must confess," she glanced away with an innocent coyness, "I'm rather intrigued with . . . how did you put it?" She looked at him with wide eyes. "Tea by candlelight?"

"Why?" Jess asked, his mouth dry.

"Why am I intrigued?" She watched her fingers trace patterns in the dust particles on the desk.

"Before the race, you turned me down flat." His eyes narrowed. "Why did you change your mind?"

"Did I?" She gave him a teasing smile. "I just asked if your offer still—"

"Yes," he interrupted, "it stands."

"Then give me half an hour to freshen up." She started toward the door. "Do you want me to bring the tea?"

Jess shook his head. "I think I can manage. I'll be in the room just south of the dining room."

Alexa nodded and hurried back to the carriage house. While she washed up and changed into a fresh shirt, Alexa reminded herself to be straightforward with Jess, but to also let him know that she trusted him. She pulled the ribbon from her hair and brushed it out, allowing it to hang free. Little more than half an hour later, she knocked at the specified door. Getting no response, she tentatively pushed it open and caught her breath.

What appeared to be a breakfast room was illuminated with the glow of a candelabra on the fireplace mantel, two others on a sideboard, and another in the center of a small table where a tray with china tea service waited. Jess occupied one of the two chairs, his long legs stretched out, a fresh shirt clinging to shoulders that leaned back comfortably. His hair was damp and a clean, masculine scent permeated the distance between them.

"Your hair looks pretty like that," he said quietly.

"No," she laughed softly and sat down, "my hair looks better like this. Nothing on earth could make my hair look pretty. Believe me, I've tried."

"It looks pretty now," he said.

Alexa turned her attention to the tea service, taking it upon herself to pour. "You didn't make this yourself, did you?" she asked with a sideways smile.

"You can thank Mrs. Brown for that," he said, fascinated with the way her fingers handled the delicate china as if they were made for each other. When she passed him a cup, their hands brushed for a moment and their eyes met like a match to tinder. Jess leaned back and held the warm cup close to his face, feeling the steam rise while he peered over the rim at Alexa, surrounded by candlelight. He wanted her now, and he wanted to savor each moment of anticipation. He wondered if she would stay the night, or turn away again when faced with the possibility. He knew he must tread carefully, but oh, how he wanted to touch her!

"Here," he said, setting down his cup and picking up one of the little cakes left by Mrs. Brown, "try this." He leaned forward and held it to her lips. Alexa took a bite and made a pleasurable sound as her tongue flicked out to lick the cream filling from the corner of her lips.

"That's wonderful." She took another bite. Jess popped what was left into his own mouth, then noticed more of that cream on her lower lip. Impulsively he wiped it away with his thumb, then showed it to her, making her smile. With a gentle hand she guided his thumb to her lips, where she licked the cream away.

Jess heard pulse beats in his ears that became deafening when their eyes met, and he realized she was feeling this way, too. He watched her in awe as she fed cake to him. She took a careful sip of her tea, then with the cup cradled in her palms she urged it to his lips. Jess wrapped his hand around hers and tipped the cup while his eyes held hers. He felt as if they were participating in some ancient mating ritual. Perhaps, in a way, it was. The sensation intensified when she took the cup back, turned it in her hands, and placed her lips over the rim in the very spot where he had just drunk. Their eyes met again, and he could almost believe she was a part of his own flesh and blood by the way her presence alone filled him completely.

He leaned back nonchalantly, while inside he wanted to jump out of his chair and carry her to his bed. "So, we've already gone riding in the moonlight, and now we've shared tea by candlelight." He tapped his fingers on the table at his side. "But wasn't there something about . . . firelight?"

Familiar stirrings became nearly unbearable beneath Jess's heated gaze. In Alexa's heart she wanted to cross boundaries with him that she'd never crossed before, but she had to have more. She glanced helplessly toward the cold grate in the little fireplace at her side, almost wishing she didn't know what he was implying. But the details of his offer came back to her clearly. And if there was any doubt, Jess erased it when he added, "Oh, there's a perfectly incredible fireplace upstairs . . . in my bedroom."

"Jess, I . . ." She came abruptly to her feet, ready to spill any thoughtless excuse to get out of here. Jess caught her arm, and she felt cornered.

"Am I wrong in assuming you want to be with me tonight?" His voice was quiet but determined.

"I *do* want to be with you," she retorted, "but not just tonight, Jess. I'm not sure that what I want out of this is something you're willing to give."

"And what is that?" he asked severely.

"You're no fool, Jess Davies. You figure it out. What I want is nothing more than any respectable woman would."

She moved toward the door, but he stopped her. "Alexa, wait. Please sit down."

Alexa did as he asked but remained on the edge of her seat. Her palms began to sweat as she considered what hinged on this moment. If only he would say something, anything to indicate he wanted the kind of commitment she needed. She wrung her hands nervously. Was she a fool to be here in the first place? How could she make him understand that she wanted him, wanted to be close to him, but giving herself to him completely was something she just couldn't do until—

"Alexa," he interrupted her thoughts, seeming nervous, "I want to say something that's not easy to say. I hope you will hear me out."

Alexa nodded, feeling a degree of hope. He'd never found it difficult to ask her to go to bed with him.

"Alexa, I'm asking you to take a gamble." Her eyes widened, but he persisted. "You see, I've hesitated to ask you because everything I have seems so precarious. I mean . . . I've made one more payment, but I can't be certain what will happen before the next is due. In a sense I've been living for the moment, but I can't live that way any longer, Alexa. When I thought I might lose everything, I realized the only thing that would make it bearable is . . ." He set a hand to her face and looked at her deeply. "Alexa," he whispered, "am I worth the gamble? Will you stay with me no matter what happens? If I ever have to leave here, will you go where I go?"

Attempting to keep hold of her reason, Alexa felt she had to say, "Don't patronize me, Jess. Don't you dare sit there and tell me what I want to hear so you can—"

"I hear Chad talking," Jess interrupted curtly. Alexa leaned back with a guilty sigh, wishing she could explain her fears without sounding prejudiced.

"What will it take, Alexandra, to convince you that what I am saying is genuine? Do I have to get down on my knees?" he asked in mock gallantry, then did just that.

"Stop it," she insisted, not amused.

"Then tell me what to do!" he insisted, taking her upper arms into his hands. "Tell me what you want me to do, Alexa, and I'll do it. Not to patronize you, but because I want you. I want you in my life so badly that my heart threatens to break if I just think of never seeing you again. I know it sounds trite. That's why I haven't said it before. But it's true, Alexa." He clenched his teeth and leaned toward her. "I need you. *I love you.*"

Alexa was momentarily stunned. It all felt too wonderful to be true, which prompted her to test it further. "What if I told you I want something you can't give?" He drew back, but his grip remained firm. "What if you were to lose everything, and—"

"You wouldn't." His voice became edged with anger. "I can't believe that you, of all people, would base such a thing on whether or not I—"

"No," she broke in, "I wouldn't. But now perhaps you know how it feels to wonder. Don't try to make me believe that one night would hurt you more than it would me. If you and I care for each other enough to want what we are wanting, then there is no gamble. No bets. No speculations. What I want from you, Jess Davies, is something any man can give. But I don't want it unless your full heart is behind it. If you give it to me, I will give you everything I have in return. I will follow you to the ends of the earth, if need be."

"Name it," he said huskily, his eyes burning with male challenge.

Alexa felt the words at the edge of her tongue, but she couldn't bring herself to say them. It wasn't her place. She would not spend her life wondering if his commitment was a matter of bargaining in a passionate moment.

"You figure it out." She pushed him away and ran into the hall.

Eleven

DISCLOSURE

"Alexa!" Jess caught up with her just below the stairs and grabbed her arm. "Where are you going?" he demanded.

"I . . . shouldn't be here so late . . . this way . . . I . . ." Her voice began to tremble and she stopped before it cracked.

"You don't trust me?" he questioned, but she gave no response. Seeing a rise of panic in her eyes, he hurried on with his original purpose. "You promised to hear me out. I'm not finished yet."

Alexa relaxed slightly and he took a deep breath. "Perhaps it's too soon, but I have to know." He glanced down uneasily, then he lifted his eyes to hers, conviction filling his expression. "As soon as the racing season is over, we'll be busy harvesting the wool, and . . . if all goes well, I'll have enough to pay another mortgage payment then, and . . . Alexa, what I'm trying to say is, when we get past all that, when what I have is a little more secure . . . Alexa, will you marry me?"

Relief engulfed Alexa and left her momentarily speechless. Vulnerability brimmed in Jess's eyes. She set a hand to his face and reached up to kiss him. "Yes," she said against his lips. "Oh, yes." Jess laughed and kissed her again, easing her closer, holding her tighter. Apparently he'd figured out what she wanted.

Passion quickly seeped into their embrace, and Jess didn't hesitate to admit it. "Stay with me, Alexa," he whispered. "Don't leave me alone tonight. I . . ."

She drew back, and that panic rose again in her eyes.

Jess spoke immediately. "If you've got something you want to say, you'd best say it. I'm getting tired of you looking at me like that."

Alexa hesitated.

"You *don't* trust me," he stated rather than asked.

"It's not a matter of trust, Jess."

"Then what is it a matter of?" he demanded.

Alexa took a deep breath. She knew he was right. She had to say it and let him know where she stood, but it was so difficult to talk about. Reminding herself that she *did* trust him, she drew courage. "I simply cannot allow such a thing . . . to happen outside of marriage." There. She had said it. She nearly expected him to protest or get angry, but his eyes were unreadable.

"All right." Jess folded his arms. A brief flicker of disappointment appeared, then vanished. "If that's what you want, I can respect it. May I ask why?"

Alexa drew up her chin. "I've seen too much pain as a result of children being born where they weren't expected, and likely not wanted. I will not allow that to happen to any child of mine."

Jess stiffened visibly and stuffed his hands into his pockets. Was she speaking from personal experience? Did she have a clue what that statement meant in regard to his own life? Looking at it that way, he felt like a fool for not thinking of it himself. But he intended to make one point clear. "I hope you know I would not leave you to face such a thing alone. Of course I would marry you."

Alexa straightened her back and snapped at him. "Then marry me *first,* Jess. Marry me because you love me, not because you're obligated to give my child your name."

Jess's first impulse was to snap back. But all anger and disappointment fled in the face of his growing respect. His father would have loved this woman. Here she stood, reminding him of the values he'd been raised with, teachings that had somehow become lost in the oppression he'd suffered since Ben Davies' death.

With gentle purpose he took Alexa's hand and urged her close to him, looking into her eyes with profound intensity. "I *will* marry you, Alexa." He spoke close to her face and brushed his fingertips over her temple, into her hair. "I'll marry you because you're the best thing that ever happened to me. I love you. I need you." He kissed the corner of her mouth tentatively. "And I want you." He drew back and added firmly, "But I will wait. We'll have a family the respectable way, Alexa."

Relief left Alexa weak in his arms, fighting back tears of joy. She clung to him and savored every intricate sensation of his kiss. Her tears spilled in the midst of it, but Jess smiled as he pulled back and caught one with his fingertip. "Just don't expect me to stop holding you this way," he insisted and kissed her again.

Alexa sighed, reveling in the feel of his lips as they skittered over her face, lapping up the salty tears. "Never," she whispered and urged her mouth to his. It was easy to release her affection without reservation. His promise to heed her wishes evoked complete trust.

"You know," she tipped her head back, allowing his lips to play over her throat, "my mother once told me that the truest intimacy is not physical."

Jess wove a hand into her hair and lifted her face to his. Their eyes met, their breath mingled. The spectrum of their conversation tempted Alexa to blush, but instead she tingled with the anticipation of being his wife.

"I think I'd like to explore that theory." His green eyes glowed with mischief. "How about right now?" Alexa looked up, wide-eyed. "You do trust me, don't you?"

"Of course I do, but—"

"Alexa," he rubbed a thumb over her cheek, "do you know how many years I have spent in this house alone? Stay with me, Alexa. Be with me. Just for tonight. Let me hold you through the night, wake up with you in my arms. I swear to you nothing will happen that shouldn't. It's just that . . . I keep thinking about the night we spent together on the mountain, and how our feelings have blossomed since then, and . . ." Not wanting to sound overbearing and push her into something she didn't feel comfortable with, he coolly motioned toward the stairs and set one foot onto the bottom step. "You can stay or you can go. Either way, I'm going to marry you."

Alexa's heart raced. Their eyes met, and the intensity of the moment descended as two strong wills melted beneath a mutual desire for being together.

Jess held up a hand in resignation. "The choice is yours."

Alexa gave him a defiant glare and walked toward the door. Jess felt his heart sink as he watched her go, but she stopped with her hand on the knob. He held his breath. Was she staying, or did she just want to say something more?

A turmoil of emotion rose in Alexa's throat, telling her she was being ruled by her pride. Jess had pledged his heart and life to her. He had accepted her desire to wait, and he had promised to respect her wishes. It *was* a matter of trust—and leaving now would only make him believe she was giving credence to what Chad had told her. Hadn't she once accused him of doing the same to her, and resented him for it?

Alexa hesitated only a moment, then walked past Jess and up the stairs as if she owned the place. With any luck, it wouldn't be long before she did. Jess inwardly whooped with eager excitement as he followed Alexandra Byrnehouse up the stairs. He didn't even care that they had to wait to make love. This night would be sublime just in being with her. Her willingness to stay demonstrated a trust that he would not betray.

Alexa stopped at the landing, and he reminded himself that she didn't know the way from there. "Second door on the right," he said, taking up a lamp from the hall table.

Alexa pushed the door open, and light shone into the room from behind her. "It's marvelous," she said as he set the lamp down and closed the door.

It was like a bedroom, sitting room, and study, all put together in one huge room. The decor was in deep maroon and forest green, the center of which was a high, old-fashioned bed, covered with a satiny comforter of paisley, coordinated with the drapes. But the incredible thing was the way it made her feel. There were paintings of horses, a couple of pairs of riding boots here and there, books left open, a snifter of brandy partially drained, pillows propped against the headboard, and a riding crop on the bedside table. This room was Jess Davies. She could almost imagine him sitting up in bed with a book in one hand and twirling his crop in the other. And then there was the fireplace, which he'd given the humble description of "incredible." It reminded Alexa of those she'd seen in books about castles. It took nearly half the wall; the grate was level with the floor, with mosaic tiles laid out in front and an ornate brass screen set upon them.

Jess took off his boots and stockings while Alexa absorbed her surroundings, walking about, touching his belongings, occasionally glancing his way. Was his bedroom so fascinating? It looked a mess to him.

"You like it, eh?" He chuckled, bending to light the fire.

"I do." She continued to look about with interest, perhaps to distract herself from the reality. She was in Jess Davies' bedroom—with Jess Davies.

"Good," he said lightly. "Before long we can move your things in."

The implication made Alexa's heart jump. Jess stood and brushed his hands on his breeches. Her eyes went to his bare feet, then back up again to meet his gaze. She prayed the night would not see her a fool. She turned her attention to the fire, already burning in vibrant hues of orange and red. "That didn't take long." She realized he must have had it prepared.

Jess smiled nervously. "Make yourself comfortable."

Alexa glanced around. The chairs were situated too far from the fire, and the bed seemed too blatant. She opted for the thick braided rug near the fireplace, and sat on the floor. She stretched out her legs and leaned back on her hands.

Jess sat beside her and watched her while she stared into the flames. "You don't look very comfortable." He lifted one of her feet into his lap to pull off her boot, then her stocking. She glared at him dubiously. When her foot was bare, Jess looked at it contemplatively, then he looked at her, then at her foot again. He grinned, and Alexa grasped his intention an instant before he started tickling.

"No," she protested, "please don't! Jess!" she screamed, and squirmed while he laughed and continued mercilessly until she kicked him. She lay back breathlessly while he bared the other foot and began again. Alexa managed to scramble out of his grasp. She ran to the other side of the room, then over the bed and back again, where Jess finally grabbed her leg and sent her sprawling onto the comforter in a heap of giggles. Jess laughed as he wrapped her in it and dragged it over to the braided rug. Alexa threw the comforter off and lay breathlessly in the middle of it. She laughed helplessly until she looked up to see Jess standing above her. His expression was so intent that she absently put a hand to her heart in an effort to calm it.

Suddenly weak from the scene before him, Jess went to his knees. Seeing his own emotions mirrored in her eyes, he felt compelled to admit, "I've had fantasies like this, Alexandra."

Alexa smiled timidly as she absorbed his aura in the firelight. "So what happens next?" she asked.

"I don't know," he chortled. "You tell me."

"It's your fantasy."

Jess lay beside her, but not too close. "I'll tell you about it when we're married."

"I can't wait." Alexa looked into his eyes and wondered how she could bear waiting when she wanted him so badly. But it was not a matter of what she wanted. Her motivation ran deep. Still, she convinced herself as his lips came over hers, there was no harm in a kiss.

"Alexa," he murmured and kissed her again. She tensed slightly, and he reminded himself not to get carried away. "Alexa," he repeated with assurance, "I promised—and I meant it."

She nodded subtly and closed her eyes, inviting him to kiss her again. Then she sighed and laid her head on his shoulder, reminded of the night they'd spent on the mountain in the storm. Jess wrapped his arms tightly around her, and she tried to comprehend the life they would share. They lay in peaceable silence until only a few smoldering coals remained to give the room a dark, reddish glow. Alexa nuzzled closer to Jess's warmth as she began to feel chilled. Jess threw the excess of the comforter over the top of them and brushed his lips through her hair. "I love you, Alexa," he whispered, and she turned her face toward his, silently beckoning a kiss. Jess was quick to comply.

Alexa drifted to sleep in his arms, and her next awareness was dawn flowing into the room. She realized she was in the bed, but she couldn't remember getting there. The fire had died but the comforter was still spread over the floor. She turned to look at Jess, and was surprised to find him watching her.

"Did I wake you?" he asked, setting his fingers to her face in greeting.

Alexa shook her head and Jess bent to kiss her. He sighed and laid his head next to hers on the pillow. With a poetic tone that surprised her, he said, "Heaven is like unto Alexa. The brilliance of dawn is lessened by her presence."

She nuzzled closer to him and slept again until she heard the door close and looked up to see Jess setting a breakfast tray on a small table near the window. He smiled and pulled the drapes back further to let in the sun. Alexa sidled toward the edge of the bed and swung her legs over. She stretched and yawned, then looked up to find Jess standing before her, his eyes betraying all he felt.

"Morning becomes you, my love." He touched her face and she kissed the palm of his hand.

A knock at the door startled them both, and Alexa looked panicked. "It's all right," he chuckled softly. "We have nothing to hide."

Alexa nodded, but quickly stood and smoothed her clothes. Jess grinned wryly at her as she hurried across the room to pick up his brush and attempt to straighten her hair in the bureau mirror.

"Have you seen Alexa?" Richard asked sharply before the door was completely open.

"Why?" Jess retorted in panic. "What's wrong?"

"We can't find her," he shouted. "That's what's wrong! I don't think her bed's even been slept in."

Jess lifted his brow. "I didn't realize you kept such close track of her."

"Someone's got to," Richard insisted. "I can't imagine what might have—"

"I can assure you that Alexa is perfectly fine," Jess interrupted. Richard looked at him, suspicion crossing concern in his expression. "I saw her just a minute ago."

"But how could you, when—"

Alexa appeared beside Jess to clear up the confusion, though she knew Richard was not going to like the evidence. "I'm fine, as you can see," she said.

Richard's gaze went slowly down over her wrinkled clothes to her bare feet and back up again. He glared at Jess, then turned back to Alexa. "You spent the night here?"

Jess put a protective arm around her, wondering what had gotten into Richard. "She is perfectly chaste, I can assure you, though I see no reason why I should have to. You, of all people, have no right to judge my spending the night with a woman."

The anger in Richard's eyes melted into astonishment. "I'm not asking you to justify anything, Jess." Alexa sensed the barely detectable hurt not far below the surface. "I was just concerned." He glanced at her again, then hurried away.

"Did you understand any of that?" Jess asked, staring into the empty hallway.

Alexa shook her head, genuinely wishing that she didn't understand. To be ignorant of Richard's feelings would only add to her bliss. She was relieved by the distraction of Jess's lips against hers.

"Breakfast is waiting," he said close to her face. His eyes sparkled, and she was glad she'd taken the risk. Their night together had strengthened their trust and added to the comfort of their relationship. The love she felt for him threatened to burst from its fullness as she sat across from him and enjoyed a simple breakfast and a spectacular view of the distant hills.

"I love you, Jess." She reached across the table to squeeze his hand. The warmth in his eyes added to her determination to have a life with him. Not even Chad Byrnehouse could keep them apart.

❦ ❦ ❦

Only Richard looked perturbed when Jess seated himself at the bunkhouse table and began to eat lunch. Alexa could see that he was genuinely irritated, but she chose to ignore Richard and concentrate instead on Jess.

During a lull in the conversation, Jess spoke up. "Just so you all know where we stand, I want you to continue working with Crazy and Demented as you have been. They're both registered to compete in local races in the near future. We'll also be doing the maintenance work we discussed the other day. I'm putting Crazy in the derby, and—"

A number of approving gasps interrupted.

"Tod will be riding her," Alexa clarified.

"When the racing season is finished," Jess continued, "we'll take care of the wooling as usual. When that's done, we ought to have a little time to be lazy." Jess winked at Alexa, and a variety of sniggers surfaced.

"Any questions?" Jess added, coming to his feet. No one responded. "Oh," Jess stopped at the door, "by the way, Alexa and I will be getting married this summer; December maybe."

His announcement left the group momentarily stunned. "Blimey," Murphy grinned, "what a lucky son of a gun he is."

"Amen to that," Fiddler added.

"I saw it coming." Edward smiled warmly.

"Isn't this a bit rushed?" Richard's cynical tone turned all eyes toward him.

"If they were gettin' married tomorrow," Murphy spoke on Alexa's behalf, "I'd say that was a bit rushed."

"I feel confident I'm doing the right thing," Alexa stated, "if that's what you're wondering."

Richard threw his napkin to the table and walked out.

"What's eatin' him?" Jimmy asked, dumbfounded.

A sickening sadness enveloped Alexa as the evidence deepened that she was hurting Richard, however unintentionally. If she had any doubt, it vanished when Fiddler set a hand over hers. "He'll get over it, Alexa. You have to follow your own heart." Alexa managed a smile, knowing he was right. But weeks passing didn't ease the tension. If Jess noticed, he didn't say anything. Alexa did her best to ignore Richard's terseness and learn to live with it. She felt relieved when he began spending more time on the range with the sheep, and she rarely had to encounter him at all.

Gradually the boys became accustomed to the new Jess Davies and his desire to be wherever Alexa was. Murphy confided to her that they thought the changes in Jess were great. He had always been a good man to work for, but now he was the best. Often it didn't seem they worked for him as much as with him. Alexa knew he had always lent a helping hand, which was something Chad would never do. But it became more common to see Jess push up his sleeves and work side by side with any one of the boys.

During this time, Crazy competed in two local races where she placed in the first and won the second. Tod's confidence began to build, and prospects of winning the derby looked hopeful. They traveled to New South Wales for a race and had the time of their lives. Crazy's reputation was wrapped up neatly when she won the eight furlong by half a length. It was all so enjoyable that Alexa couldn't help but anticipate going to Melbourne with Jess, as well as the derby.

As Jess became the center of her life, Alexa found fulfillment in a way that even horse racing couldn't compare to. They became friends by their common interests. It was as easy to talk to him about almost anything as it was to laugh and play and feel like a child again. Yet far deeper was the prospect of what the future held. Jess often spoke of the time when they would be partners in every respect, but words were not necessary for Alexa to know beyond any doubt that Jess wanted her for much more than friendship. His kisses never ceased to leave her breathless, and she knew it was only her conscious effort to maintain careful boundaries that kept him from having her completely. She wasn't certain if Jess knew her reasons; he had never asked. But with an obvious respect for Alexa, he seemed content to let time take its proper course.

While Chad vacationed in the south, the only dark cloud hanging over Alexa's life was the hurt in Richard's eyes. When he was out with the sheep for days at a time, she could forget about it and feel the full spectrum of her love for Jess. But Richard inevitably returned, and it would hit her all over again.

"He must be tired of his own cooking again," Jess commented casually, and Alexa looked up in question. He nodded toward the horizon, where she could see Richard riding slowly toward them.

"Is it necessary for him to be gone so much?" She maintained a light tone and distracted herself by observing Tod as he rode Crazy around the gallops.

"Not usually." Jess removed his hat and wiped the sweat from his brow with the back of his sleeve. "But it's typical for him to be moody. He gets into low spells for no apparent reason." Jess replaced the hat and straightened it, keeping a concerned eye on Richard. "He can be difficult to figure out, so I stopped trying a long time ago."

Richard galloped past them with no more greeting than a casual wave. Alexa could hear disappointment in Jess's sigh, and she became freshly aware of the friendship she had intruded upon. Her thoughts churned over the situation until it nearly drove her mad. When Richard came into the bunkhouse for supper, his expression made her want to slap him. How could he claim to care for her and silently manipulate her into feeling this way?

"Hello, Richard," Jess said as he was seated. "We've missed your jovial company." Despite his light tone, the sarcasm was evident by the scowl in Richard's response.

"So, how's the mob?" Murphy asked.

"Still there," Richard retorted.

"How are you?" Jess added.

"I'm still here, too," Richard stated.

After a miserable silence Jess persisted, "Aren't you going to ask us how we're doing?"

"No."

"I'm going to tell you anyway." A hint of anger seeped into Jess's voice. "Murphy's got a nasty bruise and a new bump on his head from trying to break in that stallion. Fiddler's been a little down lately. Jimmy's had a touch of the flu. Edward's heart has been giving him some trouble, but he manages to keep going. Sam's doing okay as far as I know. Alexa is as perky as ever, and I'm a little worried about an old friend of mine."

Richard finally looked up from his meal. "There's no need to worry about me, Jess, if that's what you're implying. I'm a big boy. I can take care of myself."

"In that case, maybe you would honor us by standing up with me at my wedding?"

Richard swallowed hard and set down his fork. Alexa knew he was fighting emotion, and for a moment she nearly feared anger would erupt and provoke contention. He calmly rose from the table and said tonelessly, "I doubt I'll be here."

The disappointment in Jess's eyes drove Alexa to a breaking point. She was tired of this, and decided that now was just as good a time as any to get to the heart of it once and for all.

"Excuse me," she said tersely and followed Richard out.

Jess rose to go after her, but Fiddler stopped him. "I think she might be able to handle this one better on her own."

Richard answered his door expecting Jess. He froze when he saw Alexa. Her eyes moved unobtrusively over his bare torso, then back to his face. "If I had known it was you, I'd have put on a shirt," he said but didn't move.

"It's me," Alexa stated. He still didn't move, certain she wouldn't be staying. "Put on a shirt, Richard," she added. "I'd like to come in."

Richard hesitated a moment then took a step back, elaborately motioning her inside. He closed the door and leaned against it while she casually sat on the edge of the bed and crossed one knee over the other. He felt almost dazed, not certain what to expect.

Alexa watched Richard for several awkward moments before she leaned forward to grab a shirt off the back of the chair and throw it at him. He put it on but left it unbuttoned and stuffed his hands into his pockets, pressing one bare foot against the door behind him.

"What do you want?" he finally asked.

"I want to talk to you, Mr. Wilhite."

"My, but aren't we formal," he said cynically.

"If I'm not mistaken, you are the one who started these formalities. Personally, I've had about all I can take. I keep waiting for you to deal with this, but apparently you're not going to, so I figured we ought to find out exactly where we stand. If we're not going to be on speaking terms, I'd like to have it established so I can stop waiting for you to say something to me."

"Like what?" he asked tersely.

"Like, 'Hello, Alexa.' That would be a good place to start."

"Hello, Alexa," he said, but she wasn't amused.

"Richard," she said softly, though her eyes penetrated him, "if I have hurt you, I—"

"You're jumping to conclusions," he interrupted curtly.

"Am I?" She feigned astonishment. "Richard, since my relationship with Jess became personal, you have hardly spoken a kind word to me, or to Jess. You glare at me as if I were leprous when you look at me at all. Don't stand there and tell me I'm jumping to conclusions."

Richard looked away, leaving the good side of his face to her view. "What do you want me to say?" he asked quietly.

"I want you to tell me how you feel." He said nothing and she persisted, "This is not like you, Richard. Where is the warm, sensitive man I came to care for?"

He looked at her sideways. "You have no idea what kind of man I am, Miss Byrnehouse."

"You're playing games with me." She pointed an accusing finger.

"And who is losing?" he retorted.

"Stop acting like a child and talk to me!" she demanded, standing abruptly.

Richard put both feet on the floor and straightened his back. He didn't seem prone to talking, so Alexa prodded him further. "Have you got something against Jess?"

Richard gave a dry, humorless chuckle. "Jess is one of the finest men I know."

"It must be me, then," she guessed. "Don't you think I'm good enough for him?"

"Alexa," he said in astonishment, "now who's playing games?"

"I am not playing games, Richard. I asked you a genuine question."

Richard sighed audibly. "I'd say you and Jess are pretty well suited for each other."

"Then what's bothering you?" she insisted. Though she dreaded hearing him admit it, she knew it was the only way to get him to face it.

"Who said anything's bothering me?"

Alexa threw her hands in the air and sat down again. "Here we are, right back where we started." She looked at him severely. "Why don't you just talk to me, the way you used to? Tell me what you're feeling."

Richard stepped thoughtfully toward the chair and sat down, straddling the back of it. "Alexa, there is nothing I can say that will make any difference."

"Any difference to what?" she asked pointedly, feigning innocence. She wished they could just get to the heart of it.

"Why don't you just say what you came to say and get it over with?" he said sharply, and she wondered if he could see through her as easily as she could see through him.

"Why won't you answer my questions?" she retorted.

"Because I don't want to talk about it!" he shouted.

"You've got to!" she shouted back.

"If you want to argue with someone, go argue with Jess."

"Frankly, I'd rather not. Why don't you just tell me what's bothering you, and get on with it."

"Why should I," he retorted, "when you know perfectly well what's bothering me?"

"I can only guess," she said quietly. "But if you tell me, then we can work it out."

"You might as well start guessing, because I don't want to say it," he stated coldly, then his brow furrowed. "And no, Alexa, we cannot work it out."

"Why not?" she persisted, knowing if he didn't admit to the problem, he would never be free of these resentments.

"Alexa," he said gruffly, "don't try to convince me that you are not well aware of how I feel about you."

Alexa looked down, and her heart thumped painfully. It was what she'd suspected, but hearing it was more difficult than she'd imagined. She was tempted to blink back the tears burning into her eyes, then decided that he needed to know that she cared. Shamelessly she met his gaze as the tears trickled down her cheeks. "Do you want me to apologize for loving Jess?"

"What I want doesn't make any difference, Alexa." She looked down again and he added, "I can't help how I feel."

Her eyes shot back up. "Neither can I." Richard looked away sharply. "Talk to me," she nearly pleaded.

Richard leaned his brow against the back of the chair and sighed. "I've asked myself a thousand times why it was him and not me, and I can only come up with two possible answers."

"And what might they be?" she asked, not liking the way he was putting comparisons on her feelings.

"Well, for one thing," he looked at her harshly, "you're a Byrnehouse."

"What has that got to do with it?" she demanded.

"I should have expected you to marry into your own class, but—"

"Now, wait a minute," she interrupted. "You're lying to yourself if you think I'm the kind of woman who cares for such nonsense. This is Australia, Richard, not high European society. And don't forget that whatever I once was, I am no longer. I am as much an employee here as you are."

"But not for long," he said bitterly.

Alexa paused a moment to grasp the implication. "Oh, I see. So now I'm a fortune hunter. I lost my birthright, so I'll marry somebody with something to offer." She sighed with disgust. "Any fool can see that a woman out for fortune would not want to marry Jess Davies. Everything he owns is hanging by a thread until that mortgage is paid off. We could be on the street by next year, for all we know. Don't you dare say that—"

"All right, Alexa." He held up his hands in defeat. "You've proven your point."

When it became evident he wasn't going to say anything more, Alexa said firmly, "You said you came up with two answers."

"The other is obvious."

"Perhaps to you."

"Alexa," he leaned forward, "it stares you in the face every time you look at me."

Alexa's eyes narrowed to perceive what he was saying. She was appalled to think that Richard would give her so little credit. But reaching deeper, she realized that for him it was an undeniable reality that was difficult to deal with.

"Richard," she said gently, "would you believe me if I said that it makes no difference to me?"

He looked at her severely. "If you were me, would you?"

While Alexa thought about it, he misinterpreted the silence. Alexa winced when he groaned and came to his feet, kicking the chair over with such fervor that it slid across the floor. He turned his back to her and pushed his hands through his hair. "You will never convince me that it isn't easier to love a man who doesn't look like a monster!"

Alexa frantically searched for the right words to express what she felt without hurting him further. "Richard," she said gently, "I will not try to compare my feelings for you with those I have for Jess. It would be impossible. But I can tell you with all sincerity that what I feel for both of you goes far beyond skin-deep." She rose and touched his shoulder. "Richard, I can't explain to you why I love Jess the way I do. I only know that what I share with him is something that many people only dream of. I can't question destiny, Richard. I can only be grateful for being so fortunate. I never intended to hurt you, and I can only say that feelings cannot be chosen or changed. They just happen."

"I'll have to agree with you there," he stated, then turned to look at her. "I can't begrudge your loving Jess. He's a good man. And I certainly can't blame Jess for loving you. He'd be a fool not to. But as long as we're getting past the games and pretenses here, you might as well know that seeing you with him is one of the most difficult things I've ever had to face. You know what the other is. Before you came to live here, I had resolved myself to living alone. A man like me does not have a social life, Alexa. You're the only woman who has ever looked at me in the last ten years and seen something besides these scars."

"Perhaps I'm the only woman you've allowed to get close enough to see anything else."

He gave a dry chuckle. "It's not that easy, Alexa. You could never understand without seeing the world from my point of view."

"You're likely right," she admitted. "But I want you to know something, from the heart." She reached a hand up to touch his face, relieved that he didn't pull away. "You're a wonderful man, Richard. As much as I love Jess, there is a part of me that only you can fill. I miss you. I miss what we shared. I'm not going to ask you to continue our friendship if it would be too difficult for you, but I want you to know that I will always care for you. I have never had such a friend as you in all my life."

Alexa went on her tiptoes to kiss him, just to the side of his mouth. She looked at him deeply as she stepped back, but he pushed an arm around her and urged her against him.

"You're an incredible woman, Alexa," he said close to her face, "and I can't say that I don't appreciate everything you've said. You have a good heart." He pressed the fingers of his free hand over her face, as if to memorize it forever. Alexa took hold of his upper arms, fearing she might fall if she didn't. She felt a need to pull away, but she found no will to do so. She could feel his heart pounding in time with her own, and she became conscious of each breath she took, as if it might be her last.

"You're right, I've got to stop acting like a child and just admit that you will never be mine. But there is something I want to say to you before you walk away; something you have to remember." Richard sighed and pushed his hand into her hair, lowering his voice to a seductive whisper. "There are two men who love you, Alexa, but you can only have one. Choose carefully, my love. Till death do us part can be a long time."

Alexa watched Richard fade behind the mist in her eyes, then she felt his lips come over hers with a guarded urgency. She closed her eyes and the tears fell while she allowed him to kiss her. She lost her breath and drew back to catch it, but she could find no motivation to protest when he kissed her again.

"I love you, Alexa," he whispered, his lips still touching hers. "I will forever be here if you need me, no matter the circumstances. But don't you ever—ever—expect me to feel anything less for you than I do right now."

Alexa looked up at him in wonder, feeling lost and dazed. When the numbness wore off she became keenly aware of his presence, and the reality frightened her. She stepped back and touched her lips as if they'd been burned. Something subtly triumphant filled Richard's expression, and she could do nothing but run.

Twelve
THE TRAP

Alexa stood just outside the stable, watching Richard ride away. With the gear he carried, it was obvious he intended to be gone for several days.

"There you are." Sam's voice startled her. "Fiddler's lookin' for you."

"Thank you," Alexa said.

"Gone again, eh?" Sam nodded toward Richard's disappearing figure.

"He seems to enjoy being alone," Alexa commented. She followed Sam into the stable, where Fiddler was hammering freshly cut lumber to repair a broken stall.

"You wanted me?" Alexa said.

Fiddler glanced up and grinned. He set aside his task, cleared his throat elaborately, and bowed from the waist. "I have a message," he said, mimicking a stuffy butler.

"From who?" Alexa laughed.

"Mr. Davies requests the pleasure of your company this evening to dine with him at seven precisely."

All thoughts of Richard fled as a flutter of anticipation seized her. "Tell Mr. Davies I would be honored."

Fiddler nodded and picked up his hammer, then added in his normal tone, "Oh, and he said to tell you it's formal."

"Formal?" Alexa laughed again.

"I just give the messages, dearie," he insisted, and returned to his work.

Alexa left Tod with orders to give Crazy a good workout while she went to the carriage house and dragged one of her trunks out from under the stairs. Drawing a nostalgic breath, she lifted the creaking lid and folded back the tissue paper. There it was, right on top. She'd had the gown custom made for a social that should have taken place soon after her father died, but his death had brought a very different sequence of events.

Alexa lifted the silvery blue gown and laughed aloud. She held it against her, delighting in the way it rustled. It seemed forever since she'd felt like a real lady. Tonight would be exquisite.

Taking the afternoon off, Alexa soaked in a hot bath with an abundance of lavender salts soothing every part of her. Wearing long-unused petticoats and kid slippers, she pulled the carefully pressed gown over her head and adjusted it in the tiny mirror. She tingled from the way it made her feel, and anticipation absorbed her.

Trying to put her hair up and make it look attractive, Alexa wished she had some help. She'd never asked Sarina or Mrs. Brown to help her with anything personal before, but decided she would have now if it had been possible. This was Sarina's time off when she visited family in the outback, and Alexa felt sure Mrs. Brown was busy with whatever Jess had in mind for the evening.

After several attempts, she finally felt pleased with her hair, except for one spot where blunt ends stuck out no matter what she did. Searching in her drawer, she found a wooden box she'd hidden there and pulled out a jeweled comb that took care of the problem nicely. Examining the contents of the box, she decided to wear a matching necklace, and fastened the string of diamonds and sapphires around her throat. She giggled aloud to think how dismayed Chad must have been when he realized she'd taken her jewels.

Alexa emerged from the carriage house just as the boys were gathering to go in for supper. She wasn't surprised by the whoops and hollers that came as a reaction to her appearance, but she knew they were only trying to embarrass her. "Ah, shut up," she hollered. "You're just jealous."

This brought on a whole new bout of laughter.

"Where you goin', Missy?" Murphy asked.

She bowed slightly and said with mock grandeur, "I've been invited to dine at the big house."

This was answered with comical oohs and aahs, except for Fiddler, who smiled with approval. "Turn around and let us see."

Alexa lifted her skirt and did as he asked, then she hurried into the house. Mrs. Brown eyed her curiously as they passed in the hall. With all the times Alexa had come in and out of this house, she would think that Mrs. Brown would get used to it. But she never seemed to.

Alexa paused at the dining room door and smoothed her appearance. She drew a deep breath and stepped quietly into the room. Jess stood at the far end, looking out the window with his hands in his pockets. The long dining table stood between them, lit with several candles. Alexa closed the door behind her, and he turned expectantly.

Jess didn't realize he'd been holding his breath until the pain in his chest forced him to let it out. He'd tried all day to imagine how she might look when she came through that door, but his imagination could never have concocted something so incredible. She looked like some kind of mythical goddess, her eyes sparkling with blatant affection, the silvery gown clinging to her delicate frame, the cluster of jewels shimmering at her throat. Tiny sleeves sloped downward, exposing pale shoulders and arms that until now had always been hidden by prudish blouses and masculine shirts. He wanted to take her in his arms and love her endlessly, almost as much as he wanted to stand here and look at her. The intensity of his love rose in him so fiercely that it nearly frightened him.

While Alexa openly admired Jess in the finely tailored black suit and bow tie, a reality descended upon her with tranquility. Destiny filled the room around them as surely as it filled her heart. The silence seemed endless, but there was no need for words. The love, the trust, the mutual respect were all rooted deeply. And the evidence glowed in Jess's eyes.

Feeling suddenly as if he had to touch her or die, Jess stepped slowly toward her. Gingerly he set his fingers against her shoulders, marveling at the softness of her skin as his touch skittered down her arms and back up again. His eyes were drawn to the jewels at her throat. At first thought, the reminder of the life she had known before tempted him to feel somehow unworthy of her. But time had proven that only one thing mattered between him and Alexa, and the love they shared was something he could not doubt. A clean, feminine aroma surrounded him as his arms went around her in a careful embrace. Fearing he might get carried away, he cleared his throat and eased back a step. "You should set aside those riding breeches more often, Miss Byrnehouse."

"And you," she smiled, affectionately straightening his tie.

"Thank you for coming." He moved deliberately away, knowing he had a promise to keep that was being strongly tempted at the moment. "Do you want something to drink?"

"No . . . thank you. I don't drink."

"I see." He laughed, pouring himself a glass of brandy. "Don't tell me. It's not healthy."

"That's true," she stated. "But actually I don't like it."

Alexa couldn't recall ever seeing Jess drink before, despite the availability of liquor in the house and the brandy snifters she'd seen in his room. She felt sure it was something he did minimally, which suited her fine. She'd seen too much drunkenness in her own home.

"Dinner should be coming soon." He motioned toward the table. "Shall we?"

Jess helped Alexa with her chair and sat close to her. Taking her hand across the corner of the table, he noted how straight her back remained, as if he was seeing her as a lady for the first time. They stared at each other for several moments before Jess lifted his other hand to methodically touch Alexa's face. Moving a thumb over her silken skin, he realized that the sun didn't take away its softness like it did his own. Mrs. Brown backed into the dining room carrying a tray, and Jess straightened in his chair.

Silence reigned as they enjoyed their meal, neither embarrassed by the other's obvious gaze through the candlelight. Just before dessert Alexa said, "I was thinking just today that I know very little about your family, while you likely know too much about mine."

"There's little to know."

Was it her imagination that his answer was terse? "Tell me," she prodded gently.

Alexa saw him bow his head slightly and swallow. Though it was subtle, she knew that something made the subject difficult, which likely explained why it had never come up before.

"I'm the only one left," he said.

"Your parents?" she asked gently.

"My father died of illness before I turned eighteen, and my mother was killed a year or so later."

Alexa recalled what Richard had told her of Jess's parents. She wanted to ask Jess if it was true that his mother had not been sound, but she knew it would be tactless and insensitive. "How long ago was that?" she asked instead.

"She's been gone over ten years," he said, but by his eyes it might have been last week.

"You were an only child?"

He glanced at her sharply but his answer was soft. "Yes."

"Tell me about them," she said, reaching her hand across the table to take his. When she squeezed it, he seemed to find the incentive to go on.

"They were wonderful people. What is there to tell? They gave me everything. My father was the son of Welsh coal miners. He came to Australia to make his fortune, and found enough gold in Victoria to give me all of this." He raised his hands to indicate his surroundings. "And he did me the honor of giving me his name—something I'm terribly proud of."

"Which is?"

Jess smiled and said elaborately, "Jesse Benjamin Davies. Though my father went by Ben."

"You must miss your parents terribly."

"Yes," he said distantly. "As I said, they gave much to me. I loved them both."

"That's good," she said, and he looked surprised. "I mean, I wonder how many people can say that about their parents."

Jess seemed lost in another time until Alexa asked, "How did your mother die?"

His voice turned dry. "Must we discuss such a thing over dinner?"

"You don't have to. I just . . . well, I want to know you, Jess. It's evident that you loved her."

"Good heavens, I thought you would have heard that story by now."

She'd never heard anyone mention Jess's mother except Richard, but she had to admit, "It doesn't seem to be a favorite topic around here." Jess's expression proved it.

Approaching it from a different angle, Jess leaned back a little. "She was beautiful. You almost remind me of her." His eyes softened on Alexa. "Though not in appearance, really. It's something different. She was kind and good; pure to the soul."

Jess picked up his drink and held it close to his eyes, watching the golden liquid swirl effortlessly as he moved the snifter in his hand. "She was killed in a fire," he stated tonelessly. Alexa narrowed her eyes in question. "The house that used to stand where this one is burned to the ground."

Alexa's gasp went unnoticed. "I'm sorry." Her gentle voice brought him out of a daze.

He met her eyes, and for a moment Alexa saw something that resembled fear. He took her hand and spoke in a voice that deepened the evidence. "I love you, Alexa. I would never want to harm you."

"I know you never would." She laughed slightly in an effort to shake off this uneasiness.

"Not intentionally," he said with such severity that Alexa felt chilled. Recalling that they had been discussing his mother, she wondered what was behind his statement. Before she had a chance to ask, he changed the subject.

"I built this house to duplicate the one that was here before. It was my father's dream house."

"It is beautiful," she said, "but a little . . . empty. It's so big."

"It doesn't feel empty right now," he said intently.

Alexa glanced down meekly. "Where did you live while it was being rebuilt?"

"In the old house," he stated. "It still stands, east of this one." Alexa nodded, aware of the cottage-like house that stood empty a short distance away. "My father built it when he first homesteaded this land. They lived there until the big house was built. The overseer lived there until the fire, and then . . ." He broke off, and Alexa wondered if the overseer had been killed in the fire also. "Well," he cleared his throat, "I lived there while the house was being rebuilt."

"What happened to the overseer?"

"You ask too many questions," he stated.

"You don't have to answer them."

"I suppose I should," he said. "You're the only one who's ever cared enough to ask. I'm just not used to talking about it."

She said nothing, and he realized he had a question to answer. "The overseer died in the fire, though he was getting on in years and his son had mostly taken over. His son tried to save my mother. By the time he got her out of the house, she was already gone. I'm afraid he paid sorely for his heroism." After a moment's pause he added, "Richard."

Alexa unconsciously put a hand to her mouth and leaned back. A deeper picture formed in her mind of the bond these two men shared. How did Jess feel to think of his mother dying in Richard's arms, and to see the reminder that Richard bore of the incident? And Richard had lost his father in the same fire. She tried to suppress the nagging fear that she had come between a kinship that ran deep. And then there was the evidence before her that put a whole new perspective on her feelings for Jess. Something inside him was hurting. Though she couldn't pinpoint it, she had an urge to take him in her arms and somehow soothe that hurt away. If only he would let her.

"Enough of this dismal talk." Jess pushed his chair back and stood. Alexa was relieved to see his usual self again. "You look good enough to eat in that gown." He took her hand, urging her to her feet. "I should have declined dessert and had you instead."

"As soon as I have your name, you would be more than welcome to do just that."

Jess grinned and carefully eased an arm around her. She looked so delicate that he almost feared she might break. If she didn't, what she was wearing might.

They shared coffee on the veranda, indulging in comfortable conversation and a perfect view of the stars. When Alexa became chilled, Jess removed his jacket and put it over her shoulders, almost envying the way it clung to her, giving warmth. Through a contemplative silence he wondered what life had been like without Alexa. He almost couldn't remember.

It wasn't unusual for Alexa to occupy herself by wishing that she and Jess were already married. The desire to share his life completely was her deepest dream. But through these tranquil moments, her need for him was so intense she nearly ached. She watched him unfasten his tie as if he could hardly bear the restriction another minute. He left it hanging around his neck and unfastened the top two buttons of his shirt. She cleared her throat and took a sip of coffee.

"What are you thinking, my love?" he asked. His voice startled her. He chuckled, and she felt sure he'd read the guilt in her expression and knew exactly where her thoughts were. He erased any doubt when he added, "I'm counting the days myself."

"But we haven't set a date."

"We'll do that when the shearing is done."

"It won't be much longer now." A delighted tremor laced her voice.

"Only a week until the derby," he added in nearly the same tone, "and then we'll get to those sheep."

"We're going to be very busy," she said.

"And wealthy." He laughed, and Alexa enjoyed hearing the optimism in his voice. "It's getting late. I'll walk you home."

Jess put his arm around her shoulders as they ambled slowly down the path toward the carriage house. He followed her up the stairs and paused in front of the door to kiss her.

"Please stay a few minutes," she said. He followed her into the room and lit the lamp.

"Is something wrong?" he asked.

"No, I just . . . don't want the evening to end. It's been so wonderful. I can't remember the last time I had a good reason to dress this way."

"You miss it?" he asked, pulling back the curtain at her window to look into the stable yard.

"Not really," she admitted. "It's just nice to feel like a lady again."

Jess turned to look at her as she reached behind her neck to unfasten the necklace. "You're always a lady," he said, and she warmed at the compliment.

Alexa opened her jewel box and dropped the necklace and comb in to join the few remaining pieces, then she ran her fingers through them and smiled.

Jess's eyes widened. "There must be a small fortune there."

"That's what it will cost to buy Lady's Maid back." She closed the box and put it into the drawer.

"Ah, yes. Your lovely little horse."

"I've intended to do it all along . . . since I got a job and didn't have to sell them to survive," she added with a little smile. "I know Chad won't let her go without a fight, because he knows it's hard on me to be without her. I've also hesitated, fearing it might bring on more trouble. And we don't need any more trouble."

"We haven't had any for a while," Jess smiled. "Perhaps you bring me good luck."

"Perhaps it's because Chad's been away."

Jess chuckled. "That too."

Their eyes met amidst a hovering tension, and Jess decided it was much easier keeping his promise of chastity when she wore those prudish blouses and masculine shirts.

"Perhaps I should go." He moved toward the door. "It's late, and I—"

"No, wait," she said, then sensing his concern she added, "I know I can't sleep. Let me change, and we could go riding."

Jess smiled. "I'll wait for you outside."

Alexa was relieved when she came out to find only one horse. She loved riding with his arms around her, and time flew as they roamed the hills with only starlight to guide them.

"Do you think you can sleep now?" Jess asked as he dismounted near the carriage house and helped her down.

"I'm exhausted." She laughed, leaning into him as he kissed her. "Delightfully exhausted."

"Thank you for a beautiful evening, Alexa."

"I should thank you . . . and pass along my compliments to Mrs. Brown. It was a lovely meal."

"I love you," he whispered and sauntered off, leading the horse by the reins toward the stable.

Alexa started up the stairs and heard the board crack only an instant before she fell through. Her scream seemed detached and distant as blood rushed from her head. Pain encompassed her as she found herself lying in a heap of broken planks.

On his way out of the stable, Jess heard Alexa cry out in the midst of a distant crashing. "Alexa!" He threw open the carriage house door and frantically lit a nearby lamp.

"The stairs," was all she could manage to say. She tried to move, and intense pain shot from her thigh. The light illuminated a gaping hole in the stairs above her and the heap of broken planks she'd landed in. She looked toward the source of her pain just as Jess came to her side.

"Merciful heaven!" he choked. For a moment he could only gape at the blood-soaked breeches and the broken end of a plank with protruding nails piercing her flesh. "Don't move," he said gently, kneeling beside her to survey it closer. He touched the plank and she cried out as he realized both ragged wood and nails were embedded in her thigh.

Carefully Jess moved the debris from around her head and shoulders in an effort to make her more comfortable while he figured out what to do. He rolled up his jacket and placed it beneath her head. Alexa managed a smile as he situated her against it.

"Just relax," he said. "I'm going to get Murphy to help me." She nodded. "Don't move now," he added.

"I'm not going anywhere," she said trying to keep her voice light.

Jess squeezed her hand and left quickly. He burst into the bunkhouse and shouted Murphy's name. A chorus of groans responded.

"What?" Murphy asked urgently, his breeches on before he hardly got out of his bunk.

"Alexa's hurt," Jess said in panic while Murphy pulled on his boots. "I need your help."

Murphy grabbed a shirt and flew toward the door. Every one of the boys quickly followed once they heard the reason for their interrupted sleep.

"Blimey, what a mess!" Murphy professed when he saw her. Alexa tried to smile. He knelt beside her and quickly examined the situation. "I think we can handle this," he said with confidence, and Jess sighed.

"Murphy's great at doctoring horses," Jimmy proclaimed, looking on with the others.

Jess glared at him. "Oh, that's reassuring."

"Actually," Alexa said weakly, "if he treats me as good as he does those horses, I'm not too concerned."

Murphy grinned, then turned to bark orders. "Fiddler, get the doctor out here." He left without hesitation. "Jimmy, get some clean rags, some salve, and a bottle of whiskey."

"Whiskey?" Jimmy questioned.

"Just do as you're told," Jess demanded, and he ran.

"All right, Missy," Murphy said gently. "We just gotta pull it out. It's as simple as that." Alexa unconsciously gripped Jess's arm. Murphy turned to Edward, who was standing above him. "You hold her leg here so she doesn't move." Edward nodded. "And you hold tight to Jess now, Missy. We'll try to get this over with quick, and then the doctor can fix you up."

She nodded and glanced toward Jess. "I'm scared."

"So am I," he admitted.

Jimmy returned with the specified items. Murphy set the whiskey bottle aside, told Jimmy to hold onto the rags, then he carefully smeared salve around the wound. Alexa tensed from the pain, then nodded toward the whiskey. "Give me some of that."

Murphy wiped his hands off, pulled out the cork with his teeth, and gave it to her. With Jess's help, Alexa took a healthy swallow and nearly choked on it. She grimaced and took another, then relinquished the bottle and indicated she was ready.

Jess leaned over her and put his arms completely around her. Alexa gripped his upper arms. He looked directly into her eyes and said gently, "Don't think about it. Think about something good."

Murphy surprised them both by saying, "Kiss 'er, Jess."

Jess did as he was told and decided to make it good. Her lips parted eagerly, but the distraction was interrupted by the pain and Alexa shot her head back in a cry of anguish. Part of Jess nearly died inside to see the color drain from her face and sweat bead out over her throat and brow as her fingernails dug painfully into his arms.

"It's done," Murphy said, and Jess turned to see him scornfully throw the bloodied plank behind him. Alexa fought to catch her breath. "It came out pretty clean, but she's bleedin' like mad."

Alexa held to Jess with what little strength she had left. Jess kissed her brow, wanting so badly to take away the pain.

Murphy ripped open the breeches around the wound and pressed rags over it to absorb the blood. "Are you all right, Missy?" he asked.

She tried to nod but Jess said, "That's a stupid question."

Murphy chuckled dryly. "You're gonna hate me, Missy, but it's not over yet."

"What?" Jess asked sharply.

"Hold on tight," was all Murphy said before he poured whiskey into the wound.

Alexa cried out again. Jess pulled her tighter against him, pressing her face to his chest. Murphy quickly pressed a clean rag over the wound and held it firmly with his hand. Alexa fought for her breath then muttered through clenched teeth, "You're right, Murphy. I hate you."

Edward relinquished his hold on her leg, and Jess relaxed slightly.

Murphy moved from his knees to sit on the floor, but he kept his hand firmly over the wound. He looked thoughtfully above him and said, "How do you suppose that happened?"

"If only I knew," Jess said scornfully.

"I thought they were pretty sturdy," Edward said.

"They were," Alexa insisted, gradually relaxing in Jess's arms. "They didn't even squeak." She recalled Richard saying they could hold a tribe of aborigines.

"Tell me what happened," Jess said.

"It just fell through." She glanced down at her leg and moaned. "It was as if nothing was there to hold it."

"Wasn't that trunk over here?" Jess pointed, and Alexa nodded in agreement.

"I pushed it back under today after I got the gown out."

Jess glanced around abruptly and demanded, "Where's Sam?"

"Jess," Alexa protested, "you don't really think—"

"Where's Sam?" he repeated.

"Didn't come in before I went to sleep," Edward said. "You seen him, Murphy?"

"Nope," Murphy replied, and Jess's jaw tightened.

"Don't even think it, Jess," Alexa said. "You can't just assume that—"

"I'm not going to assume anything, but I am going to have a little talk with him. Come on," his tone changed to concern, "let's get you someplace a little more comfortable." Murphy added a clean rag over the soaked one and tied it in place.

"You can't take her up there," Edward said, glancing at the absence of a good portion of the stairs.

"I'll take her to the big house, where I can keep an eye on her." Jess carefully eased her into his arms.

"Are you all right?" he asked when he had her situated.

She nodded. Murphy held the lamp to guide them up the path, while Edward remained behind to examine the stairs more closely.

"How you doin'?" Murphy asked while he held open the door.

"I'm better now that I've got that board out of my leg."

Jess carried her up the stairs and kicked open the door to a room where he laid her on the bed and propped up the pillows beneath her head.

"It might be a bit dusty," he apologized.

"Do you really think I care in this condition?" she asked.

"I'll go out and wait for the doctor," Murphy said and left them alone.

Jess carefully pulled off Alexa's boots and threw them to the floor. He put a pillow beneath the wounded thigh to elevate it, then sat beside her and brushed the hair back from her sweaty brow.

"It would seem bad luck has returned," he apologized, as if it was his fault.

"Bad luck or Chad?" Alexa retorted.

Jess's jaw went tight but he said nothing more. Noting the spreading red on the bandage, he quickly folded another rag and pressed it there, trying not to think of the life flowing out of her. She closed her eyes and appeared relaxed. He wondered if that little bit of whiskey had done her in. Keeping his hand over the wound for pressure, he relaxed by her side.

"It seems to me that you bring nothing but good luck to my life," Jess muttered, "but I only bring bad to yours."

"Perhaps it's the other way around," she said groggily.

Jess grunted in disagreement. His next awareness was Murphy's announcement that the doctor had arrived.

Jess went back to the carriage house, where Fiddler and Jimmy were cleaning up the debris. "Get some sleep," he ordered. "We'll take care of it in the morning."

"It's almost morning now," Fiddler said.

"Tell Edward we'll have breakfast at noon."

"Is Alexa going to be all right?" Jimmy asked.

"The doctor's with her," Jess replied. "I'm sure she'll be fine."

The two left, and Jess shimmied carefully up the edge of the stairs to Alexa's room. Just being there made him feel warm inside. He glanced around nostalgically a few moments before he carefully looked through her things to find what he thought she might need. He smiled as he gathered nightclothes and underthings, knowing she'd be embarrassed.

Jess pulled them into a bundle and grabbed her hairbrush, then his eye caught the pages tacked to the wall. He'd seen them before, but hadn't wanted to take notice while Alexa was with him. He took a minute to read over the different pieces of poetry, wondering what Alexa thought of it all.

Jess waited in the hall outside Alexa's new room until Doctor Lloyd appeared. "She's lost a lot of blood," he stated, "but it appears she'll be fine. Keep her down for a while and feed her well. The bandage needs to be changed frequently."

"I can handle it."

"Good, then. Keep it clean and there shouldn't be any problems." Jess nodded. "Other than that, it appears she's bruised up a little. She was lucky. I'll check back the day after tomorrow."

"Thank you," Jess said. The doctor patted him on the shoulder and left.

Jess moved timidly into the room and found Alexa resting with her eyes closed and a sheet pulled up to her waist. A lamp burned low on the bedside table. She still wore her shirt, but the breeches lay on the floor, apparently cut away.

Sensing his presence, she opened her eyes and held out a hand toward him.

"Some things I thought you might need." He set the bundle down on the other side of the bed.

Alexa lifted up slightly to see what was there. "Jess!" she said, and he chuckled.

"I should check the bandage again before you go to sleep," he said, and she nodded. Jess pushed the sheet aside to find the bandaged thigh. "It looks all right," he said. "We'll leave it until morning." Perhaps by then Mrs. Brown would be awake and willing to help, he thought, which would likely be better for both of them.

"Thank you, Jess," she said as he covered her again and stood up straight. "I'm so grateful you were there."

"So am I."

Alexa closed her eyes, and Jess bent to kiss her before he extinguished the lamp.

Thirteen
GLIMPSES

Alexa drifted in and out of sleep while the pain persisted, despite what the doctor had given her to ease it. When the heaviness finally lifted, she opened her eyes to daylight and saw Jess sitting near the window with the sun against his back. He had a book propped against his thigh where he was writing vigorously. Alexa nearly said something, but weakness tempted her back to sleep and she didn't wake again until she felt pressure on her leg. She opened her eyes to see Jess removing the bandage.

"Sorry to wake you, but this has got to be changed and I was afraid you'd sleep all day." She turned her head and relaxed but said nothing. "The bleeding's nearly stopped," Jess added. "How are you feeling?"

"Tired," she replied.

They were silent as he rebandaged the leg then sat beside her and took her hand.

"I must be a sight." She pushed straying hair off her face.

"You're beautiful, as always." He pressed a kiss to her brow.

"You're just saying that because you love me."

"I do love you," he admitted, "but you should know by now that I'm an honest man."

"Yes—I know."

"Are you hungry?" he asked.

"I believe I am." She attempted to move in order to ease the ache in her back. "Will you help me sit up? I'm so stiff and . . ." Jess propped up some extra pillows and helped situate her against them.

"That's much better." She glanced down the bed, surprised to see a sheet of paper. Picking it up, she said, "Richard was here."

Seeing the poem in her hand that he'd just finished writing, Jess wondered over the connection. "Yes, he was. How did you know?"

"Just a hunch," she said, setting it aside as if she wasn't interested. "I'll get you something to eat."

The moment Jess left, Alexa picked the page up and eagerly read the tiny block letters, a deep emotion filling her.

For Alexa
There stands a man and in his hands
*   he holds elusive dreams*
Like shooting stars and shimmering sands
*   they fall and roll to sea*
He felt them slipping from his grasp
*   and falling to the ground*
But Alexa came and picked them up
*   and turned his dreams around*
Alexa with her wild eyes,
*   those eyes that stir my soul*
She picks the little pieces up,
*   like new, she makes them whole*
Alexa, now I bare my soul
*   and leave it in your hands*
Please hold it gently with the dreams,
*   the shooting stars and shimmering sands*

The emotion surfaced with tears as she finished the unsigned piece. She marveled at Richard's perception, and his sentiment touched her. But she felt as if he was speaking more about her and Jess. Were these tender observances a way of telling her he was accepting the circumstances?

She dropped the page between the bed and bedside table when Jess came into the room.

"Mrs. Brown is sending something up for you." He glanced

toward the paper on the floor, then bent to pick it up. "What's this?" he asked, testing the reasons for her apparent uncertainty.

"It's a poem," she stated.

"Any good?" he asked satirically, wondering why she seemed hesitant to discuss it. Did his attempt to express his deepest feelings somehow embarrass her?

"It's beautiful," she said with vehemence, but she said nothing more. Jess set the page on the bedside table as Mrs. Brown entered with a tray.

Alexa had never known what to expect from Mrs. Brown, but her smile was kind as she set the tray over Alexa's lap. "Now, is there anything else you're needin'?" she asked, her voice implying that she truly meant it.

"Well, I . . ." Alexa glanced hesitantly toward Jess. Mrs. Brown picked up on the hint and saved any embarrassment.

"Get on out o' here," she insisted and shooed him out of the room.

Alexa was relieved to have some feminine assistance, and she appreciated Mrs. Brown's graciousness. "It's not easy survivin' in a world o' men out here," she said earnestly. "But it's a good life, I'll have t' say."

"You've been with Jess a long time," Alexa prodded.

"On and off since before he was born." She smiled.

"You knew his mother, then." Alexa's curiosity slipped out before she had a chance to check it.

"She was a fine woman," Mrs. Brown replied with a little too much fervency, as if she was daring Alexa to question that the deceased Mrs. Davies was anything less.

"I understand Jess loved her very much. It must have been difficult when she was killed."

"I'm certain it was, but I didn't live here at the time. I heard about it much later. There, now." She tucked the blankets around Alexa in a fresh nightgown and replaced the dinner tray. "Is there anything else you'll be needin' now?"

"Not at the moment, thank you. I'm certainly grateful there's a woman in the house."

"I'll check back regularly."

"Thank you." Alexa noticed a comical scowl exchanged between Mrs. Brown and Jess as they passed in the doorway.

Jess stood with his hands in his pockets, wondering why he felt uncomfortable. She smiled at him, and the sensation eased until Richard came into the room just as she finished eating. Jess set the tray on the bureau. Was it his imagination that Alexa tensed visibly the moment Richard appeared? He quickly forgot his speculations when Richard turned to Jess.

"Murphy needs to see you right away. I'll stay with her if you like."

"Is something wrong?" Jess asked.

"You'd best talk to Murphy."

Jess glanced hesitantly toward Alexa, then hurried from the room.

Attempting to ease the silence, Alexa asked quietly, "When did you get back?"

"Early this morning." He tossed his hat over the bedpost. "Murphy told me you'd been hurt. I came right up, but you were resting."

Another uneasy silence reminded Alexa that Richard had kissed her the last time they'd been together. Warmth rose in her face and she turned away.

"Are you all right?" he asked.

"I'll be fine," she said, "though I fear it will be some time before I'm back to normal."

"If I ever find who did this to you, I'll—"

"The stairs broke, Richard. Don't just assume that—"

"Those stairs were not weak by any means, Alexa."

"I know," she admitted quietly, not wanting to acknowledge what that meant, but realizing she had to.

"Do you think Chad had something to do with it?"

Alexa shrugged her shoulders, suddenly finding it difficult to speak. Not only had she come between the lifelong friendship shared by Jess and Richard, but she had stepped into a feud that at the moment felt as real to her as the pain in her leg. "It's becoming more apparent that Chad is capable of many unspeakable things," she uttered.

"If I had any brains, I'd kill him before he has a chance to strike again." Richard's fist curled unconsciously.

"You wouldn't."

"No," he admitted, "I wouldn't, but I'd like to."

Alexa's attention turned to her fidgety hands, smoothing the bedcovers methodically.

"Are you certain you're all right?" Richard asked.

The tenderness in his voice urged her to look up. "I'm fine, Richard. Just a little . . . shaken. How are you?"

"I think I'm doing better, if you must know."

"How is that?" she pressed.

Richard looked down at the floor. "I want you and Jess to be happy, Alexa. I really do. I apologize for my behavior. If you ever need me, I'll be there for you."

Alexa swallowed hard. "Thank you, Richard. You can't know what that means to me." She met his yearning countenance and glanced away.

"Does Jess know?" he asked.

"I haven't told him, if that's what you mean."

"Good. Let's keep it that way." Richard picked up his hat and left the room. Alexa stared at the ceiling and wondered why she felt sure this wasn't settled.

❦ ❦ ❦

"Murphy!" Jess called as he entered the stable. "What's wrong?" Panic struck when he saw Crazy out of her stall and the boys huddled around her.

"Nothin' too serious," Murphy said calmly. "I noticed her limpin' a bit. She's got a little cut there on the hock."

"How on earth did that happen?" Jess shouted.

Murphy looked at him gravely. "Jimmy found a nail stickin' out o' the side of her stall."

Jess went into the stall to investigate. The evidence was blatant. He slammed his fist against his thigh and groaned.

"If you don't mind my sayin'," Murphy's expression intensified, "somebody's been busy with a hammer around here."

"Sam isn't back yet?" Jess asked, and Murphy shook his head. "When he comes back," Jess added bitterly, "*if* he comes back, I want to know immediately."

Jess glanced again to Crazy's ailing hock and sighed. "You'd best cancel the arrangements."

"We're not going to the derby?" Fiddler asked.

"My trainer's in bed with a bleeding leg—lucky to be alive—and my horse is limping. It's not worth it. No race is worth blood, and it appears that's what somebody is out for."

"I'd wager who that somebody is," Fiddler interjected.

"Cancel it," Jess ordered abruptly and walked out of the stable, where he came face to face with Sam Tommey.

"Where have you been?" Jess asked firmly.

"I ran into some trouble," Sam replied with no expression.

"So did we," Jess stated.

"I just came to get my things." He avoided Jess's eyes. "I've got to leave."

"Why?" Jess asked, but Sam wouldn't answer. "Why?" Jess shouted.

"Like I said," he moved around him to go into the stable, "I ran into some trouble."

"I've got some questions to ask you." Jess followed him back inside. Sam stopped but didn't turn. The others remained silently observing.

"Look at me when I talk to you," Jess said, and Sam turned slowly. "There was a little accident here yesterday. I want to know if you had anything to do with it. I told you the last time something like this happened that if you—"

"I would never want to hurt Alexa," he defended immediately, and Jess's eyes widened.

"How did you know it was Alexa?"

Sam glanced around, and his demeanor became like that of a cornered animal. "She's not here," he said tensely. "I assumed that—"

"Neither is Edward," Jess said, his jaw tight and his lips pressed together, "or Richard. How did you know it was Alexa?" he shouted, but Sam didn't answer. Jess cursed through clenched teeth as his fist struck Sam's lower jaw.

"Let me at 'im," Murphy said as Sam reeled backward.

"I think that's been taken care of." Fiddler took Murphy by the arm to hold him back.

Before Sam got to his feet, Jess pulled him up by the shirt collar and backed him against the wall. "I want the truth right now or I'll kill you," he hissed. Sam hesitated, and Jess slammed him into the wall. "Alexa is lying in a bed bleeding, and I want to know why anyone would want to hurt her. Do you want me to tell you what it was like when they pulled a plank out of her leg? I wish you could have been there to hear her scream. Is that why you've been gone?" Jess slammed him again. "Couldn't take it?"

Still Sam said nothing.

"The truth!" Jess insisted.

"I had no choice," Sam shouted.

"No choice?" Jess shrieked, and the boys could tell his grip tightened by the increasing grimace in Sam's expression.

"Let him go," Fiddler said, touching Jess's arm. Jess hesitated, but slowly relinquished his grip.

"All right," Jess said while Sam took a deep breath. "Let's have it."

"You have every right to feel the way you do," Sam began. "There's no way I could ever apologize, and I'm not going to try. I didn't want to do it—any of it. But I got into trouble with a gambling debt, and—"

"Who?" Jess interrupted and Sam hesitated. "Who's making you do it?"

Sam bowed his head. "Jess, if I—"

"Who?" Jess shouted.

"If he ever found out I told you, he'd—"

"Who?!" Jess took him by the shirt again and shook him.

"Chad Byrnehouse," Sam squeaked, and Jess let him go.

"I knew it." Jess's fists clenched unconsciously.

"He's the only thing keeping me out of jail," Sam muttered. "I was cornered."

"If you needed help, you should have come to me," Jess said.

"What could you have done?" Sam retorted.

"I don't know," Jess shouted, "but I certainly wouldn't be manipulating you into rigging saddles and staircases."

"I know there is no excuse," Sam said guiltily. "I don't expect you to forgive me. I've just got to leave. All I ask is that you let me go and give me another chance to make a decent start somewhere else."

Jess's anger resurfaced, and he hit Sam again. This time Sam stood it, but Jess was ready for another blow when Richard's hand caught his arm. "Let it go, Jess," he said quietly. Jess met Richard eye to eye while too many related memories passed silently between them. "I don't think Alexa would appreciate the way you're handling this. The problem here is between you and Chad. Sam's just a victim like the rest of us."

Jess pushed Richard's hand away. "The woman I love was nearly killed last night. If you—"

"We all love her, Jess," Richard interrupted. "You're just the one lucky enough to have her love in return. Think about Alexa and let it go."

Jess straightened his shoulders and took a deep breath. Part of him wanted to hit Richard, too, but he couldn't deny the truth of what he was saying. It seemed Richard had always been there, talking sense into him when he had no reason.

Jess softened his tone toward Sam. "I want the truth. You rigged the stairs?"

"Chad didn't want her to get hurt badly," Sam attempted to justify. "He just didn't want her to ride the derby."

Jess briefly closed his eyes, trying to keep his temper under control. It was obvious that Sam had known Richard was gone, and this was a pretty sure way to guarantee that the accident would happen to Alexa.

"The nail in Crazy's stall?" Jess asked tightly. Sam nodded. "You drugged Tod's drink before the race?" Again he nodded. "You cut the girth on Crazy's first race?"

"Yes," he said with regret in his voice.

"Anything else?" Jess demanded, looking him in the eye. "Come on, Sam! The least you could do is tell me if I have any more surprises waiting around this place."

"There's nothing else," he said firmly.

"Fine," Jess said and turned toward the door. "Don't ever show your face here again."

❦   ❦   ❦

Alexa was as disappointed as Jess expected when he told her they weren't participating in the derby, *or* going to Melbourne. But she had to agree it was for the best.

"I'm sorry, Jess." She took his hand as he sat on the bed beside her.

"What reason have you got to be apologizing?"

"I know Chad's behind this."

Jess recalled what Richard had said earlier in the stable. "This is between Chad and me. You're just a victim, Alexa."

"As you are."

"Perhaps." He sighed, then forced himself to brighten up. "Maybe next year." Alexa squeezed his hand and smiled, simply from the prospect of a future with Jess, whatever it entailed.

Alexa quickly got some color back in her face, thanks to a combination of Mrs. Brown's cooking and extra surprises from Edward. Richard visited nearly every day, and even brought her a new piece of poetry, written in longhand. She wanted to ask him about the anonymous pieces, but something kept her from bringing them up. The subject of his deeper feelings for her was best avoided. She enjoyed her talks with him and felt a keen gratitude that he was willing to overlook what might stand in the way of their friendship.

With frequent visits from all of the boys, Alexa hardly had a chance to get bored or lonely, but she did get restless. She was grateful when Dr. Lloyd told her she could get up the following day. He suggested the use of a cane until she became steady on her feet, and he assured her that the limp would eventually go away.

The boys all pitched in and sent Fiddler into town to buy a cane suitable for a woman. They came in together to present it to Alexa, and she nearly cried at their sentiment. "You boys are the best family a girl could ever want," she declared, and they sheepishly glanced back and forth among themselves, seeming to grasp for the first time that they all felt the same way; at least they'd come to since Alexa had softened their lives.

Jess brought Alexa some clothes from her room, but she looked at the skirt in dismay. "I'm not hobbling around in that thing. Get me a pair of breeches . . . please."

"Yes, dear," he replied and went back.

Alexa ate an early breakfast and got herself dressed in time to meet Jess at the door when he came in to get her.

"It's sure good to see you up again." He laughed and embraced her.

"It's good to be up." Alexa held him close and relished the deepening bond between them. "It feels good to be in your arms again," she whispered, and he kissed her.

Jess put his arm around her as they moved slowly down the hall. She looked warily at the top of the stairs. "Do you want me to carry you?" he asked.

"No," she replied, taking hold of the bannister with one hand and holding the cane firmly in the other, "I need the practice."

Jess stayed patiently by her side as she descended. "Does it hurt much?"

"It could be worse," she said and continued on.

When they finally made it across the yard, Jess threw open the door of the bunkhouse and Alexa stepped inside. The boys all came to their feet with applause, and Alexa blushed. She sat to rest while they ate, then she was escorted by the whole crew into the carriage house to see if she liked the stairs they had built.

"Completely new from top to bottom," Jess announced.

"And very sturdy," Tod added.

"We tested it," Jimmy chuckled.

"Now that," Alexa said, "I would like to have seen." She could almost imagine them jumping up and down on the stairs like a bunch of natives.

Jess ordered the boys to get to work, and Alexa went carefully up the stairs to her room. "Is there anything I can get you?" he asked.

"I don't think so. I may be slow, but I think I can manage on my own now."

Jess kissed her and excused himself to see to business. Alexa tidied her room and got things in order, then she ventured on a walk to the stables, just to see how things had fared in her absence. She was talking to Crazy when it came over her that she wasn't alone. Glancing around she saw nothing, but looking down she was met by the big brown eyes of a child, watching her with interest.

"Does she understand you?" the boy asked with an endearing expression that somehow reminded her of Jess when he was in a mischievous mood.

"I think she might," Alexa replied, wondering if this was Sarina's boy. She couldn't think who else it might possibly be. The child obviously had native blood in him, but by his features and coloring, Alexa knew he had to be half white.

"Crazy is a winner, isn't she," the boy said adamantly.

"She certainly is."

"Uncle Jess told me when she was born that she was going to be a winner. I knew he was right."

"Ben!" Sarina's voice startled Alexa more than the child. "I think you have a job to be doin', my boy. Don't you be wastin' Miss Alexa's time."

"Oh, it's fine," Alexa insisted. "He's very charming. How old is he?"

"I'm seven," Ben volunteered, still lingering despite his mother's orders. "How old are you?"

"Ben!" Sarina scolded. "You mustn't ask a lady such things. It's not proper. Now run along."

"I've been living in the outback," Ben continued. "Have you ever been in the outback or—"

"Ben," Jess's voice interrupted, and the child turned abruptly to see him entering the stable. "I heard your mother telling you to do something. You'd best see to it."

"Can we still go riding?" Ben asked.

"If you get your work done," Jess replied.

Ben moved quickly toward the door. "Can I ride Crazy?" he paused to ask with wide eyes.

"That would be up to Miss Alexa," Jess stated. "She's in charge of Crazy. You can talk to her about it when I see that everything's properly done."

The boy hurried away and Sarina sighed. "It's a good thing you're around to keep him straight."

Jess chuckled. "You've just got to sound stern, Sarina. You're too sweet, and he knows it."

"I suppose you're right. But I am grateful for you takin' time with him the way you do."

"It's my pleasure," Jess replied. "It's nice to have him back."

"Yes," Sarina laughed, moving toward the door, "I must admit that it is. He's just such a little scoundrel."

"Got a little of his father in him," Jess muttered after Sarina left. Alexa turned to him in surprise and he added casually, "Or at least I would assume."

He came toward Alexa and touched her face. "You look a little pale. Are you feeling all right?"

"A little tired," she replied, "but I'm fine. He's a charming boy." She steered the conversation back, curious about the situation.

"Yes, he is," Jess agreed emphatically. "I must admit I'm rather fond of Ben. He's a good boy, too," he added with pride in his voice. She still looked curious and he said, "I assume someone's told you the circumstances."

"Richard mentioned it briefly."

"Don't hold it against him," Jess said, and Alexa caught a deep severity in his eyes. "Ben can't help the situation he was born into."

"Is it just coincidence that he has your father's name?"

Jess looked surprised. "Sarina asked me before he was born what my favorite names were, and I told her. Now come along, my dear." He took her arm and ushered her from the stable. "You need some rest."

Jess helped Alexa back to her room and tucked her into bed, insisting she take a nap.

"Not until you tell me a bedtime story." She held his hand so he couldn't leave.

Jess sat near the bed and drew her hand to his lips. "I don't know any stories, Miss Byrnehouse, but I can tell you what I've been thinking about a great deal."

"Do tell," she smiled.

"We're nearly ready to start the wooling." He grinned, and Alexa felt a tremor of anticipation. "When that's finished, my love, I'm going to take you into town and buy you the most incredible wedding gown we can find. We'll have it custom made if necessary."

"Jess, you really don't need to . . ."

Jess put his fingers over her lips, and his eyes filled with something that resembled sadness. "My mother had a beautiful wedding gown. I remember my father showing it to me. He told me when I got married, he would like to see the gown used again, and perhaps pass it along to future generations." Jess looked down. "That gown was destroyed in the fire. I know we don't want a fancy wedding, really, but it's important to me that you have a gown worthy of handing down. Perhaps one day our daughter will wear it."

Alexa leaned forward to kiss Jess, relishing the sensation and the anticipation it evoked. "I love you, Jess Davies," she whispered.

"I love you, too, Alexandra Byrnehouse." He shook his head and grinned. "Mercy, I'll be glad to give you a different name."

Alexa had to agree.

With Alexa on her feet again, everything returned to normal. It wasn't long before she was as good as new. The limp was less noticeable than the scar, but Alexa didn't let either deter her. While her love for Jess deepened, her friendship with Richard gradually returned to what it had been. She was honest with him concerning her feelings for

Jess, and he seemed to lose whatever apprehension he'd had over the relationship at the beginning.

She was delighted when he gave her more poetry, written in longhand and signed. But when she received another anonymous piece printed in tiny block letters, she felt sure that his feelings for her still ran deep. Alexa compared the different works and realized that the emotions and perceptions were much the same, though the anonymous poetry had more depth and sensitivity. Something formless stirred her when she read them, but her feelings were centered on Jess and she almost felt guilty, or at the very least confused. To think of Richard's feelings left her afraid at times. She could not love two men the way she loved Jess.

On a bright morning, Alexa returned from a long ride on Crazy. The air tasted of spring and the anticipation of her future was deepening. Fiddler met her as she dismounted. "Jess wants to see you," he said. "Go on in. I'll take care of the lady here."

Alexa entered Jess's office to find his boots planted in the center of the desk, reminding her of the day they'd met; except that Ben was sitting next to him, drawing a picture with intense concentration. Alexa leaned against the door and smiled.

"How was your ride?" Jess asked.

"Exquisite, thank you."

"Run along, Ben," Jess said and the boy obeyed immediately, pausing only to show Alexa his picture.

"That's very fine, Ben," she commented. The boy grinned proudly and left as Jess threw a newspaper onto the desktop.

"You might be interested in that." He nodded toward it.

Alexa picked it up and read the headline. *Mentor takes Cup amid Centennial Celebration at Melbourne.*

"It must have been great," Jess said.

"You're disappointed."

"Of course I'm disappointed," he stated. "But then, I know you are, too."

"Actually, I have more exciting prospects."

Jess grinned. "I can't wait."

Alexa leaned over the desk and kissed him. "You'll just have to."

Jess fingered a button on her shirt and looked at it contemplative-

ly. He lifted his eyes to meet hers and said gruffly, "Perhaps you should
. . . distract me."

Once Alexa perceived the implication, she eased away and cleared
her throat. "With what?"

"How about the piano?"

"Good idea."

While Alexa relaxed with her music, Jess lay back on the little sofa in
the room and put his feet up. She glanced at him occasionally, marveling
at her feelings. He closed his eyes and she wondered if he was asleep until
he asked out of nowhere, "Do you suppose insanity is hereditary?"

Alexa stopped playing so abruptly that he turned to look at her in
question. "What on earth has that got to do with anything?" she asked.

Jess gave her a flippant grin. "I was just wondering if Chad inherited his insanity."

"That's not funny, Jess. I'm his sister."

"No," his expression sobered, "I suppose it wasn't. I didn't mean
anything personal by it."

"I can assure you that my . . ." She hesitated, then corrected,
"Chad's parents were perfectly sane. If he is truly as demented as he
seems, he didn't get it from them."

Contemplating the way she'd clarified that, Jess wondered for the
first time in months over the reason she'd been disowned. He wanted to
ask her, but had no desire to get into a conversation about parentage.
He would not ask her questions about herself that he wasn't willing to
answer concerning his own past. Instead, he settled his head back onto
the sofa with a sigh. "I suppose that means insanity is *not* hereditary."

Recalling disjointed bits of information concerning Jess's background, Alexa couldn't suppress a brief chill. Impulsively she asked,
"Does that ease your fears?"

"What fears?" he shot back tersely.

Alexa shrugged her shoulders, feeling uneasy as she realized there
were aspects of their lives they had yet to share. They had talked so
much, but never about their deepest hurts and fears.

"I can assure you I am as sane as any man alive," Jess insisted
vehemently.

She was quick to assure him with complete confidence, "Of that I
am certain."

Jess relaxed again on the sofa, and Alexa continued to play. She felt certain that whatever wasn't right between them would take care of itself when they were married.

Fourteen
TRIGGERING THE PAST

Alexa found Jess in the front parlor with Ben. Without being noticed, she leaned against the doorframe and watched them. Ben knelt on the floor next to a table, writing furiously, while Jess sat close by, reading over his shoulder.

"Now, wait a minute," Jess said, and Ben stopped. "Does 'green' rhyme with 'sky'?"

"No," Ben replied.

"Then you have to change it. Try switching that word with that one."

Jess was silent again while Ben wrote something.

"That's better." Jess leaned back a little. "But how does it end?"

"I don't know."

"What happens when you mix blue and yellow?" Jess asked. Ben shrugged. "My mother was an artist. If she were here, she'd tell you that mixing blue and yellow makes green. Think about that while you finish it."

Ben continued to write and Alexa was content to watch Jess silently, feeling a sense of fulfillment absorb her. She felt it every time she grasped the reality that she and Jess would be married soon. The prospect left her happier than anything ever had.

Ben handed his paper to Jess, and he read thoughtfully. "Now all you have to do is think of something else that's blue."

"I can't think of anything except the sky, Uncle Jess."

"But you already said the sky is blue."

"What else is blue?"

"Alexa's eyes," Jess said with warmth in his voice. Alexa smiled as love swelled within her.

"That's it!" Ben said triumphantly and scribbled something again with his pencil. He turned and handed the paper to Jess, who leaned back and put his boots on the table to read it.

"Not bad, considering. Now copy it onto a clean sheet of paper so it looks nice. Print it very carefully."

While Ben was busy copying, Jess stretched his arms above his head and happened to glance at Alexa. He smiled in surprise but said nothing. He just held her eyes with his, further deepening Alexa's sense of fulfillment.

"Are Alexa's eyes really blue?" Ben asked, oblivious to the intense gaze being shared behind his back.

"Really," Jess said.

"Are you really going to marry Miss Alexa?" Ben persisted.

"Really," Jess repeated with more feeling.

"But I always thought you were going to marry my mother."

Alexa was stunned, but not as much as Jess. He turned abruptly toward Ben and put his boots on the floor. His face reddened visibly at the awkwardness of the situation.

"Uh . . . ," Jess stammered, "I think you and I need to have a little talk. Finish your poem, and we'll go for a ride."

"I'm done." Ben stood and gave it to Jess, finally noticing Alexa in the doorway. "Hello, Miss Alexa. I've been writing a poem. Do you want to read it?"

"I'd love to." Alexa stepped into the room and took the paper from Jess. She caught something wary in his eyes as he was obviously wondering how Ben's statement had affected her. Alexa was certain that if anything had ever existed between Jess and Sarina, it was long over. She didn't feel threatened, but she wondered if there was something she didn't know.

Alexa read the poem and smiled, mostly to think of Jess coaching him through it.

The sky is blue, the grass is green
The greenest grass I've ever seen
The yellow sun shines from the sky

Sky as blue as Alexa's eyes
Yellow sun comes from blue sky
And makes me always wonder why
When I see the grass I've seen
I know that out of blue comes green

"That's very nice, Ben." Alexa thought of Richard's poetry and how touched she had been by it. "You should keep practicing. By the time you're grown, you'll be a very fine poet."

"What are you going to do with it?" Jess asked Ben.

"I don't know. What do you think I should do with it?"

"If I were to write a poem," Jess said with a subtle smile, "I would give it to whoever it was written about. As long as you keep a copy for yourself."

Ben smiled at the idea. "Would you like to keep it, Miss Alexa?"

"I would be honored." She kissed the boy on the cheek, and Jess grinned.

"Should I sign it first or something?" Ben asked as if it was a very important matter.

"If you want," Jess said. "But she'll know it's from you."

Ben decided to sign his name, then he gave it to Alexa.

"Come along now, Ben." Jess stood and ushered him toward the hall. "Let's have that little talk."

"And perhaps we should have one, too," Alexa added lightly.

Jess nodded satirically and left with Ben.

Alexa went to her room and tacked Ben's poem up with the others. Richard came by to see how she was doing, and she pointed it out to him. "I thought it was sweet," she commented as he read.

"I agree," Richard said. "It was Jess who encouraged me to write."

"Really?" Alexa's voice betrayed her interest.

"When I told him I had trouble expressing myself, he suggested it." Richard glanced over the other poems with interest. "You're getting quite a collection."

"Thanks to you," she remarked lightly, hoping he'd admit to the anonymous ones.

"I enjoy it." He shrugged. "Not that I'm so good."

"Oh, but you are. I enjoy your work very much."

"Thank you." He seemed surprised. "I feel that . . ."

Alexa was hoping for some kind of confession, but his words were interrupted by boots ascending the stairs. Richard stepped into the hall just as Jess reached the doorway.

"Am I intruding?" Jess asked, pressing an arm around Alexa's waist and kissing her cheek.

"I was just leaving," Richard said with a stilted smile, then went into his room.

Alexa smiled at Jess, hoping to cover her concern for Richard. "I hear there's some fresh lemonade in the bunkhouse," she said. "Care to join me?"

"Sounds delightful." He took her hand and led the way.

"So," Alexa said, pouring out two glasses, "did you have your little talk?"

"We did." Jess sat down and took off his hat. "And I know you're dying of curiosity, so I'll get to the point and tell you what I told him."

"And what is that?"

"I told Ben that his mother is a good woman with a lot of fine qualities, but it takes a special kind of love for two people to marry. I simply told him that I had never felt that way for his mother. That's not too difficult to understand."

Alexa shook her head and he continued. "Now I'll tell you something I didn't tell him. When Sarina first came here, she'd been hurt very badly. Typical story. She thought he loved her. He took her to bed and let her go. When she asked me for a job, she was barely pregnant and scared to death. She didn't want to go home and bring shame to her family. I gave her a job and let her have the baby here. She's faithful and works hard, and Ben has added to our lives when he's around."

"But what made him think that—"

Jess interrupted with a sigh. "There was a time when Sarina got a little carried away with her feelings. She interpreted my help as something deeper. We talked about it, and I was completely honest. She got over it. Ben was at an impressionable age when it happened, and I fear the boy has an impeccable memory. It's as simple as that."

Alexa smiled and took Jess's hand across the table. "Thank you, Jess."

"For what?" He took a long swallow of his drink.

"Your honesty is reassuring. Knowing what little I did, I couldn't help wondering if . . ." Alexa faltered and Jess's eyes narrowed.

"Wondering what?"

"I'm embarrassed to admit it now." She laughed tensely. "Everything you said makes complete sense, and . . ."

"Wondering what?" he repeated.

"Well, I must confess that it crossed my mind that Ben . . . might be your son."

Jess choked on his lemonade. "What on earth," he coughed, "gave you that idea?"

"He reminds me of you a little."

"You're seeing things, my dear," he insisted. "If Ben were my son I'd have married Sarina a long time ago, whether I loved her or not."

"I'm sorry," Alexa said gently. "As I said, I'm embarrassed to have even thought it. It's just that . . . I know so little about you in some respects, and—"

"Next time, just ask."

She nodded. "I suppose the two of you just go so well together. You almost seem like a father to him in a way."

"I've tried to make up for the circumstances a little." Jess chuckled and shook his head, astounded by her assumption. "But the only thing I have in common with that boy's father is the color of our skin."

"You know who the father is," Alexa stated.

"What gave you that idea?" he asked tersely.

"The way you talk about him. It's subtle, but I can tell."

"You're too perceptive for your own good," he said.

Alexa met his eyes and saw regret.

"Yes, I know who Ben's father is. The man's probably in a different bed every week. I wouldn't be surprised if Ben had two hundred half brothers and sisters roaming the country. Most of them probably starving because their mothers are left in the cold." Anger seeped into his voice. "If I had half that man's money, do you know what I would do with it?"

Alexa shook her head, sensing something personal.

"I would find a way to provide for children like Ben, and see that they got a proper education and such. It's unfair for children to grow up with disadvantages because of circumstances they had no control over."

"You're a good man, Jess." Alexa squeezed his hand.

"Ben is a good boy."

"Yes, he is. I've only gotten to know him a little, but I must admit I feel something strongly. It's as if . . ."

"What?" Jess asked intently when she faltered.

"I don't know," she laughed slightly. "I can't explain it."

"I can," Jess stated, and Alexa's eyes widened curiously. Jess bent his head forward and tapped his fingers against his glass. "There's no reason you shouldn't know, though you must understand that it's confidential. I'm certain Sarina would be upset if she thought you knew." Alexa nodded and Jess met her eyes. "Alexa, Ben is your nephew."

"Chad?" she asked breathily, and Jess nodded. She leaned back. "I don't believe it. I mean . . . I should believe it, I suppose. It doesn't surprise me, but . . ."

"If the man had any scruples," Jess rose from the table, "he'd take his tight fingers from around all that money and do something to rectify his philandering ways."

Alexa held her glass tightly, still stunned. "Scruples are something my brother will never have."

Jess put his arms around her from behind. "And there is something else your brother will never have."

"What's that?"

"He will never experience the joy of his own posterity. Now, when I have a son . . ."

"And what if you have a daughter, Jess Davies?"

"How about some of each?" he whispered behind her ear.

Alexa turned to kiss him, settling a little further into a contentment that words could not describe.

Life became hectic as they jumped into the wooling process. The days were long and hard for the men, and Alexa did what she could to help. She always made sure they had plenty to drink and helped with odd chores so they could concentrate on the shearing. The process was not unfamiliar to Alexa, but she couldn't help being impressed with Jess as he worked side by side with his hired hands. By the way he could get an animal down and shear away the coat as quickly as any of them, it was apparent he'd been doing it the better part of his life.

Watching the last of the wool being loaded, Alexa's mind turned to the future. Today it would be finished, and they could set a date and soon be married. Jess had told her he was pleased with the harvest this year; he'd profited enough to make another mortgage payment, cover expenses for the coming months, and have ample for a fine wedding and honeymoon. Alexa felt life could be no better as she watched Jess helping the boys finish the project.

At a vague rumbling in the distance, Jess stopped to look at the sky. "Let's hurry it up, boys," he called, lifting a sack onto his shoulder. "Looks like we're in for a storm."

Bored with watching, but knowing she couldn't help, Alexa decided to supervise. "Stack 'em neat, boys," she teased, and got a response of histrionic wails and moans. "Let's pick up a little speed now." Jess gave her an affectionate grin. "How about some rhythm? Don't put it there, Murphy. Let's make this look tidy."

"Haven't you got anything better to do?" Fiddler asked.

"Actually—no," she replied.

"I was afraid o' that," Jimmy added.

"I'm not complaining," Jess said.

"Of course you wouldn't," Murphy retorted, pausing to hoist a sack on his shoulder, "she's your woman."

Jess lifted a brow toward Alexa, warmed by her expression.

"You're just jealous," Alexa said.

Murphy grinned. "Now, why would I be jealous?" he asked impishly.

"Because," Jess threw a sack down, "she's the most beautiful woman in the country."

"Amen," Richard remarked lightly, but Alexa caught a smile that added to her contentment.

"Now, that's more than I can take," she said in mock embarrassment. "I think I'll go to my room and find something to occupy myself."

"Splendid idea," Fiddler said, but she knew he was teasing.

"Will I see you later?" Alexa asked, looking at Jess.

"If you insist," Murphy gushed, batting his eyelashes.

"Not you!" she laughed. "I see too much of you as it is."

"Of course," Jess replied. "As soon as we're finished."

Alexa sauntered toward the carriage house. Jess paused a moment to watch her until Jimmy stopped to elbow him in the ribs.

A short while later, Tod rode in from a quick trip to town and hollered, "Hey, Jess. You might like to know—I just saw Chad

Byrnehouse. Apparently he came to visit his sister."

Jess tensed visibly. "Thanks, Tod," he muttered, and nearly ran to the carriage house.

☙ ☙ ☙

When Alexa heard the knock at her door, she assumed it was Jess and called for him to come in. "Hello, love," she said without turning.

The door closed, but only silence answered. She looked up abruptly just as Chad said, "Really, little sister, I wasn't aware you held such affection for me."

"What are you doing here?" she snapped.

He dropped a faded hat box onto a chair. "Some things of Mother's," he said. "Thought you might like them."

"What things?" she asked warily.

"Just some old letters and stuff. I figured they'd be of more interest to you than me."

"What makes you so concerned about my sentiment all of a sudden?"

"Well," he glanced down nervously but she sensed something phony, "I must say . . . I've done a lot of thinking, and I . . . I owe you an apology, Alexa." He remained silent for several moments and Alexa waited, not believing that he could say anything worthwhile. She pondered briefly that he was Ben's father and felt a mixture of emotions.

"What I did was wrong," he finally admitted. "I want you to come home—where you belong."

Alexa couldn't believe what he was saying, but it didn't take long for her to grasp his true intentions. "Home?" she tested. "You said I had no home."

"I came to apologize. What I said was—"

"You told me you would never give me the time of day; that I was no better than a serving wench, and I'd best find a position or starve."

"Alexa, I—"

"Well, I found a position—and a good one at that."

"Alexa, you're a lady. You should be home with me, and—"

"And what? What are you offering? How much, Chad? I want to know how much it's worth to you."

"Are you saying I have to buy you back?"

"I'm saying the only reason you want me back is because your plan backfired. You wanted to be free of me, and you ended up giving Jess Davies an asset. It took you long enough to figure it out."

"And now I hear that Jess Davies is going to have a wife," he said cynically.

"Oh, now that explains the timing of your visit. I love him, Chad, and I will starve here with him before I ever come groveling for whatever you decide I'm worth."

"Calm down, Alexa." He chuckled as if it was all quite amusing, and he expected her to see his reasoning any moment. "Listen to yourself. You can't really mean that you would want *him*. I know you were just using him to—"

"You don't know anything!" she shouted. "You're so blinded by greed and some warped obsession of hatred that you can't even see your own nose. Well, I'll tell you something. Jess is a good man and the best thing I've ever had in my life. And all of your hired ploys to destroy us will never change that."

He gave an innocent chuckle, and anger seethed in Alexa as she recalled all she'd gone through because of him. She regretted that she couldn't show him the scars on her thigh. "Get out of here!" she cried.

Chad glanced toward the box he'd brought with him, seeming complacent. "You're making a mistake, Alexa."

"Get out!" she repeated.

"I think you'd best look these things over before you make any decisions. Don't do something stupid that you're going to regret, just to—"

The door flew open, and Chad turned to see Jess Davies filling the frame. His hair was damp with sweat, making the curls tighter around his neck. Perspiration gleamed over his face and trickled over his chest where it showed through his dampened shirt, partially unbuttoned. "What are you doing here?" he asked dryly.

"Just paying a little visit," Chad replied easily.

"You were just told to leave," Jess stated.

Chad chuckled. "Think about it, Alexa," he added as he turned to leave. "And I wouldn't wait too long to look those things over."

"Get out!" she shouted, and Jess's hands went onto his hips, fists clenched. Chad nodded toward Alexa, then smugly tipped his hat to

Jess as he walked past him and down the stairs.

Alexa sat on the edge of the bed and put her face into her hands. Jess closed the door and knelt beside her, fondling her fingers with his. "Are you all right?" he asked gently.

"Yes," she said sharply, but he gave her a dubious glare. "No," she added more softly, then she stood and picked up the hat box from the chair.

"What is that?" Jess asked.

"Nothing to be concerned about, I'm sure." She slid the box under the bed then stood before the window, fanning her face with her hands. "Why is it so blasted hot?"

Jess stood behind her and touched her shoulders. "Alexa, do you want to tell me what he said?"

"What made you show up when you did?" She evaded the question, her voice tinged with anger.

"Tod saw him come in. I was going to wait in the hall until I heard you shouting."

"He had the nerve," she turned toward him, "to ask me to come home." Jess lifted his brow. "But I can see right through him. He knows he made a mistake, because my being with you is a threat to him. Though I can't figure why our winning a few races should make any difference to his life."

"It's impossible to figure why he does what he does, Alexa, but don't let yourself get hurt by—"

She stopped him with a sharp look. "I told him I would rather be with you and starve than grovel for his money. He can have it, Jess! He can have it all, and . . ." Her voice faltered, and she put her face into her hands and groaned.

Jess reached out to take her shoulders and she pulled his shirt into her fists, pressing her face to his chest.

"I'm all sweaty," he apologized.

"I don't care," she said softly, but he could still hear the tension in her voice. She pushed her arms around him and he eased her closer, feeling emotion in her firm embrace. He sensed something deeper bothering her. Chad's visit had triggered some kind of hurt that she evidently meant to keep to herself. But Jess could not begrudge her keeping secrets when he had so many of his own. Instead he just held her, doing his best to offer comfort.

"Jess," she said intently, pulling back to look up at him, "I need you. I can face anything if I have you."

"I'm here," he promised. "Always here."

"Hold me, Jess." She pressed her face against his chest, and he tightened his grip around her. Carefully he lifted her chin to meet his gaze, searching for the deeper cause of her pain. She met his eyes with a longing for comfort. Her lips parted and her eyes closed. Jess could do nothing but kiss her.

Alexa drew the needed comfort from his kiss and sought for more. Instinctively she pulled his face into her hands and pressed all of her fear and pain into her response. Jess drew back breathlessly, surprised by her reaction. Alexa impatiently brought her lips against his again, moving closer as his kiss deepened. She felt his breath quicken with his heart. He braced his feet apart to support himself as she melted against him, blindly seeking the assurance that he loved her. It seemed no one else ever had.

"Alexa," he whispered hoarsely, but she only tipped her head back and gave an emotional moan, fiercely pressing her fingers into his shoulders. Jess brought his lips to her throat and attempted to urge her closer. She felt weak and helpless, overpowered by her emotions. Jess tightened his arms around her as her knees gave way, and she would have fallen had he not held her.

"I love you, Jess," she whispered, her face against his. He kissed her cheek, her brow, her lips again. He pulled at her earlobe with his lips, and she trembled. With purpose her hand moved down his chest. Her touch brought forth a passion in Jess that almost frightened him. Alexa had always been the one to keep him in line and stop such things from getting out of hand. But she didn't seem interested in stopping him now, and Jess had to admit that when it came to Alexa, he had no self-control.

"Alexa," he whispered in warning, but she silenced any question by putting her lips over his. Amidst the fury of their kiss, Jess lost the ability to keep them both standing any longer. He was glad the room was so tiny when he only had to urge her two steps backward before he pushed her onto the bed and lay beside her.

"Jess," she cried, and he lost all reason. His only conscious thought was that he wanted her. He could only wonder if he'd gone mad as he explored the intensity of his desires.

Alexa gasped as she realized how close they were. Wondering how it had come to this, she recalled Chad's visit, then her mind went to the box she'd shoved beneath the bed. "No, Jess," she cried.

Consciously, Jess didn't want to hear it and ignored her. He felt her go tense, but it only made him want her more, and he drowned her plea in a torrid kiss.

Alexa thought of her mother and knew this could not happen—not yet. She had vowed she would never have a man unless she was his wife. She would not leave a child to face what she herself had endured. She would not!

"Please, Jess," she murmured, trying to push him away. She knew she had provoked this and it wasn't fair, but she just couldn't go through with it. "Jess," she cried, but he only kissed her. She turned her face away but he devoured her throat, while everything inside of her erupted with volatile emotion. A tangible pain developed between her eyes as the hurt and confusion centered there. Questions of her troubled childhood had been answered with the devastating realization that her mother had been too involved with a clandestine lover to care for her children, and the father she trusted and looked up to was not her father at all. She was the product of deceit, and her very existence had spurred drunkenness and shouting that had thundered all too often through the walls of her home.

"Jess, please," she sobbed, her chest heaving with unvented pain. But Jess mistook her labored breathing for passion, and persisted with his desires.

"Stop it!" she screamed, using every bit of strength she possessed to push him away.

Stunned to his senses, Jess drew back to look at her. Alexa's pained expression was amplified by an acute fear in her eyes. Tears streamed into her hairline while she shuddered with uncontrollable sobbing. Checking his sanity, Jess wondered if he had lost it somewhere in the last few minutes. What had he done to bring this on? Was he doing the very thing a part of him had always feared he might?

In panic, Jess went to his knees. Once free of Jess's weight, Alexa recoiled against the headboard, frantically trying to cover herself while she pressed a hand over her mouth that didn't begin to hold back the wailing that rose from her chest.

Alexa wanted to tell him how sorry she was for allowing this to happen. She wanted to tell him how much she loved him. But her emotions had taken complete control, and she could only cry and hope that he understood. In an effort to convey her regret, she met his eyes and saw something visibly change there. It was as if a trigger had been fired in his mind, and the resulting explosion had left him devastated.

"No!" Jess said from low in his throat. He turned his eyes shamefully to the floor as he inched away. "No, no," he repeated. "Please, no."

Fear engulfed Alexa, squelching all other emotions as Jess backed against the wall and covered his head with his arms. She bit into her knuckles as he fell to his knees with a self-punishing groan that far surpassed what she considered a normal reaction to such a situation.

Alexa rushed to his side. "Jess, what is it?" She knelt on the floor beside him and touched his shoulder. He made no response, and she pressed her fingers gently over his face. Seeing the blatant fear in his eyes, she had to bite her lip to keep from crying out. "What?" she whispered intently.

"Alexa," he said hoarsely, "I . . . I . . . What I just did . . . I . . . Don't let me hurt you, Alexa. I . . . must be . . . crazy. I don't know what came over me . . . I'm sorry! You must believe that I'm so sorry. I . . . didn't intend to—"

"Jess," she said in a soothing voice, easing his head to her shoulder. "There's no need to be so upset. I lost my reason. It wasn't fair of me to act that way and expect you to stop. *I* should apologize, Jess, not you. Forgive me, Jess, but I just couldn't do it. Not yet. When we're married, we can—"

"No!" he interrupted and stood abruptly, nearly pushing her away. "You can't marry me, Alexa. You can't!"

"Jess," she reached out a hand to touch him, "calm down."

"Don't." He recoiled. "No. You can't marry me, Alexa."

Alexa's heart sank into her stomach. What had gone wrong? "It's all right, Jess." She tried to remain calm on the surface for his sake. "Everything will be fine." She stepped toward him, but he backed away and held up his arms like a frightened child.

"No," he muttered, "I'll hurt you."

"Don't be absurd," she said gently. "I know you would never hurt me. You love me. I know you do."

He looked dazed and bewildered as he sat on the edge of the bed. "I love you, Jess," she said, and he looked up in surprise. She sat close beside him and tentatively took his hand into hers. He briefly attempted to pull it away, then he gripped it so tightly it hurt. "It's all right," she said gently and kissed his brow. His shoulders slumped from apparent exhaustion, and he took hold of her as if he needed her to breathe.

Painful tears pressed into Alexa's eyes as she held him close. He nuzzled his face against her throat and seemed to draw comfort from her nearness, though his breathing remained sharp, his every muscle taut with nerves. Alexa lay back carefully on the bed, urging him with her. She could almost feel his mind racing in circles. Her heartbeat synchronized with his as his fear absorbed her. If she only knew what he was afraid of! He repeatedly groaned in anguish and pressed his face against her, as if he could bury his pain in her nearness.

Alexa was aware of the clock ticking as Jess's torment continued. More than an hour later, he gradually relaxed. As dusk filtered into darkness, rain started to fall and the curtains blew wildly at the open window. Jess lay completely still, and Alexa wondered if he was asleep until he leaned up on one elbow to look at her. She could barely see the outline of his troubled expression in the dark.

"Where are your thoughts, Jess?" She pressed gentle fingers over his face.

"What did Chad say to upset you so badly?"

"I asked you a question first." She wondered where the pain she'd just witnessed had gone.

"You asked where my thoughts were. I was wondering why you were so upset."

Alexa sighed. "It isn't so much what he said as . . ." She looked toward the evidence of the storm intruding through the window. "It's the whole blasted thing."

"Tell me," he whispered, and Alexa wished she could perceive his thoughts. She knew now what she had vaguely suspected. Something in Jess was hurting very badly—something their intimate encounter had brought painfully close to the surface. Yet here he was, content to ignore whatever it was, concerned only for her.

"I don't want to talk about—" she began, but he interrupted.

"I have to know," he said strongly, despite a soft tone.

Alexa *didn't* want to talk about it. Though she assumed Jess would accept her circumstances, she wondered how he'd feel about them. And too, the subject was painful for her. Thinking of Jess's anguish, she decided to tell him her feelings with the hope that perhaps he would do the same.

"I was disowned," she stated. "It's not an easy thing to live with."

"I knew that much. But you've never told me why."

"Yet you still accept me."

"Why shouldn't I?"

"How do you know I don't have some wretched secret that makes me not worth having?"

"No," he said too soberly. "If anything, it's the other way around." Alexa wanted desperately to know his thoughts, but his tone changed as he quickly added, "There is nothing you could tell me that would make me feel any differently about you." The confidence in his voice made her believe him.

Alexa tightened her arms around him to express appreciation, and he responded with a warm embrace, settling his face against her shoulder. He waited silently for her to go on, while the air hung heavy with tension.

"I only found out after my father was killed, or rather . . . what it boils down to is that Tyson Byrnehouse is not my father."

Jess only tightened his arms around her, full of comfort and acceptance. Tears brimmed in Alexa's eyes, evoked from a mixture of emotions.

"Your heart is pounding, Alexa," he whispered. "Why?"

"Oh, Jess." A gentle sob escaped her. "All my life, I thought things were as they appeared. My mother and I were never close. She was distant; never seemed happy. Still I loved her, and I grieved when she died. As a child I recall my father being distant as well, and he was easily cross with me. He treated Chad and me differently, but I always assumed it was because they were both men. As I grew older, things changed. My father and I became close; he became gentler and stopped drinking. And I sensed distance growing between him and Chad. They became very different as the years passed."

Alexa paused and shifted on the narrow bed. Jess put his arm around her shoulders, bringing her face to rest against his chest. "It hurt terribly when they told me he'd been killed. He was such a good horseman, and the last thing I expected was to lose him that way. In terms of an inheritance, I had always assumed that Chad, as the eldest and a son, would receive the majority of Father's holdings. But the will . . ." She stopped in an effort to control her emotion, then went on falteringly. "The will stated that I was not his blood daughter; that I was the result of an ongoing affair of my mother's that he had resented. There was no provision left for me at all, but the matter was left in Chad's hands. And of course, you know Chad. He did the very worst." Alexa drew a deep breath and finished, "So here I am."

"Stuck with me," Jess said with no humor.

"I don't consider myself stuck," she retorted and leaned up to look at him. "If only I understood," she added intensely. "I thought Tyson Byrnehouse cared about me. I would swear by all I hold sacred that this was not his intention."

"How old was the will?" Jess asked.

The question struck her deeply. "I don't know."

"It's too bad he didn't know he was going to die. He probably would have redone it."

At his words, a formless peace settled into Alexa's heart. It made sense. "Perhaps you're right."

"I love you, Alexa. I hope you know that."

"Even though I'm not a Byrnehouse."

"Perhaps it's the very reason I always liked you—even though you were a Byrnehouse. Actually, it's a relief."

"It is?"

"It only makes it easier to hate Chad and love you at the same time."

"Why do you hate him so much?" she asked, and he became so physically tense that she feared his recent anguish would return. Still she pressed him, thinking it might be better if it did. Perhaps it would help them both understand the reasons. "What do you know that you're not telling me, Jess, that keeps feeding this feud?"

"That's too long a story to get into tonight."

"Too long—or too hard?" she asked cautiously.

He turned his head away and said without tone, "Both."

Alexa said nothing more and Jess drifted to sleep on the narrow bed, wrapped protectively in Alexa's love. She awoke to daylight and found Jess sitting on the edge of the bed, pulling on his boots.

"You're leaving?" Her disappointment was evident.

"Don't you think I should?" he said without looking at her. "The rumors are already going to be impossible."

"I don't care." She sat up to kiss him. "We've spent the night together before. Let them think what they want." Alexa looked into his eyes and sensed something different. There was a glazed coldness that kindled her fear. "Are you all right?" she asked.

He stood to tuck in his shirt and pull his braces over his shoulders. "Of course I'm all right. Why wouldn't I be?"

Alexa moved to the edge of the bed, saying cautiously, "What happened last night was hard on you, for reasons I don't understand."

He looked toward her sharply but said nothing.

"I just want to know that you're all right," she added.

"Yes, Alexa," he said dryly, "I'm fine." He moved to the door and put his hand on the knob. "I'll see you later."

Alexa moved across the room to kiss him, but she was disappointed by his lack of response. He opened the door at the same time Richard's came open across the hall.

"Good morning," Jess said coolly.

"Good morning," Richard replied. "A bit early to be checking up on her, don't you think?"

"It's never too early to see Alexa," Jess replied, then he closed the door and hurried down the stairs.

Alexa watched from the window as he walked up the path, ignoring jibes from the boys about his visiting hours. Jess had never let their teasing bother him, but Alexa wondered why he was ignoring them completely. She knew something was very wrong, and a rush of emotion made her fear what it might do to their future.

Fifteen

BEAUTY AND THE BEAST

Right after breakfast, Alexa went to the stable to begin her work, hoping to distract herself from the nagging oppression she felt. She found Ben sitting in a corner, crying. "Whatever's wrong?" she asked gently, sitting beside him.

At first he seemed embarrassed, but his emotions got the better of him and he gladly accepted Alexa's embrace. It was hard to believe this child was related by blood, but she felt close to him in spirit as she held him.

"Do you want to tell me what's wrong?" she asked when his crying quieted.

"Uncle Jess yelled at me," he said, and dread stabbed at Alexa.

"Were you doing something you shouldn't have?" she asked, determined not to jump to conclusions.

"No, I just asked him if we were gonna go riding today. He said he didn't know. I told him he promised, and he . . . he . . . just yelled at me and told me to find something to do."

Ben became upset again, and Alexa made an effort to console him. "I'm certain that Jess isn't angry with you. Sometimes life is difficult for adults too, Ben. I know that's hard for you to understand, but I would bet that Jess has something on his mind and needs to be left alone. If you know that you didn't do anything wrong, then just leave him be and I'm certain he'll come around."

Ben seemed comforted and was soon off to play, but Alexa was left with a deepening concern. She had to force herself to take her own advice. Perhaps if Jess was left alone, he would return to his old self.

Jess didn't come around that day, but Sarina came out to the paddock to tell Alexa that he wanted her to join him for dinner. Alexa took the opportunity to tell Sarina what a fine boy Ben was.

Sarina seemed surprised. "Why, thank you," she said. Their eyes met, and Alexa was certain that Sarina realized she was Chad's sister.

"Jess thinks a great deal of him," Alexa added, "and I can see why."

"Mr. Davies is good to us. You'd never convince Ben that Jess isn't really his uncle. It were him that taught Ben to read and write." She chuckled. "Actually, he taught me, too. I could hardly speak English when I came here."

"He is a good man," Alexa agreed. It was several moments before Alexa realized her mind was wandering with blanketed fear.

"Are you all right, Miss Alexa?" Sarina asked, startling her.

"Yes, of course."

"You're a very lucky woman," Sarina added.

Alexa wondered if Sarina's feelings for Jess had faded with time, or if she just kept them concealed. "Yes, I am," Alexa said with confidence.

"I should get back inside," Sarina said. "Remember, dinner is at seven."

Alexa went in at the appointed time and found Jess already seated at the dining table with a snifter in his hand. He drew his attention from it to smile at her when she entered, motioning for her to sit down. "Hello, my dear," he said without rising, which was unusual.

Alexa sat down. "I missed you today. What have you been doing with yourself?"

"A little of this," he took a long swallow of his brandy, "and a little of that."

Alexa's fears settled heavily upon her as she observed him through a silent meal. He drank more than ate, and paid little attention to her. The hurt rising inside made her wonder why he'd even invited her.

When they'd finished eating, Sarina came in to ask Jess if they would like coffee on the veranda. He made no response.

She timidly glanced toward Alexa in question. "That would be fine, Sarina."

Alexa forced the glass from Jess's hand and set it aside while he looked at her in dismay. She urged him to his feet and led him to the veranda, realizing he was more than a little drunk by the way he leaned against her to walk. She was more concerned than angry as she pushed him into a chair. He glanced up at her and grinned as he caught his arm around her waist. "Hello, Alexa," he said impishly, as if she'd just arrived.

"Hello, Jess," she retorted with disgust.

Sarina brought out the coffee tray, and Alexa eased away from him to pour it. She gave him a cup, which he set down immediately to take her hand as she was seated. "You're beautiful, Alexa," he said, but there was mischief in his eyes.

"You're drunk," she retorted.

He acted surprised but didn't argue. "Come here," he said, "and kiss me. It'll make me feel better."

He said it with sincerity, and Alexa complied with a gentle kiss. Before she could pull away, he took her face in his hands and his kiss turned hard, nearly bruising her lips. When she finally broke free, he looked hurt. "Why won't you let me kiss you?"

"You were hurting me." She tried not to sound upset.

He looked pointedly away and his cheek twitched. "I need a drink." He tried to stand with little success, then he looked at her. "Will you get me another drink?"

"No," she stated calmly, "I will not. You've already had more than enough to make you sick." He looked like a scolded child, reminding her too much of Tyson Byrnehouse during the years he'd spent trying to drown something or other in a bottle of liquor. Alexa knelt beside him and touched his face. "Why, Jess? What makes you want to do this to yourself?"

"What makes you care?" he snarled.

Alexa moved toward the door. "There is no point talking to you when you're like this. You don't even know your own mind." Before she could leave, he rose quickly to catch her and pulled her into his arms. In the process, he tipped over the little table and his cup of coffee shattered on the tile floor. Alexa glanced toward it in dismay, but Jess ignored the mess and backed her toward the wall, where he leaned his body against her.

"Don't leave me," he said hoarsely. "I need you. You must believe me when I say I need you. Please don't leave me."

"Jess," she said tensely, "let me go, please. We'll talk when you're sober."

He ignored her plea and attempted to kiss her. His mouth tasted of warm brandy.

"Come on, Jess," she said gently, "let me help you to your room, and you can sleep it off."

"I don't want to sleep it off." He urged her closer. She gasped with a combination of excitement and fear. "You want me, too," he whispered. "I know you do."

"Jess," she insisted as his grip tightened around her, "you're drunk. Don't treat me this—"

He pressed his mouth over hers harshly, and his hand moved over her throat until he found the top button of her blouse. He tugged awkwardly at it while Alexa pressed her hand over his, trying to urge it away. In his mindless state the gesture frustrated him, and he used all the force he could muster to move her to the bench near the veranda rail. He obviously had no intention of stopping with a kiss. Recalling the pain he'd exhibited from a similar situation yesterday, Alexa knew he had no idea what he was doing. When her protests were ignored and her efforts to move him were in vain, Alexa drew back her hand and slapped his face as hard as she could. A brief soberness rose in his eyes as he slid to his knees. Alexa sat up to look at him sharply.

"I deserved that, didn't I," he stated dryly.

"You most certainly did." She stood and helped him to his feet. "Now come along. I'm putting you to bed."

"No!" he protested and jerked his arm away. "Go home, Alexa. Leave me alone."

"Jess, I . . ."

"You're crazy!" he shouted. "You must be mad to be in love with me. You don't deserve me. Look at me. You've made a mistake," he ranted. "It was a mistake to fall in love with me."

"Jess," she attempted to soothe him, "please—"

"Get out of here," he shouted so angrily that she could do nothing but comply. Tears bit into her eyes as she hurried toward the carriage house, wondering what had gone wrong with their lives.

Alexa rose from a sleepless bed and rode out of the stable before dawn. She returned in time for breakfast, then ordered the boys to take the horses out for a trial run.

"What for?" Murphy asked.

"To keep them in shape," she said sharply.

Murphy did as he was told, and they all took a break to watch Alexa and Tod ride the track. As Alexa dismounted, she realized Jess was leaning against the fence, watching. Even from a distance she could see that he was tense. She tried to walk past him as she went to the stable, not knowing what to say or how to act. He called her name, and she turned hesitantly toward him.

"Can we talk?" he said. She glanced around at the boys, who were heading toward the stable, pretending that nothing was out of the ordinary. Alexa stood before Jess silently, waiting for him to speak. "I don't know what to say. I must have made a fool of myself last night."

"You did," she stated. He sighed and looked away.

"What did I do, Alexa?" he asked, looking her straight in the eye.

"What difference does it make?" she retorted.

"It makes a lot of difference." He took her arm firmly. Alexa glanced toward his hand, then looked into his eyes. He let go abruptly. "Tell me what happened," he pleaded, but she made no response. She wanted him to sweat it out. "Come on, Alexa. I have this recurring flash of you slapping me. Did I dream it?"

"Don't you wish you had?" she snarled, and he looked down.

"Why?"

"Don't you remember anything else?" she asked.

He leaned against the fence with a guilty sigh. "I remember you sitting at the dinner table with me, and then walking out to the veranda."

"That's it?" she nearly shrieked.

"I threatened Sarina into telling me what she knew."

"And what is that?" Alexa fought to remain calm.

Jess looked away and stuffed his hands into his pockets. "She said that she heard us shouting, and . . . a table was tipped over, and there was a broken coffee cup on the veranda."

"And what, exactly," Alexa said satirically, "did she say we were shouting about?"

He sighed guiltily again and looked skyward, folding his arms. "She said you told me I was drunk, and—"

"How very perceptive of me," she interrupted, and he glared at her.

"And that I . . . accused you of being crazy and . . . well, something like that."

"That about sums it up."

"But what did I do?" he asked, and she realized he was fearing the worst.

"How would you feel if I told you that you did it all?" His eyes widened in horror. "And how would you feel if I told you how unforgettable it was?" She brought her face close to his and said through clenched teeth, "And you don't remember a blasted thing!"

"Alexa," he whispered, "please tell me it's not tr—"

"It's not true!" she said angrily. "That slap you so fondly remember is the only thing that saved you . . . or rather me."

"Oh, Alexa." He reached out to touch her face, then retracted his hand tensely. "I'm so sorry. I—"

"Sorry enough to stay away from it?"

"What do you mean?" he asked.

"I mean," she said with strength, "that I don't know what made you decide to personally dispose of all the brandy you could get your hands on, but I'm going to tell you something, just in case you haven't figured it out by now." She put her hands on her hips. "It was pointless! Whatever you were trying to solve isn't, and whatever you were trying to prove, you didn't. If you love me and I love you, and something is bothering you, then you can talk to me about it, Jess Davies. Don't you dare look at me and tell me that everything is fine, then turn around and drown yourself in brandy, and subject me to a mindless brawl.

"Now," she pointed a finger at him, "I'm going to give you an opinion. There is nothing more pathetic or stupid than a grown man—especially one who carries so much natural dignity—lowering himself to a state where he has no control, no brain, and no memory. I'll admit that I've seen drunk men act worse than you did, but I didn't relish seeing the man I love unable to stand up straight or talk without a slur, and so possessed with who knows what that he practically forced himself upon me. Well, I won't be subjected to it again, Jess Davies; so you can vow here and now that it won't happen again, or you can find another woman to share your life with."

Jess stood like a guilty child while Alexa gave her heated speech. When a moment's silence made it evident she was finished, he said sheepishly, "Does that mean you'll forgive me?"

"I could think about it," she said sharply, then her voice softened as she met his eyes. "Of course I'll forgive you. How could I possibly live without you?"

"I am so sorry, Alexa; so very sorry. I can assure you it won't happen again."

Alexa glanced down, emotion replacing her anger.

"Did I hurt you, Alexa?"

"Yes," she said, putting a fist in the center of her chest. "You hurt me right here. It hurt to see you have so little respect for yourself—and for me."

"I understand," he said quietly, "but did I—"

"Yes," she interrupted, and a smile seeped into her countenance. "My hand hurt for quite a while after I slapped you."

Jess chuckled, and Alexa reached her hand toward him. With hesitance he took it, and she eased into his arms. He embraced her fully, deeply grateful for her unending acceptance and love. He bent to kiss her, and applause came from the distance.

Alexa blushed and turned away. Jess bowed his head and chuckled before he yelled at the boys gathered in front of the stable, "Get out of here! Can't a guy have any peace?!"

"We wasn't listenin'," Murphy shouted. "We was just watchin'."

"If you can't find anything better to do," Jess called, "I'm sure I could find some extra work that—"

"All right, boys," Murphy said, and they disappeared before he finished, "let's get to work."

Jess chuckled, then turned to Alexa. "How long has it been since we went riding together, Miss Byrnehouse?"

"Far too long," she replied, keenly aware of the change in his eyes. He was trying to be the same man, but he wasn't and she knew it.

"Let's go." He ushered her to the stable as if nothing had ever been wrong. His very indifference over what had happened in the last two days was the most frightening thing of all. Instinct told her that Jess was holding within him a deep, festering wound—so deep that it would eat away at him until it destroyed them both.

After a long ride with Jess, Alexa returned to her room and found a poem slid under the door. As always, she was touched by Richard's sentiment. She tacked it to the wall before she read it, then abruptly pulled it back down as the words almost haunted her.

In the mirror I see a man,
   but the reflection shows a beast
Does my soul show through my eyes
   or do my eyes only hide my soul?
From the distance I watch you there,
   and I see nothing but beauty.
Beauty through and through.

I have heard through legend's tongue,
   from books my mother read,
The only thing that changes beast to man
   is true love, pure love, Beauty's love.

Tears brimmed in Alexa's eyes, though she didn't understand why. Her thoughts were with Jess, and it made her feel guilty knowing that Richard wanted her thoughts to be with him.

Carefully she tacked it to the wall with all the others. She compared the two types of writing and was intrigued to think they had come from the same man.

❦   ❦   ❦

Jess lay staring into the darkness. His recent encounters with Alexa stormed through his mind. What had gone wrong? When had it gone wrong? Logically, everything had seemed perfect until a few days ago. But searching deeply for the truth, Jess knew the problem had been there long before he'd even known Alexandra Byrnehouse existed.

Jess could look back through his youth and know with certainty that he'd never wanted for anything. As a young child, he had assumed that all mothers were like his. Emma Davies had been the perfect mother to him. She was so involved in his child's play that he'd never noticed the absence of other children, isolated as they were. Only when Jess turned twelve did he realize that he'd surpassed his mother's maturity, and she was somehow different. He remembered asking his father about it, and Ben had reverently told him that Emma's mind was not whole. She had a keen ability to love and she was a good woman, but her perception of life was childlike and unrealistic.

It never crossed Jess's mind that such a thing could be inherited until Chad Byrnehouse challenged him to a pointless fistfight behind the stables during a particular race. It was only at the races that the Byrnehouses and the Davies ever encountered each other, which was likely for the best. A silent rage singed the air each time Ben Davies and Tyson Byrnehouse were within sight of each other. But Chad's hatred was not so suppressed. Apparently following his father's example, he took it upon himself to persecute Jess, while Jess's father taught him adamantly to turn the other cheek, that vengeance was for fools and cowards. Jess tried to do as his father asked, but there were times when he just couldn't resist giving Chad a bloody nose. Even in his youth Chad was shrewd, and if Jess got the better of him, Chad inevitably dug deep with retaliations that Jess was still not free of. Sneering words haunted him at moments when he felt the lowest. *Crazy mothers have crazy babies. The older you get, the crazier you'll be.*

Jess had never felt crazy—until now. But in the back of his mind, he had always wondered. There had been consolation in Ben Davies' example of strength and unquestionable sanity. Jess found peace in believing he could be like his father. And until Ben died, Jess felt confident that he was. But little more than a year later, the bottom fell out of Jess's life. At first Chad's taunting was passed off as an absurdity, but something inside Jess had to know for certain. His searching had proved Chad right, and Jess had to admit that he could not claim Ben Davies' blood in his veins. He *was* a bastard, just as Chad had said he was. But even worse, the means of his conception only deepened the possibility. What chance did he have of believing he could be anything *but* crazy?

Jess had never wanted to believe it, and in all honesty he had never seen himself behave in a way that warranted any doubt. Until now. Something had snapped in him when he'd met the fear in Alexa's eyes. What had he done to upset her so badly? Was he capable of doing to Alexa what the man who had fathered him had done to his mother? Had he gone mad without even realizing it?

The questions pounded through his head relentlessly, and with them a tangible pain formed somewhere between his heart and his stomach. How could he begin to tell her? What could he possibly do? Just thinking about it left him so consumed with fear that the very thought of admitting it verbally squelched any possibility of ever facing it. Could he live a normal life, knowing what he knew, fearing what he feared? It all left him so confused that he could only find one conclusion: he would have to try. And perhaps if Alexa loved him enough—or if he loved her—he could find happiness in spite of it all. He would just have to try.

❦   ❦   ❦

Alexa's relationship with Jess slipped quickly into a well-formed pattern. She and Jess spent a great deal of time together, but his affection never went beyond a quick kiss. With the wooling taken care of and another mortgage payment made, Alexa kept waiting for him to bring up marriage, but he never did. Whenever she tried to approach the subject, Jess either became flippant and started making jokes, or he quickly changed the subject. Alexa tried to rationalize that he was dealing with something, and eventually he would come around to the only possible turn their lives could take.

To Alexa, it was so logical and easy to think of being married to Jess that it was difficult for her to be patient. But she loved Jess with all her heart, and knew that patience was essential to a relationship.

When the mood seemed right, Alexa urged Jess to tell her what was bothering him. She became concerned and frustrated as he looked away with blatant pain in his eyes and flippantly told her that everything was fine. Her attempts to pursue it were answered with subtle anger, and Alexa felt she had no choice but to let Jess deal with it on his own. She only prayed that he would.

Sixteen
A GIFT OF FRIENDS

Alexa entered the bunkhouse at mealtime, but only stood at the head of the table until all eyes turned toward her.

"Aren't you gonna eat?" Jimmy asked.

"Not right now," she said. "I've got something to tell you. Jess is too proud to tell you himself. The bank just upped the deadline for the next payment because Chad Byrnehouse has offered a staggering amount to buy the property and free the mortgage. By moving the deadline up three weeks, it misses the upcoming race, which Jess needs in order to make the payment. Unfortunately, my brother has too many friends at the bank. Simply put, Jess doesn't have the money. He's resigned himself to losing it, boys. I know you're all thinking that you wish you could help, but you wouldn't know how, right?"

They all agreed.

"Well, you can. I have some things I'm going to sell, and with any luck it will make the payment. I don't need much from you except someone to take me into town, and . . . let me put it this way. If I go into the bank and make Jess's payment, the gossip is going to kill him. But if we can honestly say that we all pitched in, then there won't be anything shameful in it. It's our home as much as it is his, and he's given us all much."

Without a word spoken, each of them rose from the table and went to their bunks. Alexa started to cry as Murphy took off her cap and shoved a handful of money in it. "I've been savin' it, but there's nothin' to spend it on anyway."

Each in turn made his donation with a similar statement, Richard being last since his room was farthest away. But he made the biggest donation.

"When do you wanna leave?" Murphy asked.

"As soon as you're finished," she said, and he nodded. Alexa glanced down at the cap in her hands as they all sat back down to eat.

"Miss Alexa," Fiddler said as she turned to leave, "I think I can speak for all of us when I say that we appreciate your insight and courage. We are all truly grateful." His statement was followed by a chorus of amens and warm smiles in her direction.

"Thank you all," she said and hurried to her room. She put the money into a small satchel along with the bits she'd collected from Sarina and Mrs. Brown. Even Ben had made a donation. She then emptied her jewel box into it and changed into a skirt. With her hair quickly pinned up, she met Murphy just as he finished harnessing a horse to the trap.

Gallantly he helped her in and sat beside her. The drive was occupied with Murphy's stories of horse races and herding mobs that kept Alexa laughing much of the way. When they arrived in town, Murphy drove her to the appointed spot and drew the trap to a halt.

"What on earth are we doin' here?" he asked, noting they were at the boot-maker's shop.

"Surely you know that Mr. Lubin doesn't live in that nice house of his because of his skill at making shoes."

Murphy laughed and helped her down. He stuck close to her as she went into the shop and discreetly told Mr. Lubin she had something to sell that he might be interested in. The proprietor ushered them into a back room while Murphy whispered to her, "How did you know about this, Missy?"

"I sold some earrings once to bet on a race," she replied quietly, and Murphy chuckled.

"Did you win?"

"Enough to buy them back and more."

Murphy and Mr. Lubin both gasped as Alexa reached into her satchel and brought out piece after piece of fine jewelry. Mr. Lubin examined each one carefully and told her she was lucky, as he happened to have a buyer in mind and the cash on hand. Alexa knew it wasn't luck. She'd prayed about this.

Mr. Lubin quoted her a price and Murphy chuckled. "Come now, sir. You might can convince the lady that's all they're worth, but not me."

Mr. Lubin upped his price, and again Murphy bartered with him. When he quoted his third price, Alexa had to fight to keep a straight face.

"That's more like it," Murphy said. Mr. Lubin left the room and came back with a handful of bills that they counted through carefully. Alexa stuffed them in her satchel, and they left the shop with almost twice the amount she had hoped for. And she didn't feel the slightest remorse over the loss of her jewels.

As they drove toward the bank, Alexa said, "You know, Murphy, I'm not sure, but I think we might have enough to make a double payment." He looked toward her in surprise. "That would free him for another year, and then there would only be two more payments left. Think how far ahead he could be in a year."

"I think it's a great idea," Murphy grinned.

Alexa followed Murphy into the bank, where he took over the transaction in order to keep talk to a minimum. Mr. Hemming, the banker, seemed both surprised and disappointed, but there was little he could do when they dumped the bag of money on his desk and started counting. Alexa laughed when they came up with one pound over the amount for two mortgage payments, and Murphy made the banker sign a statement that Jess Davies was free and clear for another year, with the balance due clearly recorded along with the dates payments were expected, so that no more discrepancies could come in by way of Chad Byrnehouse.

On the way home they planned how to let Jess know, and returned just in time to gather up the boys before they all went to bed. With some quick work they fixed their gift for Jess, found Mrs. Brown and Sarina, and all went to the office together. Only Ben was absent, as he'd already gone to sleep.

Alexa knocked on the door, and Jess responded with a weary voice. She peeked her head in and grinned.

"Alexa—you're back. Richard said you'd gone into town to get yourself a few things, and—"

"Yes, I'm back," she interrupted, "and we want to talk to you a moment."

"We?"

She opened the door wide and the group sauntered complacently into the office. They gathered around the desk while Jess looked on, baffled.

"We have something for you," Alexa said, and Edward brought forward a large box wrapped in brightly colored Christmas paper. "I know it's the wrong time of year," she said as he set it on the desk, "but consider it early—or late—either way."

"What is it?" Jess asked, wary to touch it.

"Just a token of our appreciation," Murphy said.

"For a roof over our head," Jimmy added.

"And entertainment," Tod chuckled.

"And food to eat," Richard piped in.

"And someone who cares whether or not we're in the gutter," Fiddler stated warmly.

"And because we all love you," Alexa finished.

"Some more than others," Edward said, and they laughed.

"So open it," Sarina said. "I hate waiting."

"What is it?" Jess repeated, still dazed.

"A puppy," Fiddler said soberly.

"Oh, good," Jess laughed. "I always wanted one."

Still he hesitated, and Alexa said, "Come on, Jess, or I'll order Mrs. Brown to start watering your soup."

"She might have to anyway," Jess said a little too seriously, which made it difficult for the rest of them to keep from sniggering.

"I already do," Mrs. Brown said in a rare attempt at humor.

Jess finally tugged at the paper too slowly and opened the box lid with hesitation. He chuckled to find only an envelope in the bottom of the big box. His fingers trembled slightly as he picked it up.

The room became deathly silent as Jess pulled out the single page and unfolded it to read what it said. Feeling suddenly weak, he sat down. Jess felt ashamed when the tears spilled from his eyes, until he looked up to see that everyone else in the room was crying, too.

"I don't believe it," he said breathlessly. "What can I possibly say? How did you do it?" He chuckled. "I just don't believe it."

"We all just pitched in." Murphy mopped his face dry with his shirtsleeve.

"But two payments?" Jess said dubiously. "Do you know how much money that is?" They all grinned. "I guess you do."

"We'll be off," Edward said suddenly, ushering the group out the door. "It's past my bedtime." He feigned a yawn and they all did the same. Jess laughed at their ridiculous performance.

"Wait," Jess said and they all paused, huddled in the doorway. "Thank you. I owe you all my life."

"Now we're even," Fiddler stated, and Jess was left alone. He stared at the document for several minutes, trying to grasp the reality of it. Then he closed his eyes in humble prayer to give thanks for what he could only perceive as a miracle.

It wasn't until the middle of the night that Jess finally figured out where the majority of the money had come from. Without thinking his reaction through, he donned breeches and boots and grabbed his coat. He went into Alexa's room without knocking, and she didn't wake until the room became light and she saw Jess blowing out the match.

"What are you doing here?" she asked groggily.

"I want the truth," he said angrily, and she sat up straight.

"What are you talking about?"

"Where did you get the money, Alexa? I know that none of you have made enough from me to ever come up with half that amount. I want to know where you got the money."

"It's none of your business." She got out of bed and threw on a wrapper. "It was a gift, Jess. The money came honestly. That's all you need to know. Why don't you let your pride go and just accept it?"

He ignored her and turned to pull open a drawer. Alexa sighed as he picked up the jewel box and opened it to find it empty. He said nothing as he slammed the lid shut, put it back in the drawer and closed it.

"Go ahead," she insisted. "Let's have it. Lecture me, Jess. Tell me I'm a fool and I'm crazy and I must be out of my mind. You tell me little else these days."

Jess sat down and leaned back in the chair. He looked up at her with a depth of emotion in his eyes. "Why?" he asked.

"Because this station means a lot more to me than some stupid race horse. That's why!"

"Sometimes . . ." His voice was unexpectedly gentle. He paused and leaned his forearms on his thighs, cupping his hands in front of him. "I feel like everything I have is right here, and no matter how hard I try, it runs between my fingers and I can't hold on to it." His eyes shifted toward Alexa. "But you, Alexa, you put your hands beneath mine and catch it all as it slips through, then you give it back to me and help me tighten my grip a little. And if it falls again, you're there to catch it."

The theory sounded familiar to Alexa, but she was too touched to ponder where she'd heard it before.

"Why?" he asked again.

"Because I love you."

"I believe you do," he said, "and that makes me want to ask again: why? What is it about me that makes you give everything you have on my behalf?"

"Words could not explain, Jess," Alexa said gently.

"Oh, but they can," he said wistfully, and Alexa sat on the edge of the bed. "I am a man with empty pockets. I'm a dreamer. I'm a fool. I bet my life on eighty-to-one odds. I go through life year after year, existing on dreams that just sift through my fingers.

"But you, Alexa," his eyes filled with wonder, "you are like a series of endless rainbows that filter through the storms. During the day your eyes reflect the moon, and at night the sun burns through them. You have common sense and the ability to be positive about every-thing you touch. You love and you give. You give to me. A man with empty pockets.

"That allows me to draw only one conclusion." His voice turned cynical. "You must be out of your mind."

Alexa rose and moved across the room. She touched Jess's face and his eyes softened. "If I'm crazy," she said, "I don't ever want to know sanity." Jess came to his feet and embraced her. "Aren't you hot?" She pushed his coat open and realized he wasn't wearing a shirt. Alexa pushed the heavy coat to the floor and put her arms around him. "Take off your boots, Jess. Please stay a while. Hold me."

Quietly he sat on the edge of the bed to remove his boots, then he lay back as Alexa blew out the lamp. Jess sighed and pushed his arms around her as she lay close beside him.

"I love you, Jess." She laid her head against his shoulder and idly ran her fingers over his chest.

"I love you, too," he said, but he lay tense until he slept.

When Jess began to snore softly, Alexa allowed her emotion to overcome the painful barrier holding it back. She cried silent tears while her mind wandered through all of the questions that had drummed on for months now. What had gone wrong? How could she fix it? When would it end? The usual fruitless answers finally put her back to sleep.

She awoke when a knock at the door made Jess jump. "What time is it?" he asked groggily as Alexa came to her feet.

"Almost time for breakfast." She hurried to the door, tightening her wrapper around her.

"Good morning, Richard," she said easily, and he glanced over her shoulder to see Jess pulling on his boots.

"Do you think we could talk—sometime today?" he whispered.

"I don't see why not," she said warmly. "Why don't you come along when I take Crazy out for a run right after breakfast?"

"Thank you." He took her hand and squeezed it.

Jess moved to Alexa's side with his coat thrown over his shoulder. Richard eyed him speculatively. "Why don't you just marry her and get it over with?" he asked lightly, but Alexa caught the edge in it.

"Mind your business, Richard," Jess said without tone or humor. He kissed Alexa on the cheek, then eased past Richard and went down the stairs.

"Are you all right?" Richard asked.

"Of course," she said easily. "Why do you ask?"

"If you could see your eyes right now, you wouldn't have to wonder."

Alexa glanced down uneasily, not wanting her feelings read.

"Get dressed," he said, "and I'll walk with you to breakfast."

Alexa nodded and closed the door to change.

❧ ❧ ❧

Jess entered the stable to find Richard saddling Crazy and Alexa watching.

"Where you going?" Jess asked, ignoring Richard as he pulled Alexa into his arms and kissed her.

"We're taking Crazy and Demented out for a run."

"Will you have dinner with me tonight?" Jess asked quietly.

"I'd love to." Alexa smiled up at him and touched his face.

"Come early," he added, "and we'll go to the music room."

Alexa felt warm inside as she watched Jess leave, but reality broke in when Richard said, "I wish he'd stop playing games with you and get down to business."

"So do I," Alexa said wearily as Richard helped her mount. It wasn't until they'd galloped far into the hills and finally slowed to a trot that Alexa said, "So what did you want to talk about?"

"You," he said, and she looked surprised. "It's you that needs to talk, Alexa. I can see it every time I look at you."

Alexa dismounted and left Crazy to graze. Richard did the same and stood beside her. "It's Jess, isn't it. I heard the two of you arguing in the middle of the night."

"Of course it's Jess," she admitted. "But for the life of me I don't know what's wrong. I suppose I just have to be patient." Her voice turned hopeful. "I believe he just needs time."

"And in the meantime," Richard's tone betrayed a hint of anger, "he comes and goes as he pleases, and—"

"Richard," she interrupted, "if you think that because he spent the night with me—"

"Don't say it." Richard held up his hands. "I don't want to know."

Alexa realized he was thinking the worst, but she didn't know what to say. How could she tell Richard that, if anything, she feared Jess wouldn't have her if she forced herself upon him?

"Alexa," his tone softened when he saw her distressed expression, "perhaps I shouldn't say anything. Maybe it's none of my business." He touched her chin to make certain she was looking at him. "I am speaking as a friend, Alexa. Whatever may have happened between us in the past is irrelevant. Do you understand?" Alexa nodded firmly. "I'm concerned for you. I can tell you're not happy, and so can everyone else. You don't have to put up with it, Alexa." He paused and said strongly, "Don't let his insecurities destroy your happiness."

Alexa's eyes turned sharp, wondering how he had managed to voice what she hadn't wanted to admit. Was he so perceptive?

"It's good to be patient with him, but you've got to draw the line somewhere. How much can you give to him when you get so little in return? Eventually I fear you'll go dry and end up hating him."

His words kept driving the truth a little deeper, and Alexa had to lean against a tree as she suddenly felt weak. Richard took her hand as silent tears trickled down her face. "It's your happiness that concerns me, Alexa. Jess is a good man, and he likely just needs a push. But I don't want to see you stand back and watch precious time slip by while you're not happy."

"You're right, Richard," she said after a long silence. "It's not easy to face, but I know you're right."

"If there's anything I can do . . . ," he said in a tone of offering, and Alexa smiled up at him.

"You've already done so much." She squeezed his hand and looked at him with an expression of warmth. He wiped at her tears, and a tension she hadn't felt between them for months suddenly rushed back. When Richard turned quickly away, she knew he felt it too.

"Perhaps we should get back," he said and helped her mount.

"Let's race," Alexa challenged, and Richard laughed.

"You expect me to race Crazy and Alexandra Byrnehouse?"

"Just for the fun of it."

"Fine," he said, breaking into a gallop to give himself a head start. She won anyway.

Alexa felt good as they returned. Richard had said just what she needed to hear. Through the day she contemplated his advice, and decided that something had to change. She looked forward to having the evening with Jess, and rehearsed in her mind what she might say.

With some extra time, she impulsively rummaged through her trunks and found a pale pink gown that she'd not worn since her seventeenth birthday. It was simple but elegant, and it made her feel feminine as she surveyed her reflection in the tiny mirror.

She passed Richard on her way down the stairs, and he smiled in approval. "You look beautiful. If Jess Davies doesn't want you, he *is* crazy."

"Thank you, Richard." She kissed his cheek. "Thank you for everything."

Alexa went to the music room and sat to play while she waited for Jess. She rose when he entered the room. So many memories rushed back. All of the reasons she loved him flooded over her. Instinctively she moved into his arms and felt hope to see the affection in his eyes. Abandoning all rehearsed statements, she whispered close to his face, "Let's get married, Jess. Let's leave tonight; right now."

Jess chuckled and tried to ease away, but Alexa held her hands firmly against his back, making his attempt awkward. "Give me one good reason why we shouldn't," she urged.

Panic rose in his eyes and she wondered why.

"Tell me, Jess." She attempted to move closer. Jess took a step back, but she persisted. "Talk to me. If there is a reason we shouldn't elope tonight, tell me."

"The boys would be hurt if you didn't invite them to the wedding."

"If they want to go to a wedding, they can find their own brides. Try again."

"Surely you don't want to elope," he said lightly. "A girl like you should have a—"

"I want to get married, Jess."

"Must we discuss this now?" he asked, beginning to get edgy.

"When did you want to discuss it?" she asked, and he turned away. He made no response, and Alexa's desperation began to show. "It has been eight months—*eight months,* Jess—since you asked me to marry you. I'm starting to feel like there's something wrong with me, and you just don't want to hurt my feelings."

Jess's expression filled with alarm. "That's not true. You're a wonderful woman, Alexa. I love you."

"Then why are we still living this way?"

Jess made no attempt to answer.

"There was a time when I believed that you wanted me."

"I do want you," he protested.

"That's not the impression I get," she retorted calmly. "You kiss me as if I were your sister, and your embraces are tense and withdrawn."

"And tell me, Alexa my dear, what happens when they are not?"

"It's been so long I don't remember."

"Oh but you must," he retorted, "or you wouldn't have said what you just did." Alexa remained silent, wary of the edge in his voice. "You know very well what happens. You, who have made it clear you will not be had until you are wed, have no right to tell me that my affection is dispassionate."

"That isn't what I meant."

"What exactly do you mean?"

"I wonder why I feel nothing at all when you kiss me. Does there have to be passion for me to feel loved when I'm in your arms?" He didn't answer. "I don't feel loved, Jess. Why?" Still he hesitated. "You're holding something back from me, and I want to know why!"

His silence left Alexa frustrated, knowing from the past that she would get nowhere with this approach. It was as if a brick wall stood between herself and the reasons that kept him from loving her completely. While a part of him seemed afraid to be away from her, another part was afraid to get close. The result left her feeling utterly trapped.

Following her intuition, Alexa wondered if toying with his passion might spark enough feeling in him to broach the problem. However unfair it might be, she had to fight fire with fire.

Wearing seduction in her countenance, Alexa eased into his arms and looked up at him, hoping to convey the bewitching quality that Jess had said her eyes held. "Don't you want me, Jess?" she asked breathily. Jess tried to back away, but she held him tightly.

"Yes," he said coldly, "I do."

"Show me, Jess," she challenged. "Give me just enough to let me know you want me."

"You're playing a game with me, Alexa."

"You've been playing a game with me for months." Alexa kissed him but got little response. "If you could have me now," she breathed in his ear, "would you take me?"

"I can't have you now," he stated. "It's a pointless question."

"Not from my point of view," she said brashly, and kissed him with anger tainting it. She felt something spark in him but knew he was fighting to hold it back.

Jess saw fire in her eyes when she pulled away. She could see the moisture she'd left on his lips as he pressed them together. "I hate this, Alexa."

"So do I!" she said angrily, moving toward the door.

"Where are you going?" he demanded.

"*We* are going nowhere! That's why I'm not going to stand here and throw myself at your feet so you can trample on my heart and let it bleed all over the floor."

Jess caught her around the waist and kicked the door shut. "What do I have to say, Alexa, to make you believe that I love you?"

"I want honesty," she insisted. "You are hiding something from me that is tearing you apart inside, yet you stand before me and deny it time after time. What do I have to do to make you trust me? What can I say to make you believe that we could work it out if you'd only talk to me?"

"I don't want to talk, Alexa." He pulled her fiercely against him and she gasped. His kiss stirred fond remembrances that left her breathless.

"Jess," she cried as his lips went rampant over her throat. He found her lips again, and Alexa became powerless within his grasp. His kiss spoke of intimacies yet unexplored, and Alexa wondered why they weren't married by now.

Jess pressed his kisses over her face and tugged at her earlobe. "I want you," he whispered, and his breath rushed through her in a wave of goose bumps. "I love you. I need you. I want you with every fiber of my being."

Alexa trembled with delight and felt her conviction crumbling. She nearly hoped he would force himself upon her and take the decision from her hands. She was weary of fighting something she wanted so desperately, even though she knew it was wrong.

"Jess," she whispered, "I—"

Their escapade was interrupted as Sarina knocked at the door but didn't wait to open it. Without relinquishing his hold on Alexa, Jess looked up in question. Sarina didn't do well at hiding her astonishment as she stated, "Dinner is served, Mr. Davies."

"Thank you," he said, finally easing away. "We'll be in just as soon as . . . we're finished here."

Sarina nodded and left quickly. Jess met Alexa's eyes, and the rekindled passion hung thick in the air between them. Alexa longed for him to take her in his arms and start where they'd left off, but he only took her hand and led her to the dining room.

They ate mostly in silence, but a spark of passion lingered as he held her eyes through the candlelight. His expression became intent as he watched her more than ate.

"What are you thinking, Jess?"

"Honesty?" he asked, and she nodded. "I was exploring the urge to take you to my bedroom."

Alexa's heart quickened. "Marry me and I'll move in."

"That's an enticing thought," he said coolly.

"But not enticing enough?" she challenged. "Honesty?" she added when he made no response.

"I'm not ready to be a husband worthy of you."

Alexa was surprised but tried to understand. "If there's a reason you feel that way, we should talk about it."

"I can't."

"Perhaps it would be easier to talk about if we were married."

"It's not that simple, Alexa." His voice was smooth with sincerity. "Please try to understand. I realize I haven't been fair with you, but you must believe me when I say that I need you in my life."

"We can't go on this way."

"I know."

"No one can change it but you."

"I know that, too."

"But I will help you."

"I believe you would. But I have to take care of this myself."

"Forgive me if I'm jumping to conclusions," she said cautiously, "but does it have anything to do with my brother?"

His cheek twitched but he stated firmly, "No."

"Does it involve anyone else?"

"No," he stated, "just me. I'll take care of it."

"Will you?"

"Yes."

"When?"

"Soon," he said warmly, "I promise." He lifted his glass toward her and smiled. "I'm looking forward to sharing my bedroom."

Alexa lifted her glass in return, wondering why his promise left her feeling empty.

Seventeen
THE ULTIMATUM

The morning Sarina left to take Ben back to his grandparents, Alexa realized it had been over two months since Jess had promised this problem would be resolved. A sense of hopelessness seeped into her. Their relationship had fallen deeper into a pattern so unintriguing that she had to wonder if she wanted her whole life to be this way—married or not. Where was the Jess Davies she'd fallen in love with? The question struck so harshly that she began her day with the determination to end this waiting one way or another.

"What is it?" Alexa asked Jess as he slapped a saddle onto a stallion's back.

"What?" he replied blandly.

"What is it about me that makes you not want me?"

She couldn't tell if he was angry or just surprised, as his brow went up slightly. He bent to tighten the strap beneath the horse's belly. "What makes you think I don't want you?" He ducked beneath the horse to stand beside her. Without warning he kissed her with a hint of passion. If he kissed her like that more than twice a month, she might have believed he wasn't simply trying to make a point.

"Just look at us." She ignored the effect he had on her and stepped back. "Why are we going on like this?"

"We've discussed this before."

"But you never give me any answers. I want to know why I should sit here waiting to get on with my life, when there's no life left between us at all. If you need time, so be it, but if you're just putting off something that will never come about, let me know."

"Are you trying to tell me something?" He pulled on his gloves tersely.

"I'm telling you that I don't want my life to be like this forever. Is this all you want?"

"No."

"What do you want?"

"I want you." He grinned in an attempt to lighten the mood, but it didn't work.

"Under what terms?" she asked pointedly. Jess only mounted the stallion and looked down at her as if he didn't have a clue what she was talking about. Impulsively he took her arm and pulled her into the saddle with him.

"Where are we going?" she asked as he broke into a gallop with his arm protectively around her waist.

"Crazy," he stated, heading toward the hills.

"Jess," she said after an unbearable silence, "talk to me."

"What do you want me to say?"

Infuriated and upset, Alexa took hold of the reins and drew them back. She slid down from the horse and turned to glare at him. "Get down here, Jess Davies, and talk to me!" she demanded. He calmly swung his leg over and stood with his hands on his hips.

"I want to know," she persisted angrily, "why you don't want me!"

"I've told you—I do want you."

"And I ask again—under what terms?"

"Why do there have to be terms?"

"You just want it to be like this forever?" He looked away and his cheek twitched. "I want more than this, Jess. I want a home. I want children. What do I have to do to convince you that we could be happy together?"

"We are happy."

Alexa turned away and clenched her fists. "I'm not!" She turned back to face him. "We're going nowhere."

"Then why do you stay?"

"I love you, Jess."

"And I love you."

"So, let's get married."

"We will."

"When?"

"I don't know. When we're ready."

"I'm ready."

"I'm not!"

"Why?" she demanded. "I have a right to know why." He made no response but a blank stare, and she lowered her voice as she added, "A year ago you were more than ready to have a woman in your bed, but even that isn't enough to make you accept commitment."

"Oooh," he chuckled, "that's a good one, Alexandra."

Alexa swallowed her emotion and said straightly, "One day that attitude will destroy you, Jess. And I don't want to be around to see it."

She mounted the horse and turned it homeward. "Are you coming, or do you want to walk?"

His expression faltered slightly as he took hold of her waist and brought her back to the ground. "Why do you love me, Alexa?" he asked close to her face.

"Does there have to be a reason?"

"I want to know why you're willing to give your whole life to a man like me."

"You make it sound as if something's wrong with me."

"There's nothing wrong with *you,*" he said and let her go.

"Jess, I—"

"I don't understand why you want to marry me, Alexa. There's nothing in it for you."

"Are you trying to convince me or you?"

"I'm trying to tell you that perhaps it's a mistake."

"I thought you loved me."

"I do love you," he said directly. "That's why I have to wonder if I should let you marry me."

Alexa shook her head, and her eyes narrowed. She couldn't believe what he was saying. After all they had been through, would he dismiss their relationship so easily?

"Look at me, Alexa. I'm a streak of bad luck."

"And that's it?" Her hurt turned to anger. "In other words: Go away, Miss Byrnehouse. You're not worth the trouble to make this work."

"I didn't say that!"

"If I've misunderstood, you'd best clarify yourself. Talk, Jess! Make me understand."

"There's nothing to say," he stated, and she moaned in frustration.

"It's an excuse. It's all just a trail of excuses and rationalizations! I love you, Jess, but I'm not going to beg you to be mine. You want love without commitment. You want comfort without commitment. You want it all without taking any risks. Well, you won't get it from me."

"Alexa!" He grabbed her arm firmly. "I do love you."

"Show me!" she demanded. "Stop telling me and show me."

"How?" he asked just innocently enough to make her frustration unbearable.

"You figure it out!" she shouted. "All I ask is an opportunity to spend my life with you; a chance to prove to you that you are worth loving. You've got an ultimatum, Jess Davies. Either you marry me or it's over. I'm not wasting my time with this any longer."

"You make it sound so easy—so cut and dried."

"You make it too blasted difficult! I love you. You love me. Nothing else matters."

"I don't see it that way."

"There was a time when you did!" she shouted.

"Well, I don't anymore."

"Then find someone who can see it your way. I can't!"

Again she tried to mount, but he pulled her into his arms. "Don't give up on me, Alexa. Just give me more time."

Alexa sighed and attempted to swallow her anger. "How much more?"

"I don't know. I just need time."

"I've been giving you time, yet nothing changes. At this rate I'll be an old maid before you decide you don't want me."

"Soon," he said. "I'll come to terms with this soon. I promise." His eyes bored into hers, searching for a response. She sighed again and nodded slightly. Jess smiled with relief, then moved his face toward hers.

"Must you kiss me?" She turned away. "I lose all reason when you kiss me."

"Your problem, Alexa," he said, tilting her face to meet his so closely that his lips brushed her cheek as he spoke, "is that you're too blasted reasonable."

His mouth came over hers, warm and demanding. He pressed his hands to her back, urging her closer with a rare kiss that made her believe he truly did want her. "I do love you, Alexa," he whispered. "You must believe me."

"And you must believe me when I say that I can't take this much longer."

Jess nodded, then gave a flippant laugh as he helped her mount. They rode home in silence, and Alexa resigned herself to more waiting.

🐾 🐾 🐾

It happened when she saw the baby. Alexa went into town with the boys to pick up some things she needed. While she waited to be helped, a young woman stood close by with a tiny baby girl. Alexa marveled at the beautiful little hands and started a conversation with the mother. On the way home, she counted up the months and realized that she could have easily had Jess's baby by now, had they been married when they'd originally planned.

Long past her bedtime, Alexa sat in the trap where it rested in the dark carriage house. She didn't know what had gone wrong, but she knew that she couldn't fix it. She thought of that baby, and her arms nearly ached with maternal instinct. She thought of Jess telling her they would be partners in all respects, and wondered what had happened to the man who'd said that. They had talked about having children, about sharing all aspects of their lives. But all those dreams had somehow shattered, and she didn't even know why. She had the skill and knowledge to win his races, but she was baffled about how to change his heart.

The darkness seemed to tighten around Alexa as she swept all hopes and aspirations from her mind to see the situation as it really was. Jess was not going to change. He was a good man, but would loving him be worth it if he couldn't see his own value? Would he ever let her love him if he didn't? At first, she felt too numb to cry. It was as if she'd just learned that a loved one had died. But as she stopped to ponder the reality that had to be faced, a smoldering emotion rose up to choke her until she had no choice but to cough it out. An acute loneliness left her weak, and she curled onto the seat of the trap, sobbing helplessly against her arm.

"Alexa." A warm hand touched her shoulder and startled her. She lifted her head enough to recognize the shadow looming above her.

"Richard." Embarrassed and afraid, she sat up abruptly and mopped her face with her sleeve.

"Don't tell me." He stepped into the trap and sat beside her. "Jess is at it again."

"I suppose he's at it still," she managed to say between whimpers. Richard's arms came around her, and Alexa hesitated only a moment before she allowed the emotion to spill. Time had no essence as she cried and held to him. One by one, the dreams she had woven with Jess became unraveled in her mind until there was nothing left but a mass of tangled yarn that only Jess could untangle. But she knew he wouldn't do it.

For a long while after the tears had gone dry, Richard held her in silence. Comfort encompassed her in his embrace, finally urging her to admit aloud, "He'll never change, Richard."

Richard sighed. "It's hard to change a man, Alexa. It takes circumstances to change a man." Alexa lifted her head to look toward him. "Circumstances changed me," he went on, "and I'm grateful for them, however horrible and drastic they were. I believe suffering endured makes a better man."

"Then surely you are one of the best."

Richard chuckled. "I'm just an ordinary man, Alexa. I know there are always ways to strive and improve."

Alexa wanted to tell him he was everything Jess Davies wasn't—or rather, everything Jess used to be. But she couldn't bring herself to outwardly compare them. It was impossible.

Another long silence made Alexa's embarrassment return, and she sat up. "I'm sorry," she muttered. "It seems I'm always unburdening myself on you."

"It is my pleasure to ease your burdens." He took her hand.

Alexa squeezed it with affection. Their friendship had been so comfortable these many months that she had almost forgotten he'd once admitted to deeper feelings. It was easy to relax against his shoulder and present her problem.

"I gave him an ultimatum, Richard," she sighed, "and still he will make no commitment. Am I to spend my life only longing for him and gaining no fulfillment at all? Is it wrong of me to be so impatient?"

"I'd say you've been more patient than a hundred other women would have been." His voice lowered melodically. "You are entitled to seek out your own happiness, Alexandra."

His words buoyed Alexa with a formless hope, but silent tears of regret accompanied the feeling.

Through another silence, Richard contemplated the moment. For months he had struggled daily on where to stand as he observed the relationship deteriorating between the two people he cared for most. He'd done his best to just stand back and allow them the room and the time to work it out. He'd long ago accepted the fact that Alexa's love for Jess was something he couldn't change and couldn't resent. And his own commitment to Jess was something he didn't take lightly. They might as well be brothers for all they'd been through together. He only hoped that Jess would forgive him for what he was about to do. Richard's conscience told him he'd done nothing to influence what had happened here. But he was about to change that.

"Alexa," he whispered, feeling his heart come to life, "I can give you what you want."

Alexa held her breath, then slowly eased away from him. "What are you trying to say, Richard?" Her voice trembled.

Richard took a deep breath. "I'm giving you an option."

His implication assaulted Alexa with such force that she scrambled out the other side of the trap and ran up the stairs to her room. She leaned against her door as if it might protect her from the feelings she'd just tampered with. Her mind raced in heated circles. The paths lay open before her, and the consequences of taking each one glared blatantly. She couldn't deny the light glimmering on the path she'd just been offered. Or had she? Perhaps she had misunderstood.

Richard's boots on the stairs startled her to the moment. How could she have been so rude, to dash away like that when he'd been so kind? Ignoring the dark side of this situation, she experimentally pushed Jess out of her mind and opened the door as he reached the top step. He stopped, and she felt his questioning gaze through the darkness.

"I'm sorry," she muttered. "It's just that I—"

"I understand," he said when her words faltered. "Really, I do. But perhaps I should clarify myself."

"Perhaps you should," she said with a calm voice that belied what was happening inside her.

"Alexa, my deepest wish is for you to be happy. If Jess is what you need to make you happy, then I have every hope he will change and be able to give you what you want."

When he said nothing more, Alexa felt the need to test him. "It appears he will never change."

Richard's hesitance made her wonder if he was as afraid as she to admit what was happening. "As I said, I'm giving you an option. Think about it." He moved toward his door, but she stopped him with a hand on his arm.

"Richard," she sought quickly for the right words, "I'm tired of not knowing where I stand. Don't walk away from me with vague allusions."

A moment of fragile stillness preambled the words upon which Alexa's future hung. In one swift movement he eliminated the space between them and took her arms into his hands.

"I love you, Alexa." His voice cracked with a combination of ardor and fear. "I've done my best to stand back and let you love Jess. I've tried to be your friend because that's the way you wanted it. But I can't stand by any longer and let him hurt you this way. I love you." He pulled her close to him and rummaged his hand through her hair. His lips bathed her brow with an unconcealed adoration that stirred Alexa to respond. She clutched his shoulders, starved for what he offered. The intensity of his affection reminded her of how long it had been since she'd experienced any at all.

"Close your eyes, Alexa," he whispered.

"But it's dark."

"Not dark enough. Please—close your eyes."

She did as he said, and his lips hovered over her ear. "I want you to imagine the man I am beneath the surface. Don't look at me with your eyes, Alexa; see me with your heart."

"I see you," she whispered, and he took hold of her chin to tilt her face upward. Alexa held her breath as he timidly touched his lips to hers. His kiss was reserved until he felt her respond, then something seeped into it that left her breathless.

"Marry me, Alexa," he whispered against her face. "I don't expect you to forget Jess, or even stop loving him. I understand how you feel, and I don't ever want you to stop sharing those feelings with me. All I ask is that you accept me for what I am, and I will do everything in my power to make you happy."

A part of Alexa ached to accept his offer immediately, to settle her future once and for all. But thoughts of Jess left an empty hole. She had to step back and look at all aspects carefully. By returning Richard's affection, she had already stepped into a circle of betrayal. Whichever road she chose, one of these men would end up hurt.

"I . . ." She opened her eyes but still could hardly see him, "I don't know what to say."

"I don't want you to make a decision under duress, Alexa. We're talking about a lifetime. Think about it in the light of day. Take as long as you need. I'll still be here."

Alexa nodded and stepped back. "We should try to sleep."

Richard pressed a final kiss to her brow and went quietly into his room. Alexa spent a sleepless night pondering her dilemma. She was glad when the sun finally came up and she made the decision that she would get on with her life, one way or another.

She was brushing through her hair when a page slid beneath the door, and there was no sound at all following it. Before she picked it up, she opened the door but saw nothing, which made her certain that Richard must have quietly closed his door. There seemed no other explanation.

Alexa closed her door and picked up the paper. Richard's offer made the words tug at her heart more poignantly as she realized it was an extension of one she'd received earlier.

> *In the mirror I see a man*
> *but the reflection shows a beast.*
> *Beauty is not afraid of the beast in me.*
> *She entices it to come out and show itself.*
> *She, with her courage wants to battle it out—*
> *The winner takes my heart and soul.*
> *Beauty's love can conquer the beast in me.*

Alexa tacked it up with the others and said nothing about it when Richard came to her door a few minutes before seven.

Despite his lack of sleep, Richard's heart raced as Alexa opened the door. Still clad in a nightgown and wrapper, she looked almost angelic, even with the weariness about her eyes. He was surprised when she motioned him inside and closed the door. Her normal response would have been to ask him to wait while she got dressed. When she didn't seem prone to speak, he finally asked, "Are you all right?"

Last night's emotion resurfaced, and Alexa shook her head. She put a hand over her mouth in an effort to control it, and was relieved when he took her into his arms.

Richard wondered if her emotion was an attempt to tell him she couldn't marry him. He hardly dared breathe without some indication of how his offer had affected her. He lifted her tear-stained face to his view with a questioning gaze.

"I love you, Richard," she murmured. He swallowed hard and let out a long breath. "I can't compare my feelings for you with those I have for Jess. And I won't try. It's just too different. But I . . ." She closed her eyes and nuzzled her face against his chest. Richard pressed his hands to her upper back to hold her tighter. "I need you," she cried.

"I'm here." He pressed his lips into her hair. "Tell me what you want me to do, and I'll do it."

"Just hold me," she whispered. Richard still wasn't sure if she was considering his offer, but the likelihood increased when she tilted her face upward and beckoned him to kiss her. Genuine affection poured from her, and he thought he'd melt into the floor from the ecstasy. Though his years of loneliness protested, he kept his passion carefully guarded, knowing he was treading into a delicate situation. When she drew back to look at him, there was a light of hope in her eyes that mirrored how he felt.

"I have to talk to Jess," she said firmly, though her voice was tainted with ardor.

"I understand." He wiped at her tears with his fingertips. "Alexa," he took a deep breath, knowing it was something he had to say, "if you decide to decline my offer, whether you marry Jess or not, I will not let it change the way I feel about you. We will be friends forever—no matter what happens."

Alexa felt peace settle into her. She marveled at his goodness as she recalled all they had shared.

"And Alexa," he continued, wanting to be free of any doubt between them, "you must consider what it would be like living with a man like me." Her eyes narrowed in question. "You're the one who would have to look at me—every day, every hour. We could not go into public without—"

Alexa put her fingers over his lips. "I can see you with my heart, Richard. It is irrelevant." He sighed and pulled her closer. "If I marry you, it will hurt him terribly. He won't understand the reasons. It will tear him apart."

"I know."

"And it will be hard on you, Richard."

"And you."

"I fear it could end up coming between us."

"Not if we don't let it." He touched her chin to look at her. "Don't ever stop telling me how you feel, Alexa. Don't let secrets interfere."

Alexa nodded stoically and stepped back. "I should get dressed. We're missing breakfast."

Richard waited on the stairs until she was ready, and they walked together to the bunkhouse. Nothing appeared to be out of the ordinary, but she wondered if the boys could sense the changes taking place. They all knew of the tension between her and Jess, but how would they react if she decided to go through with this?

As the boys finished eating and left, Alexa found herself alone with Richard. He took her hand across the table. "I'm riding out to check some fence lines. Would you like to come along?"

"No, thank you." She squeezed his hand tightly, as if it might sustain her. "I've got to find Jess. I'll see you later and . . . we can talk."

Richard nodded his understanding and left for the stable. Alexa found Jess in his office, and he smiled widely when he saw her.

"Good morning, my love," he said jovially, and she wondered what reason he had to be happy. Did he know that his indifference was on the verge of drastically changing his life?

"Good morning," she replied.

He turned his attention to his book work, muttering that he'd be done shortly and they could go out for a ride.

"I don't want to ride," she said, and he glanced up in surprise.

"What?" He laughed. "Alexandra Byrnehouse doesn't want to go riding? Are you ill?"

"We need to talk," she said, and his expression faltered.

"About what?" he asked dryly.

"About us, Jess. You said you needed a little more time. You've had ample in my opinion. What will it be?"

"I love you, Alexa, but I—"

"No more buts, Jess!" she shouted, leaning over his desk. "Either you love me or you don't. If you love me, you can give me more than a room in the carriage house and a good-night kiss. I want more!"

"So do I," he said quietly.

"Then take it! Good heavens, I'm offering you everything. I don't understand why marrying me is so utterly distasteful to you."

"I never said it was."

"You didn't have to!"

"Calm down, Alexa. There's no need to be angry and—"

"I *am* angry! I'm sick to death of having you toy with my emotions because you're not willing to face yourself enough to know what you want from life. There is something in you that you're using as an excuse to hide from reality, and you'll let it eat at you until it destroys us both. I have tried to help you find yourself, Jess. I have tried to show you that I'm not afraid of what you fear, that together we can face it. I have tried to love you. But I can't! I can't because you won't let me. And I won't fight it anymore."

She hit her fist against the desk, then stopped to catch her breath. Jess stared at her in dazed silence.

"What do you want me to do?" he asked with no emotion.

"Let's talk about it, Jess."

"Talk about what?"

"There is something hurting you. You know it as well as I. You've as much as admitted it. Let's talk about it, Jess."

"You're taking a lot for granted," he accused, moving his eyes away.

Her voice lowered fiercely. "You expect honesty, but you won't give it to yourself, let alone me. And until you do, we will never be happy."

Jess met her eyes with something cold hovering in his. "Maybe you'd be better off without me. Maybe I'm doing you a favor to let you go."

Alexa took a step back from the desk as if she'd been struck. She was grateful for Richard's confession of love that caught her heart as it fell. "Are you saying that you're letting me go?"

Jess bit back the emotion and wondered if he meant what he was saying. He wanted Alexa so badly. He loved her. But could she ever begin to understand the reasons behind his concern? He didn't want to let her go, but he felt certain they would have another chance. She was upset, but she'd been upset before and she'd always come back. He wanted to believe that he could put all of this behind him, but he needed time. It was all so painful that he didn't know where to begin.

"Well?" she insisted.

"I don't want to let you go, Alexa. I want to marry you, but I'm just not ready. I need time."

Anger tightened Alexa's jaw, and she turned away abruptly. "Time to do what?" she demanded. "Put it off? Stall a little longer? Let the problem go a little deeper?"

"Alexa, please don't—"

"I think I need to get away for a while." She turned again to face him.

"Where will you go?" he asked in alarm.

"I don't know. It doesn't matter." She swallowed hard. "Jess, if you think there's a chance we can work this out, then let's talk about it. If not, then I just need to leave and deal with it. It's up to you." She attempted to penetrate him with her eyes as she added, "I give you no promises once I walk out this door."

Alexa saw the panic in his eyes, but was it enough to make him stop her?

"Good-bye, Jess." She put her hand on the knob.

The silence hung so tensely that Alexa felt the room would collapse. In her mind, she could hear the words she longed to have him say. *You're right, Alexa. Let's talk. Please help me.* Her heart fell a little further when he came to his feet with a terse, "Will you come back?"

"I live here," she stated. "I need this job."

Alexa gave him one last, hard glare, then drew all her courage and left the room, closing the door loudly. The finality bit at her, and she had to put a hand over her mouth to keep from crying out. She leaned against the wall for a moment to support herself, then she ran down the hall.

Jess finally found the momentum to move out from behind the desk. He wanted so badly to stop her, but he didn't know what to say that would make any difference. Instinctively he walked to the door and hesitated only a second before he opened it and stepped into the hall.

"Alexa," he called and she turned breathlessly, not daring to hope.

Jess sensed the expectation in her stance, but he was at a loss for words. Deciding that he would come to terms with this soon and talk to her about it when she came back, he simply said, "Take care of yourself."

Alexa swallowed her hopes and lifted her chin. "That is exactly what I'm going to do," she called back, then turned and ran outside.

Frantically, Alexa packed. Only one thought focused in her mind: she had to get out of here. The pain of Jess's rejection blinded all else. A knock at the door startled her. She both hoped and feared it was Jess, but she was not disappointed to see Richard.

It was easy for Richard to see that Alexa had been crying. The question was why. There was so much he wanted to know but didn't dare ask. Before he could think of a place to start, his eye was drawn to the evidence that she was packing.

"Where are you going?" His voice became frantic. Was she leaving both him *and* Jess?

Alexa resumed stuffing things into her bag, hoping to fight back any more tears. "There's a train to Brisbane."

"Brisbane? But . . . why? Alexa, if anything I said has—"

"I just need to get away, Richard."

He took hold of her arm. "Alexa, what happened?"

Alexa closed her eyes and bowed her head. "It's over, Richard. I'm not going back to him."

Richard's heart missed a beat. "Alexa." He took her shoulders and forced her to look at him. "Don't walk away and leave me wondering."

Alexa's expression changed abruptly as she forced Jess deep enough that she couldn't feel him, and replaced the pain with her love for Richard. "Meet me there." Hope glimmered in her eyes with the tears. "Give me a few days to gather my wits, and . . . we'll get married right away."

"Alexa." He breathed more than spoke her name. "This is happening so fast. Are you certain? Do you want to think about it, or perhaps—"

"Richard," she interrupted, "just wait a week, then take the next train to Brisbane. I'll meet you when you get off."

"Are you certain?" he had to ask again.

"Yes." She bit her lip. "Don't tell Jess. I don't want him to know until it's done."

"I understand," he said quietly, then he couldn't hold back any longer. He pulled her into his arms and laughed. "I can't help being happy, Alexa. I only pray he'll forgive us."

"He'll have to."

The spectrum of what they were doing descended as Richard bent to kiss her, holding nothing back. Alexa fused to him, losing all fear in his affection. She marveled at the way it stirred her. The way he held her made her long to live life completely, to experience all a woman was intended to. For the moment, it was easy to forget Jess and all he meant to her.

"Alexa," he murmured against her face, "I love you. I love you with all my heart and soul."

Alexa buried her face against his throat. "I love you too, Richard. I do."

Reluctantly she eased away. "I've got a train to catch." She returned to her packing. "Murphy is taking me to the depot. I thought it would be better that way. You probably should tell the boys, but as I said, I don't want Jess to know. Not yet."

"I promise."

Alexa closed her bag and looked around the room to make certain she had all she needed. Finally, her eyes rested on Richard. "I'll meet you in Brisbane."

"I'll be there."

"I must go."

Richard stepped aside and motioned toward the door. Alexa walked past him, then turned back in the doorframe. Looking up at him, she recalled the moment they'd met, in this very spot.

"Richard," she felt the need to clarify, "I can't promise that I'll stop loving him."

"I know."

"And I won't apologize for the way I feel."

"I wouldn't expect you to."

She sighed. "Do you really believe we can be happy, in spite of everything that's happened?"

She didn't like the way he hesitated until he answered firmly, "I'm absolutely certain of it."

Alexa nodded and started down the stairs, pausing again to find him right behind her. Their lips met by some instinctive gravitation.

Alexa laid a warm hand over his chest and felt the quickened rhythm of his heart.

"Be careful," he whispered. "I'll be counting the hours."

Richard walked her outside and helped her into the trap. Murphy scrambled up beside her and took the reins. She squeezed Richard's hand, then turned and waved as they moved away. A bittersweet peace settled inside her until she caught a glimpse of Jess standing on the side veranda. She pretended not to see him as they rode past. Instead, she set her eyes on the road ahead as they wound away from the house. In that moment, she vowed to never look back.

Eighteen

IRREVOCABLE CHOICES

As soon as Alexa left, Richard set out to build a future for her. He'd had a private plan formulated in his mind for months, but he never dreamed it would come to pass—and so quickly.

When his work was finished, Richard went to the big house to talk to Jess. He wasn't surprised by the glum mood he found him in, but he ignored it and pursued his request.

"I have something I'd like to ask you," he said, and Jess showed polite attention. "You know, of course, that the old house hasn't been used for years. I was looking at it recently and had an urge to fix it up. How would you feel about that?"

Jess shrugged his shoulders. "Why?"

"It was my home once. I must say I miss it on occasion. And there are times when the carriage house gets a bit gloomy. I've got a little money put away that I could use. I just wanted to know if it's all right with you."

"I don't see why not," Jess said. "Someone might as well live in it. I can help you out some."

"We'll work it out." Richard smiled. "Thank you."

"No problem," Jess said distantly.

"Is anything wrong?" Richard asked.

Jess looked surprised. "No, why?"

Like Alexa, Richard wanted to know they had given Jess every chance. As an extra precaution he asked, "Nothing you'd like to talk about . . . with another man?"

Jess hesitated and Richard held his breath. "No, but thank you anyway."

Richard thought how easy it would be to turn away and justify to himself that this was right. He'd promised Alexa he wouldn't say anything to Jess, but still, he had to be sure.

"Jess," he said carefully, "I know there are problems between you and Alexa that—"

Jess glared at him sharply, then sighed. "It's that obvious, eh?"

"Did you think it wouldn't be? We're all concerned for you, Jess. But we're concerned about Alexa, too."

Jess pushed a hand into his hair, then scratched his head as if it might make him think clearly. "As you should be, I suppose." He sighed again. "Did she tell you why she left?"

Richard nodded and fought the urge to tell him the whole truth. If he ignored Alexa's wishes and confronted this now, would it make a difference?

"She's pretty disgusted with me." Jess leaned back in his chair carelessly, but Richard sensed the anxiety he was trying to mask. "I can't say that I blame her." His eyes became distant. "But I'm going to miss her." Jess swallowed hard and met Richard eye to eye. "She's a strong woman, Richard. She'll do all right."

In spite of everything Alexa had told him, Richard was surprised. "Can you let her go so easily?"

"I can't see that I have any choice."

"Choices are what you make them, Jess." He took a deep breath and said what his conscience demanded. "I can tell you when and where to find her if you—"

"I can't, Richard." Jess's voice bordered on fear. "Not yet. She'll come back."

"Can you be so sure?" Richard asked severely.

Jess chewed his bottom lip a moment. "Maybe she would be better off if she didn't."

"And what about you?"

Jess looked at Richard harshly, a blatant coldness seeping in to replace any fear or regret. "What about me?" he asked defensively. "I can take care of myself."

Richard felt a deep empathy for Alexa's frustration. He wanted to take Jess by the throat and choke some sense into him. "I'm sorry you feel that way, Jess," he stated firmly. "But I can't be sorry for whatever Alexa decides to do with her life." At the risk of sounding brash, Richard added, "She deserves a man who will not leave her to face the world alone."

Jess wanted to be angry. He wanted to take all of this pain out on Richard. But Richard was only reiterating a truth that Jess knew all too well. Ignoring all emotion, Jess chuckled and shrugged off the reality. "You're likely right about that." He looked at the wall and his cheek twitched. "She's probably better off without me."

"I hope you're saying that because it's what you truly believe, not because it justifies something you're hiding from. If you don't go after her now, Jess, you could end up a very lonely man."

Jess gave him a blank stare. "Was there anything else?"

"I'll leave you to your business," Richard said tersely. "Thank you again. I'm going to start working on the old house tomorrow."

"Oh, Richard," Jess added and their eyes met, "leave the studio as it is. You understand."

"Yes," Richard said gently, "I understand."

Jess was amazed at what Richard managed to do with the old house in just a few days. He coerced the boys into helping him, and Jess even put in a little time on the project. The house brought back memories for Jess. As it came together, he couldn't help recalling the childhood he'd spent there.

He was surprised when Richard went into town and bought new lace curtains for the windows and a spread for the bed. In less than a week, the house was almost like new.

"What's the hurry?" Jess asked as he walked through to survey the results.

"I'm going out of town for a few days," Richard said, "and I wanted to move right in when I get back."

"Where you going?" Jess asked. This was not like Richard to venture into the world.

"The city," he replied as they stepped out onto the porch. "You can do without me for a week or so, can't you?"

"Oh, of course." Jess was certain it would probably be good for Richard. He didn't understand this change in his lifelong friend, but at the moment there were other matters pressing on his mind. He looked toward the hills and wondered when Alexa would come back—if she came back.

❦   ❦   ❦

Alexa waited tensely at the depot, hoping Richard would be on the next train as he'd said he would. Her time alone in Brisbane was the most difficult she had ever faced. Worse than either of her parents' deaths, or even being disowned, was the anguish she faced in making this irrevocable decision.

She wondered if she was being impatient, if she should give Jess more time. But instinct told her he would never change, at least not under these circumstances. And she didn't know how to change the circumstances.

The questions were difficult to answer. She loved Jess and knew she always would. The road she was choosing would not be easy for any of them. But an undeniable peace settled into her when she thought of a life with Richard. Through much prayer and contemplation, she felt certain, for whatever reason, that her decision to marry Richard was right.

Alexa's heart thumped audibly when the train whistle sounded in the distance. She wrung her hands with nervous excitement as it ground to a halt. She felt a fluttery rush to see Richard step off, wearing a flat-brimmed hat pulled low over the left side of his face. He smiled when he caught her eye, and she beamed. They laughed as they came into each other's arms and he kissed her.

"I feared you wouldn't be here," he admitted.

"Why wouldn't I?" she asked, and kissed him again.

"You made your decision quickly, Alexa—and under stress." They walked together alongside the parked train. "You were very upset with Jess when you left."

"And I have thought it over carefully in the time since."

"Have you changed your mind?" He stopped and took both her hands into his. Alexa was aware of people regarding him oddly, but he paid no mind.

"Richard, I feel strongly that whatever I once shared with Jess is over. It has reached a dead end. I do love you, Richard, and the prospect of becoming your wife makes me very happy."

Richard laughed and embraced her.

"I already bought a gown," she said with enthusiasm, and he smiled. "I hope you don't mind. I found exactly what I wanted."

"Why would I mind?" He laughed. "I just can't believe this is happening to me."

"I have a room nearby. You can freshen up, and then we'll make plans over dinner."

Richard kissed her again and they walked on, holding hands. His presence alone gave her a growing reassurance that she was doing the right thing.

They were married quietly in a little church on the outskirts of the city. As the ceremony began, Jess crowded into Alexa's mind, making her momentarily angry. She didn't want anything to mar the happiness of this experience. But as she looked at Richard, a warm peace filtered over her. His aura seemed to tell her that he could read her thoughts and he understood. Alexa's anger melted into compassion. She felt sorry for Jess. It should have been his wedding, his ring on her finger, his kiss sealing a lifetime commitment. But he had thrown it all away for the sake of his fears. With perfect confidence, Alexa spoke her vows and embarked on a new life as Mrs. Richard Wilhite.

The reality of being his wife struck fully as he carried her over the threshold of a dimly lit hotel room and kicked the door closed. Alexa turned to look at him, her husband. She certainly had been aware that this would be a part of their marriage, but perhaps in the way this had all come about, she had not stopped to ponder it as thoroughly as she should have. She simply did not feel prepared, and she knew that he sensed it.

Searching for a distraction, she thought of the young man who had ushered them to their room, and the way he'd regarded Richard as he was given a generous tip. "It's difficult for you, isn't it," she said. He looked bewildered, and she clarified her statement. "The way people don't know how to react to you."

Richard sat on the edge of the bed to remove his boots. "You can't blame them. You must admit it's awfully gruesome."

"It doesn't bother me," she said, and he smiled.

"That's only one of the reasons I love you."

The conversation stopped there, but Alexa expected something to be said or done to preamble what was meant to take place. Richard only extinguished the lamps and began unfastening the long row of buttons down her back. The gown fell in a heap around her feet. Despite the darkness, Alexa felt vulnerable. The expertise he had once admitted to became evident. She soon became oblivious to anything but this, and grateful to finally know what it really meant to be a woman. Then, just when she thought something wonderful was going to happen, she realized it was over.

Richard kissed her once more and eased away. He could see now that he'd been a fool to assume she'd done this before. If he'd taken the time to consider the possibility, or even ask her, he might have been more careful. He realized then that his experience with women had been during a time in his life when he was not proud of his character. Looking back, he was often appalled at his behavior. Perhaps he needed to forget what he knew and learn to be a lover that meshed with the man he had become. He wanted to say something to Alexa, to somehow apologize. But any conversation he could begin on the subject would bring them back to Jess. Alexa nuzzled close to him, and he kissed her brow. They could talk about it tomorrow, he decided, and slept in her arms.

Serenity filled Alexa as she pondered what had just taken place. It was not as she'd imagined it to be, but there was consolation in recalling her mother's frank discussions of such things. Lovemaking evolved with time and a growing familiarity. Alexa felt sure that time would help her understand and appreciate an intimate relationship.

Recalling the events of this day, she had to admit that everything had been wonderful. Richard loved her, and she knew it. His adoration was evident each time he looked at her. The prospect of their life together filled her with peace. Then why, she wondered as she stared at the ceiling above her, did she feel this subtle, lonely ache?

Alexa awoke to daylight, tangled in Richard's arms. Just seeing him made the ache fade, and she moved closer. She watched as he came awake, and she greeted him with a kiss.

"Good morning," he said.

"Did you sleep well?" she asked, and he grinned.

"Never better."

Alexa's expression sobered, and she gingerly lifted her hand to touch the scarred side of his face. Abruptly he turned his head, but she urged him to face her and continued to study the scars with her fingers.

"You mustn't be ashamed," she said gently. "They are a part of you, and I love you as you are." His expression showed disbelief at her indulgent attention to what he considered ghastly and grotesque. "How would you feel," she asked cautiously, "if you could go into public and not feel uncomfortable?"

"It would be great," he said, "but it's impossible to—"

Alexa touched her fingers to his lips. "I've been thinking, for quite some time actually, that I could take a soft, thin piece of leather, and if I worked it just so . . ." She moved her fingers over the border of his scars, across the bridge of his nose and onto his cheek. "I think you would feel more at ease."

"A mask?" His voice betrayed intrigue.

"A very distinguished mask. Of course, it would just be for going into public. I prefer you this way."

"I never would have dreamed of such a thing."

"If you like the idea," she smiled, "I will start working on it as soon as we return home. I'm not terribly skilled with a needle, but I think I could manage."

"Yes," he touched her face with adoration, "I most certainly like the idea."

Alexa kissed him, and he urged her closer. The thoughts he'd fallen asleep with came back to him. "Alexa," he hesitated, "I'm sorry if I . . . hurt you last night."

Alexa put her face against his shoulder to avoid any eye contact. She kept waiting for him to continue, but his silence made it evident he either didn't know what else to say, or he was expecting a response. She had often considered her mother to be brash and unconventionally open on such matters, but she was grateful now for the things she'd been told at a young age. "Such a thing is expected the first time, is it not?" she asked quietly.

"That's the point, Alexa," he said, and she lifted her head to look at him in question. "I'm trying to apologize. I should have taken more time." When she still didn't seem to understand, he added carefully, "I didn't expect to be the first for you."

"What made you think otherwise?" She tried not to sound disturbed.

"Forgive me, Alexa," he said gently, "but I know how much time you spent with Jess. I had to assume by the hours he often kept that—"

"Must we discuss this?" she asked sharply and backed away.

"Alexa, there is no point pretending that things are different than they are. We're not going to stop talking about Jess just because we're married. You will never convince me that what you felt for him has magically disappeared because of what you and I have now shared."

"I don't want to talk about him." She sat up and pulled the sheet beneath her arms.

"I know you don't, and that's why I brought it up. Don't start hiding your feelings from me. If we talk about it and you don't have to feel like you're keeping secrets, it's less likely to come between us." Alexa's expression softened but she said nothing. "We have to go back and face him, Alexa. We can't ignore his feelings for you—or yours for him."

Alexa marveled at his wisdom, but didn't know what to say.

"Talk to me," he whispered, "the way you always have."

"I'm afraid to go back," she admitted. "I don't want to face him. I don't want to hurt him, but I know it will. And I'm afraid of how his pain will make me feel."

"And how is that?" Richard squeezed her hand.

"It takes so little for him to push all my anger away." She leaned her head back and sighed deeply. "He has a way of making me feel so . . . oh, I don't know. I can't explain it." Her focus turned to Richard. "But you must understand that those feelings have nothing to do with you. They don't make me love you any less, and they will never make me regret marrying you. But you are right. I cannot deny that I . . . ," she closed her eyes, "I love him, Richard."

He leaned over to kiss her in a way that spoke of the intimacies they had shared. "Then I'll just have to keep you distracted," he smirked. "But," he kissed her again, "I have every hope that one day you and Jess will be friends—just as you and I have been."

"Do you really believe that's possible?"

"I do," he replied with confidence, "though it may take time. I doubt he'll accept this easily."

"I can't even comprehend what it will be like when we go back." She pushed her fingers into his hair as his lips blazed warm trails over her shoulder.

"It will be incredible." He lifted his head and grinned. "I fixed up the old house for us."

"You did? When?"

"This last week, of course. The boys helped. Even Jess did a little."

"You didn't tell him that—"

"I promised I wouldn't."

"You are so good to me," she said, and he kissed her warmly. Taking time to savor each moment, Richard saw a new perspective of himself emerge. This was a new experience for both of them. For the first time in his life, Richard was making love to a woman he loved. He wondered how he could have ever done it for any other reason.

Alexa's contentment deepened as the tension of the previous night receded. She became totally absorbed with Richard, and thoughts of Jess faded into oblivion. When it was over, they held each other quietly until Alexa's stomach rumbled and Richard laughed.

"I think that means it's time to begin the honeymoon." He swung his legs over the edge of the bed to pull on his breeches.

Alexa leaned against his back and wrapped her arms around him, gently kissing his shoulder. "I love you," he murmured, and Alexa knew she could face anything.

❦ ❦ ❦

Murphy stopped Jess on his way out of the stable. "I think Richard will be back today," he said in a cautious tone.

"How do you know?" Jess asked, wondering why it seemed so important. The uneasiness in Murphy's eyes wasn't natural.

Murphy hesitated before answering. "He sent a letter from Brisbane." Jess lifted a curious brow. "Says he got married and he'll be home today."

"Married?" Jess laughed. It was the last thing he'd expected to hear, though it certainly explained his interest in the house. "I didn't think he had it in him," he said idly. "Where did he come up with someone to marry? He doesn't know any women except . . . Alexa." The name pressed through his lips hoarsely, but Murphy had turned away and gone into the stable.

"Murphy!" Jess grabbed his arm. "What else did he say?" Murphy appeared calm, but something in his eyes made Jess nervous.

"That's all the letter said." He told Jess the truth, but he didn't bother to mention the talk he'd had with Richard before he left.

Not wanting to look like a fool, Jess let Murphy go and tried to tell himself the idea was ridiculous. He hit a fist against his thigh and moved briskly toward the house, feeling something inside tear at him as he pondered the coincidences. Alexa was gone. Richard was gone. She'd left saying this was the end. She had given him no promises.

"She wouldn't!" he said aloud as he strode into his office and slammed the door, leaning against it heavily. "She wouldn't do it!" He covered his head with his arms and clenched his teeth.

Jess paced the office tensely, wondering if it could be possible. Richard didn't know any other women—except Mrs. Brown and Sarina. Not only was Mrs. Brown here, she was old enough to be his mother. Maybe it was Sarina, he thought with a ray of hope, but he couldn't recall seeing them hardly exchange a word. And Sarina was in the outback with her family. It just didn't feel right. Perhaps Richard had been exchanging letters with an old acquaintance, and it had come to more. But if that were the case, wouldn't he have said something? Richard had always been open with Jess about the happenings in his life. Or had he? He'd said many times that the only people he knew were on this station. He'd hardly shown himself in public for over ten years. He'd been afraid of women since the day he lost half of his face. But not Alexa; he was often with Alexa. Alexa cared for him. She'd admitted it a number of times. Jess had always assumed it was no more than that. But now he wondered if something had been there all along that he simply hadn't seen. Going over the months since Alexa had come here, he recalled the dark mood Richard had fallen into when he had first become involved with Alexa. Jess had attributed the tension to Richard's typical moodiness. Had Alexa known even then that there was more to it? It all began to make sense. Now he understood. Had Richard loved Alexa right from the start?

"No!" Jess cried, and his pacing quickened. "They wouldn't do this to me! They wouldn't!"

The office gradually got dark, but he didn't feel the motivation to even light a lamp. He sat in his chair, then went to the window, then sat in another, then paced again, wondering what he'd done to deserve this. Finally he tried to tell himself he was blowing this out of proportion. There was no evidence that it was true; there were only his deranged ideas.

"It's ridiculous," he said aloud, then he wondered if Richard had returned yet. Quickly he went out, certain that he would realize it was all a mistake. Richard would be here with some other woman. Alexa would come back soon, and they could somehow work all of this out.

His heart quickened when he saw a light on in the old house. As he got closer, he could hear the sounds of celebration floating out. The familiar fiddle was playing, and Jess realized the boys were having a wedding party. He wondered why he hadn't been invited.

The question stuck in his throat as he pushed open the door without knocking. The fiddle stopped, and all eyes turned toward him as the front room became still. Jess felt his knuckles turn white as his grip tightened on the doorknob. He met Richard's gaze, full of empathy but no regret. Then he met Alexa's. She was in Richard's arms, her hand resting against his shoulder. She wore a gold band on her finger that caught the lamplight sharply. Her eyes showed compassion—and something else. What was it? Contempt?

"Hello, Jess," she said with genuine warmth, but he gave no response. It took moments of silence for Jess to pull himself together enough to dare move or speak. He wasn't about to give even a clue as to how he was crumbling inside.

Finally he drew back his shoulders and stated, "Let's not party too late, boys. I want everyone on the job an hour early tomorrow." He calmly turned and closed the door, then lumbered toward the house, dazed, shocked, and completely alone. This feeling could only compare to the night he'd lost his mother. But then, his pain had been caused by his enemy. Now, he'd been betrayed in the deepest way by the people he loved most. He numbly made his way to his bedroom, where he locked the doors to be alone in his anguish.

❦ ❦ ❦

Life quickly settled into a familiar routine for Alexa and Richard. Alexa spent her time working with Tod and the horses. Richard went quietly about his business. The boys were always around. They ate in the bunkhouse, and Alexa wore breeches the majority of the time.

She was undeniably happy. She loved the little house and relished living there with Richard. Each moment with him deepened her con-

tentment, and she hoped that life could always be this way. She began
working on a leather mask, and found it slow but rewarding. It added
to a sense of peace that was only impaired by one thing—the complete
absence of Jess Davies.

Alexa kept watching the big house expectantly, waiting for Jess to
appear, feeling afraid in a way she couldn't define. She knew the marriage would hurt him, but surely he had the strength to face it. What
could possibly make him not show himself for four days?

She casually inquired of all the boys, but no one had seen or heard
anything, and no one dared ask. Finally, Alexa made up her mind to
face him. She couldn't change what she'd done, and would not let herself wonder if she wanted to. But she couldn't deny that she loved Jess,
and she was concerned for his welfare.

"Where is Mr. Davies?" she inquired of Mrs. Brown.

"Holed up in his room," she reported. Alexa moved past her and
bounded up the stairs, with Mrs. Brown following. "He's not eaten for
days." Her voice betrayed relief at having someone to share her burden of concern. "I keep askin' what's amiss, but he just yells at me and
wants t' be left alone."

"Fine, thank you," she said, but the housekeeper lingered as Alexa
approached his door. She knocked loudly but no answer came. She
tried the knob but it was locked. "Jess!" she called, hitting the door
with her fist. Still no answer.

"The sittin' room door's locked, too," Mrs. Brown reported.

"Get me the key," Alexa demanded. "Hurry."

With sweating palms and a pounding heart, Alexa persisted with
no response until Mrs. Brown returned. She turned the key in the lock
and pushed open the door. The rank odor of liquor made Alexa wince,
and Mrs. Brown scrambled in her apron pocket for a handkerchief to
cover her nose.

The room was dark and stuffy, and it took a moment for Alexa's eyes
to adjust. The bed was torn apart and empty liquor bottles were scattered
about, but she couldn't see Jess. Searching frantically, she found him
sprawled over the floor on the other side of the bed. Mrs. Brown gasped.
Alexa was almost sure he was dead as she went to her knees beside him.

"Jess," she cried and turned him over, pulling his head into her lap.
He showed vague signs of life, but she couldn't get him to respond.

"Get Richard," Alexa ordered Mrs. Brown, "then prepare a bath—now!"

Mrs. Brown scurried away. "Jess," Alexa repeated over and over. Her tears fell over his face as she tugged at his hair and gently slapped him. "Please, Jess," she cried. "Don't you dare die on me."

"What is it?" Richard nearly ran into the room. The scene before him answered his question, and he took over trying to rouse Jess. "Stupid fool!" he said under his breath.

"I didn't think he'd react this way," Alexa muttered.

"I didn't either," Richard admitted.

When Mrs. Brown had the bath prepared, Richard hoisted Jess up beneath the arms and dragged him to the tub, where he literally pushed him in. Jess choked and gasped himself awake to avoid drowning. He shook his head with a breathy, "What the . . ."

"Stupid fool!" Richard repeated, shoving his head under the water and dragging it back up while Jess choked and spit water. "What are you trying to do, kill yourself?"

"Oh, leave me alone!" Jess snarled and tried to sit up in the tub. His hand went over his eyes and he gave a guttural moan. He moved his hand to see Richard still there. Pointing to the door, he shouted, "Get out of here!" Jess moaned again and leaned back in the tub, pressing his hands over his temples.

"Maybe we should talk about this, Jess," Richard said.

Jess scrambled awkwardly out of the tub. "I have nothing to say to you," he growled, teetering a little.

"I can't blame you for being upset, Jess, but if we—"

"You deceived me." Jess staggered toward him.

"You're drunk, Jess."

"Not drunk enough," he retorted. "You were the only man alive that I believed I could turn to, and you betrayed me." Jess swung back and launched a fist into Richard's face.

In Jess's condition, Richard hadn't expected the blow to have much impact, but he reeled back against the wall, briefly dazed. Fortunately, the effort did Jess in and he fell to his knees, pressing his head into his hands with a painful groan.

Alexa rushed to Richard's side. "Are you all right?" she whispered, and he nodded.

"Get out!" Jess muttered without looking up.

Alexa read more concern than hurt in Richard's expression. "Perhaps you should leave us alone," she whispered. Richard looked hesitant, but he nodded his understanding and ushered the curious Mrs. Brown from the room.

By the way Jess cursed under his breath, he apparently thought he was alone once the door closed. He groaned and pushed his hands through his wet hair.

"You *are* trying to kill yourself," Alexa said. He looked up gingerly, as if the pain in his head was unbearable.

"What are *you* doing here?" he hissed.

"I want to know why you're up here drinking yourself to death."

Jess came awkwardly to his feet and looked at his wet clothes with disgust. "What I do is my problem."

"Oh," she retorted, "and you really believe you can become a martyr and gain something by this?" He said nothing. "Look at yourself, Jess. What are you doing?"

He sat on the floor abruptly, as if he couldn't stand any longer. His hands went into the air in a defeated gesture, then he tugged brutally at his hair and groaned.

"Jess," she said, but he made no response. "Look at me!" she demanded, and he did. "You can't do this to yourself. It won't change anything."

His expression deepened, and he looked suddenly sober. She felt his eyes absorbing her fully, as hard as green ice. "Get out of here," he demanded in a voice so low she could barely hear him, but with an edge to it that bit deeply. The confusion she had been fearing rose up to choke her. All she could do was run.

In the darkest hour of the night, Alexa stood at the window of her new home, staring toward the big house.

"Are you regretting it?" Richard's voice startled her.

"I'm sorry if I woke you." She softly evaded his question.

"I never went to sleep." He paused and cleared his throat. "Are you regretting it?" he repeated.

Alexa looked toward the sky and answered with a firm, "No." She rubbed the chill from her arms. "But I have to talk to him."

"I know." After a long moment's silence, Richard quietly went back to bed.

At first light, Alexa dressed and moved to the porch steps to watch the sun come up. When it had filled the sky, she closed her eyes and basked in its warmth, almost dozing from exhaustion. A door closing across the yard startled her as the first evidence of human life broke the stillness of morning. She watched Jess lean against the veranda rail and press a hand over his eyes, as if the light was torturous. His other hand cradled a snifter of brandy. She knew she'd get no better chance than this.

Deftly and with determination, Alexa crossed the yard and stepped quietly onto the veranda. Without so much as a glance in her direction, Jess muttered, "What do you want?"

"We need to talk, Jess."

"There's nothing to say."

"Nothing?" She couldn't hide the emotion in her voice.

A minute later, he finally turned to look at her. He staggered to a chair, more weak than drunk, and took a long swallow of his liquor. Their eyes connected, and she stepped slowly toward him. "Alexa," he said breathily, "why?" She turned away, and he came unsteadily to his feet. "Why?!" he shouted and took her arm firmly, leaning on it for support. "I want to know why!"

"I love Richard," she stated, trying to remain calm.

"More than you love me?" he questioned.

"As much as. It's different."

"Couldn't you have at least . . . warned me . . . or something?"

"I gave you an ultimatum. You let me go."

"You said you were going away to think about it!" he shouted. "I only needed time."

"Time?" she retorted, pulling her arm from his grip. "I gave you time. I gave you everything, Jess Davies, that I could possibly give." Her voice softened and she looked down. "I had no more to give. But Richard . . . he gives back to me. He *revives* me." She met his eyes courageously. "There. That's my honest answer. That's why I did it. I did it for me. I knew it would hurt you, and I knew it would be hard on Richard. I did it for me. I'm not going to let you hurt me, Jess, and I pray you'll have the sense to not hurt yourself. I'm not worth the anguish."

"And that's it," he stated dryly, backing toward a chair to sit carefully. "I'm just supposed to forget what it felt like to hold you in my arms and hope that we could always be together. Do you think I can walk out there every day and pretend I don't see you with him? Am I supposed to come home every night and pretend the house doesn't feel empty? Don't stand there and tell me this is going to be easy."

"I didn't say it would be easy, Jess, but it's done."

"Yes," he said satirically, "it's done. You've done it, all right. You've neatly ruined both of our lives."

"My life is not ruined," she protested. "You know Richard is a good man."

"Yes," he said bitterly, "Richard is a good man. What does that make me?"

"Do you want to hit me, too?" she retorted.

"My life is ruined!" he shouted.

"Only if you let it be."

"Oh," he chuckled dryly, "no problem. It's all in my hands. Now I should pick myself up and start over, when I didn't have anything to start with in the first place. My life was *nothing* before you came into it. And now it's worse!"

"Jess, you can't blame me for—"

"I can do whatever I want! You work for me. He works for me. And work you will."

"Oh, so you're going to punish us?"

"Punish?" He laughed. "I'm going to *torture* you. Do you know how I'm going to do that, Alexa? Every time our eyes meet, you're going to remember—just like I'll remember. You're going to think about what might have been. You might be happy, Alexa, but you'll never be content. What we had, Alexa, was a once-in-a-lifetime magic. You'll never find it again."

Alexa fought tears as truth rang in his words. With a cracking voice, she spoke in her defense. "What we had once was gone, Jess. You let it go, and I could do nothing more."

Jess retaliated truth with the venom of his hurt. "I didn't turn my back and leave you, Alexa, but this is not over yet. I hope you're miserable. I want you to be every bit as miserable as I am right now."

"You're mad," she sneered.

"Yes," he laughed, "I am. In fact, I'm downright crazy. You're better off without me, Alexa. You made the right choice, but I hate you for it. There! That's honesty. That's how I feel. I *hate* you, and I *hate* Richard."

"Jess," she said as gently as she could manage, "you can't destroy yourself with this. I know you're hurt, but—"

"Yes!" he shouted. "I am hurt beyond endurance. But I'm not going to let anyone destroy me—especially you!" He stood carefully and pointed a threatening finger at her, saying through clenched teeth, "I will not let a Byrnehouse destroy me."

Alexa gazed numbly at him, failing to cover the pain, not knowing what to say. He met her eyes, and his cold expression faltered. "Alexa," he whispered and lifted a hand toward her. Before she had a chance to take it, he glanced toward it and his eyes hardened. Clenching his fingers into a fist, he pulled back with a groan of frustration. "Go away, Alexa," he said coldly. "Get out of here. Leave me in peace."

Alexa forced herself to walk away and try to forget how much she loved him. Her tears quickened with her footsteps. She had to get home. Home to Richard. She needed him now more than ever.

"Richard." She was breathless as she came through the door.

He turned expectantly, obviously waiting for her. Had he been watching from the window? "Are you all right?" he asked.

Alexa shook her head and moved into his arms. He held her while she cried, then she urged his lips to hers and kissed him urgently. "Love me," she whispered, holding desperately to him. "It always goes away when you love me."

Without hesitating, Richard pulled her into his arms and carried her to the bedroom. He kicked the door closed and placed her on the bed. "Everything will be all right," he whispered, lying beside her. "Don't worry, my love. Everything will be fine."

Richard kissed her and pulled her closer, but a part of her just couldn't believe him.

Nineteen
SHADOWS FROM THE PAST

Jess quickly made good on his promise to torture Alexa. But she wanted to tell him that every time he met her eyes with pain in them, or made a biting comment about the circumstances, he was only driving her closer to Richard.

Alexa inevitably turned to her husband for love and comfort. He gave her the sustenance she needed and more. They were both aware that Jess was hurting, and they continued to discuss it openly. But they had to agree there was nothing they could do. Jess simply had to face it on his own.

From outward appearances, Jess seemed fine much of the time. He came and went and saw to his business, but they all knew he was drinking more than he should, and no one hardly dared speak to him. His tongue was sharp and his attitude cynical.

Alexa often wondered how the boys felt about this turn of events. They were openly supportive of this marriage, and each in turn had let her and Richard know that they understood. But still, it was easy to see their concern for Jess. They cared for him as she did, and the situation was not easy for any of them.

Alexa kept telling the others they should be patient and kind to Jess regardless, and eventually he would get over the hurt. But it seemed he never would. Alexa was at least glad that Ben had gone with Sarina. He would never understand the situation, and Jess's attitude would have likely hurt him.

Richard and Alexa traveled with Crazy and Tod to participate in a race in Victoria. Murphy and Fiddler went along to assist. They all invited Jess to come, but he boldly declined. Still he was pleased when they returned with a healthy purse for winning. He said he was going to put it away for his next mortgage payment, but Richard suspected he didn't. He commented once that it was a good thing Alexa had made two payments on Jess's behalf, since it appeared he was drinking up the money that should have paid the next one.

Gradually Jess lost his cynicism, or at least became not so apt to show it. Instead, he became melancholy and seemed lost in another time. Only then did Alexa begin to comprehend where the real hurt lay.

She generally never had trouble sleeping. Her days were always full, and it was rare that she didn't go to bed exhausted. One night, hearing noises above her, she wondered if this was the first time they had occurred since she'd moved into the house, or if she'd just slept through it previously.

"Richard," she whispered. The pounding of her heart compelled her to nudge him. "Richard—wake up."

"What is it, love?" he asked groggily.

"There's a noise upstairs in the attic."

Richard tilted his head to listen, then he sighed. "It's Jess."

"Jess?" she asked in surprise. "What on earth is he doing in the attic?"

"Probably . . . looking around," he said noncommittally, then rolled over in an effort to go back to sleep.

"What's up there?"

"Just some . . . storage. Don't worry about it, Alexa. Go back to sleep."

Richard was soon snoring softly, but Alexa found it impossible to sleep as subtle noises continued filtering through the ceiling. She speculated on what it could mean. Was there a side to Jess she didn't even begin to understand? Yet Richard seemed to take it for granted. Wouldn't he have told her if it was worth knowing?

Quietly she slipped out of bed and put on a wrapper. Coming into the parlor, she saw Jess's shadow move past the window, and her heart quickened a little. She waited a few minutes, then lit a candle and went out to the side of the house where stairs led to the attic.

Carefully she moved up and tried the door. It came open easily and she peered in, almost afraid of what she might find. Holding the candle high, she was pleasantly surprised to see that it was nothing more than a studio. There was a partially finished painting on an easel, with a stool in front of it and oils and brushes scattered as if they had been used today. Thick dust was the only evidence that it had sat untouched for years.

Other than the painting paraphernalia, there was little else in the room. A small sofa and a couple of chairs were the only furnishings. The ceilings sloped nearly to the floor, except for a single gable with a large, curtained window. The room felt cozy, but there was a haunting quality that sent a shiver through Alexa.

"His mother," she whispered aloud, and her heart went out to Jess. Did he feel so alone that he had to come here in the middle of the night to feel close to his deceased mother? How he must have loved her, to have left this room as it was after her death. Of course everything else of hers would have been destroyed in the fire. Perhaps she'd kept the studio here from the days when they had lived in this house.

Suddenly chilled, Alexa left the room and closed the door tightly. She wished there was something she could do to help Jess find the peace she knew he was seeking. But past evidence told her she was powerless in that respect.

The following morning, Jess paraded into the bunkhouse to interrupt breakfast with some instructions. His hard expression made it difficult for Alexa to imagine him pondering over his mother's studio in the middle of the night.

It wasn't unusual for him to assign a specific job to each of the boys when extra maintenance was needed, but Alexa was surprised when he said, "Richard. Could you and your *wife* please clean out your rooms in the carriage house so they'll be ready if we ever need them."

Richard nodded, but Alexa avoided his eyes and was grateful when he left. "I'll see to it," Richard said as they rose from the table. "You'd best get Crazy out for her run, then you can help me finish up."

Alexa kissed him and Murphy said from behind, "You two are always kissin'."

Alexa blushed and Richard laughed. She returned from riding and went to her old room in the carriage house. Richard met her at the top of the stairs.

"Good timing," he said and kissed her. "I just finished up. There are some things of yours I left on your bed. You can do what you want with them."

"Thank you. What are you doing now?"

"Fiddler and I have fence lines to check. I think we're taking lunch out with us, so I doubt I'll see you before supper."

Alexa gave an exaggerated moan of disappointment, and he laughed. "I think you'll live until then, love." He pulled her against him and gave her a demanding kiss that left her weak with longing. "But that'll give you something to look forward to."

Richard left and Alexa went into her old room, relishing some memories and wanting to be free of others. She wondered what she might have left here, since she'd been certain to take everything to the house right after her marriage. Lying on the bed were a hair-comb she had lost months ago, a pair of shoes that she hated, and the box Chad had given her that she'd slid under the bed in an effort to forget it.

Alexa scooped up her belongings and took them to the house to put away. She nearly slid the box under the bed again, but something compelled her to at least look inside. She found nothing but letters. There were several, in handwriting she didn't recognize, and some in her mother's hand that appeared to have never been sent—or perhaps returned to her after they'd been read.

Impulsively she picked one up and opened it, wondering what Chad might have hoped to accomplish by giving them to her. The script was eloquent and distinctive, but the letter was old, and Alexa had to move into the sun to read it.

My dearest Faye,

I saw you today at the races. Like so many times before, it was difficult to not just take you in my arms and let the secrets go. I'm not certain you saw me there. If you did, I must say you did well in acting uninterested. I know that's the way it has to be, but I hate it.

I couldn't help noticing the child. She's growing beautifully, and I am still astounded to realize she is mine.

Alexa stopped when she realized these letters were from her father. Hurriedly she glanced over the rest of them, finding the content much the same. He spoke of longing for Faye, of hating the lying and hiding, wishing he could claim his daughter, and a great fear of being found out, brought on by something awful that had happened to someone named Emma. The name struck a chord of familiarity, but Alexa couldn't recall at the moment where she'd heard it.

Since the day Alexa had learned she was not Tyson Byrnehouse's daughter, she had inwardly resented the man who had fathered her. But reading his letters filled her with the poignancy of his love for her mother. Still, she was certain they had gotten involved by choice. But even that rationalization was squelched when she read on.

You know it should have been me, Faye. Your marriage should have never taken place. What you and I shared is a once-in-a-lifetime magic. He came between us knowing full well that you loved me, and I wonder if I can ever forgive him.

Empathy rushed through Alexa so strongly that she almost dropped the letter, as if it had burned her hands. Perhaps she understood her mother more than she wanted to believe. Perhaps Faye hadn't been selfish and wanton, but unhappy and preoccupied. Still, Alexa deeply resented the choices made by her mother that had brought so much pain into so many lives.

The letters written by her mother were much the same, full of longing, frustration, and an equal amount of concern over how their daughter's life would be affected if she were to know the truth.

Alexa became so lost in her emotions that she missed lunch. She longed to know the identity of her father as a warmth filled her on his behalf, but each letter was only signed with an artful letter B.

Written on a bulky envelope at the bottom of the box were the words, *You said you wanted one of these.* Alexa looked inside and found an engraving used for sealing wax. Examining the letters more closely, she realized that each one her father had written was sealed with it, but they had been broken and were difficult to decipher. The engraving was backwards and she had trouble making it out, so she went to her desk and melted wax that she pressed the stamp into. Clearly she read JBD.

The initials meant nothing to her right off, but the insignia looked dreadfully familiar. Alexa pondered over it briefly while she rummaged through a drawer and found the blue silk scarf Chad had passed along to her. She felt sure it was a gift from her father. As her thoughts were carried further away, Alexa scolded herself for getting so caught up in this. She stuffed the scarf into the box with its contents and shoved it under the bed. She hurried to the bunkhouse, hoping lunch wasn't too long over. Her emotion had left her feeling a little lightheaded and extremely hungry.

"I thought you'd get here sooner or later," Edward said as she entered the bunkhouse. He set a plate before her with a flourish.

"Thank you, Edward." She smiled warmly. "You are good to me, as always."

"Nah, it's the other way around," he said and returned to the kitchen.

When Alexa was finished eating, she hurried to the stable to catch up on some of her missed work. But thoughts of her mother's letters kept filtering through her mind, and she found it difficult to concentrate. She was most disturbed by wondering what Chad had hoped to gain by giving them to her. She knew him too well to believe it was just a kind gesture, as he'd pretended. Had he simply hoped to get her to return home by stirring her sentiment? But those letters contained nothing but an affirmation that she didn't belong at Byrnehouse.

Alexa stopped and sighed, leaning her head against a saddle hanging beside her. The lightheadedness hadn't gone away. She opened her eyes as she lifted her head, and directly in front of her, like the answer to an unspoken prayer, lay an exact replica of the wax engraving. The only thing that made the coincidence believable was that she'd seen the insignia many times each day she'd been here. It was embossed in the saddles, branded on the animals, and carved over the door of the stables. She wouldn't be surprised to find it monogrammed on handkerchiefs.

"Oh, no," she whispered aloud as the only possibility struck her harshly.

"What was that?" Murphy asked from behind and startled her.

"Nothing," she said distantly. "I was mumbling. Murphy?" she added, and he paused to give her his attention. "What does the insignia stand for?"

He glanced at it and chuckled. "You haven't figured that out by now?" She was almost certain, but wanted to reassure herself. She shook her head and he said in mock grandeur, "Jesse Benjamin Davies." She looked contemplative and he added, "I'm certain it's been around for years."

"Of course," she said quietly, and he went back to his work.

A painful knot grew in Alexa's stomach as she attempted to comprehend the reality.

"What's up?" Murphy asked Fiddler when he rode into the stable. Alexa was distracted by a brief surge of panic. She knew Richard was supposed to be with him.

"Fence lines are down," he said, and Alexa relaxed. "We've got mobs roaming the mountains. Richard's gone up to start looking, but it could take a while. We need some food and bedding and one more man."

"I'll go," Murphy said.

"I'm glad you're here," Fiddler said to Alexa as he dismounted. "Richard told me to tell you he's fine, he loves you, and you have something to look forward to."

"Tell him I already knew that," she smiled, and Murphy chuckled.

Still absorbed with her recent discovery, Alexa left the stable and idly wandered to the other side of her house where a tiny cemetery was situated, surrounded by a black iron fence. She wasn't surprised by what she read on the stones, but the reality made her nearly sick. Side by side were the stones of Benjamin Davies and his wife, Emma.

Tears blurred Alexa's vision as she knelt and brushed her fingers over her father's name. The knot in her stomach suddenly tightened and she wrapped both arms around her waist, curling around them with an anguished groan. The knowledge of her paternity left her stunned. But far outweighing it was a bewildered gratitude that she had not married Jess, or made love with him. Oh, the treachery they had fallen into because of their ignorance! If only they had known the tangled web their parents had woven. She understood now the feud that had existed between these two families. It was easy to see why Tyson Byrnehouse and Ben Davies hated each other. They had both loved the same woman.

Is that why Chad had given the letters to her? But it seemed that he had been doing her a favor to try and keep her and Jess apart. If he had known about this, why hadn't he just come out and said something?

Numbly, Alexa rose from her knees and wiped her tears away. It wasn't going to be easy, but she had to tell Jess.

Alexa threw open the dining room door and Jess rose abruptly, startled by her entrance.

"What's wrong?" he questioned. Not only was it evident by her appearance that she'd been crying, but she hadn't stepped into this house since the day she'd found him drunk soon after her marriage.

"I have to talk to you." Her voice trembled as she came toward him.

"What?" He moved to meet her, and their hands clasped instinctively.

"Oh, Jess." She met his eyes fearfully. At his expression she quickly averted her gaze. What business did he have to look at her that way? He might be unaware of the blood they shared, but she was still another man's wife. "Finish your dinner," she said, "then we can talk."

"I've had enough," he stated. "Let's go in the other room." He silently led her down the hall to the east parlor, where he urged her to a sofa and sat beside her. "Now, what is it?" he asked gently.

She met his eyes, seeking courage, but her shoulders slumped weakly and her face turned pale. "Jess," she finally said, "tell me about your father."

"My father? You came here like this to talk about my father?"

"Please."

Jess couldn't guess her motives, but he did his best to comply. "He was a wonderful man. What can I say? He was a hard worker, a good example. He was like a friend to me. What has that got to do . . ."

Alexa put her hand over her mouth and began to weep, leaving Jess frustrated by his ignorance. "Alexa, please tell me!"

"Do you remember," she began falteringly, "when Chad brought me a box of my mother's letters?"

"I remember. You put it under the bed, and . . ." He trailed off as the memory caught him sharply.

"I came across that box today. Richard found it just where I'd left it. I started reading her letters, and . . ." She looked at him deeply, her expression pained. "Jess," she cried, "Benjamin Davies is my father."

Jess narrowed his eyes, trying to grasp it. "Are you sure?" he asked softly.

"It was all there. Letters from him to my mother. He talked about me, the affair they'd had, the torment he felt, and . . . Jess, do you know what this means?"

Jess stood abruptly as he realized her implication. "It's a lie!" he muttered. "It's nothing more than one of your brother's ploys to destroy me."

"It's not a lie. It was all there in the—"

"Do you remember when he brought those letters?" Jess shouted.

"He was trying to tear us apart." He laughed cynically. "Too bad he went to all the trouble."

Alexa's hurt deepened, but she pushed it away. "Jess, it's true. You are my half-brother."

He looked at her dubiously, dazed and confused.

"Face it, Jess. It's better that it turned out this way. I am grateful, Jess, that we never . . . I mean, when I think how close we came to . . ."

His eyes hardened. She saw anger rise in them.

"Tell me what you're feeling, Jess," she said gently, perhaps hoping this revelation might do for him what it had done for her. Despite the poignance, it eased her regrets concerning Jess to know it would have been wrong for them to be together. "Please, Jess," she urged. "Talk to me. It's so—"

"I am *not* your half-brother, Alexa."

"I know it's difficult, Jess, but—"

"I am not!" he repeated and stormed out of the room.

Alexa tried to swallow her emotion and left the house as quickly as possible. She wished Richard was here. She needed his shoulder that was so accustomed to her tears, and his sensitive heart that was well-rehearsed in absorbing her troubles. Not understanding Jess's reaction, or why he wouldn't believe her, she hardly knew what to feel and longed to talk it through.

Past midnight, a knock at the door roused Alexa from a sleepless bed. She wondered if Richard was all right as she went to answer it. She was surprised to see Jess standing on the porch. He hadn't been here since the night he'd discovered her marriage. He said nothing until she motioned for him to come in, and he sat in the overstuffed chair, leaning back wearily.

"I apologize," he said with his eyes closed, "for the way I reacted earlier. I can understand how you must be feeling."

Alexa hadn't seen him behave so rationally since her marriage. She had every hope that this would help him face up to the circumstances and get on with his life.

Jess opened his eyes to look at her standing nearby, holding her wrapper tightly about her. He wondered when Richard would be back, then he reminded himself of his reason for being here.

"It's quite a shock, Alexa, to think of my father being . . . Well," he glanced away uncomfortably, "I'm several years older than you. If it's true, then I have to look back on my childhood and realize that my father was . . ."

When he faltered, Alexa said, "I understand, Jess. I know it's difficult."

He met her eyes, and for the first time since her marriage, there was an absence of his hardened pain. Memories absorbed her, and she wondered if it was simply habit that made it hard to believe he was her brother.

"May I see one of those letters?" he asked, and she went into the bedroom to get the box. Cautiously he opened it and saw the silk scarf lying on top. He looked at Alexa while he slid it through his fingers. He remembered Chad giving it to her and what she'd said about it. But something lurched inside of him to see it now. Jess knew Ben Davies, and this was just the kind of thing he would give the woman he loved. Watching the silk slide over his hand, he became distracted by the color—as blue as Alexa's eyes. His gaze shot back to her. *Those eyes.* His heart quickened. He never would have recognized it without knowing. But sure enough, those were Ben Davies' eyes.

Jess set the scarf aside and rummaged through the pile of letters. He first pulled out the bulky envelope and removed the engraving to examine it. While he fingered it, he caught her eyes in an exchange of poignancy. "I have one just like it in my own desk," he said almost scornfully, and stuffed it back in the box.

Though Jess needed no further proof, he pulled out a letter and opened it. He closed his eyes and swallowed hard. "It's his handwriting," he admitted. He looked at it long enough to read a few paragraphs, then returned it to the box with the scarf and closed it.

Alexa took the box from his lap and set it aside. She knelt beside him and took his hand into hers. "It's a shock for both of us," she said. "I'm glad we have each other to turn to."

Jess nodded firmly, and she put her arms around him with a forceful embrace that he returned with desperation. Alexa pulled away and touched his face. A familiar desire rose in his eyes, and she pulled back. "Must you look at me like that?"

"How am I supposed to look at you?" he snapped.

"I'm your sister, for crying out loud. This changes everything."

"It changes nothing, Alexandra." His voice deepened with spite as he took her hand, fondling her fingers intimately.

"Are you mad?" She jerked away and stepped back.

"Perhaps," he stated, "but I'm not your half-brother."

"You just admitted that—"

"I should go, Alexa." He stood abruptly. Coming so close to the truth pushed a tangible pain to the surface that he'd rather face in privacy. He left saying nothing more, and Alexa wanted to die inside from the turmoil of confusion and emotion. If only Richard were there.

Twenty
THE GABLED ATTIC

Moments after Jess left, Alexa caught a glimpse of his shadow moving past the window. Instead of going home, he went around the house and up the stairway to his mother's studio. Quietly Alexa followed and found the door ajar. She hadn't known what to expect, but what she saw made her heart sink. Jess was kneeling on the floor, his head bowed over the seat of a chair. His fists were clenched and his shoulders shook with silent anguish. What was it about today's discovery that had brought his pain so close to the surface?

Instinctively wanting to offer comfort, Alexa closed the door loudly with her back to him. By the time she turned to face him, he was on his feet and the tears had been mopped away. "What are you doing here?" he asked angrily.

She glanced around, pretending she'd never been here before. "Richard said it was just storage. I had no idea that—"

"It is storage."

"For what? Ghosts?" Jess looked away and she added with empathy, "I'm sorry if I disturbed you. I only wondered if you're all right."

"I'm all right," he stated.

Knowing he wasn't, Alexa moved farther into the room, reverently touching the brushes and oils. "Your mother?"

"Yes," he said after a long silence.

And then Alexa remembered the signature on the painting. Emma Davies. "Tell me about her," she urged.

"Why?"

Alexa recalled her father's letters mentioning something awful that had happened to Emma. Maybe Jess knew what that was. "I want to know about her, and perhaps talking would make you feel better."

Jess turned toward the window but didn't bother moving the curtain to look out. He doubted anything would make him feel better, but now that she was here, he didn't want her to leave.

After several moments of silence, Alexa felt certain he would say nothing, but the eerie quality of the room deepened when he spoke in a hushed voice. "She didn't like to paint as much as she liked to just come here and be alone. Though she had talent, it was just an excuse. It took her months to finish a painting." He glanced toward the canvas on the easel. "She never finished this one."

Alexa asked stoically, "Why does her absence make you hurt so much?"

His sharp glance penetrated the darkness. "It was my fault," he stated, as if discussing the weather.

"That's ridiculous." She nearly laughed. "Richard told me about it. You were nowhere near when the fire—"

"That's irrelevant. If I had done things differently, it wouldn't have happened."

"Jess, you can't blame yourself for—"

"I can if I'm the one to blame," he shouted. "I did *nothing* but cause that woman grief from the moment she conceived me." His voice softened, and he looked toward the ceiling. "She didn't deserve it. She didn't deserve me."

"What are you trying to say?" she asked, wondering where such feelings could possibly come from.

"Why are you asking me so many questions?" he growled. "You want all the answers. You want me to bare my soul to you, while you're sharing your life with another man."

Alexa sensed the anger rising, but she couldn't begin to comprehend the long-suppressed truth erupting in that moment.

"You want the answers?" He strode abruptly toward her and she backed away. "Well, you can have them! But I don't think you're going to like it."

"Jess," she whimpered, finding herself cornered.

"You are not my half-sister, Alexa." He took her forearms into his hands. "Not even close." His angry breathing seared her face as he spoke through clenched teeth. "I'm a bastard, Alexa."

A wave of relief briefly overcame her fear. They shared no blood. Her feelings for him had been natural and justified. But why was he so upset? Wanting to offer empathy, she reminded him of what should have been obvious. "So am I, Jess."

His grip tightened until it hurt. "But at least," his voice lowered, "you can look at yourself in the mirror and know that you're the product of love. You came about because two people cared for each other. You have no idea where my feelings are coming from, so don't try to tell me."

"Why don't *you* tell *me?*" She failed to sound calm.

Jess shook her as he pulled her closer. "She was raped, Alexa. Some crazed beast forced himself upon my mother—and I am the result. That is where *my* blood comes from. A crazy, raving maniac took everything my mother had to give, and left me in return. There!" He pushed her from his grip and she nearly tumbled backward. "Now you know the truth. Now you know why I was scared to death to marry you; why I hated myself every time I found you in my arms, wanting to . . ." He broke off with a groan and turned away, pulling brutally at his hair.

"You should have told me before," she said gently, her voice trembling with emotion. "We could have—"

"I know that!" he shouted, turning to face her. "I know I should have told you. I know we could have worked it out. But we didn't! And here I stand."

Regret softened his voice. "I used to be the one who held you when you needed to feel safe. But I'm not anymore. I believed you were the one chance I had to redeem myself from what I was born to be. But that chance is gone."

Jess came toward her again. Despite her fear, she didn't recoil. "I know I should have told you." He took hold of her arms. "I know I should have talked. But I couldn't! It hurt too much to even think about it, Alexa." His voice softened but his grip tightened. "And now it's too late. The boys tell me to forget about you. They say I'm wasting my life away. I'm fooling myself." He pulled her closer. "They tell me I can't change it. You're gone forever."

Alexa found herself crushed against him as his voice lowered to a whisper. "What am I supposed to do, Alexa? Keep going on this way? Can I pretend I'm not lonely? Can I possibly believe that my nights will be filled with anything but shadows?

"The ghost of you sits on my shoulder, Alexa. I close my eyes and see all the things you used to do that made me so happy. I hear words you said that filled me with wonder. It breaks into my mind when I least expect it.

"Yes, Alexa," he muttered, his lips against her face, "I am obsessed with you. I know I shouldn't be. I've tried to fight it. Sometimes I wonder if I'm crazy."

Jess backed her against the door and pushed his arm around her waist as he studied her face with his fingers. "My father was crazy," he said cynically. "A man would have to be crazy to do something like that to a woman so good. He left my mother crazy. She was like a child after it happened. I've been told how vibrant she was before, so full of life. And then she conceived me and her world fell apart. She became mindless; sensitive as a frightened child."

Jess brushed his lips over her face as he spoke. Alexa's shoulders rose and fell with each stilted breath she took. "Imagine how she must have felt, Alexa." He pressed her against the wall and swept a hand over her hip. "Imagine how it must feel to become powerless to save yourself from a man crazed with passion."

"Please—no, Jess," she muttered, but he ignored her.

"Both my parents were crazy, Alexa." She whimpered and tried to push him away, but it was impossible. "How do I know if I'm crazy or sane? How do I know what I felt when I held you in my arms? What am I feeling right now? Grief? Passion? Pain? Or is my mind too far gone to feel anything but vengeance?

"There is only one thing I know for certain, Alexa." His voice became hoarse, and she felt her heart pounding. "I know that I love you. I love you, Alexandra, with all my soul." His lips came over hers.

"No," she cried and turned her face away. Jess took her chin and jerked her lips within his reach. "No," she repeated, but he muffled it with a forceful kiss.

Alexa tried to tell herself she hated this, but truthfully she was drowning in the internal struggle. What was it about Jess that made her feel this way, even when he was behaving so irrationally?

"Alexa," he said gruffly as any remaining reason dissipated behind his pain. Jess went to his knees, and Alexa had no choice but to fall within his grasp until she found herself lying helpless in his arms.

"Jess, please," she sobbed. "You mustn't." Outwardly she protested. "Jess," she pleaded, but his determination only increased with his ardor. "I know you don't want to do this. Listen to me. It's not true, Jess. You're not crazy. You are whole. I know you are."

"You don't know anything about me," he snarled, and kissed her harder. Alexa's will to fight lessened. His nearness made her burn with longing, and she felt herself betraying Richard in her mind.

"Jess," she cried but he paid no mind, "please don't hurt me. I love you, Jess. Please don't hurt me."

Alexa didn't know what suddenly sobered him, but she was relieved as he went to his knees, easing her up with his arms securely around her.

"You're lying to me, Alexa. If you loved me, it wouldn't be like this."

"You can think what you want, but it will not change how I feel about you."

"No," he said bitterly, "and what I think or feel will not change the fact that you married my best friend behind my back. Whatever we once had is lost forever."

"It doesn't have to be," she said, and his grip tightened.

"Tell me what my options are," he muttered close to her face. Alexa hesitated and he demanded, "Tell me! I put my life into your hands a long time ago, Alexa. Now you tell me what my options are."

"We can be friends, Jess, if only you would—"

"Friends?" He gave a demented laugh, then eased her to the floor again with a harsh kiss. His actions clearly indicated that the idea was preposterous from his point of view.

"You and I," he whispered, moving his fingers over her throat, "should be much more than friends." Alexa's breathing became sharp and raspy. "Tell me, Alexa, do you ever close your eyes and remember what it was like to be in love with me? Do you ever wonder what it might have been like to let me love you?" His voice lowered. "Let me love you now, Alexa."

"No," she insisted, attempting to move away, but his strength outdid her. Outwardly she continued to protest, but inside she longed for it to go on. "Please stop," she cried. "You would regret it."

"I have too many regrets to ever regret such a thing."

"I would regret it. I can't hurt Richard this way. I know you wouldn't want to hurt Richard either."

"But it's all right for me to hurt," he insisted brashly.

"You're not thinking clearly, Jess. You would hate yourself tomorrow."

"I already hate myself. If I could get you to hate me too, then we would have something in common again."

"You're mad!" she breathed, and immediately regretted her choice of words.

Jess threw back his head and laughed. "Yes, I am," he said almost proudly.

"No, you're not mad. You just want me to think you are. You're just hiding behind it, using it as an excuse to justify the way—"

Alexa knew she'd hit a nerve when he stood abruptly and kicked over the stool. She scrambled to her feet and rushed toward the door, but he grabbed her arm. "We're not finished yet, Mrs. Wilhite."

"Please, Jess," she sobbed, "I can't fight this any longer. You're torturing me." His grip only tightened and she cried out, "Let me go!" Weak from the strain of their encounter, she nearly collapsed in his arms. As her knees buckled, she was grateful Jess caught her before she hit the floor. Gently he eased her down and lay close beside her.

"Alexa," he muttered, rummaging his fingers through her hair. "My sweet Alexa." His lips brushed over her brow, and she had no will to fight when he eased her closer. She lay cold and still, unable to protest, but not wanting to betray what his nearness did to her. Jess bathed his lips in her tears and held her so tightly that she could hardly breathe.

"Take me if you must," she sobbed, "but don't torture me any longer. I can't bear it."

Jess put his mouth forcefully over hers and felt Alexa respond. He eased back slightly, wishing he could see her face through the darkness. The evidence of her response had a calming effect on him, and he stopped to wonder what he was doing here.

Alexa fell asleep in the midst of her tears and woke up in her own bed. She sat up abruptly to look at the clock and was overcome with a wave of nausea. Through scattered memories of the night before came the realization that something in her had changed. She analyzed the symptoms and briefly forgot about Jess as she felt sure she was going to have a baby. Richard's baby. A fresh peace eased her anxiety over yesterday's happenings as she got dressed and brushed through her hair.

"Any word yet?" she asked Edward, coming into the bunkhouse late.

"Not so far." He set a plate in front of her. "But I'm sure they're fine. Should be back later today, I assume."

"Thank you, Edward." Alexa examined the breakfast in front of her. "I bet you don't give any of the others a hot meal when they don't make it on time."

"They're not as pretty as you." He smiled, then his voice turned cautious. "You've seemed a little under the weather for a few days now, I've noticed. Are you all right?"

"I'm fine," she said, but he looked dubious.

"Perhaps I should send for the doctor, eh?" He sat down.

Alexa nearly insisted that he shouldn't, but if her suspicions were correct, it would be wise to be examined. "That might be a good idea," she said warmly.

Edward's eyes narrowed. "Is something wrong, Missy?"

"No." She couldn't suppress a smile. "I have a feeling it's all quite normal." She met his eyes, and he seemed to perceive what she was implying as a grin spread over his face. "But," she placed a hand over his, "we'll keep that a secret until we know for certain."

Edward nodded and patted her shoulder as he rose from the table and left her to eat. The discomfort eased in her stomach as she filled it, but her anxiety over recent happenings was still with her as she went to the stable to begin her work.

"Good morning," Jess said, and she turned abruptly. "You don't look so good." He sauntered toward her. "Have a bad night, Mrs. Wilhite?"

"I guess you could say that." She eyed him warily and backed away as he came closer.

"So did I." His tone was complacent. "But," he continued elaborately, "I have to admit it was nice to be with you again, however unpleasant the circumstances."

"You carried me to bed," she stated.

"Yes." His voice lowered seductively, and she found herself between the wall and his body. "You looked so beautiful, so warm. It was tempting to crawl in with you, but I was afraid Richard might come back and kill me."

"Please, Jess." She pushed her hands against his shoulders but he wouldn't budge.

"Think about it, Alexa. If you ever change your mind—"

"It's ridiculous," she insisted. "I will never betray Richard."

"Oh," he smirked, "but you already did."

Alexa looked away and closed her eyes. She couldn't deny what she'd felt in his arms, and he knew it. "I love Richard," she said firmly. "I am *his* wife." It was her only defense.

Jess ignored her and took her chin in his hand. "Please, no, Jess," she insisted as he bent to kiss her, but it was too late.

Murphy heard Alexa's plea as he walked into the stable unannounced and witnessed his employer's indiscretions. He cleared his throat ridiculously loud just as Alexa managed to push Jess's face away with her hands. They both turned in surprise and Jess backed away from Alexa, though his expression remained straight.

After an unbearable silence, Murphy said, "If I was Richard, I'd give you the beatin' o' your life." He glanced toward Alexa then back to Jess. "You're playin' with fire, Jess—takin' liberties with another man's wife. I'm not gonna say any more, but I'm not gonna stand here and pretend I didn't see it either."

Jess turned away but said nothing.

"I can assure you it won't happen again," Alexa said indignantly and walked away.

"You're a fool, Jess," Murphy stated dryly.

"I thought you weren't going to say any more," Jess came back defensively.

"Someone's got t' tell you!" he shouted. "How many times have I said it's over? How long will it take to get it through your thick head? She's gone, Jess. She's—"

"Shut up, Murphy," Jess interrupted quietly.

"I'm not gonna shut up until you do somethin' about it and stop wallowin' in your own grief. You can fire me if you want, but it won't change anything. And," he attempted to lighten the mood, "admit it, you'll never find help as cheap as me."

"Did you find them all?" Jess changed the topic after a long silence.

"Every one," he said proudly. "Richard and Fiddler are pushin' 'em down."

"Good." Jess walked away, but Murphy knew he hadn't absorbed a word of his lecture today any more than he had before. He decided he was going to keep an eye on Jess, whether Jess liked it or not.

❦   ❦   ❦

The doctor confirmed Alexa's suspicions, and she was waiting expectantly on the porch when Richard returned.

"Hello," she said as he set his foot onto the bottom step. He lifted the saddlebags off his shoulder and threw them over the porch rail.

"Hello." He moved up a step and pushed an arm around her waist and a hand into her hair. His kiss made her forget anything but how much she loved him, and the news she had to share.

"Hold still." She took his chin and turned his face so the scars weren't visible. "Such a handsome man," she said. "I want my baby's profile to be just like that."

Richard looked at her abruptly. She was grinning. "Your *what?*"

"My baby." She took his hand and pressed it over her belly, correcting with a whisper, "*Our* baby, Richard."

"Are you sure?" he asked. She nodded. He laughed. "Really?" She nodded again and he lifted her into his arms with a forceful hug and a jubilant laugh. "Really?" he asked again.

"Really," she repeated, laughing with him.

Richard made the announcement at the supper table, and the boys all cheered. Richard beamed as the duration of the meal passed with endearing speculations on having a baby around the place. They teased Alexa about being a *pregnant* trainer and jockey, but in truth they all knew this would bring about changes.

After supper, Richard prepared himself a hot bath in a galvanized tub that he dragged into the kitchen. It was typical for Alexa to sit quietly and do her needlework while he soaked after a long day. But tonight she didn't bother with her sewing.

"Richard." The tone of her voice made him raise his head to look at her. "There's something I need to tell you."

"I'm listening." His pulse quickened. It occurred to him that last night was the first he'd spent away from her since their marriage. By her severe expression, he wondered if Jess had taken advantage of that. He was relieved when she brought up something else.

"It's about my father."

"Tyson Byrnehouse, or the man who—"

"My blood father," she interrupted. He waited patiently while she swallowed hard and took a deep breath. "The box you found in my room was filled with my mother's letters. I'd never read them before, but I did yesterday."

"And?" he urged, certain she was trying to get to a point despite the way she hesitated.

"Richard," she swallowed again, "Ben Davies is my father."

"Good heavens," he muttered. "Are you sure?"

Alexa nodded and looked down, fighting the emotion back.

"That certainly explains the great Byrnehouse-Davies feud, now doesn't it." Richard shook his head in disbelief. "Then you and Jess are—"

"That's what I thought," she interrupted, then met his gaze, "but we're not, because. . ." Alexa put a hand over her mouth and closed her eyes as memories of the previous night flooded into her mind. Gaining some control, she tried to explain. "After I figured it out, I went to talk to Jess. He refused to believe me, but he looked at the letters and admitted it was true. He stormed out, insisting we were not related, and went up to the attic. I followed him. I was concerned, and . . ."

Alexa hesitated, and her eyes revealed something bordering on guilt. Uneasiness crept up the back of Richard's neck. He wanted to demand to know what had happened, but he just waited quietly for her to continue.

"Jess was upset, but he did manage to tell me that . . ." Alexa began to cry, then wiped at her tears with an embarrassed laugh. "The doctor said that pregnancy could make my emotions more sensitive. Maybe that's why I'm crying so easily."

"Maybe you're crying because what happened last night upset you." Her tears increased at the suggestion and he added, "What *did* happen, Alexa?"

Her emotion prevented her from speaking for several minutes. Realizing this was serious, Richard rose from the tub and dried himself off. Wearing a clean pair of breeches, he squatted beside her and took her hand.

"I understand now, Richard," she cried. "I know why Jess drove me away. He was afraid because . . ." She hesitated, and he began to feel impatient.

"Why?" he pressed, but it was the least of the questions drumming in his mind. What had happened between them last night? Was she regretting their marriage? Could he give her enough to compensate if she did?

"He believes he's crazy, Richard."

"What?" He almost laughed. "Why? Because of his mother?"

"That's part of it, I suppose. But did you ever know why she was like that?"

"I just assumed she always had been."

"According to Jess, she wasn't. I never met her, but it seemed odd to me that a man like Ben Davies would marry a mindless woman. Apparently he didn't." Alexa looked searchingly at her husband, perhaps hoping he already knew and she wouldn't have to say it. But her promptings only made him appear all the more baffled. Alexa bit her lip and squeezed his hand. "Jess told me last night that she was raped."

Richard leaned back and inhaled sharply. He absorbed it while Alexa sniffled and wiped her face with a handkerchief. "I see," he finally said. "And her mind never recovered from the trauma."

"Perhaps she was not terribly strong to begin with," Alexa speculated. "I suspect some women would be able to deal with such a thing better than others, but apparently it . . . ruined her." She fidgeted with the handkerchief in her hands and thought of Jess crying in the attic. "Apparently Jess cared very much for his mother."

"He was the center of her life. She adored him, and he took very good care of her. He looked just like her."

"And when she died, he took it very hard."

Richard nodded. "He blamed himself for reasons I'll never understand."

Again Alexa's mind went to Jess in the attic. Hadn't he said it was his fault, but given no explanation?

"Did Jess tell you when it happened?" Startled, Alexa looked at him deeply and he clarified, "When she was raped?"

A new batch of tears welled up silently in her eyes. "The man who did it is . . . Jess's father."

Richard put a hand over his brow, then pushed it into his hair as the pieces fell into place. "And that's why Jess is not your half-brother." Richard stood up and sighed, stuffing his hands in his pockets. "I can't believe it." His voice betrayed emotion. "I've known Jess for twenty-five years, and I had no idea. I don't understand where he would have possibly discovered such a thing. Emma wouldn't have told him; the concept couldn't have existed in her mind. And I know Ben wouldn't have said anything. Until Ben died, Jess was always so happy, so secure. It doesn't make sense."

"It's obvious he found out later in life. But who else would have known? And what good would there be in telling Jess?"

"There's no use speculating. If Jess is telling the truth, then the problem is serious." Richard tried to steer the conversation back to the heart of this. "But you said you understood what drove you apart. I'm afraid I missed the connection."

Alexa hesitated, and her emotion surfaced again.

"You said he was afraid of something." She nodded but didn't respond. Richard fought to remain patient. "You said he believes he's crazy."

Alexa nodded. "At first the things he said sounded so ridiculous, but as I got thinking about it, I recalled odd things he used to say now and then. Everything was fine until . . ." The memory choked her and she couldn't speak.

"Are you trying to say that he *is* crazy?"

"No," she insisted, "of course not. He just wants to think he is. But when I remembered what had changed him, it all made sense. Richard," she looked up, bewildered and concerned, "he was afraid of his own passion." Richard kept a straight face, but he didn't like this conversation. "He misinterpreted something that happened between us, and he was terrified. Something I said or did triggered what he knew about his parentage, and I believe he honestly feared he would hurt me. He thinks that something in his blood is prone to committing crimes of passion."

Richard sat down and crossed his ankle on his knee. He folded his arms over his chest and watched his wife cry. The way she wrung her hands increased Richard's uneasiness. He felt certain she hadn't told him everything, but he wasn't sure he wanted to know. If something had happened between her and Jess, wouldn't ignorance be easier? Easier perhaps, but not right.

Attempting to push aside his own concerns, Richard tried to concentrate on Alexa. "So," he said with compassion, "you had a rather trying experience while I was away. You discovered Ben Davies is your father, and from what you've told me, the time you spent with Jess was not pleasant."

Richard watched her eyes closely. The guilt rose as fast as his heart sank. She looked away abruptly and bit her lip. "Alexa," he drawled, "what else happened?" She tried to stand up, but he grabbed her arm and forced her to stay seated. His voice lowered with a desperation he wasn't ashamed to admit to. "Don't keep secrets from me, Alexa. If something happened last night, I want to know about it."

Alexa knew he had a right to know, and she wanted to tell him. It was just so difficult to find the words, to know where to begin. She sensed anger rising in him and knew she had to get it over with. Recalling that Murphy had seen Jess kissing her this morning, she didn't want it to reach Richard through other sources.

While Alexa tried to find the words, her tears increased. Impatience merged into anger as Richard began to assume the worst. For the first time since he'd made the decision to marry her in spite of Jess, he felt an emotion creeping into him that he'd rather not harbor. But how could a man not be jealous? True, he was the one married to her, but he knew beyond any doubt that she felt something for Jess she would never feel for him. Everything tangible in their relationship was good, but an abstract fear hung over Richard that he couldn't deny. He didn't believe it was in Jess to do something horrible. But then, Jess had been prone to drinking too much. And he knew well enough that when a man was drunk, there was no telling what might happen. When minutes passed and Alexa didn't speak, that dreaded jealousy pushed him over the edge.

"Alexa!" He tightened his grip and moved to the edge of his chair so their faces nearly touched. "Tell me what happened!"

"I . . . I . . ." Alexa closed her eyes, unable to face him but unable to turn away. "I shouldn't have followed him to the attic. But I was concerned and afraid for him, and I . . ." She hung her head. "Oh,

Richard, I'm so sorry. I tried to fight it, but he . . ." She sobbed into her hand. "He just . . ."

He cursed, then pulled her closer, held her tighter. "Did you sleep with him?"

Alexa shot her head up. "No, no. Of course not."

Richard sighed audibly. "Did he harm you . . . in any way?" he asked more softly.

Alexa shook her head slowly. Richard pulled her head to his shoulder and held her tightly. The relief was indescribable.

"Richard," she eased back to look at him, "I can't say that nothing happened." He looked at her sideways. "But it was not my choice." She could see the hurt combining with question, and she knew she had to tell him the whole truth—now. "He was extremely upset, Richard. We argued, and he . . ." She searched carefully for the right words. "He became physically aggressive."

Richard bit back the impulse to demand every detail. Had he touched her? Had he kissed her? Then he realized he didn't want to know. Any detail she repeated would only haunt him. He was relieved when she wrapped it up neatly.

"His behavior was not appropriate, Richard, but I did my best to let him know that I disapproved, and I am committed to you. Nothing else matters."

Richard nodded to acknowledge her explanation, then he opened his arms in acceptance. A primitive instinct suggested a need for jealousy, but holding Alexa close, a need to be more civilized overruled. In Jess's present state of mind, any exhibition of envy would likely spur him to fight harder. Richard had not come into this situation ignorant, and he was not about to lose control of it by losing his senses. He'd partly expected something like this to happen. He should be grateful it hadn't been worse.

With complete acceptance, Richard urged Alexa's lips to his. As the kiss gained fervor, he lifted her into his arms and carried her the short distance to their bedroom. Relief mingled with love in her eyes, reaffirming how he needed to handle this. From this day forward, he would never give her a reason to stray. He would be there for her, no matter the circumstances. He would listen and nurture and care for her enough to compensate for anything that might come between them in the future.

"I'm sorry, Richard," she murmured against his face.

Richard met her eyes stoically. "Now that you're beginning to understand what came between the two of you, do you regret marrying me?"

"No," she answered firmly, surprised at the question. "I have no doubt that I did the right thing. I don't believe he would have ever faced up to this if I hadn't."

"Good," he smiled. "Then you have nothing to be sorry for."

"I love you, Richard." She touched his face and kissed him.

"I know you do," he replied. "You're going to have my baby. And I hope she looks just like you." He looked at her eyes as if he'd never seen them before. "You know," he said, "I do believe you have a look of Ben Davies, especially around the eyes."

"Really? The thought still seems strange. But I must admit, in spite of the circumstances, there's a degree of comfort in knowing it was him. I didn't know Ben Davies, but I believe I would have liked him. It shouldn't take too long to become accustomed to the idea of being his daughter."

"I shouldn't think so," Richard said. And then he kissed her.

Twenty-one
LEAVING

Richard found Jess in his office with a bottle of brandy. While part of him would rather avoid this encounter, logic told him it was necessary. He took a deep breath and closed the door loudly to make his presence known.

Jess looked up, indifference changing to disdain when he saw Richard. "What do *you* want?"

Richard pressed both hands flat on the desk and leaned over to look Jess in the eye. "I have something I want to say."

"About what?" Jess demanded, taking a healthy swallow.

"Concerning my wife." Jess chuckled without humor, but he stopped when Richard added, "She told me about your little escapade in the attic."

Jess's eyes widened. When it became evident that Richard expected a reaction, he said spitefully, "So, did you come to give me a whipping, or what?"

"Should I?"

"I guess that depends on how much she told you."

"Enough to know that she was not to blame."

"Not entirely." Jess gave a self-satisfied smile that left Richard uneasy. But he pushed it away along with the jealousy.

"Why don't *you* tell me what happened?" Richard urged.

"Why should I?"

"We're in love with the same woman, Jess."

With an unnatural cough, Jess attempted to disguise the emotional noise that escaped his throat. "Is this supposed to be a great revelation?"

"The only way we're going to make it through this is to face it head-on. No secrets, Jess. If you think you're entitled to take liberties with my wife, I'd like to know about it." Richard paused but got no reaction. "Are you sober enough to hear what I'm saying?"

"I'm not drunk enough to be able to ignore it," he said with distaste. "So you know. Not only am I a bastard, but I force my affection on other men's wives." Jess set his eyes directly on Richard. "She wanted me." He turned in his chair to stare at the wall. "But her heart was with you."

"Is that what you resent?" Richard asked.

Jess thought of a thousand biting responses, but none of them could justify what he'd done. He'd driven Alexa away from him, then he'd tortured her for it. He emptied the glass in his hand and filled it again. "Is there a point to this conversation, Richard?"

"Only one."

"Maybe you'd better get to it and get out of here."

"I'll make a deal with you, Jess."

"What do I get out of it?"

"Exactly what you've earned. Nothing." Jess glared at him. "You can hate me for saying it, like I used to hate you when you told me I looked bad enough to scare a horse into winning. Then one day I confronted the truth and realized you'd been right. You said things like that to me because you wanted me to face up to reality. So, hate me, Jess, but one day you're going to figure out what happened and why."

"You were getting to a point." Jess was obviously irritated.

"We both love her, Jess. I'm doing my best to make her happy, but I'm no saint. Sometimes I just want to shake her until her feelings for you are all gone." Jess squeezed his eyes shut as Richard added in a whisper, "My point is this. I won't hurt her, if you won't."

Jess's voice was suddenly sober. "I know you would never hurt her, Richard."

"No, I wouldn't," he replied, "and neither would you." Jess gave him a dubious glare, but Richard just turned and left the room. He'd said what he wanted to say, and saw no reason to antagonize the situation any further.

❦ ❦ ❦

Jess opened his eyes and saw a pillow about to swallow him up. "Good morning," a feminine voice said somewhere on the brim of his headache.

"Alexa," he murmured.

"No, it's not Alexa."

Jess forced his head around to find the source. "Sarina! When did you get back?"

"Late last night. I came in and found you half drowned in a bottle of brandy, so I helped you up to bed and thought I'd better stay around and be sure you was all right."

"Were, Sarina. Were all right."

"Stop correcting my English and drink some of this coffee."

"Where's Ben?" Jess attempted to sit up.

"He stayed with my parents."

"Is he all right?"

"Of course he is. They nearly went mad without him. Couldn't wait to get him back."

"This coffee is terrible. You must have made it yourself."

"I never could make coffee. I were sure surprised to—"

"Was, Sarina. I was sure."

"Was. Were. Make up your mind. I was sure surprised to hear about Richard getting married."

"So was I." Jess abruptly set his cup on the bedside table and swung his legs over the edge of the bed. Gaining coherency, he realized Sarina was in his bedroom. "What are you doing in here?" he demanded brashly.

"I told you. I were looking out for you until—"

"I'm fine, as you can see. Leave me in peace."

Sarina rose from her chair and put her hands on her hips. "If you don't mind my saying so, I think it's pathetic for you to be pining away like this for a woman."

"I do mind you saying so."

"Even *I* didn't pine away like this for you."

Jess looked up inquisitively. "Now that," he came unsteadily to his feet, "is the smartest thing you ever did, Sarina. Go away so I can change my clothes and attempt something worthwhile today—after I have a drink."

"Isn't there anything I can do for you?" Sarina asked intently.

"Yes. Get me a drink."

"Besides that?"

"No. Just leave me alone."

"Jess," she said, and he glanced up sharply. She hadn't called him anything but Mr. Davies for years. "If there's anything I can do . . ."

She left the offer unfinished, and Jess wondered about her feelings. "Come here," he said, and she did. Carefully he took her chin in his hand. Her black eyes widened. Jess looked searchingly into them and considered long and hard whether or not to kiss her. He wanted to. He wanted to lose himself in her and never look back. But he knew it wouldn't change anything, and it wouldn't be fair to either of them. His heart would always be lost in eyes of blue.

"Go away," he said in a low voice, pushing her chin from his grasp. Sarina made no attempt to hide her disappointment. "Go away," he repeated more strongly when she hesitated, "or you might discover that I'm no better than Chad Byrnehouse."

Sarina scurried from the room, and Jess moved unsteadily to pour himself a drink. He emptied the glass and set it down abruptly to pour another. "You should have known, Jess," he said aloud. "The first time Chad Byrnehouse told you that you were crazy, you should have known."

❦ ❦ ❦

Jess walked into the stable to find Alexa leaning her head against the wall, her hand over her mouth.

"What's the matter?" he bellowed.

Her head shot up. "Nothing serious." Alexa tried to gain control of her smoldering stomach, at the same time hoping she wouldn't have to fight off any more bold advances.

"You've looked awful for days now." A cold tone in his voice covered the concern. "Perhaps you should see a doctor."

"I already have." She looked away and attempted to appear busy. "I would have thought you'd heard by now."

"Heard what?" he asked tensely. "I'm always the last to know anything around here."

The statement bit, but Alexa drew back her shoulders and looked at him directly. "I'm pregnant." Hurt seeped into Jess's eyes, and she added with a humorless chuckle, "Surely you can't be so surprised."

"I suppose deep inside I'd hoped it was platonic."

"Really, Jess," she said, trying to keep this light, "you should know Richard better than that." Her voice mellowed. "You should know *me* better than that."

"Yes," he said coldly, "you'd think I would."

Jess turned and walked away with no expression, but Alexa could feel the hurt he'd left hanging in the air.

Jess wondered how much more of this he could take as he slammed the door to his bedroom and poured a full glass of brandy. Ever since Alexa had come to him with confessions of her paternity, it seemed that everything bad had gotten steadily worse.

It was true, he thought as he emptied the glass and poured another. He was crazy. Any sane man wouldn't let himself be eaten alive with anguish over a woman. Looking back over his life, he saw nothing but anguish since the day Benjamin Davies had died. And soon afterward, Chad Byrnehouse had taken the opportunity to tell Jess he was the product of a vile crime.

He still wondered how on earth Chad had found out before he did, but it was only one of so many questions haunting him that it was hardly worth dwelling on. Foremost, his mother's tormented life pressed through his brain in repeated flashes. And overshadowing it all was the numb realization that he was indirectly responsible for her death.

And then there was Alexa. Beautiful Alexa. Here he was, a man fool enough to attempt doing the very thing to her that had destroyed his mother. He *was* crazy. He was absolutely certain of it. No one in his right mind would hurt a woman like Alexa. But he was hurting her. He hurt her every time he turned around. What was he trying to accomplish? Vengeance? Retaliation? Or was he just desperately in love?

Jess swallowed his third glass of brandy and was frustrated to find the bottle empty. He went downstairs to find another, wanting only to drown the questions—or at least put them where he couldn't feel them.

❦　　❦　　❦

Alexa and Richard were awakened in the night by a pounding at the front door. Richard pulled on his breeches and stumbled to answer it. Alexa could hear Fiddler. They exchanged typical greetings for the middle of the night, then their voices lowered so drastically that she knew they didn't want her to hear. She put on a wrapper and moved into the room. "What is it, Fiddler?" she asked.

He stared at her with no expression while Richard said, "It's nothing to concern yourself over, my dear. Go back to bed. I'll take care of it."

"It's Jess, isn't it," she stated, and Fiddler's eyes betrayed the truth. "What happened?" she demanded, moving toward the door.

"Alexa," Richard stopped her with his arm, "please . . ."

"Where is he?" she insisted.

Fiddler glanced expectantly at Richard, who reluctantly nodded his consent. "The stable," Fiddler stated, and Alexa led the way.

She found Jess lying in the dirt. The blood on his face made her panic. The feeling deepened when she saw Murphy unloading a revolver. "What happened?" she cried, going to her knees beside Jess.

"Not much," Murphy said casually, and she gave him a hard glare.

"Why is he bleeding?" She pulled his head into her lap.

"That would probably be because I hit him good and hard," Murphy announced, and Alexa's eyes widened.

"Why?"

Murphy threw the empty gun onto the ground, then added the bullets to it. "What else could I do?" He shrugged, then his expression became sober. "He was going to shoot himself."

"He *what?!*" she shrieked as she stood, sending Jess's head back to the ground with a thud.

"He's drunk, of course, which isn't unusual," Murphy said. "I heard some strange noises and came out to check. He was havin' a devil of a time tryin' to mount a horse. I asked him what he was doin' with the gun, and he told me to mind my business and to tell you good-bye. Then he said he should have done it years ago. Said we'd all be better off without him. So I hit him."

"Stupid fool," Alexa murmured.

"I'm glad you were here," Richard said.

"So am I," Murphy added.

"Wake him up," Alexa insisted, and they all looked puzzled. "Wake him up!" she repeated, and Fiddler threw a bucket of water in Jess's face. He gasped and shook his head, moaning from the pain in his jaw.

His eyes focused on Alexa, and she lost no time in slapping the left side of his face. "That is for being stupid enough to get drunk—again!" She slapped the right side and he groaned.

"That's the side I hit, too," Murphy said proudly.

"And *that,*" Alexa added, "is for being stupid enough to think you could solve your problems by shooting yourself in the head."

Alexa stood, leaving him dazed. "Get him to bed, boys," she ordered, "and I want somebody with him all the time until we convince him what a fool he is."

❦   ❦   ❦

Alexa managed to squeeze into a pair of breeches that had once been baggy before she went quietly into the bunkhouse. Jess was sleeping with Edward sitting nearby, absorbed in a book. "I'll take over for a while," she said.

"So far he's slept like a baby. Wonder what he'll do when he finds out he's under quarantine."

Alexa tried to smile as Edward left her alone with Jess. Her heart ached for him as she watched him sleep. She allowed her mind to wander briefly over the times when they had laughed together and loved each other with the hope of a bright future. She couldn't allow herself to regret her choices, but at moments the irony tore at her.

She sat for nearly an hour before he finally moaned himself awake. "Have I died?" he asked when his eyes focused on her.

"No such luck," she said satirically.

He sat up slightly to survey his surroundings. "What am I doing in here?"

"Here is where the people who care about you are going to keep an eye on you for a while."

"Why?" He sat on the edge of the bed. Alexa glared at him and he added, "I seem to recall that famous slap again."

"Two of them," she growled.

"What did I do this time?" He almost chuckled, and put his hand over his eyes when it hurt. Alexa took his forearm into a firm grip and he looked at her deeply, surprised at the angry tears showing.

"You're a fool, Jess Davies. But I'm not going to let you ruin my life any further. You think that through your drunken mindlessness you can become a martyr and leave me with guilt to face all my life. Well, you're wrong. You are responsible for you, Jess. You make your own choices. I'm not going to pity you anymore. I'm not going to care!"

He gazed at her dumbly and she lowered her voice. "What were you doing with the gun, Jess?"

"What?" he laughed, then groaned when it made his head hurt.

"The gun, Jess. Tell me what you were going to do with it."

He obviously didn't remember, and Alexa's grip tightened, her fingernails digging painfully into his arm. "You don't even remember!" she shouted. "You were ready to shoot yourself, and you don't even remember!" He looked disbelieving and she said through clenched teeth, "How dare you!"

"Looks like I missed the good part." Murphy entered and stood beside Alexa.

Jess glared at him but Alexa said, "You can thank Murphy for saving your life last night." Jess glanced at her like a frightened child, and Alexa relinquished her grip. "Keep an eye on him, Murphy." She moved toward the door. "I've had all I can take."

Alexa returned to Richard and poured her heart out to him, just as she had so many times before. It was always Jess that caused her anguish, but Richard was unfaltering in his comfort and understanding. Alexa was in awe that any man could be so good.

With her heart spilled, Alexa made up her mind not to concern herself with it any further. It took all she had just to accomplish her work and deal with the physical effects of this pregnancy. She didn't have the strength to worry about Jess any longer.

As it neared bedtime, Alexa and Richard sat together in the parlor, speculating over their child. Alexa giggled as Richard professed they would have a daughter built like her mother, and she would be a world-famous jockey. He pulled her onto his lap to kiss her, but it was interrupted by a knock at the door. Alexa moved off Richard's lap and he went to answer it. "Jess," she heard him say, and she quickly pulled up her sewing to look busy. "What a pleasure. Come in."

"Thank you," came a sober reply, and Alexa glanced up as he moved into the room.

"Hello, Jess," she said quietly.

"Alexa." He gave a barely detectable nod.

"Please, sit down," Richard said as he sat near Alexa.

"Thank you," Jess said, but he remained on the edge of his chair.

"Did you need something?" Richard asked.

"Actually . . . yes. I need to tell you . . . both of you," Alexa shot her head up, "that I'm leaving . . . for a while."

"Where are you—" Alexa began to ask, but Jess interrupted.

"I don't know where I'm going, and I don't know when I'll be back. But I think it's what I need to do. If you're willing, Richard, I'd like to leave it all in your hands. You're familiar enough with everything. I know I'll have nothing to worry about if you're in charge."

"Are you sure you're doing the right thing?" Richard asked with the sincerity of a true friend.

"I'm not sure about anything, Richard, but I can't stay here and . . ." Jess stood abruptly to pace the room. "It's stupid of me to sit here and pretend that we don't all know what's happening. You both know how I feel. I suppose I just need time to . . . well, just time."

All was silent until Richard stood and held out his hand. Jess hesitated, then shook it firmly. "Everything will be fine," Richard said.

Jess gave some semblance of a smile. "I'll be leaving early tomorrow."

"Is there anything we can do for you; anything you need?" Richard asked.

Jess glanced toward Alexa and stated dryly, "No."

"Take care of yourself," Richard said, and Jess knew he meant it.

Alexa put her work aside and stood by her husband. "You will come back?" she asked, and Jess saw emotion brimming in her eyes.

Jess chuckled tensely. "Of course I will. This is my home."

Alexa touched his face, and he closed his eyes as she kissed his cheek. "Do take care," she whispered, and he nodded.

"I guess that's all, then." Jess moved abruptly to the door. "I'll be leaving at dawn."

Richard nodded, and Jess left.

Despite Alexa's conviction to not be concerned, she spent a sleepless night and was sitting on the porch when Jess rode out of the stable just after dawn. He paused when he saw her, and Alexa wanted to run across the yard and beg him to stay. In her heart she knew this would be good for all of them, and she had to respect Jess for his decision. It was just so hard to see him go. She kept expecting him to ride away, but he continued to stare at her across the distance, defying the horse's urge to run. For the first time in months, Alexa pushed away all logic. He was leaving, and she loved him.

In a flurry, she lifted her nightgown around her knees and ran with bare feet toward him, her wrapper flying untied behind her. He reached out a hand, and she took it in a desperate grip.

"I understand why you have to go," she cried, unconscious of the tears streaming over her face, "and I can't blame you for feeling the way you do, but I . . ." The words became lost in emotion as she realized he was crying, too.

"I'll come back, Alexa," he said. "When I can face it and not feel this way, I'll be back."

"Please be careful." She maintained her grip on his hand, despite the vacillating of the impatient horse. "You will always be in my prayers, and in my heart."

In one easy movement, Jess bent to kiss her. Alexa accepted it with parted lips, hoping somewhere deep inside that Richard would forgive her. She braced a hand against the back of his neck and went on her tiptoes to accommodate him. Their kiss was brief but harsh with reality. For moments after, Jess held her head firmly, his brow pressed to hers, his eyes closed.

"I love you, Alexandra," he whispered, then eased away. As he straightened his back, Jess saw Richard leaning against the porch rail. Jess briefly touched the brim of his hat in a gesture that he hoped Richard would understand. He was doing his best to accept this and leave Alexa in his hands. Richard nodded in his direction and Jess turned his attention to Alexa, who was oblivious to anything but the moment.

"I have to go." He squeezed her hand and stirred the horse forward before he had a chance to talk himself out of it. Alexa took a few steps with the horse before she finally let go. Jess paused a short distance away to look back once more. He adjusted his hat and stirred the horse into a gallop. Alexa watched until he disappeared into the hills.

In the quiet of early morning, she finally accepted that he was gone and turned toward the house. She stopped when she saw Richard, wondering how long he'd been there. She hesitated, fearing he might be angry. In truth, he had a right to be. But he stepped off the porch and walked toward her, taking her into his arms with an embrace so full of love and acceptance that Alexa could only cry in his arms, overwhelmed with the bitter-sweetness of her life.

Weeks flowed into months, and Alexa's condition worsened as her weight increased. It was unanimously decided that the boys would keep the horses in shape, but for the time being, they couldn't afford to concern themselves with any racing.

As shearing season approached and Richard knew how badly the money was needed, they took every precaution to make certain it went smoothly. But like a bad omen, the sheep were scattered at the worst possible time, and it took every man to bring them in while it rained continually. They were pleased to end up with a decent price for the wool after all, but in the process Jimmy broke his leg, Edward's heart condition worsened drastically, and Richard came down with a cough that Alexa credited to all that mob herding in the rain.

As Alexa's pregnancy progressed, she found more time for sewing and finally finished the leather mask for Richard. Her heart quickened when he tried it on. It gave him a handsome, mysterious appeal that left her nearly breathless. As it molded to his face and the side of his head, covering the scars completely and tying above his right ear, he appeared almost a different man. Richard declared that it made him feel different, and he liked the confidence it gave him. The boys were quick to agree that it was well worth Alexa's effort. Mrs. Brown swooned over it, saying he was the most handsome man in the country. But still Alexa preferred he didn't wear it when they were alone, and it left him assured that she truly loved him for the man he was inside.

They all wondered where Jess had gone and when—if ever—he would come back. He was mentioned occasionally, but an hour hardly passed when Alexa didn't think about him, always keeping a prayer in her heart for his safety, and that he would find the peace he was seeking.

With Fiddler's help, Alexa took over the cooking when Edward became confined to bed. As long as Alexa was careful and got plenty of rest, she was able to manage. But each day was a struggle as aches and swelling consumed her. Even so, her concern was more with her husband as his cough worsened daily, and one morning he collapsed while he was getting dressed. The doctor declared he had pneumonia, and Alexa wondered if life could get any worse.

With Jimmy's broken leg finally healed, they managed the work well enough without Edward or Richard. But this, along with caring for the patients, was a mutual strain. Alexa became close to the boys in a way she never had before, and was continually grateful for all they did. Murphy never complained and always kept the mood light, and Tod spent most of his time with either Edward or Richard, seeing to their needs and making sure they obeyed doctor's orders.

As Alexa worked with Fiddler in the kitchen, she came to care for him even more. He opened up and told her of the life he'd had before with a wife and young son who had been killed. She discovered then that his name was actually Robert, but he preferred Fiddler, as few people other than his wife had ever called him that.

Alexa spent every spare moment by Richard's bedside, and often her mind was in silent prayer that he would recover rather than worsen. She prayed, too, for Edward and the rest of these people who were more of a family to her than she had ever known elsewhere.

In quiet moments she would think of Ben Davies, the man he was and the way he had raised Jess. She wondered what he might think to see her now, knowing she was his daughter. It seemed ironic that events had left her practically in control of her blood father's station. Despite the difficulties, she was grateful that Chad had forced her to come here.

"What are you thinking?" Richard's voice startled her. He'd been mostly delirious with fever for days. She took his hand and smiled, but his occasional coherency had ceased to give her hope, when it always seemed to worsen.

"Actually," she admitted, "I was thinking about Chad. I wonder what miserable thing he's up to now. Do you suppose he knows Jess is gone?"

Richard's voice came raspy and with effort. "He seems to keep track of us one way or another. I'm sure he was responsible for the sheep being scattered and . . ." He started to cough, and Alexa held her breath. Each time it consumed him like that, she feared he'd never take another breath.

When he quieted and lay back on the pillow, she spoke as if she wasn't scared beyond words that he might die. "I was thinking," she began, and he weakly squeezed her hand, "Jess said to me a time or two that he was nothing but bad luck." Richard chuckled weakly as if he knew what she was going to say. "But look at what's happened since he left. Do you think when he comes back, he'll bring good luck with him?"

"I don't know," Richard said, "but I wish he'd come back."

"So do I," Alexa said, and Richard squeezed her hand again. She kissed his face and held him close for a long moment. "Do you suppose he's all right, Richard? He's been gone so long."

"It's hard to say," he whispered, "but we have to believe he is."

"If something happened to him, I almost believe I would know."

Richard tried to smile. "I'm sure he's fine," he assured her, but Alexa continued to worry. She turned her attention to her husband, and her worry increased as he drifted again into a weak delirium. "Please, God," she whispered aloud, "don't let him die. I need him."

Twenty-two
HIS RETURN

Considering the horrid memories plowing through Jess's mind, he was remarkably calm as he hurried from the burning hotel. Perhaps his inner despair left no room for the fear that consumed others around him. With a bandanna over his face to filter out the thickening smoke, he quickly scoured each room, encouraging frantic occupants to safety. There was no thought of himself as he instinctively lifted a frail, middle-aged woman from her bed and carried her outside. Scarcely into the street, a young boy, barely a man, came rushing forward to claim the woman Jess held. Jess observed the tearful reunion, then turned to watch the flames rise higher into the sky. He barely nodded to acknowledge a hearty slap on his shoulder from the elderly hotel owner. "Many thanks, young man. You really kept your head in there."

His attention returned to the rising inferno. He knew fires just happened sometimes, and this one was likely an accident. But what rotten antic of fate had made it necessary for him to be present now? Looking around, it seemed that everyone was accounted for and no one had been hurt, but the memories sickened Jess. The last fire he'd witnessed had not been so sparing.

Another hard gaze at the flames tore at his insides. He pushed his long coat behind his arms and stuffed his hands into the pockets of his breeches as he walked away.

"Wait!" A hand touched his arm, and Jess turned in response. "Thank you. . . for saving my mother. You can't know how grateful I am."

"I think I can," Jess muttered and hurried on, as if putting distance between himself and the flames might get rid of the pain. But three hours and several drinks later, he was still feeling it. Observing how steady his hand was as he lifted the glass, Jess realized he wasn't even slightly drunk. Idly he watched the golden liquid swirl in concert with his thoughts.

Jess had lost track of the time since he'd seen Alexa. The weeks and months merged together in a mindless void. He had wandered through mountains and vast, flat lands, sleeping under the stars and living on practically nothing. He had aimlessly explored city streets, hiding in dark corners of pubs and dully absorbing the wretchedness of life through senses that were too punished to care. He had somehow believed that time and miles would ease the hurt and betrayal. And the fear. But here he sat, so keenly in touch with his emotions that he felt only death might free him.

Jess could see now that his months of wandering had only buffered and insulated his pain. He had left hoping to face up to it and get on with his life. But all he had done was hide, until the fire brought it all back to him. The smell of smoke had urged the taste of mourning into his mouth as if it had been yesterday. He could see his home lying in rubble, feel his hatred for Chad—a hatred that seemed to have spurred him to insanity. And then there was Alexa. She had taught him how to live again, had filled his life with hope. He still couldn't bring himself to believe she was gone. And of all the men she could have turned to, why did it have to be Richard? His only friend since childhood, the man he'd trusted more than any other, had married the woman he loved behind his back. But hadn't he deserved it? In truth, wasn't he a product of madness and deception, destined to live his life as an outsider, never understanding the way a normal man might think?

"Why me?" Jess muttered under his breath and emptied another glass. But the liquor, hard as it was, didn't begin to dull the reality. His feelings were smoldering close to the surface, making it evident by their intensity that he'd felt nothing at all for a long time. It was all so blasted uncomfortable, but it was becoming apparent that he couldn't push it down or bury it any longer. Why couldn't he just admit that he was what he was? Insanity was in his blood. It had provoked Chad Byrnehouse to do unspeakable things, and it had forced him away from Alexa.

Part of Jess wanted so badly to go home, to resume the life he loved so dearly. But going back meant facing the truth. If he didn't face it first, he could never exist there in peace. *Peace.* The very idea seemed to mock him, as if a voice whispered in his ear that he was not worthy of peace. Something in that voice reminded him of Chad Byrnehouse.

As if to counter that voice, something deep inside him felt compelled to pray. His plea for help was brief but intense. He couldn't fathom anyone but God himself getting him beyond this. But then, he couldn't fathom even God caring one way or another for such a fool as himself.

Jess downed another drink and was relieved to feel a vague lethargy behind his eyes. But still the hurt hovered relentlessly. He cursed under his breath and pressed his brow into his hands, wondering what he'd ever done to deserve the life he'd been born to live.

"Did you say somethin'?" A feminine voice startled Jess and he looked up, disoriented and uncertain.

"I don't know. Did I?"

The pretty face hovering above him smiled. He remembered then that he was in a pub, hundreds of miles from home.

"You look . . . lonely," she said, tracing a finger over his stubbled face.

"Do I?" he asked, wondering if she was impressed with his vocabulary.

"I know about lonely men." She sat on the edge of the table and leaned over him. "It's my job."

Jess quickly surveyed this woman as she wound her finger into a curl behind his ear. He'd encountered many of her profession in his travels, but most of them had a hard edge to them that added years to their faces. There was a subtle element of softness in the eyes hovering above him, and something about her vaguely reminded him of Alexa, though he couldn't quite pinpoint what. There was nothing about her build or coloring that resembled the woman he ached for.

"I've got some time," she said with a coy smile that made Jess's eyes widen. "I'll make it worth your while." It had never crossed his mind to pay for what she was offering, but at the moment it seemed an

appropriate thing to do. He *was* lonely. The woman he loved was having another man's baby, and there was nothing in his life to steer him
away from such an encounter. If he truly was the demented man he
believed he was, wouldn't this prove that he'd deserved everything he'd
gotten and he'd do well to accept it?

Without a word, he rose from his chair and motioned for this
woman to lead the way. She took his hand with a triumphant smile
and sauntered up the stairs. They stepped into a dimly lit room, and
she closed the door.

"Oh, my goodness." She gave an embarrassed chuckle. "I was in
such a hurry to get downstairs that I forgot to tidy up. Have a seat,
and I'll just be a few minutes." When Jess hesitated, she gently pushed
his coat from his shoulders and laid it over the back of a chair. She
removed his hat and hung it on a hook by the door. "Sit down." She
motioned with her hand. "Make yourself comfortable."

Jess did as she'd asked, but he didn't feel comfortable. When he
realized she was changing the sheets on the bed, he swallowed hard
and tried to distract himself. She stopped in mid-chore and added a
log to some smoldering coals, urging it into flames with an ornately
handled poker. As he stared into the fire, horrid images flashed
through his mind, and squeezing his eyes shut only edged the memories closer. He opened them and diverted his attention to this woman.
With practiced efficiency, he managed to temporarily push the emotions away, ignoring the way they protested and threatened to erupt.
Jess watched her set a screen on the hearth and straighten some objects
on the narrow mantel before she returned to the bed.

"What's your name?" he asked, watching her kneel in the middle
of the mattress to smooth a clean white sheet over the upper corners.

"Lizzie," she reported. "What's yours?"

"Jess," he stated tonelessly. He couldn't remember the last time he'd
heard it spoken aloud. Looking around the room more carefully, it was-
n't what he'd expected. His knowledge of such things had come from
overhearing other men talk, but the impression he'd always gotten was
not so homey. He could well imagine the dingy rooms, the smell of
cheap perfume, the lack of warmth. But this room reminded him of
the changes Alexa had made in her room above the carriage house. The
furnishings and decor were simple, but it was clean and cozy.

His attention turned to Lizzie. What made a woman do such things? He suspected that for some it was enjoyable, but she didn't seem like the type.

"You're not from around here," she said, tossing the dirty sheets into a basket before she went behind a dressing screen.

"How could you tell?" he asked.

She gave a little laugh. "I don't see many gentlemen in this place." When she emerged, she was tying a silky blue wrapper about her waist. More than a hint of something red and lacy showed above the sash. "And it's apparent you're not a city man."

"You're right about that," he admitted.

Lizzie made herself comfortable on Jess's lap and began playing with his curls again. "So what brings you here?"

"Just . . . wandering," he stated, trying to get used to this.

"Ah," she smiled again and he decided he liked her, "I think I understand that look now."

"What look?"

"You've got that broken heart look."

Jess surprised himself when he admitted, "It only hurts when it beats."

"Who was she? A real lady, I'd wager."

"Actually," Jess took a lock of Lizzie's golden hair between his fingers, "she was a jockey."

"Really?" Lizzie leaned back to look at his face. "I didn't know women did things like that."

"Neither did I."

Without permission, Lizzie pressed a hand beneath Jess's shirt collar and kissed the side of his throat. It took courage to put his arms around her, but once he did, the contact urged him on. It felt good just to share human touch. He nuzzled closer and inhaled her sweet, feminine fragrance. As he felt himself responding to her nearness, he began to wonder if he might fly into a passionate rage and do her harm. There was no doubt he wanted what she was offering, but he relaxed as it became evident that his mind was in control, and his emotions were simply elsewhere.

As Lizzie began to unbutton Jess's shirt, those emotions threatened to become involved. "Why do you do this?" he asked, partly from curiosity, but mostly to distract himself from the feelings he'd been confronting with liquor downstairs.

"Do what?"

"What makes you live this way?" She looked so surprised that Jess briefly lost his own pain in a sweep of compassion. He touched the back of his fingers to her face. "Tell me, Lizzie," he said gently.

"It's not often I get a man who wants me to talk," she admitted. Lizzie straightened her back but remained on his lap. While she fondled the leather braces over his shoulders, she spoke without looking at him. "My father told me if I believed I could be anything but a whore, I was crazy." Jess's compassion deepened as she added, "When he turned me out, I had no choice." She met his eyes almost reluctantly. For a brief moment, two lost souls touched in spirit. "It's not so bad." She shrugged her shoulders and gave a little laugh. "I try to avoid the undesirables and make do with what I've got."

Jess watched her a long moment, contemplating the injustice. Her profession could be questioned, but could she be judged so harshly, considering what had brought her to it? He briefly wondered what might have happened to Alexa if he'd not given her a job when Chad turned her out. The thought made him sick. Jess knew little about this Lizzie, but what he saw left him with one conclusion. This girl was not what he considered a whore, and he had seen many of them these past weeks.

In an effort to console her, Jess cupped one side of her face in his hand. With little thought, he urged her lips to his and kissed her as if it was her first. Lizzie looked at him deeply, as if to question his motives.

"To the devil with what your father says," he muttered. "You are what you believe you are."

Lizzie's eyes widened, and Jess heard the words come back to him. If he believed what he'd just told her, then what was he doing here? The Jess Davies sitting in this chair was not raging with demented passion, forcing himself on this woman. Funny that he would recall the hotel owner saying just this morning, *You really kept your head in there.* Other memories flooded through him with clarity, telling him his anger had been justified, his passion only human.

True, Emma Davies' mind had not been whole, but she had certainly not been a raving lunatic. Jess's mother was kind and good, and she'd loved him. And if the man that fathered Jess was crazy, perhaps there was room for doubt, but not for fear. Jess had grown up with the example of Ben Davies shining before him. Ben was strong and sane. Jess only learned after Ben's death that he was not his father; but never once while he'd lived had he been treated as anything less than a son. Ben had loved Jess and raised him well.

And Alexa. Sweet, beautiful Alexa. Wasn't it plain for any fool to see that he'd forced her away? His reasons were understandable, but so were hers. He should feel grateful that she had someone like Richard to turn to. If he truly loved her, he could learn to accept whatever was necessary for her happiness.

It only took an instant for the circumference of his thoughts to fall into place and bring him to one conclusion. The only crazy thing Jess had ever done was pay heed to Chad Byrnehouse.

It all made such perfect sense that Jess had to wonder what he'd been thinking all this time. What had been keeping him from finding peace with himself? What had kept him from loving Alexa completely? And then it hit. Like a volcano that had threatened and sputtered until the pressure couldn't be held back, Jess felt a tangible pain tremoring and bubbling inside of him.

"I've got to go." He stood so quickly that Lizzie barely caught her footing as she slid off his lap. "I'm sorry, Lizzie," he muttered, fumbling to put on his coat. "You're really a wonderful girl, but I . . . I've got to get home, and . . ."

At her bewilderment, Jess paused long enough to consider what he might have overlooked. Seeing pen and paper on a little table close by, he hurriedly scratched something in a barely legible hand. "This is where you can find me if you ever need anything." Jess put on his hat and added firmly, "I mean that, Lizzie." He reached in his pocket and drew out a roll of bills, all he had left in his possession since the fire. He peeled off a fiver and handed her the rest. Lizzie took it reluctantly, questioning him with moist eyes.

"I just need to get home," he muttered and opened the door. In an effort to soften his abruptness, Jess paused long enough to touch her face. "Remember, Lizzie, the only crazy thing you ever did was pay heed to what your father said."

Jess rode hard and fast through the deepest part of the night. At first he succumbed to habit and tried to suppress the years of pain attempting to assault him in explosive thrusts. But the struggle eventually became too great, and he allowed it to happen. He rode until the pain blinded him and he numbly slid off the horse and fell to his knees. A groan of agony rose from the innermost part of him, bringing with it an eruption of pain so intense that he felt certain no man-made torture could compare to it. As if a Pandora's Box had opened inside of him, the toxic afflictions of a lifetime rushed up to hit him between the eyes. Every hurt he'd ever endured and not confronted, every loss he'd ever suffered and not mourned came back to him now, claiming the right to be felt and acknowledged. Thoughts and memories oozed through his mind in volatile chaos, like the seepage from a long-festering wound, stinging a trail across his heart and soul until they found a way to escape and leave him in peace.

Jess awoke to shards of light that made him squint and cover his eyes. For a moment he thought he had died, but aching muscles and a growl of hunger convinced him he was very much alive. Sitting up to face the daylight, he found himself in a sparse grove of trees. The horse he'd ridden grazed on moist grass a short distance away, its reins hanging free. Disorientation gave way to clear memories of the night before, and Jess groaned as he lay back on the grass. He didn't have a clue where he was or how far he'd ridden. He might have felt lost, except that he'd never been so completely at peace. The path of his life was perfectly illuminated in his mind. The past no longer haunted him, the future didn't make him afraid. *Perhaps God had heard his prayer after all.* And only one thing mattered now. He had to get home.

Jess stretched and mounted his horse, keenly aware of the physical effect of what his emotions had done to him in the night. But as he calculated the most likely route toward home and headed that direction, the lightness of his spirit more than compensated for any temporary discomfort. Jess might not have consciously realized the weight he'd carried inside him all these years, if he didn't now feel the absence of it. All those bottled emotions had weighted his conscience with the fear of one day confronting them. And now they were gone. There remained the nagging doubt of his paternity, but it no longer made him afraid of himself. He had yet to face Alexa, and he knew he would forever love her. But life was too precious to waste on pining for a woman—even Alexa.

Jess urged the horse to a steady gallop, and laughed at the wind in his face. He would take on life the best he could and make the most of it. He was going home.

When he finally arrived, Jess halted at the crest of the hill and inhaled the scene before him. *Home*. Memories and fears had assaulted him through his journey; he'd even begun to wonder if Chad had done something unspeakable in his absence. But there it lay before him, as perfect as he'd remembered.

With an anxious leap of his heart, Jess heeled the horse into a gallop. He was so close he could almost taste it.

❦ ❦ ❦

A bright morning came when Alexa felt at least some of her prayers were being heard. Richard had taken a turn for the better, and with a little more nursing he was back on his feet enough to at least catch up on the book work.

Jimmy declared at breakfast that Richard and Alexa made a fine pair these days. Neither of them hardly had the strength to carry their own weight about, and they both looked a little peaked. "But still," Murphy added, "I swear I could walk on what shines between them when they look at each other." Alexa smiled timidly at Richard. She knew Murphy was right.

With the meal finished, Alexa and Richard left together. "Come along, my love." He took her hand. "If you can hold me up as far as the garden, I think I can hobble into the office."

"It's not as bad as all that," Alexa chortled.

"Think of all the practice you'll have for when you're old and crippled," Murphy called, following the boys toward the stable to begin their work.

"That's not funny," Alexa called back as she and Richard moved up the path toward the house.

A short while later, Murphy caught sight of a lone rider approaching from the hills. He studied the distant figure with squinted eyes, then hollered, "Hey, Jimmy. Come out here."

Jimmy and Tod emerged from the stable, and Murphy pointed toward the horizon. "Do you suppose that's Jess, or am I seein' things?"

"Blimey, it is Jess!" Jimmy cried.

"I was beginning to think he was dead," Tod added.

"Well, he's not," Murphy said with a jovial lilt to his voice as the certainty deepened.

They could hardly resist walking out to meet him. But as the horse slowed, they sensed uncertainty in Jess. The closer he came, the more they realized he looked different. There was no visible alteration; he even wore the same coat and hat he'd left in. But it was undeniable. Jess had changed.

Jess pulled the reins back to stop when the boys stood before him. He wondered for a moment if his absence had brought them to conclusions that were less than favorable. Unable to bear the suspense, he dismounted and held out a hand toward Murphy.

Murphy laughed and shook it heartily. "Blimey, it's good to see you."

"I must admit," Jess chuckled, "it's good to see you, too." With the tension broken, a round of greetings were exchanged, and Jess wasn't ashamed to admit, "I actually missed you boys."

"You look great, Jess," Tod said. "We were beginning to wonder what had become of you."

"I was beginning to wonder myself," Jess said soberly, but they laughed. Jess laughed with them, and they walked toward the stable.

"So how is everything?" Jess asked.

"Not too bad," Jimmy replied in spite of the blatant limp Jess was quick to notice. "Considering."

"What do you mean by that?" Jess wondered if Chad might have done something that he'd not yet seen evidence of.

"I think you'll find things in good shape," Murphy reported. "Richard's handled things well."

"Where is he now?"

"In your office, I believe," Murphy said, "catchin' up the book work. That's about all he's done since he got over the pneumonia."

"Pneumonia?" Jess stopped walking, and the others were two steps ahead before they realized it and turned around. "How did he get pneumonia?"

"Probably out herdin' sheep in the rain," Jimmy said and they began to walk again, more slowly.

"And why, dare I ask, was he doing that?"

"Mobs got scattered at shearin' time," Murphy provided.

"But we got 'em all in," Jimmy said proudly. "Got a good price, too."

"Where are the rest of the boys?" Jess asked, glancing around nostalgically. Oh, how he'd missed this place!

"Fiddler would probably be in the kitchen," Tod said.

"What's he doing in the kitchen?" Jess was bewildered.

"Cookin', of course," Jimmy stated.

"Edward's not feelin' too well," Murphy said before Jess had a chance to ask. Their eyes met with a mutual concern.

Tod took Jess's horse as they approached the stable. "Thank you," Jess smiled. "I'll go and talk to Richard now and . . ." Warmth filled his eyes. "It's really good to see you, boys."

They laughed to indicate they felt the same as Jess turned and walked up the path toward the house, going slowly to absorb his surroundings and the way they made him feel. He paused when the old house came into view. Was Alexa there now? Had she changed? He swallowed hard and moved up the steps and through the back door.

Jess walked into his office without knocking. Richard stood from behind the desk as Jess threw his hat onto a chair.

"Jess." He laughed and came around the desk to shake his hand, sensing immediately that he seemed different. "Am I glad to see you!"

Jess took notice of the leather mask. "You look nice."

"Alexa made it," he said humbly, and Jess smiled.

Tension briefly filled the silence hovering between them. "I heard you've not been doing so well," Jess finally said when they were both seated.

"I'm doing better now," Richard said. "But I must admit, for a while I wondered if I'd make it."

"How did you manage everything if you were—"

"I had a lot of good help."

Richard met his eyes, and the evidence deepened that something in Jess had changed. That cold, hard look was gone, and there was a warmth about him that was indescribable.

"How is your wife?" Jess asked gently.

"Better some days than others."

"Is something wrong?" Jess asked intently.

"The pregnancy," Richard stated. "It's been hard on her."

Jess nodded with concern, then he cautiously moved to something he knew he had to say. "Richard, I want you to know that I've come to terms with all of this." Richard glanced down and the tension returned. "I love Alexa," he admitted, "and I believe I always will. It's only right that you know. But I understand now why she couldn't marry me, and I'm grateful she had you to turn to. I think she's better off." Richard looked up at Jess in search of sincerity. "I want the two of you to be happy together, and I will never do anything that might cause problems."

Richard overcame his stunned reaction to say, "You can't know what that means to me."

"You're a good man, Richard, and I thank you for all you've done for me. I know that Alexa's life is in good hands."

Richard cleared his throat, then chuckled humbly. "You must go and see her. A day doesn't pass without her talking about you. She's been terribly worried."

Jess smiled tensely and rose from his chair. "Perhaps I should get cleaned up first."

"And Jess," Richard said, "tell her what you told me."

Jess nodded and shook Richard's hand again. He left Richard with the book work and went to his room to freshen up and change. It felt good to be home, and he knew he could never take any of it for granted. He loved this land, and he loved his life. And most importantly, he felt peace within himself.

It felt good to dress in his favorite pair of breeches and riding boots, then he walked idly through the house and came out the side entrance. He stopped a moment to gather his courage and realized he'd been stalling. This was not going to be easy.

Approaching the house, he saw Alexa kneeling in a little garden that hadn't been there when he'd left. His heart reacted far more intensely than he'd thought it would. Stoically he moved on, pausing at the gate to just absorb her presence. Her hair was wound loosely into a knot at the back of her head, and straying wisps circled her face. She wore a dark, loose-fitting, sleeveless dress that billowed around her, with a striped blouse beneath it. The sleeves were rolled up to her elbows and smudged with dirt from the chore she was busily engaged in. A basket at her side was filled with a variety of fresh vegetables.

When he couldn't bear the anticipation any longer, Jess finally found his voice. "Good morning, Mrs. Wilhite," he said, and she looked up abruptly.

"Jess," she said, her voice barely audible. After a moment of stunned silence, she came to her feet—with difficulty, he noticed. The weight she had gained was apparent, and he had to stop and remind himself she was going to have Richard's baby. But maternity only made her more beautiful. There was a serenity about her that had been absent before.

Jess opened the gate and walked through. Alexa brushed the dirt from her hands and came toward him. Her heart beat so hard she feared she would faint. She couldn't get to him fast enough.

"Jess," she repeated and came into his arms. Jess embraced her firmly, not eager to let her go, but doing his best to keep his affection within the proper bounds. He pressed a kiss to her brow, then forced himself to take hold of her shoulders and step back.

Tears brimmed in Alexa's eyes as they silently soaked in the passage of time. Searching his face, she saw an evidence of change that warmed her. But compassion joined the warmth as she noted the subtle deepening of lines around his eyes. He had aged five years in a matter of months.

"What happened?" She touched his face. He closed his eyes and kissed her hand. "Are you all right?"

"I'm fine, really," he said, and she knew he meant it.

"I've missed you, Jess." She embraced him again, then stepped back and took his hands into hers.

"I missed you too, Alexandra." He smiled, and she saw an absence of pain in his eyes that stirred her. "I hear you're not doing so well."

"Oh, it comes and goes," she said as if it were nothing. "So, tell me where you've been."

"Just . . . wandering. No place worth mentioning."

"You seem . . . different."

"I am," he stated with confidence, then he saw a weakness envelope her as she unwillingly leaned on the support of his hands. "Are you all right?" He shot an arm around her shoulders.

Alexa put a hand over her eyes. "I believe I've been in the sun too long, that's all. Let's go inside."

Jess picked up the basket of vegetables, and they walked slowly toward the house. "Are you sure you're all right?"

"It's nothing too serious." She smiled up at him. "Same old thing."

Jess watched her carefully and didn't know whether to believe her or not.

"Would you like something to drink?" she asked as they entered the side door into the kitchen. "Port? Brandy?"

"No, thank you," he said. She set the basket on the table and glanced toward him in question. Without looking at her he stated, "I don't drink."

Alexa caught his eye, and they exchanged an emotional smile. "Lemonade, perhaps?"

"I'd love some," he replied and moved into the parlor. Alexa followed a few minutes later with two glasses and sat beside him on the sofa. He saw her grimace slightly as she situated herself, and he impulsively took her hand.

"What's wrong?" he demanded.

"Nothing, really," she assured him. "The doctor says it's going to be a big baby. I fear it takes up too much room already, and I've still got a number of weeks left."

"You're too little to have a big baby," Jess said with concern.

"That's what the doctor said." She laughed, but worry seeped into Jess.

"Alexa," he said intently and she met his eyes, "there is a lot I need to say to you, and I hope you will hear me out." She nodded and squeezed his hand. Jess chuckled tensely and glanced down. "I have so many apologies to make that I don't know where to begin."

"There's no need to—"

"Alexa, please hear me out."

She waited patiently for him to go on, despite the emotions churning inside her.

"I could generalize it all and tell you how very sorry I am for all that I did to hurt you. I look back and see so many mistakes I made. I just didn't understand myself, and . . . well, there's no reason to make excuses. I hurt you many times and I know it. I hope you can find it in you to forgive me, Alexa."

Tears reappeared in her eyes as she put a hand to his face. "Of course I'll forgive you, Jess. How could I not? I'm so grateful to see you here and safe."

Jess glanced down humbly. "I want you to know, Alexa, that I understand why you married Richard. I don't resent that decision anymore. In truth, I admire the courage it took for you to do it. I know the two of you are happy together, and I will never do anything to take that away from either of you. I sorely regret the times in the past when I attempted to do just that, and for that, too, I ask your forgiveness."

"It's all in the past," she assured him, then pushed her arms around his shoulders with full acceptance. Jess squeezed his eyes shut as he held her, so grateful for all she had given him.

Alexa suddenly pulled away, looking alarmed.

"What?" he demanded.

"I just got kicked," she laughed. Jess studied her rounded belly with wonder. "Do you want to feel it?" she asked, then she placed his hand against her without waiting for his permission. "Don't look so concerned," she chuckled. "All the boys have felt it move. What else can we do to pass the time?"

Jess could feel nothing but the pulse beating in his ears from being so close to her. He hadn't counted on what being with her would do to him.

"It is a stubborn child," Alexa said when nothing happened. "Just be patient." Jess nodded. Their eyes met and she added, "I can't believe you're here, Jess."

"I can't either," he chuckled. Alexa kissed his cheek, not afraid to show her affection. She knew he wouldn't take unfair advantage of it.

"Won't you tell me what happened?" she urged quietly.

"Perhaps one day," he said, then an abrupt movement pushed against his hand.

Alexa laughed. "Did you feel that?"

He nodded, his eyes wide. "It's incredible." Jess was tempted to wish it was his baby, that she was his wife, that . . . He stopped himself, knowing such thoughts would bring about nothing good.

Alexa eased away but continued to hold his hand as she told him of all that had happened in his absence. Gradually she became accustomed to the soft expression in his eyes.

Jess didn't change his demeanor or even take his hand from hers when Richard came in. Knowing he had nothing to hide or feel guilty for, he just smiled and thought how good it felt.

"Hello, my love." Richard bent to kiss Alexa and pressed an affectionate hand over the baby.

Emotion rose in Jess as he observed them. Even with all the changes, his hopeless love for Alexa still remained. In his absence he'd begun to think it would be easier, but just seeing her made his heart go mad. He knew it would always be with him. Still, that didn't change his conviction to do just as he had promised both Richard and Alexa. His emotions didn't give him the right to intrude upon their lives. He simply had to deal with it on his own.

Twenty-three
NO REGRETS

"I believe it's nearly noon," Richard said. "Are you brave enough to try Fiddler's cooking?"

"After what I've been living on," Jess came to his feet, "it's got to be wonderful."

They walked together to the bunkhouse. Richard put his arm around Alexa, and she kept Jess's hand in hers. As Jess came through the door, he was greeted with such enthusiasm that he felt choked up. Richard commented that Jess had surely brought good luck back with him, and within days the theory proved itself. Edward's health improved, and he returned to the kitchen; it appeared he still had some time yet to live. And Alexa declared she felt better than she had in months.

Jess began eating in the bunkhouse again and gradually felt at ease. It nearly felt like old times as he spent the majority of his days helping with the work. He quite naturally found opportunities to help Alexa, and they began to talk. His deepest feelings emerged progressively, and he told her everything that had happened. He was surprised to find that Alexa had been right long ago when she'd suggested they could be friends. She became more dear to him in that respect than he believed anyone ever could. There was only one thing he couldn't talk to her about. He figured his feelings for her were better left unspoken.

Jess was pleased to know she'd been using the piano in his absence. And now that he was back, he took the opportunity to listen. Often he and Richard would visit and share coffee while Alexa played. They shared Alexa's enjoyment of her talent, especially while she was unable to ride or work with the horses.

Jess did well hiding his feelings for Alexa. Though he knew they would never go away, he found it possible to live with them and still be at peace. He was astounded at the complete acceptance Richard showed him. No matter how much time he spent with Alexa, Richard didn't seem disturbed in the least. It left Jess baffled enough that he had to ask one day as they worked together in the stables.

"Why doesn't it bother you when Alexa and I spend so much time together? If I were you, I think it would bother me."

Richard kept working, but Jess caught a slight smile. "I love Alexa, and she loves me. But a man would be a fool to think he can fulfill every need of a woman. We have a good marriage, and it's strong enough that I have no reason to feel threatened or . . . jealous. I know how the two of you feel about each other, and I also know that nei-ther of you would ever do anything to destroy this marriage." Richard paused and looked directly at Jess. "Alexa has been happier since you came back, Jess. There is an emotional need in her that you fill. I am not so selfish that I would deny you the right to have her in your life." Richard grinned. "To a degree, of course."

Jess was momentarily speechless. "Thank you, Richard. I will not betray your trust."

Richard smiled. "I know."

❦ ❦ ❦

As Jess became reaccustomed to his life, he knew he couldn't put off something he considered inevitable. He'd found peace with those he loved, but he also had to find it with his enemies. Sooner or later, he had to face Chad Byrnehouse and let him know where he stood. Whether it changed Chad's attitude or not, Jess knew he had to do it for his own peace of mind—despite how much he dreaded it.

Waiting in the elaborate entry at Byrnehouse, Jess recalled coming here and trying to kill Chad over a decade earlier. As the memories rushed through his mind, Jess thought of something he'd forgotten. His eyes were drawn to the bannister posts, where a young girl had observed the confrontation.

"Alexa," he whispered aloud. He wondered if she remembered the incident. He knew it must have been her. If he had only known then that . . .

"The maid said I had company." Chad's voice grated on Jess's nerves as he sauntered arrogantly down the stairs. "I should beat her for lying."

"Come now, Chad," Jess attempted to keep it light, "surely you can muster a degree of social grace."

Chad feigned a hospitable grin and motioned Jess into the drawing room. "I'd heard you were gone," he stated, pouring himself a drink.

"Well, I'm back."

"Want one?" Chad waved his glass toward Jess, who shook his head firmly. "If you didn't come to swindle me out of a drink, why did you come?"

"Oh," Jess sat down before Chad did, crossing his legs casually, "I just thought we could have a little chat."

"Feeling lonely, eh?" Chad chuckled. "That's understandable— since my sister married that beast she claims to love." He took a long swallow. "But then, she claimed to love you, as well."

Jess covered his anger well. "There's a little beast in all of us," he said in Richard's defense.

Chad gave a demented laugh that stung Jess's nerves. "How true, old pal. How true."

"I'll get to the point," Jess said.

"I wish you would. My social graces are only good for so long."

"I think it's time we both grew up and put a stop to this ridiculous feud."

"Feud?" Chad laughed. "What feud? I was under the impression that we were the best of friends."

"Sarcasm isn't going to change the facts."

"And what facts are those, old pal?"

"I know as well as you do that you've been out for my hide for years. I understand why our fathers hated each other, but I don't know why you insist on—"

"And why," he interrupted, *"did* our fathers hate each other, Jess?"

Chad's self-satisfied grin waned slightly when Jess stated, "They loved the same woman. What's *your* problem?"

"Interesting, isn't it," Chad leaned back and put his boots on the table, "to think how Alexa could have been your sister."

"But she isn't." Jess ground the words out, wondering if he would ever find peace with the fact that his father was a rapist—and Chad knew it.

"No," Chad laughed, "but I'll bet it gave her a good scare."

"You really enjoy this, don't you," Jess snarled.

"I really do," he said proudly.

"Well, I'm lowering my pride enough to tell you that I don't. I'm asking you to stop. It's pointless."

"Oh, but it's not," Chad grinned. "It's actually quite fun. You wouldn't want me to lose my main source of pleasure in life, would you?"

"Why?" Jess asked intently, and Chad looked perfectly ignorant. "Why do you hate me so much?"

"Now that," Chad gave his intolerable laugh again, "is the key to all of this, isn't it? If I told you that, I really would lose all my fun."

"You're playing games, Chad. One day it will catch up with you, and you'll lose."

"Oh, I'll admit I'm a game player," Chad said soberly. "A man's got to do something for sport. But I wouldn't go so far as to say I'd lose. I won't lose, Jess, because I'm competing with you, and you haven't got the guts to win. In fact," he chuckled, "you could hardly keep me at bay when you haven't even got what it takes to keep Alexa where you want her."

It took every ounce of self-control to remain calm. The statement bit, but Jess wasn't about to give Chad the satisfaction of showing it. "Well," he stood and pushed his hands into his pockets, "I should have known you'd be fool enough to let it go on. But you can't say I didn't try to settle this peacefully."

"There's only one way this feud—as you call it—will end."

"And how is that?"

"When one or the other of us stops breathing." Chad smiled complacently. "Which could be arranged, if you're really determined to have it over with."

"Were you planning to commit suicide in the near future?"

Chad laughed unbearably. "That's a good one, old pal, but unfortunately for you, I've got too much to live for."

"Are you threatening me with my life?" Jess asked coolly.

"Would I do something so brash?" Chad chuckled. "Then again, perhaps you might be grateful if I put you out of your misery." Jess said nothing. "We both know how miserable you are these days. There's no point denying it. And if you were out of your misery, I'd be out of mine, too." Chad finished off his drink and slammed the glass down. "This game is to the death, Jess. Winner take all."

"All of what?" Jess asked dryly.

Chad only threw back his head and laughed.

"You're insane," Jess said under his breath with a pitiful shake of his head. "Thank you for your offer," he added more loudly, "but no thank you. I'll leave this life when the good Lord sees fit. I don't need you to intervene. And I hate to disappoint you, but I am not miserable. At least I won't be, once I've removed myself from your social graces. Besides, if I were dead, you wouldn't have any fun at all."

"It was nice chatting with you." Chad smiled complacently. "Stop by anytime, and we'll do it again."

Jess left the house abruptly and took his fury out on the speed at which he rode home. Once the anger filtered away, he felt good to know that at least he'd tried. If this feud continued—and he knew it would—it would not be at the expense of Jess's conscience.

❦ ❦ ❦

It wasn't unusual for Jess to find it difficult to sleep. As always, his mind was with Alexa and his heart ached. It was becoming easier to be with her and keep up the proper facade, but his time alone was continually filled with longing. The nights were long and dark, and he hated them. He wondered at times if another woman in his life might make a difference. But it was difficult to comprehend any woman taking Alexa's place. Perhaps time would make such a prospect easier.

Just as he had on many nights since his return, Jess sat on the side veranda and lifted his boots onto the rail. He had a perfect view of

Alexa's house and the yard, and he found serenity gazing at the stars, concentrating on feeling peace within himself. It was the only thing he had. If he sat here long enough, he could almost fall asleep. And then he could find his bed and slip away in exhaustion before the loneliness crept in.

Jess stretched and set his boots on the tile floor. From the corner of his eye, he saw a figure in white floating across the yard. If he hadn't known better, he'd have thought it was a ghost.

"Alexa." His heart quickened as he wondered what she was doing out so late. She was in no condition to be wandering around in the middle of the night. He saw her disappear into the stable, and instinctively he followed.

Jess slipped through the door and heard an unfamiliar sound. She was crying. Quietly he lit a lamp, but she didn't respond to the light. His heart went out to see her sitting next to Crazy's stall, her face buried in her hands, ignoring the gentle nudging of the horse's muzzle, as if it sensed her need for comfort. Jess knelt beside her and touched her shoulder. She looked up, briefly startled. He held open his arms. She hesitated a moment, then accepted his embrace willingly.

Jess sat on the ground and eased her closer. She took hold of his shirt and cried harder. "What is it?" he asked gently, brushing her hair away from her tear-stained face. She was too upset to speak, and he waited patiently for her to release her emotion.

"Your hair has grown," he murmured, running his fingers through it. Since his return, he had only seen her hair put up. "I'll never forget the way it looked the first time I saw you leaning against the fence."

When her crying ceased, he asked quietly, "Where is Richard?"

"He's at home. I told him I needed to be alone."

"Perhaps you should be crying in his arms."

"I already did." She sniffled and laid her face against his chest.

"Did you talk to him?" he asked.

"He knows what's wrong. There's nothing he can do about it. It's my problem."

"Do you want to talk about it?" he urged, wondering if he was stepping onto thin ice.

"No," Alexa lied. She ached to tell him, to pour her heart out. But what good would it possibly do? In the months Jess had been gone, she'd missed him terribly. She'd told herself—and Richard—that she was concerned for his welfare and feared what might happen to him. Of course that was true. But deep inside, she knew there was more to it. And she felt certain that Richard knew it, too.

Before Jess had left, it was easy to turn to Richard and feel confident in her marriage. Jess's childish behavior was tangible evidence that she'd done the right thing. To this day she knew she'd not made a mistake in marrying Richard, and she'd do it again if faced with the same dilemma. She believed Jess would not have changed without such drastic consequences to face. But he *had* changed. Here he was, the man she'd fallen in love with—everything she had ever dreamed he could be.

There was no denying that Alexa loved Richard. Everything tangible in their relationship was good. Which made it all the more difficult to face up to what she had just done. Her thoughts brought the tears back, and she sobbed against Jess's already wet shirt.

"What is it, Alexa?" he asked, frustrated and concerned.

Alexa knew she shouldn't tell him. She had no idea what the consequences might be. But the burden was so heavy; the temptation too strong.

"I'm so ashamed, Jess; so humiliated."

"Tell me," he urged.

"Jess," she looked up at him, tears streaking her face, "don't misunderstand me. I love Richard."

"I know you do."

"It could be no other way. You know that, too, don't you?"

"Yes, I do," he admitted firmly, but not without emotion. His heart began to sink as he realized he was the cause of her pain. Whatever had happened, it had to do with him. "It's all right, Alexa. I understand."

His words gave her courage. "He was holding me, Jess," she cried, "kissing me, and I . . ."

Jess swallowed hard. "You what?"

"Oh, Jess." She buried her face against his shoulder. "I cried out your name."

Her crying increased with her confession. Jess brushed his lips over her brow and closed his eyes. Did she have any idea what it meant to him to know she thought of him the way he thought of her?

"I try to hide it, Jess," she cried. "I try not to think about you that way. But sometimes I can't help but remember, and I wonder if I will ever be what he deserves. He is so good to me, Jess. He deserves a woman who loves him with her whole heart."

"What did he say?" Jess asked gently.

She sobbed gently and bit her lip. "I apologized, but I felt so . . . so . . . How can I possibly explain it? He told me it was all right. He told me he knew it would be this way when he asked me to marry him. He said he's grateful to have me at all. Oh, Jess. Why does he have to be so good?"

"To keep us both humble." Jess had respect in his voice. "He has the character to be a shining example for any man."

"And that's why I love him, Jess."

"I know."

"And you, Jess. I love you for the same reason."

Jess felt a burning behind his eyes and fought to hold it back. "Don't say things like that to me, Alexa."

"It's true," she said. "You are so much like him."

She looked up to meet his eyes, and he could see the love glowing in her face. The emotion in her expression pushed his own feelings too close to the surface. Tears brimmed in his eyes as he bent to kiss her, doing his best to express affection and comfort while holding the passion back where it belonged.

Alexa sobbed when he pulled away, and he immediately regretted what he'd done. "I'm sorry," he whispered. "Forgive me, Alexa. I shouldn't have—"

"Shhh." She pressed her fingers to his lips. "Don't apologize, Jess. It's all we have."

"Come along." Jess rose to his feet and helped Alexa up. "We mustn't be alone this way. Let me take you home."

Alexa walked slowly within his embrace. She felt as if her emotion had drained all her strength. A heaviness settled into her lower back, but she felt sure some rest would ease the discomfort. It merged into something bordering on pain as they cut across the lawn to the old house.

Jess felt Alexa lean weakly against him as they walked. "Are you all right?" he asked.

"Yes," she said without much conviction, then she stopped abruptly. Even through the darkness, Jess felt her panic.

"What?" Jess tightened his grip as she nearly collapsed.

Something wrenched inside Alexa, and the blood rushed from her head. "No," she cried, "I'm not all right."

"What is it?" Jess asked frantically.

"I don't know," she said with fear and doubled over, moaning deeply. Jess scooped her into his arms and headed for the house. He threw open the door and hollered for Richard, who appeared immediately.

"What happened?" he demanded.

"Something's wrong. Send one of the boys for Dr. Lloyd."

"Put her on the bed," Richard ordered and headed out the door, knowing his wife was in good hands.

Jess set her carefully on the bed, then turned to light a lamp. He felt something wet on his arm and reached over to touch it. He gasped to see that his sleeve was soaked with blood where he'd carried her. "Alexa." He went to his knees beside her.

She moaned and weakly turned her face toward him. "I'm bleeding," she whimpered. "I can feel it. Something's wrong with me."

"You're going to be all right," he insisted. "We'll get the doctor. Everything will be fine."

Alexa moaned again and clutched at the sheets as if they might save her. They both knew it would be hours before any help arrived. Jess prayed silently for a miracle. The front door slammed, and Richard rushed into the room. "Fiddler's gone for the doctor," he reported. "What happened?"

"I was walking her home. This pain just hit her, and . . ." Jess discreetly drew Richard's attention to his bloodied sleeve.

"Good heavens." Richard moved to the bedside and Jess backed away. He'd never been so scared in his life. He didn't have any idea what to do, and it was evident Richard didn't either. On intuition, he ran to the bunkhouse.

"Murphy!" Jess shouted before he slammed the door.

"What?" He was already up and dressed, pacing the floor. "Is she gonna be all right?"

"Not if we don't do something." He grabbed Murphy's arm and dragged him outside.

"What are we doin'?" he demanded.

"You'd know what to do if that was one of my prize mares bleeding to death. So get in there and do something!"

Murphy stopped walking to protest. "But I don't know nothin' about . . . *that!*"

"You know more than anybody else around here."

"But it's . . . Alexa."

Jess took him by the shoulders and shook him. "It's Alexa's life! You've got to try."

Murphy sighed. He looked toward the old house, then he nodded. "I'll do my best."

"And wash your hands first, for crying out loud."

Murphy hurried into the house, and Jess sat on the porch to wait. Over an hour later, Richard came out and sat beside him. Jess didn't dare ask, and it was several minutes before Richard spoke. "I've never seen so much blood in my life."

Jess winced at the thought. "How is she . . . so far?"

"The bleeding's slowing down. I don't know if it's what Murphy did, or just plain miraculous."

"Probably a little of both."

"That's likely." Richard pushed his hands into his hair. "She's in labor. It's getting steadily worse."

"But it's too soon," Jess protested, "isn't it?"

Richard didn't answer. Jess cleared his throat to say something that had to be said. "Alexa told me what happened earlier." Richard looked at him sharply. "I know how difficult it must be for you to—"

"It's difficult for all of us, Jess. Least of all me."

"Why do you say that?"

"In spite of it all, I have been blessed with far more of Alexa in my life than I ever could have hoped for. Why should I begrudge that? It upset her a lot more than it upset me."

Jess didn't know what to say. They sat together in anguished silence until Richard muttered, "I'm ashamed to admit what I was just thinking."

"If you admit to the same thing I was thinking, then we could be ashamed together."

"After all we've been through, wouldn't it be ironic if we both ended up without her?"

Jess turned to Richard, not surprised at the thought, but by the way he'd expressed it. "If I could," Jess put a hand to Richard's shoulder, "I'd go in there and die in her place." Their eyes met with the unspoken bond they'd shared since childhood. "But she's not going to die, Richard. We just won't put up with it, that's all."

Richard looked toward the sky, black and starless. "I appreciate your optimism," he said, "but that doesn't explain this feeling I keep having that my time with Alexa is nearly over."

"I'd say it's your imagination," Jess said, then Richard went back into the house.

Their worst fears ended when Doctor Lloyd finally arrived. He dismissed Murphy with compliments on the way he'd handled the situation, and told Richard to stay close by. Whether they liked it or not, this baby was coming. He gave them no promises as to whether or not the mother would make it through.

The night moved into day with a mutual dread. Jess waited in the bunkhouse with the others. Looking around at his sober company, he wondered if so many men had ever been this concerned over one woman in premature labor. He kept his mind filled with silent prayer, but the hours dragged incessantly. They managed to pick through their meals, but not one of them had the will to get out and do more than what was absolutely necessary. It was as if the whole world hung in the balance of Alexa's life.

They were all on their feet before Richard even came through the bunkhouse door. Not a breath was drawn as they absorbed the wearied look about him, the mourning in his eyes.

"Alexa's fine." The expectant stares dissolved into a mutual sigh of relief. Then Richard bowed his head and Jess moved toward him. "The baby didn't make it." A hush fell over the room. Jess put a compassionate hand on Richard's shoulder, but he didn't know what to say.

"It was a little girl," Richard added more quietly. Jess ushered him to the table and poured him a cup of coffee. "Alexa held her for a minute, but she . . . ," he faltered slightly, "she just didn't have the strength to live."

"How's Alexa taking it?" Jess asked gently.

"It's difficult to tell," he said. "She's in so much pain right now that . . . Oh, Jess!" Richard put his face into his hands. "I will never understand why a woman would go through such a thing."

"That's what life is all about, I suppose," Jess said, then he glanced around. "What's everybody looking so glum for? We still have Alexa, don't we? I was under the impression, from the first day she came here, that nothing was impossible as long as we had Alexa.

"Look to the future, boys. If she can make it through this, we certainly can. And I know she can." Jess nudged Richard in the ribs. "The woman can make apple pie out of peaches."

❦   ❦   ❦

Alexa stared at the ceiling above her, fighting back the tears that came each time she stopped to think about it. Her baby was gone. How grateful she was for Richard, who never left her side for long. Though she knew he shared her grief completely, he was full of bright hope for the future and made every effort to ease her anxieties.

"We will have more chances," he whispered, brushing his lips over her brow as she lay with her head against his shoulder. "The most important thing right now is your health. When you get feeling better, perhaps we can go away for a while; a second honeymoon, maybe."

Alexa moved closer and wished she had the strength to hold him tightly. "I love you, Richard. I don't know what I would ever do without you."

"Nah," he laughed softly, "it's the other way around. Definitely the other way around."

Alexa fell asleep in his arms and awoke to sunlight streaming through the window. Richard's hope absorbed her. She had to believe their future would not be marred by the setback of losing this child.

Richard brought breakfast in and found her sitting up in bed, but she looked especially peaked and frail. The doctor had told him it would take weeks for her to recover from the loss of blood, but seeing her this way still disheartened him.

"Edward sends his love." Richard smiled and set the tray over her lap. He sat by the bed and nearly wanted to cry when it became evident that she was too weak to eat without help. He graciously took over, and she admitted she felt better after getting her stomach filled. Soon after Edward picked up the tray, Richard came in from the parlor to tell her she had a visitor.

"Hello, Alexa." Jess appeared in the doorway.

Richard smiled toward him and left the room. Jess threw his hat onto a chair.

"How you feeling?" He sauntered toward the bed with his hands in his pockets.

"Not very good." She attempted to keep the tone light, but Jess caught the anguish in her eyes as he sat carefully on the edge of the bed and took her hand.

He looked at her deeply, and Alexa read comfort in his eyes. Yearning to be in his arms, but knowing it wasn't right, she turned away. Jess cleared his throat uncomfortably as they both wondered if these feelings would ever cease to torment them.

"Is there anything I can get you?" Jess asked.

"No," she replied. "Richard takes good care of me."

Jess smiled and rose, but Alexa didn't let go of his hand.

"Please stay," she beckoned quietly, and he sat back down. "I would like to tell you how grateful I am for all you have done for Richard and me."

"I've done very little," he said humbly.

"Jess," she said and he met her eyes, pondering the severity of her tone, "I must apologize for telling you what I did the other night. Admitting such things to you could not be beneficial to either of us, and—"

"On the contrary," Jess said, "I have found a great deal of comfort in your admission." Her eyes suddenly glowed, and he had to swallow hard to continue. "I certainly have no intention of taking advantage of my knowledge. Nothing will change."

"Actually," she admitted with her head bowed, "I'm glad you know."

"Know what?" He pretended innocence.

She smiled. "That I love you still," she said, and he briefly closed his eyes. "Thank you for being strong, for my sake if not for yours. Please," her voice broke, "don't ever stop being strong."

As Jess absorbed her words, a familiar pain rose in him. "I'm not strong," he laughed in an effort to subdue it. "I just stay close to insanity."

"You're not crazy, Jess," she said gravely.

"I know," he chuckled, and she smiled.

"Jess, I was thinking about my mother. I wonder, what drove her and Ben apart? And what drove them together again?"

A pain rose in her eyes that Jess understood. "I know what you're trying to say."

"Then say it, so I don't have to."

"Whatever happened, you were the victim, Alexa. And you don't want any more victims."

"Thank you." She closed her eyes, and silent tears fell.

"Why are you crying?"

"I just lost my baby, Jess."

"Is there any other reason?"

"None I'll admit to."

"Alexa," he squeezed her hand, "everything will be all right. Richard's a good man. I'm certain he gives you everything you need and more."

Jess saw the truth in her eyes. She was not wholly content, but she didn't dare admit it; not to anyone. The pain deepened in Jess, but Alexa smiled and said, "I love Richard very much."

"Yes, I know you do," Jess said warmly as he rose and put his hands into his pockets. "If you need anything," he moved toward the door, "just let me know."

"Thank you," Alexa said, but he was gone.

❦   ❦   ❦

In a fortnight, Alexa felt good enough to get out of bed and see to her own needs. She still felt weak and sore, but late in the afternoon she ventured for a walk in the garden with Richard, needing a distraction from the continual mourning she felt at the loss of her baby. The fresh air felt invigorating. When she began to feel tired, he helped her inside to the sofa. A short while later, Jess came to the door. Alexa expected him to come into the parlor and visit, but instead Richard told her he would be back shortly, and they left together.

Richard returned a long while later, and Alexa couldn't resist asking, "What did he want?"

"He's leaving." Richard sat down and crossed his ankle on his knee. "That upsets you," he stated. Alexa looked away, not wanting her feelings read so easily.

"Where is he going?" she asked.

"He wouldn't say. He probably doesn't know. He was honest with me; he fears he's coming between us, though it's not intentional." Richard paused, and his voice softened. "I don't believe I've ever seen a man love a woman so much."

Alexa's eyes filled with wonder. "I have." He lifted a brow in question. "Would you have ever gotten over it if Jess and I had married?"

Soberly he shook his head, and Alexa looked toward the window. "Why should I be so fortunate—to be loved so much by two men, each so good, and so good to me?"

"You are worthy of loving," Richard stated.

Alexa shook her head and gave a slight laugh. "I have got to let go of him, Richard. It's not right for me to feel this way. I have to make myself be free of it."

"Perhaps that's not possible."

"It's got to be!" she insisted. "If Jess knew my feelings were gone, it would be easier for him to let go. I'm driving him away from his own home, Richard—again."

"Perhaps you and I should go," Richard suggested.

Alexa turned toward him, wondering if he meant it. "Where would we go?"

"I don't know, but we'd find something. I'm not afraid to do what I have to do to provide us a living. It could very well be the answer."

"Perhaps you're right," she admitted reluctantly. "When did Jess say he's leaving?"

"He didn't. I believe he has some business to finish up first. Probably not for a few days."

"That will give us time to think about it," Alexa said.

Richard took her in his arms. "I love you, Alexandra."

"I love you, too," she smiled, "and I always will."

He kissed her gently. "Do you regret it?" he asked, and her eyes narrowed. "Be honest with me, Alexa. Do you regret the decision we made to marry?"

Alexa glanced down briefly, but he had known it would be difficult for her to answer. She lifted her chin and said firmly, "I could never regret a moment of what you and I have shared. No," she added strongly, "I do not regret it."

Richard smiled and kissed her again. She had to believe that everything would be all right—somehow.

Twenty-four
MISTAKEN IDENTITY

Alexa lay awake, pondering whether or not it would be best to leave as Richard had suggested. She loved it here—their home, their work, their friends. The thought of leaving it all made her feel despair. But she knew Richard was right. It could well be the answer to allow Jess to be free of this torment, to find a life without her. And it would give her the opportunity to really let go of her feelings. If such a thing was possible.

Hearing thunder rumble in the distance, she hoped it would rain and cool the air. As it moved closer, she was pleased to see the curtains blowing in the breeze, and the air smelled moist with anticipation. She nuzzled close to Richard's back. He continued to sleep but she was tempted to wake him, longing to be in his arms.

White flashes illuminated the room occasionally, but the thunder followed far enough behind that it didn't concern her. The wind increased, and for a moment Alexa thought she could smell smoke. She had nearly decided it was her imagination when she heard shouting outside. Her heart beat quickly. What had gone wrong?

She was about to wake Richard when a loud banging came at the front door. Grabbing her wrapper, she hurried to answer it. "What happened?" she asked Jimmy, who stood on the porch.

"Main stable's on fire." He ran down the steps as he finished. "Wake Richard if he's not. I'm goin' to get Jess."

Alexa moved onto the porch and gasped aloud to see flames already reaching toward the sky. She turned to get Richard, but found him right behind her. "Heaven help us," he whispered, fear tainting his voice. He took hold of her shoulders with a near-painful grip. "I hate fires." Alexa looked up to see such deep emotion carved into his expression that she felt somehow alone, wondering what kind of memories it stirred for him.

🐝   🐝   🐝

"What?" Jess threw open his bedroom door while he pulled on a shirt.

"Main stable's on fire," Jimmy declared, already running back down the hall.

Jess quickly pulled on his boots and grabbed his coat and hat. He ran as if the fire were at his heels until he came through the door and saw flames rising toward the sky. "Please, no," he muttered as his fears for the future mingled with his worst memories.

Panic urged Jess across the yard, his first concern being for the animals. The boys were working quickly to get water on it while Alexa gazed on, the flames reflecting pain in her expression. Jess paused beside her, and their eyes met with unspoken horror. She predicted his question and answered it. "There are still some horses in there. Fiddler's gone in for them."

"How many?" Jess asked. Alexa turned to make a quick count of the animals running in the corral.

"Three are missing," she said, then frenzy edged into her voice with a harsh realization. "One of them's Crazy."

Jess wanted to panic, but he calmly said, "Fiddler will get her." He glanced around to survey the situation. Wind was whipping the flames toward the bunkhouse, and he knew it would get worse before it got better. He felt droplets of rain in the air, but knew they couldn't depend on that. He grabbed one of the recently rescued horses and mounted, trying not to think how many years that stable had been there, how his father had built it with his own hands, of the cost of replacing it and everything that had been inside. There was an understanding in the area that such an emergency warranted help from the hired hands of neighboring stations. And they needed it now.

"I'm going to get help," he called, and Murphy acknowledged him with a nod just as Fiddler ran from the stable leading two horses. He nearly collapsed, coughing uncontrollably as Murphy took the horses toward the corral.

"Where's Crazy?" Alexa shouted frantically.

"She's all right," Fiddler managed. "We'll get her."

Tod drenched himself with water to go in, and Jess felt sure everything would be all right until he heard Richard shout, "Alexa! No!" Jess turned to see him drop a bucket of water and run toward the stable just as Alexa disappeared inside.

Richard didn't think. He just followed Alexa toward the fire. But as he came close enough to feel the heat of the flames, he hesitated.

Jess could see the fear and dilemma in Richard's face. With his own horrid thoughts of the night his mother died, he couldn't begin to comprehend what Richard must be feeling.

Richard's love for Alexa quickly overruled his fear, and he moved purposefully toward the stable door.

"Richard—no!" Jess called, and he paused. Jess dismounted and threw his coat and hat to the ground. "I'll go in. You get help." Richard opened his mouth to protest, but Jess added quickly, "Please—let me try to repay you."

A thousand emotions boiled in Richard's mind. But the only one that made the split-second decision easy was the deep understanding he and Jess shared. With a display of trust and respect, Richard stepped back, and Jimmy doused Jess with a bucket of water.

Jess found Alexa choking from the thickening smoke, fighting to pull a frightened Crazy out of her stall. Jess grabbed a nearby saddle blanket and threw it over Crazy's eyes, then he backed out of the stable with an arm firmly around Alexa.

The rain worsened slightly, and Richard donned Jess's coat and hat. He mounted and rode a short distance, then turned and hesitated until Jess and Alexa emerged from the stable. Knowing they were safe, he galloped away.

Murphy took Crazy and soothed her. Jess felt weakness overcome Alexa as she leaned against him, coughing and gasping for breath.

"Take it slow." He coughed and urged her some distance from the fire, where she sat on the ground and leaned against a fencepost. "Are you all right?"

She nodded but continued to cough. Jess waited until she managed to say, "I'll be fine. Where's Richard?"

"He went for help."

She nodded and coughed. "I'm all right, Jess. Go help them."

Jess reluctantly left her to assist the boys in their feeble attempts to douse the fire. Despite their efforts and the continuing rain, the flames rose higher and Jess began to see that it was futile. With defeat in his voice, Jess called out, "Let it burn, boys."

They wet down the side of the bunkhouse, then grudgingly relinquished their efforts. Huddling close together, they stood back to witness a sight that tore at each of their hearts. They all wanted to somehow console Jess, but there was nothing to be said. Alexa stood quietly beside him. Murphy squeezed her hand tightly, and Jess put his arm around her shoulders. With the flames reflecting in their eyes, they watched part of their world crumble to the ground.

When just watching became too much for Murphy, he ordered Fiddler and Jimmy to help him get the animals to the other stable and see to their care. They were grateful when the rain came down harder, if only to dampen the surrounding area and keep the fire from spreading. But as Jess realized how long they'd been out here, he turned to Edward and said, "Shouldn't someone have come by now?"

"I would think so," Edward stated solemnly.

"If they're much slower," Jess observed, attempting to lighten the mood, "they'll miss the barbecue."

Nothing more was said as the rain continued and the situation appeared under control. With the animals taken care of, they all went into the bunkhouse to dry off. While Edward made some coffee, they observed the final stages of the fire from the window.

Murphy brought a blanket for Alexa and put it around her shoulders. "You shouldn't even be up and about. You'd best take care of yourself."

She smiled her gratitude and Jess handed her a cup of hot coffee. He sat close beside her to drink his own, but ended up just staring at the steam as it rose toward his face.

"Are you all right?" Alexa asked, putting a gentle hand over his arm.

"What can I say?" Alexa moved her hand into his and he squeezed it firmly, grateful to have her near him through this.

"Where do you suppose Richard is?" she asked, a note of concern in her voice.

"I was just wondering the same," Jess replied. "He's been gone far too long. "What time is it?" he called to Edward.

"Half past four," he replied. Jess glanced sharply toward Murphy, who seemed to perceive his thoughts. Alexa's grip tightened over his fingers, and he returned the squeeze in an effort to give reassurance.

"Perhaps someone else had trouble," Jess stated, knowing how good-hearted Richard was.

Alexa nodded. There had to be a logical explanation.

"What do you suppose started it?" Murphy asked.

"Lightning?" Jimmy suggested.

"It wasn't that close, was it?" Fiddler remarked.

"No," Jess said. "It wasn't."

Alexa glanced toward Jess as too many coinciding events fell into place in her mind. "Jess," she asked quietly, "do you know what started the fire when your house—"

"I know, but I can't prove it." His voice was as tight as his jaw.

"Chad," she stated breathily. When Jess's expression didn't change, she knew she was right. "And you think Chad did this?"

"I wouldn't be surprised. But as always, there's no way to verify it." Jess wondered if his visit to Chad had urged him to prove just how serious this game of his really was.

Fighting off the thought, he glanced at Alexa. She didn't look well at all. "Is something wrong?" he asked.

"I just feel . . . weak. Tired, I suppose."

"Murphy was right," Jess said. "You shouldn't even be up. Come along." He rose to his feet. "I'm taking you home."

Alexa moved with him toward the door, and Jess glanced back. "Thank you," he said quietly, and was answered with unanimous nods of acknowledgment. "I'm going to see that Alexa gets some rest." He turned to Murphy. "If Richard isn't back in thirty minutes, I want two of you to go find him." Murphy nodded. "The rest of you keep an eye on that fire and see that it doesn't go anywhere—just to be sure."

Jess and Alexa paused in the drizzling rain to survey the dwindling structure of smoking charcoal before they moved on toward the house. Once inside, he lit a lamp and sent Alexa to change into something dry. He built a fire in the parlor, and she returned to sit close to it while Jess watched out the window with expectation. "He's not come yet?" she asked.

"No," he answered dryly, and they both knew that something was not right. Even if Richard had been deterred for a good reason, he'd had more than ample time to return or send word with someone else.

"Perhaps you should get some sleep," he suggested. She looked as white as her blouse.

"I couldn't possibly," she insisted, but she reclined on the sofa. "Jess," she added, and he turned toward her, "Richard and I have been talking, and . . . well, I believe we're going to leave."

"And go where?" he asked tersely.

"I don't know," she stated. "But we both feel that perhaps it's best, and—"

"Best for what?" he questioned, but she didn't answer. She met his eyes and assumed there was no need. "This is your home," he protested.

"I know, but—"

"What brought this on?" he asked. Again she made no reply, and he said abruptly, "If you think that leaving would somehow make it easier for me, you're quite wrong. It's only you and Richard that make life worth living for me at all, so don't think that—"

"But, Jess," she interrupted, "I know why you're planning to leave again." He looked down guiltily. "This is your home more than it's ours. It's not right for you to feel the need to be away from us and have to—"

"I'll stay if you will," he said, and she met his eyes with question. "You're my dearest friend, Alexa. I'll find a way to handle the rest, but I need you here." He paused. "Please, don't leave."

"We can't go on this way, Jess. We have to get over it."

"I know."

"We can't let our lives be ruled by these feelings."

"I understand. But there must be a way to do that and still remain here together."

Alexa smiled warmly. "I'll talk to Richard."

Jess smiled in reply. She could talk Richard into anything.

Time continued to drag. Jess thought he'd go mad watching the clock on the mantel tick away the hours while Alexa gazed numbly at nothing. Her expression betrayed the fear he knew she was feeling, and his heart went out to her. His own fears were the same.

He tried to imagine what could have possibly happened. He wondered what it would be like if their worst fears came about, but he stopped the thought, convincing himself it was ridiculous. Surely there was an explanation for this. In his heart he prayed that Richard was safe and well.

Alexa heard horses approaching before Jess did. He followed her when she rose abruptly and went out. Murphy and Jimmy rode directly to the porch and dismounted. They seemed hesitant to offer any information, but their expressions revealed that they knew something. Alexa gripped the porch rail, and a part of her wanted to die inside. They looked directly at Jess, blatantly avoiding Alexa's eyes.

"Did you find him?" Jess asked.

"No," Murphy answered, "but I think we've figured out what happened to him." He glanced tensely toward Alexa. "Maybe we should go someplace else to—"

"He's my husband!" she shouted. "I want to know."

Jess put a comforting hand on her shoulder and nodded toward Murphy, who swallowed with difficulty before he continued. "I don't know where the rumor started, but . . . well, talk has it that . . . you see, they're sayin' that . . ."

"Out with it!" Jess demanded.

Murphy cleared his throat. "They're sayin' that Jess Davies is dead."

"What?!" Jess shrieked as any man might to hear of his own demise when he knew he was still standing. His eyes narrowed as he tried to read something Murphy was attempting to convey without speaking. Thinking it through, the pieces fell into place and his heart sank.

Alexa glanced at Jess, wondering if he was as baffled as she. But his disoriented expression sobered as the color drained from his face. His hand tightened over her shoulder, and his knuckles turned white where they gripped the porch rail in front of him.

"What?" Alexa asked breathily. No one responded. She took Jess's arm firmly. "Tell me!"

"Alexa," he said softly, fighting to contain his own emotion, "if someone thinks I'm dead, and I'm still here, then . . ."

"And if I'm not mistaken," Murphy added, "didn't he leave here wearin' your coat and hat?"

Alexa's eyes widened and her grip tightened painfully. When the idea took hold, she gasped for breath and leaned into Jess. He pushed his arms firmly around her and nodded toward Murphy. "Find him," he said with quiet intensity.

Murphy nodded and rode away with Jimmy at his side. Jess helped Alexa inside and sat close beside her on the sofa. She held to him fiercely, refusing to let him go.

"Maybe it's a mistake," he whispered. "Maybe they'll find him and he'll be fine. Perhaps he's just hurt and needs help. Oh, Alexa," his voice cracked, "I pray it's a mistake." He didn't tell her the full measure of his own thoughts. Were Chad's motives so deep? Had his threats against Jess's life been serious? Would he really be so low?

Time dragged incessantly as they waited. Jess felt an overwhelming rush of confusion and guilt as he realized what this meant. A painful nausea enveloped him to think of losing Richard, and it only worsened to know that it should have been him. If Richard was truly gone, he had died in Jess Davies' place. Jess didn't know if he could live with that.

Alexa's exhaustion tempted her to just fall into oblivion and never return. She'd not slept at all last night, and her emotions had depleted her already-strained body. But how could she sleep? How could she possibly rest without knowing? Confusion and fear consumed her. She couldn't even imagine what it would be like to live without Richard. She'd speculated endlessly on how to solve the dilemma of loving two men, but never had such a thing crossed her mind. Death was no answer. It was a nightmare. *No,* she insisted over and over in her head until it pounded relentlessly. She would not accept this. She would not! It had to be as Jess had said. It was a mistake. He would come home to her. He *would!*

Late in the afternoon, Jess heard horses approaching. He rushed to the door with Alexa close behind. His heart plummeted. There were three horses, but the third had a body flung over its back.

"You wait inside," Jess ordered Alexa, then walked briskly out to meet them. He caught Murphy's eye and saw the grief, then he shook his head abruptly and glanced over Jess's shoulder. Jess turned around to see Alexa running toward them. He stepped into her path and grabbed her around the waist before she could go any farther.

"Let me go!" she screamed, fighting with more energy than he knew she possessed.

"I told you to wait inside," he growled, dragging her back in the direction she'd come. Tod, Edward, and Fiddler emerged from the bunkhouse in time to witness the struggle.

Jess's arms left her waist to grab her wrists when she started hitting him, screaming and ranting as if she'd gone mad. "Let me go!" she cried again and again. "He's my husband, Jess! Let go of me!"

She kicked and thrashed until Jess shouted, "Will somebody help me before I have to hurt her?"

Fiddler ran forward just as Alexa collapsed, unconscious, into Jess's arms. He carried her back to the house, where Fiddler opened the door and followed him to the bedroom.

"I think she's all right." Jess listened for her even breathing. "But she's got to be exhausted. You stay with her, and don't let her out of this house."

"I'll take care of her." Fiddler sat in a chair near the bed as Jess hurried back out. He approached just as Murphy and Jimmy were lifting the body off the horse. He wanted to believe it was somebody else, or that Richard wasn't really dead. But there was no denying what he saw. Jess went to his knees beside the body, and an unfamiliar sound erupted from his throat. "Dear God, help us all," he muttered, biting into the back of his hand to keep from crying out.

Jess was oblivious to the comforting hands on his shoulders and the grief being shared by the others. He wanted to cry, but the tears were frozen. He wanted to scream, but his voice was choking behind the bile rising in his throat. He was glad Alexa hadn't seen Richard this way. The gaping bullet wound in his chest and the blood-darkened clothes were bad enough, but the expression etched into his face was one of shock and fear. Jess bowed his head in silent anguish. As long as he lived, he would never forget this moment. Richard was dead, and it should have been him.

Forcing himself to his senses, Jess looked up to see Murphy mopping his face with a dirty sleeve, and Jimmy leaning on Murphy's shoulder like a child. With a firm hand, Edward helped Jess to his feet. Their arms and eyes gripped one another with an unspoken emotion, while Tod sniffled and attempted to blink back the tears.

"I'd better tell Alexa," Jess said with a gruff voice.

"I don't envy you that," Murphy muttered and blew his nose.

Realizing that he was being looked to for direction, Jess tried to gather his wits. "Take care of the body as best you can," he said, "and build a proper casket." His eyes went to Murphy. "Like the one you made for my mother." Murphy nodded. "We'll see that he has an appropriate funeral." Jess glanced once more at Richard's lifeless form, then hurried toward the old house.

"I'll take over," Jess offered, and Fiddler looked up as if he'd been asleep. None of them had slept for a day and a half.

"She's been as quiet as a baby." Fiddler rose and stretched. Their eyes met. "Was it Richard?" Jess nodded, and Fiddler squeezed his eyes shut. "Blimey, it's hard to believe."

"Why don't you get some rest, and I'll sit with her."

Fiddler pressed a compassionate hand over Jess's shoulder and quietly left. While Alexa slept, Jess absorbed the grief. He had hardly allowed himself to cry when his mother had died, but he knew now that it took more of a man to face up to his pain. No man had had a better friend than he had in Richard. If the confusion of his loss didn't consume him, the guilt did. Beyond the fact that the bullet had been meant for Jess, he couldn't even entertain the thought that Alexa was now free. How could something so incredible be the result of such horror?

Daylight faded into dusk. Jess's stomach growled with hunger, but he had no motivation to eat, even if he had dared leave Alexa alone. He wondered how long she would sleep and leave him with this dread of telling her the truth. He was beginning to think the torment would never end when she moaned in the darkness.

Alexa reached to the other side of the bed and expected to feel the warmth of Richard's body. When she found him gone, she turned over and leaned onto her elbow. "Richard?" she said. Then the memories came back an instant before she heard a match strike and the room lightened as it met with the lamp.

A lump lodged in Jess's throat as he watched her. The disorientation faded into fear and question, but he couldn't bring himself to speak.

"Is it true?" she asked hoarsely, and he could only nod.

Visible pain rose into her eyes before she closed them and bent her head forward weakly. "Tell me," she whimpered from behind the hand pressed to her mouth. Jess hesitated. "Tell me!" she cried, glaring at him so he knew she meant it.

"He was . . ." He paused to draw courage. "Alexa, he was shot in the chest."

Alexa shook her head. Her chin quivered. "No." She pressed her hands to her face. "No!" she cried. "I don't believe it. I—"

"Alexa." He went to his knees and grasped her shoulders. "Listen to me. I saw him."

"No," she protested and tried to squirm away.

"Listen to me!" He tightened his grip and shook her. "He's dead, Alexa. He was shot in the chest. He's gone."

With no choice but to accept it, Alexa sank into a heap on the bed, and Jess relinquished his grip. She groaned in anguish and rolled to her side, curling herself around a pillow. Jess watched with nothing short of pity as she pressed her fists to her temples and repeatedly cried out her husband's name. Her crying turned to tormented heaves, and Jess felt helpless. He didn't dare touch her. His eyes burned painfully with tears that he thought had gone dry. Silently they fell while he watched Alexa express his real anguish. Regret consumed him. It was only a fluke that he was here to witness this instead of Richard.

Jess wondered if he should leave her to mourn alone. But he couldn't bring himself to leave. His emotion pushed him to desperation, and he finally reached for Alexa's hand, wanting so badly to give her something—anything—to sustain her through this. She seemed oblivious to his touch at first. He whispered her name, and she clutched his hand as if it were a lifeline.

"Jess!" she cried. Her fingers threaded into his, holding his hand in a grip that eased his guilt somewhat by the pain she inflicted. Abruptly she came into his arms, pressing her face to his chest, heaving uncontrollably.

Alexa's anguish continued in varying degrees, while Jess's mind raced with so many emotions that just trying to decipher them left him weak. Carefully he rolled back onto the bed and brought Alexa with him, holding to her relentlessly. His shirt turned damp from her tears, while the pillow turned damp from his. He drew comfort from her nearness, and they shared their grief until her crying was exchanged for a deathly stillness.

Alexa felt a numbness replace her tears, blanketing the reality that Richard was gone. She felt lost and uncertain, confused and weary. But she didn't feel alone. Jess remained silently holding her through the darkest part of the night.

Needing strength to make it through this, Alexa turned her mind to prayer. It was all so painful. She had just begun to think she could get beyond the anguish of losing her baby, and now this. Her prayers were barely uttered, however, when Jess tightened his embrace and she knew they had been answered. The pain was almost unendurable, but his presence alone gave her the strength she needed to face this, and enough comfort to ease the despair. When he shifted and eased away, Alexa clutched onto him and her breathing became sharp. "Don't leave me," she whimpered.

"I'm here." His voice soothed her fears, and Alexa relaxed. She felt his breathing fall into an even rhythm and wondered if he'd slept at all since the fire. Silent tears erupted again, but before they were spent, she slept as well.

Jess awoke in the light of dawn and found Alexa sleeping in his arms. Mercy! What was he doing here? He was sleeping in Richard's bed, holding Richard's wife, and Richard wasn't even buried yet.

Carefully he eased away from her and rose to stretch his legs and back. Idly he wandered the house. Seeing evidence of Richard at every turn, he wondered how Alexa was going to face all of this.

Feeling a need for fresh air, Jess went onto the porch and leaned against the post. The peaceful light of early morning was mocked by the ruins of the stable and the memory of Richard's body lying in the yard. Emotions threatened, the foremost being guilt.

"I was wondering when you'd show yourself." Fiddler's voice startled Jess from his weary thoughts.

"What are you doing up this early?" Jess asked.

"I've gone to bed several times but couldn't sleep for long. How is Alexa?"

Jess turned his head and swallowed. "She's asleep now."

"How's she taking it?"

"Not very well."

"And how are you taking it?"

Jess didn't answer.

"Don't be too hard on yourself, Jess." Fiddler sat on the steps and pressed his fingers together.

"As if losing him weren't bad enough," Jess said, revealing his deepest source of pain, "I know it should have been me."

"But it wasn't—by no fault of yours. There's no point filling yourself with questions or regret. That's what I did when I lost my wife and son, Jess. It didn't change anything. It was you that taught me I still had a life to live. No matter how you torment yourself, Jess, Richard will still be dead—and it won't help Alexa any."

"You're probably right, but it's . . ." Jess's voice broke.

"I know it's not an easy thing to face," Fiddler said with empathy. "It's not much consolation, but look at it this way. When you pulled me out of the gutter and brought me here, I wanted to die. But one day I realized I'd been given the opportunity to start over. Maybe this is your second chance at life, Jess. Put all the past behind you and do it right this time."

Fiddler came to his feet and gazed nostalgically at the brilliant hues of the lightening sky. "You gave me a second chance, Jess, and I've been careful what I did with it. I think that's why I'm happy," he chuckled, "even though I have to live with Jimmy and Murphy instead of . . ." His voice faded, and Jess knew where his thoughts were.

"Can I say one more thing?" Fiddler asked, breaking the silence.

"Sure."

"Think of it as a gift from Richard—and don't let him down." Fiddler walked away to let his carefully-thought-out words be absorbed in peace.

"Thank you, my friend," Jess said aloud, though he knew Fiddler couldn't hear him. Like a single star against an otherwise black sky, Jess felt the vaguest glimmer of hope break a tiny hole into the vast breadth of pain. He watched the sun come up, then went into the house to check on Alexa.

Twenty-five
GRIEF

Alexa woke and found Jess kneeling beside the bed. With one hand in hers and the other curled into a fist, his head was pressed to the bed. She sat abruptly and Jess's head shot up. His expression told her it hadn't been a dream. In the light of day, Richard was still dead.

Alexa's anguish continued through the following days. But even through her numbness and grief, she knew that Jess was her link to sanity. She begged him not to leave her alone, and he remained faithfully nearby the majority of the time.

Jess tried to tell himself he was hovering near for Alexa's sake. But he knew within himself that he needed her just as much as she needed him, if not more. There were times when he cried with her, and others when he spent his grief privately while she slept. Observing her pain, he wondered if she would ever get over this. It didn't seem characteristic of Alexa to be so outwardly full of despair, yet he knew from experience that mourning was an important—and necessary—process. Thinking back on his mother's death, he wondered if it might have been easier to face if he'd been willing to deal with his grief initially.

The boys were aware of Jess's coming and going from Alexa's home, but they were all accustomed to the situation and knew there was no need for speculating. Feeling it was appropriate to keep their distance for now, they inquired often about Alexa's well-being. Jess would always answer that she was doing as well as could be expected, but he was concerned.

The evening prior to the funeral, Jess went over to check on her following a late supper. He walked into the house as he'd become accustomed to doing, but he found the bedroom door closed. He knocked lightly and she answered with a terse, "What?"

Jess timidly pushed the door open to see her frantically rummaging through drawers in the bureau. He folded his arms and watched her for a few minutes as she left everything she touched in complete disarray. She slammed each drawer closed and mumbled under her breath.

"Looking for something?" he asked calmly.

As if she'd just noticed he was there, she glared at him. "You!" she grumbled. "What did you do with it? It was here."

"If you tell me what, I might be able to help you."

"The mask." She hit a fist on the bureau. "He wasn't wearing it when he left, and it's not here. Where is it?"

Jess cleared his throat and said gently, "We thought you would want him buried in it."

Alexa's frustration visibly melted into pain, and she sat on the edge of the bed. Had she gone insane? She had grieved and mourned his loss, but until this moment she had not consciously perceived the fact that there was a body. She remembered now: there was a lifeless form over the back of a horse. Had she blocked it out? Didn't she care? She looked up at Jess, bewildered and afraid.

"Where is he now?"

Part of Jess had dreaded this happening, while he feared if it didn't, she'd find facing his death all the more difficult. "The casket is in the big house," he stated.

"I want to see him," she said as if she expected him to protest. Jess motioned toward the door with his hand and stepped aside. Alexa stood hesitantly.

"Did you want this?" He pulled her wrapper from over the footboard of the bed. "Or were you going out in your nightgown?"

Alexa looked down at herself, toying nervously with the buttons at her throat as she realized he'd seen her in little else the last couple of days.

"Don't worry. My mother didn't *own* a nightgown that modest."

Alexa took the wrapper and pulled it around her, then she slipped shoes on her feet and stepped outside. A cool breeze rushed against her and she inhaled deeply, wondering if she was ready for this.

She and Jess walked quietly into the house and down the long hall toward the front parlor. "Are you sure?" He paused at the door and looked at her with searching eyes. "You don't have to do this."

"Yes, I do," she said quietly. "My mother told me that when her father died, she didn't see the body and she had difficulty accepting that he was gone. I don't want to, but . . ." She bit her lip.

"I understand." He held out a hand. "I'm right beside you." Alexa took it firmly and sucked in her breath as he pushed open the door. She expected it to be difficult, but seeing Richard brought an emotion that she simply hadn't counted on. She felt peace. She loved him and didn't regret a moment of their life together. He looked dignified and completely content.

Gingerly she set her hand to his face. When she became accustomed to the way he felt, she put her cheek to his and closed her eyes. "I love you, Richard," she whispered. "You will forever be a part of me." Meekly she pressed her lips over his, as if he was only leaving for the day. "Good-bye," she said softly and eased away. She gazed at him for a long moment, then turned her back abruptly and looked up at Jess.

"Are you all right?" he asked.

"For the moment," she said, but already she could feel the shock settling into her all over again. "Please take me home."

Jess put an arm around her shoulders and walked with her in silence back to her home. He opened the door for her, but she turned to him before going inside. "I . . . think I need to be alone, Jess."

"I understand," he said, trying to hide his disappointment. "The service will be tomorrow, midday."

Alexa nodded and quietly closed the door. Feeling somehow disjointed from the world, Jess returned to the room where Richard lay and cried half the night.

Right after breakfast, Jess went to the house and found Alexa still in bed. She'd obviously had a bad night. The mourning shadowed her countenance.

"Alexa," he said gently, and she turned to him with dazed eyes. "You've got to get dressed." She looked disoriented and he added carefully, "The funeral." Alexa bowed her head and tears spilled. "Alexa," Jess urged, "you've got to snap yourself out of this." Appealing to her natural selflessness, he added, "The boys are having a hard time, Alexa. If they see you this way, it will tear them apart."

Jess was pleased when the tactic worked. Her expression softened, and she touched her face and hair in dismay.

"I've already heated water for a bath," he said. "Is there anything else I can help you with?" She looked bewildered and he got more specific. "What do you want to wear? Can I—"

"There should be a black dress in the back of the closet." She pulled open a bureau drawer and rummaged for clean underclothing. "I wore it when Father died. I hope it's not too wrinkled."

Jess shuffled through the closet and brought it out. "You mean this one?"

"Yes, thank you."

Jess laid it over the bed. "Is there anything else you need before I go get ready myself?"

Alexa shook her head, and he moved toward the door. "We should go out in a short while, so try to hurry."

"Jess," she said, and he turned back. "Thank you."

He gave some semblance of a smile and left her alone. Jess returned to find Alexa freshly bathed, her damp hair rolled into a serviceable knot. The elegant dress left only her face and hands exposed, the stark black making her appear all the more pale. He watched in hushed awe as those delicate fingers pinned a hat into place with a netted veil that came over her eyes. She looked like an expensive porcelain doll.

"How do I look?" She glanced skeptically in the mirror.

"As beautiful as ever," he replied with sincerity and offered his arm. They came onto the porch to find the boys all waiting. Alexa had never seen them so dressed up. Murphy had even shaved. Fiddler stepped forward to embrace her, and the others were eager to follow his example. Alexa reached beneath the veil to dab at her eyes with a handkerchief, and they moved in a group toward the big house where Sarina and Mrs. Brown waited with the clergyman.

Alexa cried silent tears as Richard's casket was hoisted onto the shoulders of these six men who shared her life. She followed them outside and slowly across the yard. Holes of sunshine cast shadows of high clouds over the ground in bizarre shapes. Alexa set her pace to match the pallbearers, a marked slowness that seemed to express her hesitancy in approaching this final moment. Strange thoughts and memories flitted through her mind, ending with one unthinkable truth. She was a widow.

Alexa followed the casket to the little cemetery on the other side of the old house, and through the iron gate. Once Jess and the boys were free of its weight, they huddled around Alexa, offering silent support while a service was given. A prayer was offered, and Richard Wilhite was laid to rest near the tiny grave of his infant daughter.

When there was nothing to do but leave, Alexa looked up through mist-filled eyes and found her reason to go on living. Stoically she took Jess's hand. Together they walked away, but not without leaving a portion of their hearts behind.

Alexa insisted she needed to be alone. She was escorted home, and the rest of them went to the bunkhouse. Jess went along. Unlike Alexa, he *didn't* want to be alone. They were all glad to have it over, but a melancholy aura hung over them as they couldn't help but feel Richard's absence. And to make it worse, the skeleton of the stable stood ominously to remind them of the circumstances.

They were all surprised to look up from their cold supper to see Alexa standing in the doorway, still wearing the black dress. "I want to thank you all," she said quietly, "for the support you've given me through this." Again they shared a round of embraces, saying little but sharing a kinship that made Alexa wonder how she ever thought she could have left here.

"Do you think she'll be all right?" Fiddler asked when she had gone.

"Eventually," Jess stated. He wondered through the remainder of the meal if he should check on her. He'd stayed so close to her through this whole ordeal that the thought of being away from her was almost frightening. He walked toward the big house, still contemplating what to do. Reminding himself that his first concern was for her benefit, he pushed thoughts of himself away and knocked lightly on the door. Alexa opened the door just a crack, already dressed for bed. Jess felt suddenly uncomfortable as their eyes met through the narrow opening.

"I . . . just wanted to make certain you're all right."

"I'll be fine," she managed a smile, "thank you."

Jess nodded. "Is there anything I can get for you, or—"

"I'm fine, Jess, really; just exhausted. I'll see you tomorrow."

Jess nodded again and stepped back. "Good night, then."

"Jess," she added gently, "thank you for all you've done for me. I could not have made it through this alone."

"Neither could I," he admitted, and she closed the door.

The following morning, Alexa came to the bunkhouse for breakfast at seven. Jess walked in a few minutes later, surprised to see her sitting at the end of the bench. Typical greetings were exchanged among the group, but the air hung heavy with tension and grief.

Alexa rose to leave before the others were finished. "Thank you," she said to Edward, "it was delicious as always." A pattern was quickly established where Alexa appeared for meals, as if to make a point that she would not be a burden to anyone. Beyond that, she remained mostly distant. She was often seen kneeling in the graveyard or working in her garden, and occasionally she ventured to the stable to spend time with the horses. She continued to wear the loose-fitting dresses she'd worn during her pregnancy. Her face was still peaked and her eyes hollow.

Jess noticed that she gradually began hovering close to the boys while they worked. She helped Edward in the kitchen a little, and occasionally offered to curry one of the horses. From a distance he observed her conversing with each of them, and once-familiar feelings stirred in him. Why did she participate in these casual friendships with her fellow workers, when she wouldn't even look him in the eye? Was she simply trying to hide her feelings as she had done in the past? Or had the love she felt for him died along with Richard? Whatever it was, Jess hated this distance between them. He had grown too accustomed to her friendship to be content without her.

When she continued to look frail, Jess had the doctor come and check on her. He reported that she was doing well, but the blood she'd lost was significant and it would take time to recover. He suggested that the emotional trauma she'd suffered would likely set her recovery back immensely. She needed to take everything slowly and be careful.

Knowing where she stood physically assured Jess somewhat, but his every attempt to ask Alexa how she felt otherwise was answered with a simple, "I'm fine, thank you."

Jess inquired casually of the others as to how Alexa seemed, and they all told him the same thing. Something in her seemed scared, and perhaps bitter. Jess wondered why she wouldn't open up to *him*. Perhaps she was keeping a distance because he was the source of the problem. Whether or not that was true, Jess felt concerned for her in a way that left him feeling somehow responsible, but helpless to do anything about it.

The whole thing might have been easier if Jess could have kept his thoughts where they belonged. He loved Alexa and wanted her to be a part of his life. But she was in mourning, for crying out loud. One moment Jess would speculate over the possibilities of the future and feel a glimmer of optimism, and the next he'd remember the reason Alexa was free. The guilt oppressed him at times until he wanted to die, too. Still, he couldn't keep from wanting her. He longed for companionship, for laughter and conversation. And he ached to hold her in his arms again. He wondered if it would be as incredible as he remembered, or if too much had changed for anything to ever be as it had been before.

All he could do for now was try to keep an eye on her from a comfortable distance. His watchfulness paid off when he wandered out to her house late one evening, just to see if everything appeared in order. He couldn't figure why a horse was tied to the porch rail—until he got close enough to see the Byrnehouse brand.

"Chad," he muttered under his breath, and had to restrain himself from running right in there to kick him out. He reminded himself that Chad *was* Alexa's brother, and perhaps he had no right to interfere. On the other hand, he'd seen Chad treat her badly. Not certain what to do, Jess waited on the porch, listening carefully and hoping he could prevent any problems. When he heard nothing at all he began to feel uneasy, until he saw Alexa walking toward the house, alone. She paused when she saw the horse tied to the rail, then with a sigh of disgust she squared her shoulders and headed for the door. Jess assumed she would resent any intervention at this point, so he remained in the shadows and waited.

"What do you want, Chad?" Alexa bellowed as she threw open the door. The last thing she wanted was to see *him*.

"I was wondering when you'd come back." Chad was reclining on the sofa with a drink in his hand. "Quaint little place you've got here."

He glanced around with a wrinkle in his nose. "Though it is better than that dreadful room in the carriage house Jess kept you locked in."

Alexa folded her arms stiffly. "I like my house, and I liked my room in the carriage house. Did you come to assess my living standards again, or is there another reason I'm receiving the pleasure of your company?"

"Just came to pay my respects." He took a long swallow of the port he'd helped himself to.

"I doubt such a thing would be possible for you."

Chad chuckled. "But I understand I'm too late. The beast has already been buried."

"If you came to insult my taste in men, I'd prefer that you go now."

"Alexandra," he laughed intolerably, "there is not a woman in the whole of Australia with worse taste in men."

"Get out," she said with quiet vehemence.

"But you just got here. I haven't paid my respects yet."

"Do it and go."

"I truly was sorry to hear about your husband." He almost seemed to mean it.

"Thank you." She nodded curtly.

"So, how did it happen?"

Alexa sighed. "Chad, I'm really not up to talking about this."

"Oh, all right." He set his empty glass on the table and put his hands behind his head. "But I must say this leaves Jess sitting pretty."

Alexa's lips tightened with anger. "What is that supposed to mean?"

"Well, he's alive, isn't he?" Chad said as if he resented it. Alexa's eyes narrowed, trying to read his deeper meaning. "And now I suppose you'll be running back to *his* bed and—"

"Get out!" she said through clenched teeth. He sat up but didn't appear to be leaving. His expression was typically smug, and she wondered what he believed he'd gotten away with this time. "You had something to do with that fire, didn't you." It was not a question.

Chad laughed flippantly. "Come now, Alexa. Would I be so . . . savage?"

"Yes, I believe you would."

He smiled. "Believe what you want, sweet sister, but even if I *did* have something to do with it, you could never prove it."

Jess's similar words came back to her, kindling her fury. She moved slowly toward him like a stalking tigress. "You did it, didn't you." Her voice rose, appalled and shocked. "If there hadn't been a fire, Richard wouldn't have gone for help, and he'd still be alive."

"Alexa?" He stood and backed away as if this was all very amusing. "Don't be ridiculous. You have nothing to base such assumptions on."

"You fiend!" she snarled. The full spectrum of her grief rose up to join her anger, and she wanted to tear his eyes out. "How dare you even set foot in my house!" She nearly slapped him, but the last time she'd tried that, she'd gotten the worst of it. Instead, she picked up the fire poker and poised it near his face. "You might as well have killed him. You might as well have pulled the trigger."

Alexa saw the vague glimmer of guilt in his eyes, but credited it to the fire as she backed him toward the door. She could feel her strength waning and hoped she could hold out until she got rid of him. He was almost to the door when he grabbed the poker and wrenched it out of her hand, tossing it to the floor. "You're such a feisty little thing," he laughed, taking her wrists in a firm grip. "But one day," he hissed close to her face, "you're going to wish you'd never come here."

"Stop it, Chad," she cried, "you're hurting me."

"If you had any sense, Alexa, you would—"

"You know," Jess calmly pressed the point of the fire poker into Chad's back, "it would seem your social graces could use some refining. I'm often having to remind you that the lady asked you to leave."

Chad relinquished his grip and put his hands in the air. "Hello, old pal," he said as if they were having a friendly chat. "I hear you managed to dodge a bullet recently."

"Now, that must be a relief for you." Jess pressed the poker farther and Chad tensed. "If I were gone, you wouldn't have any fun at all."

"How true. How true."

"Tell me, Chad," Jess said behind his ear. "Did you do it yourself, or did you pay someone for what it was worth?"

"I don't know what you're talking about," Chad stated.

"You never do. But I often wonder, do you light the match yourself, or do you let someone else have the honor and just smell the smoke from a distance? Does it make your blood boil with an incomparable thrill to watch the flames? And does adding death to the event intensify the enjoyment?"

"You're as crazy as your mother," Chad sneered, though he remained as he was, apparently not certain what exactly he could feel against his back.

"Chad," Jess retorted almost indifferently, "you are living proof that insanity is not necessarily hereditary. Your parents were both perfectly sane."

"Which is more than you can say," Chad countered.

"Did you want to leave now, or do you want to have it out like old times?"

"Do you think you're up to it?" Chad asked.

"Oh," Jess chuckled dryly, "I'm almost as angry with you as I was the last time. I should have killed you then. You don't know how many times I have wished I'd just squeezed a little harder when I had my hands around your throat. I might kill you now if you stick around long enough."

"Stop it!" Alexa insisted. "I've had enough talk of killing and death. Get out, Chad. Do us all a favor and take another long vacation. We won't miss you."

Chad grinned triumphantly as he sauntered to the door. "I'll keep in touch," he said. "I wouldn't want you to think that your neighbors don't care."

When Chad's horse had galloped away, Jess calmly walked to the fireplace and set the poker where it belonged. "Are you all right?" he asked.

"You say that a lot these days."

"I'm always wondering."

"I'm fine, thank you. You always manage to step in when I need you."

"I can almost smell him out." Jess attempted a light tone, but it was lost in the severity of Alexa's eyes.

"It was you, wasn't it," she stated.

Jess looked bewildered.

"You're the one who tried to kill Chad in the entry hall. It must have been ten years ago."

He looked at the floor. "1879. February." Hoping to explain his behavior, he added, "I was very young, and my mother had just been killed."

"In the fire."

"Yes."

"It all starts to make sense."

"Does it?" Jess's voice turned dry. "I can't see any sense in it at all."

Alexa darted her gaze away, and Jess was momentarily reminded of another time. He wanted to kiss her. He wanted to just hold her until all of this pain went away.

"Thank you, Jess," she said. "As always, I'm grateful."

"Is there anything else I can do?"

"No," she stated, "I'll be fine."

Once again Jess returned to his house, feeling more alone than when she'd been married to Richard.

❦ ❦ ❦

Alexa woke in the dark, her fists clutching wads of sweat-dampened sheets. "Jess!" she cried, and gave no thought to her frenzied trek through the dark to find him. In bare feet she ran across the yard and up the steps to the big house. With only her memory to guide her, she ran up the stairs and to the door she knew was his. She didn't bother knocking.

"Jess," she murmured, feeling her way to the bed. "Jess, where are you?"

Jess sat up abruptly, his heart pounding him into coherency. "Alexa? What are you doing here?" He reached out a hand and she gripped it firmly.

"You're all right," she muttered.

"Of course I'm all right."

"Oh, Jess. It was just a dream. You're all right."

"Tell me," he urged. She sat on the edge of the bed, and he could feel her trembling.

"It was you that took the shot, Jess. It was you that fell."

"It's all right." He lit a lamp on the bedside table. "See," he smiled, "I'm here."

"But, Jess," she said intently, "someone tried to kill you."

"Someone thought they killed me. There is a difference."

"Chad?" she said breathily. "Jess, would Chad try to kill you?" Jess tried to laugh it off, but she caught the truth from his eyes. "You must be honest with me, Jess. Tell me what you know."

"I'm not sure, Alexa," he said soberly. "He's alluded to threats against my life, but I didn't really believe he'd do it."

"Did Chad kill Richard?" she asked straightly.

"I don't know. You know the police said it was motivated by robbery. Though nothing was taken, I doubt there's any evidence to change that verdict."

"It's just as well," she said distantly, then her eyes fell upon Jess. "Will he try again?" Her voice quivered. "Does he really hate you so much that he would want to be rid of you?"

"I don't know that either, but I seriously doubt he would try again. Under the circumstances, it would be too obvious."

"I pray you are right, Jess," Alexa murmured. She knew that surviving the death of one of them would be difficult, even torturous, but she could never live through losing them both.

"I should go back to bed." She stood hesitantly. Jess wanted to beg her to stay, but he knew it was impossible. "I'm sorry for disturbing you."

"You didn't disturb me," he insisted. She moved toward the door. "Do you want me to walk you home?" he offered.

Alexa shook her head and closed the door behind her. Jess lay back and sighed. No matter how familiar he became with being lonely, it never ceased to torment him.

A month beyond the funeral, Jess contemplated whether or not to go into town with the boys. They were going for supplies and a change of scenery, which he felt no need to be involved in. But he did have some business to take care of. He declined going at the last minute, concerned about leaving Alexa alone. Though Sarina planned to go with them, he knew he could ask Mrs. Brown to check on Alexa. But intuition told him he needed to be here. He knew visiting her would be futile, so he settled onto the veranda with a cup of coffee and tried to be content to keep an eye on her from a distance.

Twenty-six

SECOND CHANCE

Alexa woke at dawn and heard the boys and Sarina loading into the wagon for a trip to town. She smiled at their bantering and almost wanted to go with them. Perhaps a change of scenery would do her good. She recalled Murphy saying that Jess would likely go along. Would there be anyone at all here today except Mrs. Brown in the house? The thought almost frightened her. But she didn't have the motivation to get up and do anything about it before she heard them leave.

The contrasting silence was somehow tranquil. Alexa felt exhausted but couldn't go back to sleep. Days had merged into nights until she could hardly keep track. A relentless weakness reminded her that it had not been so long since she'd lost her baby. But the grief of that was far outweighed by her husband's death. An endless supply of tears burned into her eyes and she rolled to the empty side of the bed, wrapping herself around the pillow Richard had slept on such a short time ago.

Late in the morning, a nagging hunger drove Alexa out of bed in search of something to eat. She pulled petticoats over the chemise she had slept in, and wandered to the kitchen to find it void of anything appetizing. Certain Edward had left food in the bunkhouse for her, she perused the pile of clothes in the corner of her bedroom. With clean mixed into dirty, she could hardly tell what had already been worn. Breeches were out of the question; she still had weight to lose before she could fit into them. She shook out a wrinkled black skirt and pulled it over her petticoats. When she couldn't find a clean shirt, she pulled open the wardrobe and became distracted by the neatly hanging clothes that seemed lost without Richard to give them life. Meekly she ran her hand over the signs of hard work in his breeches, and the worn leather of his coat. Tears threatened, but she choked them back. She came across a shirt he'd worn at dinner only a few days before his death, after he'd come in and bathed. Alexa buried her face in the fabric, absorbing the lingering scent of his shaving lotion. She touched the sleeves, still rolled up by his hand. With little thought she pulled it down and slipped her arms into it, rolling the sleeves up further until her hands appeared beneath them. The shoulder seams hung nearly to her elbows, and she only had to fasten three buttons to cover herself. With a long sigh she looked in the mirror, smiled faintly, and headed for the door without bothering to look for shoes. A perfectly blue sky made it a fine day for bare feet.

The bunkhouse kitchen proved a worthy distraction, with cold beef, cheese, and fresh vegetables from the garden. Sitting at the table, Alexa's mind went back to her first meal in this room. She thought of Richard's smile from the other end of the bench and how it had warmed her. Soothing memories filled her, and she reveled in them until the inevitable intrusion filtered through.

"Jess," she whispered aloud in a husky voice. Anger came with the sound of it. He had kept her from loving Richard fully in life, and now he was there, keeping her from mourning him properly in death.

Needing a distraction, she stepped outside, surprised at the blackening storm clouds that had moved in so quickly. For a moment she just stared skyward, imagining Richard in what might be heaven, hoping he knew that she *did* love him, in spite of . . . No, she couldn't think of Jess; not now, not yet. Perhaps in time, but for now . . .

Alexa mustered up a clear image of Richard and sauntered into the yard, relishing the sprinkle of rain that somehow made the memories easier to feel.

Jess heard the bunkhouse door and looked up from his empty coffee cup to see Alexa amble into the yard. His heart quickened at the sight of her. Something about her made the confusion momentarily clear away. He was tired of wanting to be there for her but fearing what her closeness might do to him. The emptiness of Richard's death constantly put a painful knot in his throat. And while he knew Alexa shared his grief, he wondered if she also shared this longing for them to be together again, and the guilt that came along with it.

Alexa turned her face skyward and he watched her with interest, wondering over her thoughts. She lifted the too-long shirt she wore to her face, at first to wipe away the rain, then just to hold it there. Jess pulled his feet down from the veranda rail and leaned forward, wishing he could touch her thoughts, or at least see her eyes. He was intrigued when she began to move lithely in a subtle dance, gradually lifting her arms as if they were about some imaginary partner— Richard, no doubt. It was good to see her looking spry after what she'd been through, though he knew she had far to go in her recovery. It was one more reason to worry about her, but at the moment she appeared full of life and vibrancy.

Alexa's dancing gained momentum as the rain increased from a sprinkle to a healthy shower. Jess began to fear she might tire or become chilled. He sat forward as she stopped abruptly and remained still. A moment later she turned in his direction with purpose, as if she'd sensed him watching her. Jess could see no visible change in her stance or expression, but he clearly felt a glimmer of longing in her aura. For a timeless moment, Jess's heart quickened and his throat went dry. She felt it too, and he knew it. But as quickly as desire filled him, guilt replaced it. And that, too, he knew Alexa shared. Thunder rumbled and the wind worsened, pressing Alexa's skirt to her legs, revealing beneath it a hint of white petticoats and delicate ankles. She gathered her hair into one hand to keep it out of her face while she continued to stare at him, as fine and motionless as some exquisite statue in a European museum. Desire and guilt continued to battle in Jess's head, one tempting him to run and take her in his arms, the other holding him to the chair as if weights were strapped to his legs.

When he began to think she would stand there indefinitely, Alexa turned and ran into the stable. An uneasiness crept up Jess's back. If it was shelter from the storm she wanted, the bunkhouse was much closer. Nearly convinced to follow her and investigate, Jess wasn't prepared to see her emerge like some kind of avenging angel, galloping a bare-backed Crazy into the storm. A blur of skirt and petticoats cascaded about her bare legs as she sailed over one fence, then another, and headed to the gallops. Jess's pulse raced in time with the distant hooves. He came to his feet and hesitated at the veranda rail, holding his breath until the horse found sure footing. Jess jumped over the rail and ran like a madman, certain he'd find her bleeding to death in the mud before he could stop her.

Oblivious to anything but the wind and the pelting rain, Alexa drove Crazy to her limit, as if the speed might force away the torment, the longing, the guilt, the anger. But each hoofbeat drove the anguish deeper until she sobbed blindly and allowed the horse free rein. She didn't see Jess until the horse reared back to halt as he stepped into their path and took hold of the reins.

"Are you crazy?" he shouted and dragged her down. She fell against his chest as the horse trotted back toward the stable.

Alexa pulled his shirt into her fists and shook him. "I love Richard!" she screamed.

"I know you do." Jess tried to remain empathetic and ignore what her nearness did to him.

"I do, Jess!" She shook him again.

"I know!" he shouted.

"But it was always you," she growled and pushed him away from her. They both fell back a step, and the rain worsened. Alexa stumbled until one hand went to the ground to steady herself and came up muddy. "It was you!" She fought to stand straight. Jess reached out to help her and she stepped back, her eyes blazing with pain and anger.

"Let me take you inside," he insisted. "You're not strong enough to—"

"It was always you!" She struggled against his arm about her waist and shouted in his face. "It was you I wanted, and he knew it!"

"Alexa," Jess attempted to ignore her, if only to get her out of the storm, "please let me—"

"You drove me to him, and then you came between us . . . without even trying." She pushed away from him, and their eyes met in a once-familiar battle of wills. The tears running over her face became hidden in the rain, but there was no mistaking the misty clouds in her eyes that gave Jess the urge to cry himself. He wondered if she would pass out or run, but with little warning she slapped him, leaving a muddy handprint that trickled off his face with the rain.

Jess slowly turned back to look at her. His jaw went tight and his cheek twitched. For a moment, Alexa feared he might hit her back. She almost wished he would. It might give her a reason to hate him. She wanted to hate him, to hurt him, to make him suffer as she suffered. But one look into the depths of his eyes made it evident that he already was.

"Feel better?" he asked coldly.

"No!"

"Then maybe you'd like to try it again," he challenged, pointing to his face. "Go ahead, Alexa. Take it out on me." She slapped him again, but he hardly flinched. "That's it." His encouragement reeked of cynicism. "If you hit me hard enough and long enough, maybe I can forget that it should have been me!"

Uncertainty flickered in her eyes. Jess took hold of her shoulders, shaking her as she'd done him. "It was supposed to be me, Alexa. That bullet was intended to kill *me*. You don't have to tell me that all of this is my fault, Mrs. Wilhite. I'm well aware that I'm to blame for all the hell you've been through, so just go ahead and hit me. Hit me good and hard."

Alexa stood drenched and stunned until Jess scooped her into his arms and hurried toward the old house. Barely onto the porch, he became distracted by her hand pressing into his hair, fusing to the back of his head. His eyes darted to find her face so close he could have kissed her with little effort. Desire rose in her eyes like the sun rising into stormy skies. He became acutely aware of that hand in his hair until the other touched his face. He told himself to put her down and turn and walk away. Before her feet touched the porch, she meekly touched her lips to his. Jess took a step back and gratefully found a post behind him that helped support his faltering knees.

"Why, Jess?" she cried. "Why does it have to be this way?" Her eyes closed and her head fell back. Shelter from the rain left her tears without camouflage as they fell unchecked, rolling over her throat and disappearing into the wet shirt clinging to her frail shoulders. Jess touched the supple flesh of her rain-dampened brow and moved his hand down to break the flow of her tears. "I don't know," he whispered.

Alexa buried her face in the folds of his shirt, and Jess willingly offered support when she leaned weakly against him. "I feel so lost, Jess, so confused."

Jess pressed his arms around her and she responded by nuzzling closer. "It will take time, Alexa." He reminded himself if not her. "You loved him. He loved you. Nothing else matters right now."

Her eyes shot to his, full of . . . what? Anger? Contempt? "I'll tell you what matters, Jess Davies." She took a step back and raised her voice. "What matters is tomorrow. Look at me, Jess!" she screamed. "I'm a widow. I feel like my life is over."

"Do you want to hit me again?" he asked calmly.

She raised her hand to slap him, but he caught her wrist. "I know it hurts, Alexa." He pulled her close and spoke against her face. "I know because I feel it. He was my dearest friend. Richard has been by my side as long as I can remember. After all the years we'd shared, he stole the woman I loved and still managed to keep my respect. He knew what he was getting into when he stepped in. But he understood, Alexa, and he trusted us. He's gone now, and there isn't a minute that passes when I don't feel guilty for it. Guilty for wanting what he had when he was alive, and more guilty for being alive to have it now that he's dead. So go ahead and suffer, Alexandra. Suffer and mourn. Cry and scream and hit me if you must. But don't think you're suffering alone. There may be a yard and two walls between us, but we're suffering together, you and I." He paused and took a deep breath. "Still, one day, Alexa . . ."

Jess raised a finger, then found that the promise forming in his head wouldn't pass through his lips. It was too soon. For now, he could only hope that time would heal these wounds and give them another chance. Unable to bear another moment confronted by her nearness, Jess turned and walked down the steps into the rain.

Alexa watched him go, feeling the first glimmer of hope in the quickening of her heart. But so much had happened. So much had changed. "Jess!" she called, leaning her cheek against the post. He turned and stood expectantly motionless in the continuing downpour. "One day?" she repeated. "Don't walk away and leave me wondering. Clarify yourself, Mr. Davies."

Jess walked slowly back toward her while his mind tried to piece it all together. He knew she shared his longing, his guilt, his pain. Did she also share his fear that what they had once shared might have dissipated in the midst of all they'd been through?

Jess set one foot onto the step and looked up at her. "Do you think a part of Richard lives on somewhere, Alexa?"

"I don't know, but I'd like to think so."

Jess stepped onto the porch and pushed an arm around her. "Then I can only hope he'll understand."

Their lips came together like a magnetic force with no power to do anything but connect. It took no effort for Alexa to respond to Jess's kiss. She had hungered for it long before she'd even considered marrying Richard. Relief washed over her and the confusion briefly fled, taking with it all else that might keep her from relishing this. She took his face into her hands, drawing him to her as if she might die without him. Jess fell to his knees and brought her with him, while she tugged at his dripping hair and kissed the rain from his face. She sat on the smooth wood slats of the porch and leaned against the wall of the house, urging him to sit beside her.

"Jess," she murmured, and he kissed her again before he relaxed at her side, consciously willing his passion to remain where it belonged. With the tension broken between them, he leaned his head back to openly watch her. He toyed with her hair and pressed his lips to her brow.

"Are you all right?" he asked quietly.

Alexa turned her head toward him and gave a subtle nod. Their eyes met with a torrid mixture of past pain, future hopes, and the reality of the moment tying them together. Jess lifted the edge of her shirt into his fingers, realizing now why it was so big.

"Richard's?" he asked. Again she nodded, then turned to look across the yard. "Alexa," Jess touched her chin until she faced him, "all we need is time."

She nodded, and tears trickled from her eyes. Jess bent to kiss her, savoring it slowly, longing for it to never end.

"I love you, Jess," she whispered.

He kissed her again and relaxed beside her, holding her against him as if he had a right to do so. "I love you, too."

As soon as the boys returned, Jess feared Alexa would fall back into keeping the distance she'd established between them. The next morning she remained quiet through breakfast, which was not unusual. But on her way out she stopped beside Jess and smiled. "Good morning,

Jess," she said with warmth. Her eyes betrayed the memory of their passionate moment, and Jess felt as jittery as a schoolboy.

There was little more to it than that, but Jess saw a pattern develop from that morning. She kept her distance, which left him perhaps alone, but not so lonely. Her smiles and kind words gave him something to fill the empty hours, and he was grateful. Thinking back to what had transpired on the porch, Jess felt sure it had released some volatile tension. He believed emotions had been building from different sources since long before she'd married Richard. And their passion, however brief, had released much of the strain between them. Now perhaps they could stand back and see the future with a clear perspective.

With a second chance at life, Jess figured it was time to start over. He couldn't afford to rebuild the main stable at this point, but he wasn't planning to hold any races on his own track in the near future. He was able to replace the saddles and gear they needed to keep things going as they had before. With a desire to put the nightmarish episode behind them, he felt good about his decision to have what little remained of the old stable torn down and done away with. The ground was cleared with the intention of building one to replace it as soon as finances allowed.

Weeks passed while Alexa kept a safe distance, but hope filled the time. The color gradually came back to her face, and the vibrancy of her eyes slowly returned. But it was laced with a tranquility and self-possession that had been absent before. The headstrong young woman who had entered Jess's office demanding a job was gone. Alexa had experienced the pain of life first-hand and risen above it. The result was a woman worth admiring. The maturity that replaced her innocence often left Jess in awe.

On a damp, chilly day, Jess found it difficult to keep from watching her through the noon meal. He caught her eye once. She smiled and turned away, but the impression her eyes left on him eased the past a little further away.

"Fiddler," she said when they were nearly finished, "I wonder if you would mind helping me move something that's a bit heavy."

"I'd be happy to. Right now?"

"If you don't mind." She smiled sweetly and left with Fiddler, while Jess wondered why she hadn't asked him.

"What are you up to?" Fiddler asked, walking beside her toward the old house.

"Oh, I just had an urge to rearrange the furniture. I need a little help with the sofa."

It only took him a minute to do what she needed, but Alexa was hesitant to let him go. "Are you in a hurry?"

"No, why?"

"Oh, I don't know, I . . ." Alexa hesitated and was relieved when he caught on.

"Need to talk?" he asked, and she nodded. "To someone other than Jess?" he guessed, and she smiled. Fiddler sat down on the newly placed sofa and folded his arms. "So, let's talk. We'd likely feel more at home with a few potatoes to peel, but perhaps we could manage."

Alexa sat beside him. "Robert." His brow went up as she used his given name. "You know the situation here, but you're on the outside. Perhaps I'm too close to my own feelings to know what's proper when . . ."

"I think I understand," he said when she couldn't find the words to go on. "If it's advice you're after, I'm certainly no expert."

"But you have loved and mourned."

"Yes, I have," he said quietly. "And I do know you—and Jess."

"And Richard," she added firmly.

"And Richard," he repeated reverently. "In my opinion the future is the important thing here, Alexa. It's all right to look back for the memories, but don't let the memories keep you from having a normal, happy life."

"I believe that's true," she admitted, "but I . . ."

Fiddler took her hand. "I'm not sure exactly what's troubling you, but I can say that there is no reason for you to be worrying about what people might think. And least of all, you don't need to worry about what Richard would think of what you do from now on. You treated him as good as any woman could, and I don't believe you have anything to regret. You were honest with him and he knew how you felt. Don't feel guilty, Alexa, for wanting to find happiness without Richard. And you don't have to follow anyone's time but your own. Am I making any sense?"

"Perfect sense." She smiled, then bit her lip. "I loved Richard."

"We all know you did," Fiddler said with strength. "And there's something else we all know. You love Jess—and he loves you. Heaven might strike me for saying this, Alexa, but I must confess, I have wondered if this isn't how it was meant to turn out all along." Alexa's eyes widened as he went on. "We can't speculate on such things from our mortal point of view, but I believe in destiny." His eyes became slightly distant. "And I'm almost beginning to believe that destiny might just blow something good my way one of these days."

"You told me you could never love again."

Fiddler met her eyes, and the emotion was evident in his voice. "Feelings change, Alexa. It's taken me years, but I know now that Sarah would have wanted me to go on living." He squeezed Alexa's hand. "Don't waste years, Alexa. Life is too precious."

Alexa leaned forward and gave him a warm hug. "Thank you, Robert. You always say what I need to hear."

"And you always brighten my day." He touched her chin and moved toward the door. "We're glad you're here, Alexa. Life would never be the same without you."

"I intend to be here a long time," she said, and he grinned.

After supper, Alexa wrapped herself in a rarely used cloak. She ambled lazily across the lawn, feeling the recent rain seep into the hem of her skirt. It was no accident that she ended up near the veranda where she knew Jess would be having coffee. He looked both expectant and wary as she stopped nearby and looked at him deeply. "May I join you?" she asked.

"Please." He motioned toward an empty chair at his side. Alexa went around to the steps, and he was standing to meet her when she ascended. "Sit down; I'll go tell Sarina to bring another—"

"Oh, that's not necessary," she said. "I'll just share yours."

Jess sat beside Alexa and watched her lift his cup into her hands and take a careful sip. "It could use a little more cream."

"I won't dispute that," he stated.

Alexa languidly turned to absorb the view as if she'd never seen it before. "It looks as if we're in for a beautiful sunset."

"It's often that way after a storm," Jess added.

Their eyes met. "The more intense the storm, the more beautiful the sunset."

"Perhaps tomorrow's sunrise will be equally incredible."

"Perhaps." Alexa took another sip and passed the cup to Jess. Their hands brushed as it was exchanged. They settled back to quietly watch the clouds lighting up in bright hues of orange. "Do you believe in destiny, Jess?"

He looked over at her, surprised. She'd hardly spoken to him beyond casual greetings in months. "I don't believe I've ever really thought about it, but I suppose I do."

"I believe," she leaned back and lifted her feet onto an extra chair, "that I was meant to be here. I've felt so at home here, from the very first week." She looked at Jess. "Do you think that has something to do with being Ben Davies' daughter?"

"I don't know," he said, "but he would have loved you. You are so much like him." The adoration in his voice forced her to look away.

"And so are you, I hear."

"Where did you hear that?"

"Richard told me," she said softly. "He told me about Ben, and said many times that you were so much like him. He raised you well."

"He was a good man," Jess said distantly. "I often miss him."

"Jess," she said and he looked at her, "he was much more your father than mine. I want you to know that."

Jess turned his eyes to the brilliant horizon. "You were talking about destiny."

"I don't know if you'll agree with me, Jess, but I believe I was meant to marry Richard."

"I'm glad he was there for you when you needed him, Alexa. I think you did the right thing."

"I still feel confused at times," she admitted.

"So do I." He looked at her severely. "But I do know one thing. He died a happy man. For that I am grateful."

Alexa felt tears in her eyes and realized it had been a long time since she'd had the need to shed any. She took Jess's hand, and he gave an empathetic squeeze. They exchanged a warm smile and watched in peaceable silence as the sun went down in breathtaking colors. A comfortable conversation of friendship ushered in the night sky. The peace deepened as pinholes of light began to appear.

Jess was reluctant to let Alexa leave, but it wasn't until much later that he began to comprehend why she'd come. Richard's death had been a difficult adjustment for all of them, and his presence had been sorely missed. Jess wanted to give Alexa time to feel completely at ease with him again, and he had no desire to intrude upon whatever mark Richard had left on her life. Time had made the loss easier to face, but Jess had been careful not to pass the carefully made border between him and Alexa. He figured that when she was ready, she would take the first step to cross it.

Thinking back over the conversation, Jess realized she had done just that. Her talk of destiny seemed to have opened a door. By morning Jess knew that if he had any sense, he would have the courage to walk through it.

The sunrise was incredible as Jess had predicted. He only wished Alexa was there to share it with him. Over the past many weeks he had watched her emotions closely and had seen her pain slipping away, but the delicacy of the situation had made it difficult to know what was best. Grasping the full spectrum of the changes he and Alexa had lived through since the days when they had first fallen in love, he felt an ever-increasing desire to have her a part of his life—completely. But he felt afraid. Not as he had in the past, but in finding fortitude to take the first steps toward retracing some hard-lived paths.

As the sun filled the day with light, instinct told Jess it was time they moved on with their lives. And he knew he had to take the next step, no matter how difficult.

Right after breakfast, Jess followed Alexa to the stable. It was the first time he'd seen her in breeches since he'd gone away and returned to find her very pregnant. His heart gave a childish lurch of excitement when he noticed the way childbirth had filled out the clothes that used to be baggy. Then he noticed the limp. It was hardly noticeable, but a skirt had done better at hiding it than the breeches.

"I thought that was supposed to go away," he said, entering the doorway right behind her.

"What?" she asked without looking at him.

"The limp."

"I suppose doctors can't predict everything." She didn't seem disturbed by it, but Jess's mind went back to the horrible incident that had caused it, and the pointless purpose behind it. A mixture of thoughts stirred him, and he felt emotions riding high.

He watched Alexa in silence as she bridled Crazy and murmured quiet words. He liked the way she talked to horses.

"Are you going to ride?" he asked, wondering why he couldn't think of anything else to say when his heart was so full.

"I was thinking about it," she said. "It's been a long time." Alexa didn't want to admit to the memories absorbing her of the day she'd ridden Crazy out of here in a mindless frenzy soon after Richard's death. Jess had saved her from a likely accident, but since then she'd been almost afraid to ride. Other memories of that day made her pulse quicken, and she concentrated on the horse.

"How is Crazy today?" Jess eased into the stall on the opposite side of the horse, and Alexa smiled affectionately.

"Doing well." Alexa brushed her hand over Crazy's back while Jess ruffled the mane. In the midst of a tense silence, Jess noticed that her wedding ring was absent. It gave him the courage to step through that door which seemed to be opening wider.

Alexa wasn't surprised when Jess's hand came over hers where it rested on the horse, but the intensity of his grasp left her in awe. She looked up to meet his eyes, and all that had stood between them slipped away. Still, she knew they were not the same two people who had fallen in love long ago.

Jess glanced at their clasped hands, then back to her face. Alexa's blood raced through her veins as she caught the change. There was intimacy in the way he toyed with her fingers. And something in his eyes told her he would no longer be content to be friends alone.

"Jess," she whispered when his gaze overpowered her. In one deft movement, he came beneath the horse's belly to stand beside her, taking her hand into his. Alexa trembled. As much as she had loved Jess, all they had been through made her feelings for him so intense they consumed her entire being.

"Alexa," he muttered, his voice low. She held her breath when his arm shot around her waist. He looked searchingly into her eyes and felt peace from the approval he read there. He freed her hand to touch her face, and she felt his fingers tremble.

Jess watched her eyes as he lowered his head to kiss her. The desire amplified when she closed them. His kiss was timid and breathless. He barely touched his lips to hers, but it was enough to release all that Alexa had been holding back. She brought her hands to his face, touching him as if she never had. She touched her cheek to his. He sighed. She laughed. He murmured that he loved her and then he kissed her again. Again and again; timidly, longingly, urgently, until he fairly devoured her, leaving her weak and powerless. When Alexa thought she could bear no more, she buried her face against his throat and Jess tightened his arms around her, holding her as if he would never let her go.

"I hope Murphy doesn't catch us doing this," Jess said lightly. Alexa glanced up at him, amusement shining in her eyes. "The last time he caught me kissing you in the stable, he yelled at me."

"I'll protect you," she promised, and he kissed her again.

Jess wanted it to go on and on, but he reminded himself not to move too quickly. There were still steps that needed to be taken, in proper order at the proper time.

"Why don't we saddle up this horse and take a little ride, Mrs. Wilhite."

"I'll let you have the honor, Mr. Davies," she said and stood back to watch him saddle the eager Crazy. He helped her up then mounted behind her, taking the reins in one hand and holding her with the other.

"It's a beautiful day," she said as they emerged from the stable.

"Perhaps spring is not far off," he muttered behind her ear. He urged the horse forward into a smooth gallop.

Twenty-seven
THE GIFT

That evening, Jess found Alexa playing the piano. While she was unaware of his presence in the room, he watched her, relishing his memories and dreams. When she finished the piece and opened her eyes, the years fled. It was as if nothing had changed since the night they had first confessed their love in this room.

"I haven't heard you play since Richard died," he said. He didn't want to dampen the mood, but neither did he want to ignore the part Richard played in their lives.

"That's likely because I haven't."

"It's good to have you at it again." He leaned over the piano and put his chin on his fist. "I've missed it."

"So have I," she admitted.

Jess gave a nod of encouragement, and she began another piece. When it was done, he sat on the bench beside her, his back to the piano. "Alexa," he said, humor vaguely showing in his eyes, "I've got something I want to say to you, and I want you to listen closely. You know, of course, that I expect honesty from all my employees, and—"

"Oh, not one of your old honesty speeches," she teased.

"I'm trying to be serious," he laughed.

"It didn't work."

"Alexa," he looked her solemnly in the eye, "you are well aware that I expect honesty in my employees, but you don't have to worry about that anymore."

"Why not?" she asked, alarmed.

"Because you're fired." His tone came across every bit as severe as he'd hoped.

"Jess, I . . . ," she stammered, wondering what she'd done to provoke this. "I know I haven't been much of an employee these past months, but I try to help out where I can, and—"

"Alexa," he put a finger over her lips, "you worked enough in the first six months you were here to keep me indebted for years to come."

"Then . . . why?"

"We were talking about honesty," he stated, and her eyes narrowed. "I want you to think about the importance of being completely honest, Alexa. Because you can bet your life on Crazy that if I expect honesty from my employees, I'm certainly going to expect it from my wife."

Alexa's eyes filled with wonder and surprise.

"Of course you don't have to accept my proposal, and you could probably get your job back if you really want it."

"I'm not certain I understand the provisions of this offer." She imitated his businesslike attitude. "Clarify yourself, Mr. Davies."

"Let me put it this way." His voice lowered with emotion. "Will you marry me, Alexa?" He touched her face and hair. "Soon," he whispered. "Just as soon as possible. I don't want to wait any longer. We've waited long enough. I want to share my home with you, my life. I want to give you everything I have and spend my life working to give you more. Give me the chance, Alexandra, to prove to you how very much I love you."

Alexa pushed her arms around his neck and held him, burying her face against his shoulder until she was able to maintain her emotion. "It would be an honor," she eased back to look at him, tears glistening against her eyelashes, "to be your wife, Jess Davies."

Jess mingled a smile with his sigh of relief, then he carefully touched his lips to hers. The timidity gradually dissipated from his kiss, and a carefully guarded passion seeped through. Jess set her lips free to study her face, holding her so close he could feel her breath.

"Hasn't it been a hundred years since we sat here like this?" she murmured against his cheek.

"At least," he whispered. "But I don't remember it being so wonderful."

"Same lips." She brushed her fingers over them.

"But it's not the same man."

He kissed her again, and Alexa knew he was right.

❦ ❦ ❦

Alexa became convinced of the changes in Jess when he took her to town the following morning to make arrangements for the marriage, and to see that she ordered an appropriate gown. It was evident he had no intention of backing out.

The next morning at breakfast, Jess stood at the head of the table until all eyes turned toward him.

"Are you gonna eat or make a speech?" Murphy grumbled.

"Both . . . in good time," Jess stated. Alexa saw a sparkle in his eyes. "I have something to say, so you'd do well to perk up and listen."

Fiddler nudged Edward. "That's how he sounded when he wanted us to work with that woman trainer." He winked at Alexa, and she comically stuck out her tongue.

"Well, if you must know," Jess replied, leaning his palms onto the table and looking directly at Fiddler, *"that woman trainer* and I are getting married."

After a second of stunned silence, the boys whooped and hollered so loudly that Alexa was almost embarrassed. Jess laughed and motioned for her to come and stand beside him. He kissed her quickly and put his arm around her shoulders while they waited for the commotion to settle.

"The wedding has been arranged for the tenth," Jess stated. "It will be in the big house, and you're all invited, as long as you act civilized."

"Oh, Jess," Alexa smiled up at him, "I think that's asking too much."

"You just wait," Murphy insisted, apparently missing her sarcasm, "we'll show you we're not just a bunch of—"

"Murphy!" Fiddler interrupted him. "Not in front of a lady."

Murphy cleared his throat and looked embarrassed.

"Nothing you boys say could shock me," Alexa said.

"Well, how about this?" Fiddler stood and came around the table. He gave Alexa a quick embrace and extended a hand to Jess. "Congratulations. We couldn't be happier."

The boys followed with a chorus of amens. Jess kissed Alexa and Murphy muttered, "Blimey, it's about time."

❦   ❦   ❦

Alexa went into town with Fiddler and Murphy. She insisted Jess couldn't go; it would be bad luck. She picked up her completed gown and everything else she needed in order to have a proper wedding. That evening she tried the gown on privately, but it was difficult to get the effect when she couldn't fasten all the buttons. She made a mental note to ask Mrs. Brown to help her dress before the ceremony.

Hanging the gown carefully in the closet, Alexa felt the need to share her anticipation and went into the house in search of Jess. She found him in his office, his boots on the desk, tapping a riding crop against his thigh.

"The first time I saw you like that," she said to make her presence known, "I never would have dreamed I'd end up marrying you."

"No," he chuckled, "I don't think it crossed my mind that day, either."

Alexa pulled a chair close to the desk and sat across from him, putting her feet up in the same manner and crossing her booted ankles. Jess chuckled. "Does this make us partners?"

"Not quite," she smiled, "but we're getting close."

"Which brings us to a subject in need of discussing, my dear Alexandra." She was surprised when he pulled out the station ledger and removed his boots from the desk in order to open the book in front of her. Alexa put her feet on the floor and leaned her elbows on the desk. She listened intently as Jess discussed in detail their financial situation and his plans for the future. He admitted to making severe mistakes in the past, but Alexa protested. "What could you have possibly done differently?" she asked.

"The first mistake I made," he said soberly, "was investing so much in the racing. My father had always made a fair living with the sheep, and it gave us everything we needed. But when he died and suddenly it was all in my hands, I decided I was going to make it big. I invested everything I had in the racing facilities and a few good horses."

"And what's wrong with that? They've served you well."

"Yes, but I never would have needed to depend on the racing to pay mortgage payments if I hadn't mortgaged the property in the first place. And if I hadn't invested so much in the racing, I probably could have afforded to rebuild the house without going so deeply into debt. Sometimes I wonder if I even should have rebuilt the house."

"Why did you?" she asked, knowing his answer would soothe his anxiety.

"It was Father's dream house," he said easily.

"You did it for him. As far as I can see," she consoled, "you did nothing worthy of regret. I think you're losing sight of a very important factor here, Jess."

"And what is that?"

"If Chad Byrnehouse hadn't been set on some warped determination to destroy you, you most likely would have never had more than minor difficulties with the racing or the mortgage."

"Nevertheless," he said, "I'm not discussing this to hash over the past. But if nothing else, I have learned a few good lessons. I have most of the money put away to pay the last payment," he smiled, "which I will take care of as soon as we return from our honeymoon. And from this day forth, nothing is going to rely on chance. If I'm going to be responsible for a family, I'm not going into debt for anything, and the racing is simply going to be for sport. Financially I will rest nothing on it. If profits come, fine, but no more bets at eighty to one."

Alexa laughed and reached over the desk to kiss him. "What a fine husband I'll have."

"How much longer is it going to be?" He smirked.

"Three days."

Jess glanced at the clock. "Two days, fourteen hours, and twenty-seven minutes."

❧   ❧   ❧

The anticipation of Alexa's wedding day was mingled with only a little sadness. Everything seemed so perfect that it was difficult to have regrets, but a part of her missed Richard. She would have liked him to be there for the wedding, but of course that was ridiculous. If he was here, there would be no wedding.

After supper, she and Jess walked to the graveyard and spoke peacefully of the past. He took her home and kissed her chastely before he returned to the big house. They agreed on needing sleep and some time alone. But with everything under control, Alexa found she was nervous. She went to bed just after ten, but stared at the ceiling and fidgeted with the sheets. She couldn't help thinking of her marriage to Richard, which she'd hardly had time to anticipate. She speculated on what might be different, then scolded herself for comparing. It was impossible. Trying to concentrate on the positive, she reminded herself that this was the best thing she had ever done. Time and pain had proven that this love was meant to be, and together they could make it through anything.

Her thoughts turned peacefully to Jess. Butterflies rushed from her toes to her neck when she contemplated what they would share tomorrow night. They had waited so long. Surely it would be incomparable.

Alexa was startled when something tapped the window. She almost thought she'd imagined it, until it happened again. She listened carefully and heard her name being whispered loudly.

"What are you doing?" She leaned out her window and laughed.

Jess shrugged. "I thought I'd serenade you."

"I'm waiting."

He laughed again. "Actually, we need to talk."

Alexa didn't like the way his tone sobered. "All right," she said.

"It's a little chilly out here," he said. "Do you think I could come in?"

Alexa met him at the door with a lamp in her hand. She set it down and motioned him toward the sofa.

"I'm sorry if I woke you," he said, "but—"

"Oh, you didn't wake me," she interrupted.

Jess turned his face to the side and his cheek twitched.

"What's wrong, Jess?" she asked gently, not liking the uneasiness suddenly taunting her.

"Alexa," he faced her directly, "you are nearly my wife, and we have been through much together. You have given me love and acceptance since the day I met you. There is no reason why I shouldn't be able to discuss this with you." He stood and began to pace back and forth in front of her. "I thought I had dealt with all of this. But when I went to bed, the darkest thoughts crept into my mind and I . . . I have to talk to you, Alexa. I know I drove you away before because I wasn't willing to admit to what's inside of me." He stopped pacing and stuffed his hands in his pockets, looking down at her with apology in his eyes. "I can't marry you until we talk about this."

"I'm listening." She patted the sofa beside her and he sat down. He wiped sweat from the palms of his hands onto his breeches.

"This is difficult for me, Alexa," he said quietly, "but I know that I have to be honest with you, and with myself. I don't know; maybe I should have told you this before I asked you to marry me. Perhaps it would have made a difference."

"A difference to what?" she asked when he paused.

"Perhaps it's something a woman wouldn't want in a husband. Perhaps you would have been better off to—"

"Wait a minute." She held up her hands to stop him. "You're sounding a bit too much like the old Jess Davies. The new man in you knows that I love you. There is nothing you can tell me that will ever change that. And you should know it."

Jess's eyes softened. "I believe that's true."

"Tell me what you're feeling," she urged. "We can face it."

Her words gave him courage, and he took a deep breath. "Alexa, it's to do with my mother." Alexa was surprised, but she nodded with empathy. "I don't know why, but I haven't been able to stop thinking about her."

"Perhaps her blessings are with you in this marriage."

"Perhaps," he agreed, liking the idea. "But I can't help thinking of the day she married, and . . ." He faltered and looked down, then he drew back his shoulders and met her eyes again. "Alexa, their wedding night was nothing but a nightmare." Her eyes narrowed and he clarified, his voice low. "I was conceived that night. She didn't even have a chance to be with her husband before she was dragged outside and . . ." He glanced away and finished, "Well, you understand."

Alexa took his hand and squeezed it, giving him the strength to get to his point. "She was so emotionally unstable after that, and couldn't bear to . . . well, they never did share a bed, Alexa. Ben Davies died when I was eighteen, and not once did they share a bed."

Alexa touched his face with her other hand, wondering what all of this was leading to. His thoughts seemed to shift momentarily. "I suppose that's why you came about, Alexa. I know he loved my mother and he cared well for her, but you can't blame a man for wanting more." Alexa nodded as his words struck her deeply.

Jess sighed and watched his hand fidget with hers. She waited patiently for him to continue. "Alexa, if I am honest with you—and me—I hav to say aloud that I . . . I often hold you in my arms and wonder what kind of hell she went through. I've dealt with the rest of it. I know they both loved me. But I still have to wonder what kind of blood flows through my veins. And it tears me apart inside to think of her when . . ."

"I think I understand," she said when his words faded, his voice betraying deep emotion.

"Alexa," he squeezed her hands tightly and looked into her eyes, "logic tells me it's ridiculous, but there is a part of me that is scared to death I'm going to hurt you."

Alexa pulled him into her arms and he pressed his face to her shoulder. "I think I understand," she repeated, fighting to keep her voice steady.

"I hope you do," he chuckled dryly and held her tighter, "because I don't. I *don't* understand why I have to feel this way."

As Jess held to Alexa like a frightened child, she was glad he couldn't see the tears rolling over her face. He surely would have misinterpreted them. "This is where it all started, isn't it, Jess."

"Yes." The word passed his lips with great effort.

"You've never hurt me before, Jess." She discreetly wiped her tears with one hand. "Why would you hurt me now?"

"But I *have* hurt you." He lifted his head to protest. "In the attic, when you were married and—"

"You were angry and obnoxious, but you didn't hurt me."

"And in the carriage house," he whispered, as if the memory tormented him. "I don't know what I did to upset you so badly, but I—"

"Jess." She took his face into her hands. "I was upset, but it had nothing to do with you. You did not hurt me."

Jess leaned back into the corner of the sofa, as if putting some distance between them would aid in his perceiving this. "Upset about what?" he asked skeptically.

Alexa pressed her fingers to her temples, wondering how she could explain this and avoid any more pain for either of them. "Jess, have you ever . . . had a time when everything inside of you suddenly hurts unbearably?" Jess swallowed hard as he listened. "That day . . . Chad came, and . . . the things he said, his attitude . . . brought it all back to me." Alexa paused to get a grip on her emotions, proud of herself so far. "Jess, I grew up with a mother who was distant and unhappy, and a father who was either drunk or miserable. It all improved over the years, but when my father died it became very clear. My parents behaved that way for the same reason that I existed. But I was too concerned about surviving to face how much it hurt me.

"That day in the carriage house, Jess, all of the pain came back to me. I lost control of my senses. My emotions overtook me. I needed you desperately and I wanted to lose myself in your love, but then the fear struck me. I knew I couldn't go through with it and live with myself. After what I had suffered, I couldn't take the chance of conceiving a child outside of marriage.

"Jess," she touched his face as it softened from her explanation, "you didn't hurt me. What you did was nothing more or less than any man would have done. I never dreamed it would affect you so deeply. If I had known, I—"

"Shhh." Jess whispered. "There's no need to say any more. I understand, and I'm relieved."

"Then why do you still have that . . . look in your eyes?"

Jess shrugged. "Habit?" he suggested, but he knew there was more.

"Do you want me to tell you what I think, and then you can tell me if I'm wrong?" He nodded without looking at her. "First of all, I can see only one reason why it would be so important for you to discuss this now. You don't want your own wedding night to be marred by fear, and the ugly shadows of your mother's experiences."

Jess turned to look at her. Enlightenment came into his eyes. "No, I don't."

"Did you ever feel this way in another woman's arms," she asked quietly, "or just mine?" Alexa wondered what she'd said wrong when his expression filled with astonishment.

Jess turned away and pushed a hand through his hair, feeling sorely misinterpreted. "Alexa," he said, "I've never held any woman the way I've held you." Her eyes widened, and he felt suddenly uncomfortable in the wake of his confession. He stood abruptly, and a hint of defensive pride seeped into his voice. "I'm afraid if you want an experienced lover, you're marrying the wrong man."

Alexa stood to face him, moving her hand over his cheek. "Jess," she whispered, touched by what this meant, "I want *you*. I'm sorry if I insinuated that . . . well, I just assumed . . ."

"I'm baring my soul to you, Alexa, when I tell you that I've never had a woman. You will be the first—and the last."

Jess saw tears well in her eyes, and he wondered if he'd hurt her feelings. But her expression softened with love and acceptance. "I can think of no greater honor."

Jess's emotions hovered close to the surface with an overbearing intensity as he pulled Alexa into his arms. "It is only instinct that makes me want you, Alexa, and it frightens me."

"What are you afraid of, Jess?"

"Myself. If only I knew who I was, what I came from."

"It doesn't matter, Jess." She took him by the shoulders. "Look at me." He met her eyes stoically. "I'm *not* afraid of you, Jess."

Alexandra Byrnehouse never ceased to leave Jess in awe. She made it all seem so easy, so right. How could he possibly doubt her? The burden of his fears eased so significantly that he wondered why he hadn't had the courage to do this years ago. But there was no good in regretting the past. They were together now.

"Close your eyes, Jess," she whispered and he did. She eased into his arms. "What do you feel?"

"You," he replied.

"Who am I?"

He opened his eyes and smiled. "Alexandra Davies . . . almost."

"You must remember it," she said. "Follow your instincts, Jess, and don't be afraid of them. Remember that the woman in your arms loves you. She wants you. Remember who I am, Jess, but more importantly, remember who you are." He lifted a brow. "You are a man of your upbringing, Jess, not a man of your blood."

His eyes widened in pleasant disbelief. Alexa pressed her lips to his and gasped when he responded so quickly. A love more intense than anything she'd ever experienced poured into her from his kiss. She drew back breathlessly to look into his eyes, and the comparison became evident. Not since his fears had been triggered that fateful afternoon in the carriage house had he kissed her so undauntedly, so fearlessly. She had found the man she'd fallen in love with, and yet he had become so much more.

Jess lowered his head to kiss her again and pulled her against him fiercely. How long had it been since she'd been held this way? How had either of them survived without this?

"I think I'd better go now," he said, his eyes sparkling.

Alexa just sighed and watched him leave, happier than she'd ever been in her life.

❦ ❦ ❦

Jess considered the upstairs hall a perfect place for a wedding. The ethereal mood there only proved him right as his friends and servants gathered and took their seats. This time of day the sun shone brilliantly through high windows, giving a celestial aura to these moments that Jess knew would be the happiest of all his life.

Jess came from the south wing and took his place, watching with the others in hushed silence as Alexa came from the north and stood beside him. The elegant white gown that rustled around her feet was a stark contrast to the last time he'd seen her dressed so finely—in black. Jess felt nervous until her hand slipped into his. It was easy to speak the vows, and warmth flowed through him when he kissed her to seal their marriage.

While the boys celebrated and guzzled champagne, Jess watched Alexa and marveled at the reality. She was his wife. He'd wanted her for so long that he had trouble believing that a brief ceremony had changed everything. Oblivious to the commotion going on around them, he took her hand into his and kissed it with complete adoration.

"Hey," Murphy intruded, "I believe it's time we all kissed the bride."

"I'm not sure I'm up to it," Alexa teased and gave him a noisy smooch on the lips.

Tod was next. "It was nice of you to get married twice, Alexa."

"Two kisses from Alexa could last a lifetime," Fiddler said melodramatically.

"For you perhaps," Jess chuckled. "But you boys had better appreciate it while you can, because she's not getting married again."

"That's the spirit." Edward slapped Jess on the shoulder, then took his turn at getting a kiss. "You look more beautiful than I've ever seen you," he said warmly, and Alexa kissed him again.

Jimmy came last, acting as if it was nothing more than an embarrassing ritual, and Jess laughed.

"I don't think I could bear getting married again," Alexa admitted.

"I'd say that too, after having to kiss Jimmy," Edward chortled.

"Actually," she grinned, "my name is already long enough."

"Ah, yes." Jess eased an arm around her and said with pride, "Gentleman, allow me to introduce my wife, Alexandra Byrnehouse Wilhite Davies."

"Mrs. Davies would be fine."

"How about just Alexa?" Fiddler said.

"How about we eat now," Mrs. Brown piped in, and they went together to the dining room.

"For the first time ever," Jess declared as he was seated, "this table can be put to good use."

"Give yourself a few years," Edward said wryly, "and you'll have it full."

"Just as long as Alexa's always here," Jess said contentedly, "it will never be empty."

A jovial mood persisted through the meal, and was dampened only slightly when Sarina left to answer the door and returned with a wrapped package.

"What is it, Sarina?" Jess stood as she approached him.

"A wedding gift," she said, but he caught something wary in her tone.

"Who brought it?" he insisted as she turned it over to him.

"It was Mr. Byrnehouse." She spoke with distaste, and Jess glanced sharply at Alexa. "He didn't want to come in. He just handed me the package."

"It's probably dynamite," Murphy said.

"I wouldn't be surprised," Jess added too soberly.

"You open it," Alexa said to Jess.

"I'm not sure I want to."

"Knowing him, it's probably some kind of sick joke." Alexa's voice was tainted with disgust.

"Here," Murphy rose and took the package from Jess, "I'll open it. If it's safe I'll give it to you," he added in mock gallantry. First Murphy elaborately opened the card and grunted, seeming disappointed.

"What does it say?" Alexa asked.

He cleared his throat loudly. "Congratulations on your marriage."

"Sounds suspicious to me," Jess said lightly, but Alexa thought it *was* suspicious. She knew Chad too well to believe this was simply a kind gesture.

Murphy handed the card to Jess, then carefully pulled away the paper. He histrionically paused and held his breath before he lifted the lid.

"Get on with it," Alexa insisted.

Murphy opened it, and another card lay on top of folded tissue. Again he cleared his throat and read, "From one Byrnehouse to another."

"It must be for you," Jess said to Alexa.

"If you ask me," she replied, "it reeks of sarcasm."

Murphy defied his brusque manner as he delicately folded back the tissue, tilted his head and said, "It's nice."

"What is it?" Alexa asked.

"It's safe," Murphy declared and set the box in front of her.

"I don't believe it." She lifted out two silver goblets, each intricately carved with the name Byrnehouse.

Jess took one to examine. "They're beautiful."

"I don't understand," she said.

"What do you mean?"

"These have been in the family for a long time. My grandfather brought them from England and gave them to his eldest son as a wedding gift. I was under the impression these were to be Chad's when he married. It doesn't make sense."

Jess shrugged. It appeared to be a kind gesture, but Alexa grabbed the goblet from him and stuffed them both into the box. "I don't trust him in the best of circumstances." She handed the box to Sarina. "I'm certainly not going to trust him when it doesn't make sense. Put them away, Sarina—where we can't see them."

"It would be my pleasure, Mrs. Davies," she said vehemently.

"Are you all right?" Jess whispered as they were seated again.

"Yes, I'm fine." She smiled warmly and squeezed his hand. "Nothing could dampen my happiness today."

Jess kissed her quickly and grinned, knowing she was right.

When dinner was finished, Jess declared, "You boys can party all night if you want, but I'm exhausted."

They all laughed, and Alexa's eyes turned timid as Jess rose from the table and drew her with him.

"You can think what you like," Jess said as he ushered Alexa from the room, "but my wife and I are going to bed."

This brought on cheers and applause that accompanied them into the hall.

"Where did you get those characters?" Alexa laughed.

"You wouldn't want to know," he replied, then scooped her into his arms. "I suppose that's what we get for inviting a bunch of bunk-mates to our wedding," he added, carrying her up the stairs.

"Who else would we invite?" she asked. "They're the only family we've got."

Jess smiled at this, then paused as he came to his bedroom door. "Welcome home, Mrs. Davies," he said and kicked it open.   Alexa laughed as he set her down, but it was smothered by a warm kiss that filled her with breathless anticipation.

"I've got something I need to check on," he said quietly, "but I won't be long."

He left the room before Alexa could protest, but it gave her a chance to freshen up and feel prepared for what the night would bring.

Twenty-eight
WHOLE AGAIN

Emotion absorbed Alexa as she found herself alone in Jess's room. She had the best and worst of memories here, but none of that mattered anymore. The waiting was over.

She hurried to freshen up as much as possible, considering she couldn't get out of the gown without some help. Feeling as ready as she could be, a rush of nerves seized her. She reminded herself that this night would be perfect, but she felt a distraction might be in order. With curiosity she opened the wardrobe and smiled to see the familiar clothes hanging there. Touching them idly, she felt a longing for Jess and wondered what was taking him so long.

Closing the wardrobe, she caught sight of his hat hanging on the corner of the bureau mirror. She laughed as she pulled it down and impulsively put it on. Looking in the mirror she grinned, then tucked her hair up beneath it and tried to look stern. She decided Jess did the hat more justice, but she left it on as she sat down at the little writing desk and passively opened a drawer to rummage through it, half thinking she was in the mood to write her husband a memoir of these moments.

She was surprised to find the drawer filled with a disheveled assortment of pages, mostly already written on. It was definitely his handwriting, but they didn't appear to be letters or business papers. She picked one up to see what it was. The first line read: *In the mirror I see a man, but the reflection shows a . . .*

Alexa sensed more than heard the doorknob. Abruptly she stuffed the page back and shut the drawer before Jess entered the room and closed the door behind him.

"Nice hat," he smirked, and she quickly pulled it off. She shook her hair out and hung the hat up, then turned to see Jess pull off his already untied cravat and throw it on the bureau. "I'm sorry I was so long," he said, "I had to—"

"It's all right," she interrupted, not wanting to hear about trivial things tonight. Their eyes met, and her mind wandered back to the papers in that drawer. Her heart quickened as she wondered what it meant.

"Make yourself at home," Jess chortled, attempting to put her at ease. He wondered why she looked so nervous.

"I would, but . . . ," she glanced coyly away, "I can't reach these buttons, and . . ."

Jess removed his jacket and tossed it over the back of a chair. Alexa turned and lifted her hair. Jess hesitated a moment, then kissed the back of her neck before he began to work on the long row of tiny buttons. He felt awkward with such delicate work, and it was difficult to keep his hands steady.

"That should do it," he said and stepped back.

"Thank you." Alexa smiled over her shoulder, then she eased her arms out of the sleeves and the heavy gown fell in a heap on the floor. She turned to face Jess, and he unobtrusively eyed the petticoats and camisole, with bare feet peeking out from beneath.

When several moments passed and Jess realized they were still just staring at each other, he gave an embarrassed chuckle and looked down. "I've wanted to be with you like this for so long, and now I hardly know what to do."

"You can do anything you like, Jess." She stepped forward and put a hand to his face. "I'm yours now."

"I find that difficult to comprehend."

"That's understandable," she went on her tiptoes to set a quick kiss to his lips, "but I think we can overcome it."

Alexa sensed an obvious tension in him, and while she felt jittery, almost giddy inside, she knew well what to expect from this. Knowing from experience that Jess was a man of deep, innate passion, she felt sure it would take little to get past the tension.

Alexa pressed her fingers over the contours of his face, then she pushed his braces over his shoulders. Jess briefly wondered if she had been this way with Richard, but the question passed away quickly. And thoughts of his mother were completely absent. Jess's whole being became absorbed with Alexa, and he was oblivious to any past fears.

Jess lifted her chin to look at her. He smiled, then he kissed her. A familiar passion seeped in, threatening to press them into unfamiliar territory. He held her face in his hands and skittered kisses over her cheeks and brow. "Will you show me what to do?" he said against her ear, humor lacing his voice.

"I don't think that will be necessary." Alexa parted her lips and kissed him so fiercely that he had to adjust his footing.

A dreamlike sensation filtered over Jess as he slowly parted his lips from hers. He watched her eyes open languidly, and he searched them. The desire was undeniable, but behind it were the memories, the pain, the laughter, and the torment of irony, all surrounded by her perfect, unquestionable love. "If I'm dreaming," he whispered, his eyes capturing hers, "don't wake me tonight."

"If I wake you," she pressed her lips to his, "we can share the same dream."

Jess scooped her into his arms and carried her to the bed, cradling her against him. Her hair billowed out around her face as she landed in the center of the satiny comforter, and Jess paused only a moment to admire her beauty. As momentum took hold, he might have wondered if his passion was driving him to insanity, except that Alexa's behavior proved to him it was normal. He had never dreamed that lovemaking would be so thoroughly consuming. Heart, spirit, and body combined in perfect balance as the consummation of their love healed all wounds, bridged all chasms, soothed all fears.

The intensity of their physical union went beyond any earthly description, but the emotional unity they shared rose higher. The love they had felt for each other initially was only an embryo of the complete affinity surrounding them now. Their commitment was refined by pain and tempered by heartache. All they had suffered culminated now in a perfect joy that contrasted measure for measure. When the ecstasy dissipated into flawless elation, they held each other and wept—not in grief or affliction as they had become accustomed to, but with ultimate contentment.

Long after it was over, neither of them spoke, as if words might unravel the carefully woven tapestry that bound them together. Jess kissed her brow and watched her eyes pass through many phases of thought. When they welled up with fresh tears, he had to speak. "Tell me, Alexa." She nodded to indicate that she would, but he understood the complexity of her thoughts and allowed her time to gather them.

Through the continuing silence, Alexa's mind wandered through the scenes of her life since she had come to Jess Davies asking for work. She marveled at the courses she had taken, and most especially at the multifaceted relationship she shared with Jess. Looking at him now, she *did* believe in destiny. She could believe that they had loved each other in another life, and the trials of this world were only meant to make them stronger in order to bear each other up through whatever still lay ahead. She loved him with her whole heart, but she had loved Richard, too. She had long since accepted the role he played in her life, and though she missed him in a certain special way, she could not feel guilty for saying that Jess was simply the love of her life. Richard was a wonderful man, but he was not Jess Davies. Alexa had never doubted that Jess was more to her than any man could ever be, but so much had happened since their initial confessions of love. She had begun to think she had experienced it all. She had shared a rich, full life with a man who had been a devoted lover and a sensitive friend. But her true emotion in this moment lay in a harsh realization—a glorious, incomparable realization. The expectancy in Jess's eyes urged her to share it.

"Oh, my love." She cupped her hand against his face. "I have never experienced anything so completely . . . fulfilling." His eyes widened as he perceived what she meant. "I never dreamed that such an experience existed on this earth."

Jess could only hold her closer and think how grateful he was to have been given a second chance at life.

Alexa woke in the dark and oriented herself to the feel of her new bedroom. Instinctively she reached out, and her fingers met with a warm shoulder. She wondered if Jess was sleeping, but she immediately caught his attention and they came into each other's arms. He kissed her and it began again, as if to prove it had all been real. They were truly married, and what they shared was unequaled.

Alexa slept again until morning. She lay watching Jess sleep until she had an urge to further explore what she had found last night before he'd returned. Without a wrapper handy, she slipped into Jess's discarded shirt and rolled up the sleeves. Quietly she sat at the little desk and slid the drawer open. One by one she read each piece of poetry—many that she had been given copies of, some she had never seen that moved her to tears.

"Can't a man have any secrets?"

Startled, Alexa turned to see Jess leaning on one elbow. Despite his light tone, she felt somehow guilty for being caught as she was. Their eyes met, and she tried to convey an apology that she couldn't find words for.

"I had no idea." She turned her attention back to the papers on the desk.

"About what?" he questioned, if only to make her verbalize it. He'd grown tired of secrets.

"That my husband was a poet," she admitted.

"But you thought your first husband was a poet?" he asked lightly.

"Oh, he was," she insisted, her eyes softening, "though not the poet you are. But then," memories of their lovemaking glistened in her eyes, "if I had known then what I know now, I might have guessed."

Alexa looked again at the page in her hand, recalling well when she had received it—the day she had left to marry Richard. With emotion she read aloud, "In the mirror I see a man, but the reflection shows a beast."

With an eloquent voice, Jess reiterated the remainder of the idea. "I have heard through legend's tongue, from books my mother read, the only thing that changes beast to man, is pure love. Beauty's love."

"You were trying to tell me a long time ago," she stated, "but I wasn't listening."

"It doesn't matter anymore, Alexa. I'm grateful for the changes in me. Now that we're here I have no regrets, and you shouldn't either." He reached out a hand. "Come here, Mrs. Davies, and give your husband a proper greeting."

Alexa looked once more at the poem in her hand and returned the pages to the drawer. She took his hand and knelt on the bed to kiss him. Jess eased her beside him and looked into her eyes.

"Vivacious eyes," he murmured and kissed her. "Bewitching eyes, eyes that stir my soul. Losing myself within those eyes could only find me whole."

   ❦ ❦ ❦

In her marriage, Alexa found happiness and fulfillment like she'd never imagined. Just being Alexandra Davies seemed to elevate her to a new distinction, as did sharing her life with Jess in every respect. Their extensive honeymoon was a fantastic whirlwind that combined the peace she derived from her music with the breathless excitement of winning a race. Yet it was still a plane far above any of that. With Jess at her side, Alexa needed nothing else to survive. She knew that together they could face and rise above anything.

They returned home full of laughter and happiness, only to be greeted with news that put Alexa's theory immediately to the test. She followed Jess to his office first thing, as he wanted to make certain everything was in order. They came around the corner and nearly bumped into Murphy, who looked far too surprised to see them.

"What are you doin' here?" he demanded.

"We live here!" Jess laughed.

"But you weren't supposed to be back yet. I thought you were gonna have me meet you at the depot and—"

"We hired a carriage," Jess said.

"Why?" Murphy's distress increased.

"We missed you and wanted to hurry," Jess answered in exasperation. "What difference does it make?"

"None at all." Murphy chuckled uncomfortably.

"Good," Jess said and moved past him down the hall.

"Wait!" Murphy followed quickly. "Why don't you freshen up first, or—"

"Murphy," Jess stopped and faced him, "is there something you want to tell me?"

Murphy looked sheepish but said nothing, and Jess continued down the hall with Alexa's hand in his. He glanced warily toward her when they heard pounding and realized it was coming from the office. Alexa wondered if Jess felt the same nervous twitch that she did when

Murphy stepped out to block their path.

"What's going on?" Jess insisted.

"We was hopin' to have it fixed before you got back."

"*What* fixed?" Jess asked gruffly.

Murphy hesitated.

"What?" Jess demanded.

"The hole in the wall." Murphy looked at the floor like a child about to be scolded.

"Why on earth is there a hole in the wall?" Jess tried to remain calm but Alexa saw that muscle in his cheek twitch.

"I'm havin' to assume it was caused by dynamite."

"Dynamite? What the . . ." Jess tried to push past him, but Murphy held his ground.

"I'd tell you to sit down," Murphy said severely, "but there isn't a chair. And first, let me say that none of us was too thrilled about havin' this for you to come home to."

"Get to the point, Murphy."

"Somebody blew open the safe."

Jess wished he had a chair. He momentarily leaned against Alexa until he absorbed what it meant. He ran into the office where he stood in the doorway, stunned. Jimmy and Fiddler were hard at work, attempting to repair the mess.

"What's he doing here?" Fiddler shouted, and Murphy shrugged. Alexa felt nearly sick to see the condition of the office. She held tightly to Jess's arm, waiting tensely for the explanation that she knew Jess would demand.

"All right—out with it!"

The boys looked hesitantly at each other. Fiddler set his hammer on the debris-covered desk and cleared his throat. "Mrs. Brown heard it right after she went to bed. She thought the world had ended. She ran out to get us, but by the time we got here, whoever had done it was long gone."

Jess sat down, and Alexa saw the shadow pass over his face. "What was in there?" she asked warily.

"More than half the money we needed to make the payment."

"Where's the other half?" she asked, proud of herself for her calm tone.

Panic engulfed Jess as he ran from the room and Alexa followed. She found him in the dining room with a drawer to the liquor cabinet open, counting bills. He sighed as he put them back and locked it.

"It's all there," he stated, "but it's not enough." Abruptly he turned and hit his fist against the wall. "Why?" he said through clenched teeth. "Why!?"

Alexa gently touched his shoulder, and he pulled her into his arms. "I don't understand, Alexa. I just cannot comprehend why he will not cease tormenting me."

"You believe Chad did it?" she asked softly.

"I *know* he did it!" Jess drew back and pushed his hand into his hair. "I know it with every fiber of my being." He held out his hand and tightened it into a fist. "But I can't prove a blasted thing. If I tried, he'd be breathing down my neck so quickly it would suffocate me." He sighed. "I suppose I should be glad he didn't burn the house down . . . again. Oh, Alexa," his voice softened, "I don't know what to do. If I can't make that payment, we'll lose everything."

"When is it due?"

"Less than three weeks. The seventeenth."

"We're scheduled to race Crazy on the eleventh."

"Alexa," he muttered, "I swore I wouldn't—"

"Have you got a choice? I know she can win. I'll run her just to make sure."

"No."

"Why not?"

"Do you know where that race will be held?"

"Of course. It's at Byrnehouse."

"And that's exactly what Chad wants us to do. If everything is resting on that race, you can bet your life it will be rigged."

"We'll be careful," she stated easily.

Jess said nothing.

"I don't see that we have any choice, Jess."

Still he made no response, and Alexa left him standing in the dining room with his thoughts.

"This can wait," Alexa announced as she came into the office. "We've got more pressing matters."

"Like what?" Fiddler asked.

"I'm going upstairs to change. You boys get Crazy and Demented onto the track, and tell Tod to meet me there. We've got a race to win."

Alexa changed into her most comfortable breeches and riding

boots. Walking toward the track, she felt a fluttery excitement from the combination of being Jess's wife and being back at her business.

"What's up?" Tod asked as Alexa approached him.

"You know, of course, there's a race in two weeks."

"Yes."

"Well, it's now officially the most important race we've ever run." Tod's expression faltered. "It could save the station." Alexa waited for this to be absorbed before she added, "How would you feel if I ran it?"

Tod laughed. "Relieved."

"Good," she said. "You can help me train and be there for a back-up. Let's give it a try."

Alexa was leading Crazy to the starting line when she saw Jess come to the rail and lean against it. She waved toward him and he returned it, but his uneasiness was evident.

After a good trial run, Alexa met Jess at the fence and kissed him in greeting. "How did it go?" he asked.

"She made good time, especially considering how out of shape I am. You can take that worried crease out of your brow, love," she added lightly. "We've done it before. We'll do it again. No problem."

"I thought I fired you." A vague trace of humor erupted.

"No," she kissed his nose, "you *married* me. We're partners now, Mr. Davies."

"You don't have to do this, Alexa."

"I think it's exciting," she said with a lilt in her voice. "If for no other reason, let me do it for the thrill."

"You're incredible." He smiled at last. "But what if we—"

"Don't say it, Jess. We won't lose."

"I'm glad you're sure." He put his arm around her and ushered her toward the stable. He bent to kiss her as they walked, then he decided to stop and enjoy it. He marveled at how she never ceased to set him on fire.

"Don't you ever get enough?" she teased, her voice betraying that she wanted him just as badly.

"Never," he growled and patted her bottom. She laughed and jumped out of his grasp, then hurried toward the stable ahead of him. "I do like those breeches," he grinned. "You don't look too out of shape to me."

She smirked over her shoulder and he ran to catch up with her. "By the way," he added wryly, "I have something for you."

"Really?"

"A wedding gift." He stopped next to a stall and looked at her expectantly. Alexa glanced up at him, wondering what she'd missed, and Jess laughed. "Don't you recognize her?" Alexa's eyes shifted to the horse beside her. "They say when a man marries, he should get his wife a lady's maid. I knew you were quite accustomed to taking care of yourself, so I got you Lady's Maid instead."

Alexa laughed and threw her arms around his neck. "I can't believe it." She greeted the horse with affection and glanced at Jess warily. "How did you manage? She must have cost you a fortune."

"Actually, Murphy took care of the transaction. He bartered with the stable master. Chad had nothing to do with it. He probably hasn't figured out yet that she's gone."

"Oh," Alexa gasped, "I still can't believe it. Do you think we can get her in shape enough to race again?"

"Maybe, but I don't care. She's yours. Do whatever makes you happy."

Murphy walked into the stable with Jimmy, and Alexa overwhelmed him with a hug that left him baffled.

"How did you manage, Murphy?" she asked. "What kind of pressure did you use?"

"Ah, well," Murphy shrugged as he caught on, "it was pretty difficult. I walked in and said," he lowered his voice dramatically, "how much do you want for that fat, lazy horse there?"

Alexa laughed and embraced Jess again. "Thank you, my love," she said, and he kissed her.

"You're very welcome."

"But, Jess, I have no gift for you."

"Alexa," he whispered with adoration, "you have given me more than I could ever measure."

"But I—"

Jess put his fingers to her lips. "You have saved this land a number of times, and you're ready to do it again. That is gift enough to last three lifetimes."

Alexa put her arms around him tightly. She was determined to win this race, if only to prove to Jess how very much she loved him.

❦ ❦ ❦

Three days prior to the race, Alexa found Jess in his office. "It's almost back to normal," she commented, looking around as she came behind his chair and put her arms around him.

"Hello, Mrs. Davies," he said warmly.

"I have a secret to tell you," she whispered.

"Really," he chuckled, "and what might that be?"

"I'll tell you as soon as you promise that no matter what, I can still ride the race."

"I was under the impression that you were determined to do that anyway."

"You know why it's so important that I do."

"Yes, I know."

"Do you promise?"

"Very well, I promise. Now what's your secret?"

"I do have a gift for you, Jess."

"I told you that I—"

"Jess," she whispered behind his ear, "I'm going to have a baby." Jess turned abruptly to look at her. Alexa's eyes told him it was true.

"Already?" he asked breathily.

"We've had ample time, my dear," she laughed.

"I don't believe it."

"Well, it's true," she assured him, sitting on his lap. "Before you know it, I'll be so fat you won't recognize me."

"I recognized you the last time you got fat."

Their eyes met with a mutual memory, but Alexa felt warmed by it rather than pained.

"Are you happy, Alexa?" He touched her face meekly.

"More than I can say." She kissed his brow and he nuzzled his face into the folds of her shirt. "I have ached for a baby, Jess, since I . . ." Her words faded with emotion.

"You never said anything about it."

"I knew it would happen when the time was right."

Jess leaned back to look at her, his brow furrowed in concern. "How are you feeling?"

"A little nauseated if I get hungry, but beyond that, I feel great."

"That's good," he smiled and hugged her.

"Just think, my love. Your child will be winning races before it's even born. By the time it's—"

"Alexa," Jess said sharply, "you can't ride that race!"

"But you promised."

"That's not fair, Alexa," he insisted. "You can't expect me to—"

"Jess," she interrupted, "please calm down. I shouldn't have even told you yet."

"You most certainly should. What if—"

"Jess," she broke in again, "I feel fine. I'm quite accustomed to riding. The doctor said that as long as I'm careful there should be no problem. You know as well as I do that we have a better chance at winning if I ride. Please, just let me do it and don't be difficult."

Jess sighed in defeat. "I should have known the first day you walked in here that you would do whatever you pleased."

"Have you got any complaints?"

"Not usually," he conceded, and a smile seeped into his expression. "But you be careful," he added severely. "Nothing—not even this station—is worth risking you or the baby. Do you understand?"

Alexa nodded and hugged him fiercely.

"If I survive this with my sanity, it will be a miracle."

"Ah," Alexa laughed, "we'll just go crazy together."

"Haven't we already?" He smirked.

"Not completely," she whispered close to his ear then blew in it, "but give us time."

"Wretched woman," he laughed, shivering from the sensation. She kissed his nose, then his eyelids. She teased his lips while she tugged at the buttons of his shirt. "Alexa," he scolded, "I have work to do."

"It can wait," she muttered and blew in his ear again.

"Wretched woman," he chuckled.

"Going crazy yet?" She kissed his throat.

"Absolutely mad!" he growled, and she laughed as he took her into his arms. Then he looked at her with disgust. "Why can't you wear skirts like normal women?"

"There are some things you just can't do in a skirt."

"There are some things," he mimicked her haughty tone, "you just can't do in these wretched breeches."

"Nonsense," she laughed. "I would bet my life on Crazy that if a man wants his wife badly enough, he'll find a way."

Jess feigned disgust. She laughed and kissed him again. Then he proceeded to prove her right.

Twenty-nine
ALEXA'S VICTORY

At dawn Jess and Alexa started toward Byrnehouse, not far behind the boys who went ahead with Crazy and Demented. Tod would be riding Demented in the five and a half, and Alexa was legitimately registered to ride Crazy in the six.

"I'm nervous, Alexa," Jess admitted as the carriage neared their destination.

"Here," she eased closer and pushed her hand into his hair, "let me distract you." She pressed her mouth over his with immediate passion.

When the carriage passed beneath the entrance gate to the Byrnehouse racing facilities, Jess was sitting across from Alexa, wearing a complacent smile.

"Still nervous?" she asked.

"About what?"

"The race."

"What race? Oh, of course. That race." He smiled again. "Isn't it great to be married, Mrs. Davies?"

"It certainly is," she agreed as the carriage halted.

Alexa was quickly off to change into her silks, since Crazy was scheduled to run in the first race. The boys took the horses to their appointed stalls, and Jess lingered near them until Murphy got fed up with his nerves and slapped a one-pound note into his hand. "Go make a bet for me and find a comfortable place to watch."

Jess took the hint and wandered over to place a bet for both him and Murphy. He was relieved when Alexa found him.

"You look nice." He perused the pink and yellow silks. "In fact, I really like those breeches."

Alexa giggled but Jess showed no sign of humor. "Are you all right?" she asked.

"As good as could be expected, I suppose. It's too bad I don't drink anymore. I could sure use one."

"It will be over soon," she assured him.

"That's what I'm afraid of."

Jess walked with Alexa back to the stables, where it was announced that they had ten minutes before the horses would go out.

"Everything all right?" Jess asked Murphy as he led Crazy outside.

"Perfect," Murphy assured him. "I haven't let her out of my sight for a second. I've checked straps, reins, everything—inside and out."

Jess sighed and Alexa mounted. "How about a kiss for good luck?" She bent over, and Jess kissed her with a trace of passion. Their eyes met with severity, and Jess was reminded of the farewell they'd exchanged when he'd been seated on a horse, leaving to deal with the pain of her marriage to Richard. He hoped it was the memory and not some horrible premonition that sent a shiver down his back.

"Be careful," he whispered. "None of it's worth a blasted pound without you."

"I'll not only be careful," she insisted, "I'll win."

"Get out of here," Murphy laughed, and Jess returned to the track.

He was barely gone when Tod approached. "Alexa, I need to talk to you—alone."

Alexa dismounted and Murphy looked nervous.

"Don't worry," she chuckled, "I'll be right back."

Murphy was distracted by one of the stable hands who walked by with his hands in his pockets.

"So this is the famous Crazy." He paused to look the horse over with interest.

"This is her," Murphy said proudly.

The spectator pulled out a hand to pat Crazy on the rump, and the animal jumped slightly.

"Whoa there, girl." Murphy glared distastefully at this overzealous fan.

"She's ready to run, I see." The stable hand laughed.

Murphy was relieved when he moved on, and even more relieved when he saw Alexa returning. Now they could get this over with.

❧ ❧ ❧

"How was the honeymoon?" Chad Byrnehouse asked complacently.

Jess turned to face him, and contempt rose immediately. He forced an indifferent smile. "Wonderful, thank you."

"Too bad it's over," Chad added and sauntered away before Jess could think of a comeback.

When posting time was announced, Jess felt a familiar knot form in his stomach. He hated living like this. Quickly he said a prayer that if nothing else, Alexa would make it through this race unharmed. He found a place where he could see just as the horses bolted forward. Even from a distance the yellow and pink stood out boldly, and he could see that Crazy was doing well as they edged around the track. A peace began to settle into him—until Crazy suddenly lost control.

"No!" Jess cried as his prize mare reared back and twisted repeatedly. Alexa's efforts to stay on suddenly faltered. Something died inside of Jess as she landed face down on the track, and one of the horse's hooves struck the center of her back. She lay completely motionless as he shoved his way through the crowd. Pain burned behind his eyes. Even if Alexa was lucky enough to still be alive, he felt sure the baby couldn't possibly have survived.

Jess finally made it to the rail, only to see Alexa hoisted onto a stretcher and carted the other direction. It took five men to get Crazy under control.

The burning in his eyes increased as he turned back around and moved through the mass of curious onlookers, knowing he'd lost it all. But the station seemed insignificant. He only wanted to feel Alexa in his arms and know that she was alive.

Concentrating on getting through the crowd, Jess was surprised to feel familiar hands come against his chest, accompanied by a feminine voice. "What happened?"

He looked down into electric blue eyes. Suddenly everything was all right. "Alexa!" Her name spilled out with a breath of relief. He embraced her so tightly she could hardly breathe. "You're all right." He touched her face and hair. "You're not hurt." He laughed in exasperation. "Why don't I ever know who is riding that blasted horse?"

"Tod said he had a gut instinct that he should ride—so I let him."

"Tod!" Jess's thoughts shifted.

"Is he hurt badly?" Alexa asked while Jess ushered her through the crowd.

"I fear he is."

"What happened?"

"Crazy went crazy," Jess said solemnly. "And don't ask me why, because I don't know."

They were relieved to be met at the bunkhouse with a doctor's report that the jockey was badly bruised and had a cracked rib, but nothing he wouldn't recover from.

"Good instincts, eh?" Tod said to Alexa as he struggled to sit up slightly and moaned.

"Yes," Jess answered for her. "We owe you a great deal."

"Nonsense." He shrugged. "But you can't imagine how surprised I was when they told me the jockey was going to have a baby. It took me five minutes to convince them they had the wrong jockey."

Alexa laughed and hugged Tod carefully. Then she and Jess went back out to face the fact that the race was lost.

"I guess that's it," Jess said. "There is simply no other way to come up with that money in time."

"You don't sound terribly disappointed." Alexa squeezed his hand.

"I'm so grateful to have you alive that I almost don't care. I only wish I knew what happened to Crazy. It doesn't make sense."

"Nothing ever does when it comes to—"

"I can tell you what happened." A voice from behind startled them both.

"Sam Tommey," Jess said dryly. He slowly put his hands into his pockets. "Still working for Byrnehouse?"

"Yes," Sam said without apologizing, "but I'm making an honest living." He nodded toward Alexa in a silent greeting that she barely acknowledged. She'd not seen him since Jess had told her he'd admitted to being responsible for her accident on the stairs.

Unable to think of a civil word, Jess waited for Sam to speak. "I think we can get another chance for Crazy," he finally said.

"I thought you left the area." Jess was wary, not knowing whether to trust him or not.

"Circumstances change," Sam stated with confidence. "And whether you believe it or not, I've changed."

Jess had to admit it was something he could believe. "So, tell me about this chance."

"If I can prove that the race was rigged—which I can—the whole thing will be disqualified and they'll have to run it again." Sam waited for a response.

"I'm listening," Jess said, sharing the hope he felt in the squeeze of Alexa's hand.

"When I saw what happened, I knew what was going on. You see, I heard a couple of guys talking about it last night." Jess's eyes narrowed with interest, and Alexa felt formless answers to prayers settling in.

"They were talking about a tiny dart that could be soaked in a drug. You hold it between your fingers, slap the horse just enough to pierce the skin, and in so many minutes the horse goes crazy. It wears off quickly."

Jess's heart raced, but his countenance was calm and self-assured. "And you'd be willing to tell the officials that?"

"More than willing, if it could make up for some rotten mistakes I made in the past."

"If Byrnehouse finds out, it could cost you your job."

"Or worse," Alexa interjected.

"Maybe he won't," Sam suggested. "And if he does . . . well that's the price of honesty, I suppose."

"Let's go," Jess said and patted Sam on the shoulder.

❧ ❧ ❧

Just prior to the second race, it was announced that the first race had been disqualified and would be rerun after the last scheduled race was completed. From where she stood, Alexa had a perfect view of Chad. He glared at her, but she just smiled and waved. Chad became visibly upset and stormed off, obviously to protest this turn of events.

"Poor guy," Jess said with sarcasm. "It would be too bad if he lost a few pounds on a race. He might have to give himself a bigger allowance next month for his scheduled carousing."

Alexa chuckled. "I'd best go have a chat with Demented and tell him there's been a change of plans." With Tod hurt, she was riding Demented in the third race. She kissed Jess and added, "Put a healthy bet on Demented to place."

"Are you sure?" he asked as she moved away.

"Absolutely positive."

Jess laughed as Demented came in second. He went to collect his winnings and saw Chad soon after. "Why don't you just give up, Byrnehouse? One day you'll have to accept the fact that I'm surviving in spite of you."

"Now, Jess, old pal," he said complacently, "my life would be so dull if I didn't have you to torment."

"Are you ever going to give me a clue?"

"A clue?" Chad pretended to be baffled.

"As to why you're going to so much trouble."

"If you haven't figured it out by now," Chad chuckled, "you probably never will. But then," he added too soberly, "I don't really want you to figure it out, any more than I would want you to be able to prove anything."

"I can't believe you have the nerve to stand there and all but admit what you've been doing to me, and think you can get away with it."

"Oh, but I do get away with it," he smirked, "don't I, Jess. It's all a matter of power. Power comes from money. And that's something I have that you don't."

"That's true," Jess said, "but I have something you will never have."

"And what's that?"

"A good woman who loves me and doesn't care whether I have money or not." Jess slapped Chad on the shoulder and grinned. "Love can be very powerful, Chad, but it's something you will never understand . . . old pal."

Jess sauntered away and fingered the winnings in his pocket, almost feeling sorry for Chad Byrnehouse.

By the time the final race rolled around, Jess didn't feel nervous in the least. With faith in Alexa, he watched Crazy win by half a length.

Afterward he was proud to be in company with the most beautiful jockey in the world, and a horse with an insane name. Alexa squeezed his hand warmly as Crazy was paraded and awarded. Jess felt as if the world was in his hands.

With the purse and bets collected, Jess walked toward the stables to help the boys load up for the journey home.

"Mr. Davies," an unfamiliar voice called. Jess turned to be approached by a stodgy man with glasses and little hair. "My name is Morgan Speer. I was officiating today."

"Mr. Speer," Jess nodded.

"I couldn't help being aware of the happenings concerning your horse. I must say, I regret that nothing more can be done than what already has."

"And what is that?"

"The man responsible has been severely fined. But I'm certain Mr. Byrnehouse will feel no repercussions, unless the man dares to admit that he was hired to do it. Chad Byrnehouse is a difficult man to come against. I would bet he won't. But I'd wager that Sam Tommey will be without a job before the week is out."

"What has this got to do with me?" Jess asked, wary of the conversation. Beyond those who lived on his own station, he'd never heard anyone speak so outrightly against Chad Byrnehouse.

"There's no need for me to tell you that," Mr. Speer stated. "But what I really want to talk to you about has nothing to do with that—at least not directly."

"And what is that?" Jess asked.

"I wonder if you would be familiar with my practice. I am with Grant and Speer of Brisbane." Jess looked ignorant. "Solicitors."

"What? You want me to sue him or something?"

"Heavens no." Mr. Speer laughed and his whole body shook. "I want to talk to you about Tyson Byrnehouse."

An intangible eeriness crept down Jess's back. "I hardly knew the man."

"Yes, I know, though he was your wife's . . . father. And a client of mine, as well. I have a document that might be of interest to you."

"What is it?" Jess asked.

Mr. Speer glanced unobtrusively around him. "I think it might be better to discuss this privately. Would it be all right if I came to your home, say . . . the day after tomorrow, mid-morning?"

"That would be fine," Jess said, both uncertain and interested.

"Good," Mr. Speer said, shaking his hand, "I'll see you then."

Jess was left feeling a little baffled. He'd never trusted solicitors much, but that was mostly due to the fact that the ones he knew were too friendly with Chad Byrnehouse.

His mind quickly turned to Alexa when she ran out to meet him and he twirled her in an embrace. "We really did it," she laughed.

"Tomorrow," Jess kissed her quickly, "you and I will be free. No more mortgage."

"Let's go home and count the money."

Jess laughed. He'd never been so happy in his life.

❦　❦　❦

Wanting to take care of his transaction at the bank and have it done, Jess left early on horseback to make better time. After all the years this burden had been on his shoulders, it was difficult to comprehend being free of it.

When he arrived at the bank, Jess restrained himself from laughing as he imagined how it would feel to leave with full ownership of the property Ben Davies had left to him.

"Good morning, Mr. Davies," Mr. Hemming stated. "What can I do for you?"

"I'm here to make my mortgage payment." Jess set the money on the desk triumphantly.

Mr. Hemming turned pale.

"What's the matter?" Jess asked when nothing more was said.

"I'm afraid you're too late," he said dryly.

"Too late?" Jess chuckled with no humor. "What do you mean *too late?*"

"Your payment was due on the eleventh, Mr. Davies. Today is the twelfth."

"My payment is due on the seventeenth," Jess said carefully, trying to remain calm as a long-dreaded, sickening fear came to rest in the pit of his stomach. Papers were brought forth, and he was shown that the payment was due on the eleventh.

"That is a seventeen." Jess pointed at it. "There is no resemblance between that one and that seven. It is a seventeen. The payment has always been due on the seventeenth. Always!" he finished through clenched teeth.

"I'm sorry if there's been a discrepancy," the banker said as if discussing the weather, "but I'm afraid your property was sold last night just before we closed."

"Sold?" Jess's voice rose a pitch.

More papers were brought out while Mr. Hemming explained everything in just complex enough terms that Jess couldn't tell if it was legal or not. The only thing he recognized was Chad Byrnehouse's signature below a financial figure that seemed staggering and almost ridiculous. He could never buy it back in a million years.

Jess wanted to be angry. He wanted to pull the banker out of his chair and throw him against the wall. He wondered how much Chad had paid him under the table to pull it off.

Jess didn't know how long he stood with his palms on the desk, looking at the floor, while his mind went through inner phases of anger, pain, and desperation. The banker finally said something that he didn't hear, then Jess picked his money up off the desk and lumbered outside to begin the ride home.

Home? His mind silently echoed a demented laugh. He didn't have a home. He wondered how long it would be before they had to leave. Where would they go? What would they do? He was responsible for Alexa. There was a baby coming. He was responsible for these people who depended on him to make a living. How could he possibly just turn them away after all they had gone through for him and with him?

But more than anything else, Jess had to wonder why. Why was Chad Byrnehouse so bent on destroying him? What benefit would more land and tracks and a house be to Chad? He already had far more than Jess would ever dream of having. It just didn't make sense.

Jess recalled the fight that had started all of this, not long before his mother was killed. But for the life of him he couldn't understand why it had gone so far, or why Chad knew things about Jess that even he hadn't known.

The questions made Jess's head ache clear down his back as he took the long way home. He wanted to get drunk, but he knew from experience that it wouldn't change anything. It would only disappoint Alexa.

It was dark when he finally arrived, and he realized he hadn't eaten since his early breakfast. He hesitated before going into the stable, wondering how he was going to break the news to the boys. And worse, how could he possibly tell Alexa?

Jess dismounted and handed the reins over to Fiddler without saying anything at all.

"Jess," Fiddler called after him, "is something wrong?"

Jess turned and was silent a long moment, pondering his answer carefully. "Please tell everyone to come to my office right after breakfast in the morning."

"Yes, of course. Is—"

"Good night, Fiddler," Jess interrupted and walked slowly up the path toward the house, absorbing his surroundings as if he was seeing them for the last time.

"Jess?" He heard Alexa's voice before he even reached the door. "Is that you?" He stopped but said nothing. She came down the steps and into his arms, where he held her desperately. "I've been so worried," she said gently. "Are you all right?"

Choking on emotion, Jess couldn't bring himself to speak. He kept his arm around Alexa as they moved into the house and up the stairs.

Alexa hung expectantly on his silence, fearing the dazed look in his eyes that brought painful memories to the surface. They came to the bedroom without a word said between them. Jess sat numbly in a chair while Alexa lit a lamp and sat beside him. She took his hand into hers, and he looked up to meet her eyes with a silent, desperate plea.

"I love you, Jess," she said with so much sincerity that he wanted to cry. Everything inside of him just wanted to cry like a child.

"Yesterday," he finally spoke but his voice was distant, "I told Chad that I had something he would never have."

"What is that?" she asked gently.

"I told him I have a good woman who loves me and doesn't care whether or not I have any money."

Alexa laughed, and Jess wondered what she had to be happy about. He looked at her, bewildered, then he reached inside his coat and brought out a thick envelope. He placed it into Alexa's hand and wrapped her fingers carefully around it. He leaned back and sighed, then closed his eyes as he said, "Chad must have decided to try and prove me wrong."

Alexa's heart and soul swelled with empathy as Jess opened his eyes and tears rolled down his face. "That's all I have to give you, Alexa." He nodded toward the envelope. "That's all we have to start over someplace else."

Alexa's expression didn't change as she went to her knees in front of him and wiped away his tears with her fingers. "I love you," she whispered and pushed his coat over his shoulders. Jess watched her hands as they pushed away his braces and unbuttoned his shirt. She pressed them over his chest and into his hair as she moved his face within her reach and kissed him.

Jess felt love and unquestioning acceptance seep into her kiss, and he heard himself sob in the midst of it. Alexa eased his head to her shoulder. He attempted to swallow his emotion, but it caught in his throat. He cried out her name as the anguish flooded forth.

"Cry, Jess," she whispered, and warm tears trickled down her face to match his own. "Cry," she repeated, urging him to his feet only long enough to fall onto the bed and bring him with her. While Jess cried, Alexa kissed him, touched him, held him. The pain and desperation gradually turned to a passion deeper than Jess had ever known. And all of it became lost within this woman who shared his life. The anguish dissipated into oblivion as his only awareness became Alexa. Alexa's love, Alexa's commitment, Alexa's wild eyes. She was the key to his sanity, the nucleus of his life, the answer to his prayers. And she loved him.

The tears were spent with the passion, and Jess lay gazing upward with Alexa holding him, twisting her fingers in the curls at the back of his neck.

"Why are you taking it so well?" he asked quietly.

"We have each other," she said. "I knew as soon as I saw your face what must have happened. But it doesn't matter. We have each other."

"We can't live on love," he stated. "It's a nice theory, but—"

"Jess," she leaned up to look at him, "we're really not so desolate. We have quite a bit of money; probably enough to get a piece of ground elsewhere—maybe start a house. But Jess, we have Crazy and Demented. Think how much money they made for us yesterday alone. We'll invest little by little and build a new home. Let Chad have it all. We'll still have something he will never understand."

"I was right when I told him that, wasn't I?"

"You most certainly were."

Peace settled into Jess. He embraced Alexa in an effort to convey his appreciation, but it didn't seem adequate. "Alexa," he whispered. "Alexa, with her gentle hands, she wraps them firm 'round mine, and keeps the dreams from slipping through—not once, but every time."

Alexa nuzzled closer and smiled effortlessly.

"What about the boys?" Jess asked. "And Sarina—and Mrs. Brown?"

"We'll give them the option to come with us. If we all work hard and pitch in, we will find a way to survive. I know," she laughed, "we can become a band of horse-racing gypsies."

Jess laughed. "Why is it," he asked, "that I've just lost everything, and I feel as happy as I did yesterday?"

"That's easy," Alexa said with warmth. "We have something that Chad will never have—so you haven't lost everything."

❦   ❦   ❦

The boys filtered silently into the office where Jess was seated behind the desk, Alexa close by his side, her hand in his. He gave them the news straight out, then went on to explain that although he could give them no promises, he and Alexa were going elsewhere to make a fresh start, and they were all welcome to come along. With mutual interest and effort in a few good race horses, Jess expressed complete faith that they could make enough money to sustain them all. He expressed an idea he'd been contemplating for quite some time: if Demented was used as a stud for Crazy, perhaps they could come up with a horse worthy of the Melbourne Cup.

"So," Jess finished with a positive tone in his voice, "I don't know how long he'll give us to leave, but I figure we might as well just go and get it over with. We're heading south. The closer we settle to Melbourne, the better, I think."

"Well," Murphy stretched his legs and gave a wry smile, "I can't speak for the others, but I'm goin' with you."

"I go wherever Murphy goes," Jimmy added with enthusiasm.

"You'll all starve to death if I don't go," Edward chuckled.

"I beg your pardon," Fiddler piped in. "I'm coming along to take care of you."

"If Alexa's going to be having babies," Tod said, "I guess you'll be needing a jockey."

Jess laughed and turned to Alexa. "We've got something else, my love," he said quietly. "We've got friends."

Thirty
THROUGH THE GABLE WINDOW

Jess left alone to go riding, and Alexa didn't argue. She knew he needed time alone to deal with this. He was gone until mid-afternoon, when Alexa saw him ride in from an upstairs window.

"Alexa!" he shouted when he came through the door. She met him on the front stairs. "Something's not right."

"What do you mean?"

"I'm not ashamed to admit that I just spent a lot of time on my knees. I had to know . . . if our decision to leave was right. Do you understand what I'm saying?"

"Yes," she said easily, "I do."

"Alexa, I don't know why," he took both her hands into his, "but I feel strongly that we shouldn't leave—at least not yet. Suddenly I feel as if," he paused and Alexa saw fire come into his eyes, "I can't give it up without a fight. Perhaps there is a way. We have to try."

"That sounds fine to me," she smiled, "but you'd best tell the boys. They're practically packed."

"Come with me." He started back down the stairs. They heard a knock at the door, but Sarina went to answer it as they moved down the hall.

"Wait." Jess paused to see if Sarina summoned him. "I had an appointment with a solicitor today. I forgot about it until now. Perhaps that's him. Though he should have come hours ago."

"A solicitor? Is he going to help us get it back?"

"That's not the reason he was coming," Jess said. "Though that might not be a bad idea, if we could find the *right* solicitor and—"

"Mr. Davies," Sarina interrupted, "there's a gentleman here to see you."

"Thank you, Sarina," Jess said and took Alexa with him to the front parlor. But the man waiting to meet them was not the solicitor Jess had met at the track. Alexa recognized him as the local constable.

"Forgive me for bothering you, Mr. Davies, but did you know a Mr. Morgan Speer?"

"Why do you ask?" Jess inquired, feeling uneasy.

"He was killed a few hours ago, just this side of Byrnehouse Station. Carriage mishap. Your name was in his appointment book right below Chad Byrnehouse, so I had to assume you were expecting him."

"I was," Jess said dryly. Questions about Chad Byrnehouse that had churned formlessly in Jess for more than a decade suddenly came together, telling Jess this was no simple game. Chad knew something significant that Jess didn't. He thought of the lives lost, the people hurt, and all that had been destroyed. What was Chad's final quest— to drive Jess away from here forever without knowing why? Was that why Morgan Speer just lost his life?

"Figured I should let you know." The constable intruded on Jess's thoughts.

"Thank you," Jess said. "Is there anything I can do?"

"I think it's taken care of," he replied. "Thank you."

The constable left, and Alexa could feel Jess's mind roiling as he sat thoughtfully on the sofa. "What are you thinking, love?" she asked gently.

"I was wondering where it all began." Her eyes narrowed and he clarified, "Where do you suppose this feud started?"

"That's easy," Alexa declared. "Tyson Byrnehouse hated Ben Davies because he was having an affair with his wife. It's obvious he knew, because he disowned me."

"I'm sure you're right, but what reason is that for Chad to take this so far? Do you think he simply hates me because of his father's example?"

Jess stood and moved to the window, his hands deep in his pockets. "No," he said, answering his own question. "It's something more. It didn't really start until after my father died."

"Tell me about it," Alexa said softly when he remained silent. "Perhaps saying it aloud will help it make sense."

"It started when I invested in the track. My father bought me a race horse when I turned fourteen, and I raced some. Did pretty good, considering."

"You rode yourself?" She smiled.

"I did, until I got too tall."

"Imagine that."

"Chad and I were always competitive. It just seemed natural since our fathers hated each other. We were close to the same age and both racing horses. But when Father died, I decided to invest everything into racing and make it big. As soon as the facilities were ready, I hosted a race and my horse won. The next thing I knew Chad had me cornered behind the stables, accusing me of rigging it. I told him he could think what he wanted, but I had a clear conscience. He called me a few things I won't repeat, and then he hit me."

Jess chuckled dryly and turned to lean in the window sill. "The last thing I wanted was a brawl, so I laughed it off and told him how maturely he was handling it. He hit me again but I stood it. He told me I was a coward like my father. Out of respect for my father, I hit him back."

He bowed his head forward and moved his boot back and forth over the floor. "Chad swore that he would destroy me. He told me he would see me fail. I would never win another race. I would be sorry I had ever crossed him—although to this day I'm not sure how I crossed him. He told me I would never be a success, that everything I touched would fail. He told me that my mother would regret ever bearing me."

Jess leaned his head back, and Alexa saw emotion seep into his expression. "I will never forget," his voice turned hoarse, "how he looked me in the eye and called me a bastard. I laughed it off. He hit me again and told me it was true."

Jess sighed and turned again to look out the window. "You have to understand, Alexa, that I had always felt completely secure. There had never been even a clue in my life that I was not Benjamin Davies' son. But something in Chad's eyes tore at me when he told me it was true. I denied it, and he told me to . . ." Jess squeezed his eyes shut, and

Alexa came beside him to take his hand. "He told me to go home and . . . ask my mother . . . who had raped her."

Jess swallowed hard and continued. "We really got into a brawl then. It was Richard who broke it up. Once I came to my senses, I knew I had to find out the truth. I prayed it was only some sick joke, that he was just trying to find a way to hurt me. I wanted to ask my mother, but I knew it was impossible. Whether it was true or not, it would have upset her terribly—that is, if she could have even understood what I meant. And she still hadn't gotten over Father's death. I could have asked him if he'd been alive, and I believe he would have told me the truth. But he was gone. I am still amazed what a good man he was. He treated me as well as any father could, and he never let on that I didn't have a drop of his blood in me. He gave everything to me—even his name. There was so much about him to admire. Looking back, I know that much of my security came from the way he treated my mother. She had the mind of a child, and their marriage was a surface thing. But he loved her. He treated her like a queen."

Jess smiled at Alexa. "Have I ever told you what it means to me to know you are his daughter?" She shook her head, feeling peace to know that he didn't resent it. "I believe there is a great deal of him in you, which helps compensate for the lack of him in me. It only makes me love you more," his eyes warmed, "if that's possible."

"He raised you well," she said gently. "You must be more like him than you believe."

"If only he were here now." Jess folded his arms. "I bet he would know the answers." He sighed and returned to his story. "A few days after that race I went away to talk with my mother's brother, who lived near Sydney. He was the only surviving relative I knew of. He was very kind, but he told me the truth. He told me how my mother had changed. And he knew, because Ben had told him, that my parents' marriage had been platonic.

"When I realized what my mother had gone through, I wanted so badly to just hold her in my arms and tell her how I loved her; how I appreciated what she had sacrificed to bring me into the world, and how she had loved me in spite of it all."

Jess pushed both hands into his hair and bit his lip slightly. "When I got home the house was in flames, my mother and two servants were dead, and Richard was in so much pain he was nearly crazy.

"I knew Chad was responsible. But it soon became evident there was nothing to be done about it without causing myself more trouble. Once Richard recovered, he tried to convince me it was a coincidence. But there is something right here," he pressed a fist to his chest, "that makes me *know* it was connected."

Silently Jess walked to a chair and sat down. "Since then, it's been one thing after another. I mortgaged the property to rebuild the house, mostly trying to ease my conscience, I think. Then I just struggled month by month to survive, and life got steadily worse until . . . ," his eyes softened on Alexa, "until you came."

Alexa gave a serene smile and sat beside him.

"It still baffles me, Alexa. I wonder how he knew when I didn't, and what has made him so determined. I would swear he knows something about me that no one else knows."

"Except perhaps a solicitor?" Alexa said, and Jess felt something pierce him through.

"Morgan Speer was Tyson Byrnehouse's solicitor, Alexa. He told me he had a document that would be of interest to me. Whatever it was, it's probably in Chad's hands by now."

"I would guess that whatever Chad knows has something to do with your father's affair with my mother."

"That sounds reasonable," Jess said, then he glanced toward Alexa as a light came into her eyes. "What?" he asked.

"Those letters," she said. "I wonder if there isn't something in those letters that might not help." Jess remained silent as her mind was obviously churning. "Why don't you go tell the boys we're not leaving just yet." She kissed him quickly and moved toward the door. "I think I'll spend some time with those letters."

"Alexa," he said, and she paused. "Thank you."

"For what?"

"For walking into my office and demanding that I hire you."

"I needed a job." She smiled and left the room.

❦   ❦   ❦

Alexa felt frustrated as she read the letters through for the third time. Ben's letters spoke more than once of how careful they had to be that no one discovered the truth, because of what had happened to Emma. But it got no more specific than that. It was as if the situation with Emma was connected, though not really.

"Why don't you come and have some dinner." Jess sat beside her on the bed.

"I'm too frustrated." She showed him the comments about his mother, saying wearily, "It's too bad she isn't still alive. I bet she'd know some of the answers." Alexa looked directly at him. "I don't suppose she left a journal, or . . . I keep forgetting. Everything was destroyed in the fire."

"I have some poetry she wrote," Jess said easily. He had searched it deeply many years ago and found nothing, but Alexa's eyes lit up. "It was left in the studio, so it survived when the house burned. She wrote often, but it was mostly childish nonsense."

"Can I see it anyway?"

"After dinner." Jess pulled her to her feet. "You need to keep up your strength for the sake of that baby."

She smiled and put her arm around him as they walked down the stairs. "By the way, we got a letter from your brother's solicitor today." Alexa looked up at him in dismay, knowing what it must have been. "We have ten days, but . . . ," his voice turned from dry to hopeful, "that gives us a little time. I'm going into town to talk with the constable tomorrow and see what he can tell me about Mr. Speer's death. We'll go from there."

"Jess," Alexa stopped and turned to face him, "I understand why we must do all we can to find the answers, but I wonder if it will change anything."

"I wonder, too."

"Whatever happens, I will always love you."

"I know," Jess smiled. "That's why I have to find the answers."

❦   ❦   ❦

Through the gable facing east I see my source of pain
I try to hide it in the oils but it taunts me now again
Through the door laughter runs and comes into my arms
My back to the gable, I lose my pain within his boyish charms

Alexa stared at the page on her lap, reading it over and over. Something instinctive told her this was where the answer lay, but she couldn't figure it out.

"Find anything?" Jess came into the bedroom and threw his jacket over a chair. She held up the page, and he only had to glance at it to know what it said.

"What do you suppose it means?" she asked.

"She's talking about the studio window and me," he stated.

"I figured that much. But what about the 'source of pain'?"

"I don't know. It's probably nonsense, like everything else she wrote. Alexa, her mind was like a child's."

"But it doesn't sound like a child's poetry, Jess. There is something deep here. If she had completely blocked out the memory, then why would she acknowledge a source of pain?"

"I don't know," Jess said scornfully. "I've been through all of it before. There is nothing to be seen out that window but trees and bush. The leaves block out the view of everything. I tried for weeks to figure it out. I have walked beyond the trees, and the view doesn't change. It's just nonsense.

"Maybe," Jess sat on the bed beside her, "we're trying too hard. I'm going to do what I can, but I'm not going to tear myself apart over it—and you shouldn't either. Whatever comes, we'll take it on the best we can."

His words sounded hopeful, but the tone in his voice betrayed the despair. Alexa knew they could make it somehow, but she also knew there was no denying the pain it caused them both to be losing all that Ben Davies had worked so hard for.

Alexa set the page aside and extinguished the light, but her thoughts stayed with it. Her mind became filled with such horrid images of what had happened to Emma that she felt a deep empathy for Jess, knowing he'd had trouble dealing with just that.

Certain she could never sleep if she didn't stop thinking about this, Alexa deliberately turned her mind elsewhere. For no logical reason, she thought of Richard. Perhaps it was the way Jess had mentioned him today. She tried to imagine him breaking up a fight between Jess and Chad. They would have been so much younger, and of course, it had been before the fire. Alexa tried to imagine, as she had many times in the past, how Richard had looked before the scars had defiled his face. She felt a little fluttery at the thought.

Steering her mind toward happy thoughts, she recalled the love and laughter they had shared. Her days living in the old house with him were blissful in her memory, where she chose to ignore anything but the good.

Alexa was just this side of sleep when a soothing voice began to whisper suggestive phrases in her ear. She giggled and nuzzled close to the warm body at her side. She felt exhausted, but still she relished the bliss of sharing a bed with the man she loved.

As always, making love to Alexa renewed something in Jess that he could not live without. He became so in tune with his senses, so completely focused on her, that the problems in his life briefly fled. Only Alexa mattered. Whatever happened, he would have her and he could go on.

The building ecstasy made him feel desperate to have her and keep her forever. But it all shattered down into reality as Alexa clung to him, while one word escaped her lips. "Richard."

Jess stopped so abruptly that Alexa was startled. A moment's wondering made her realize what she'd just done.

"Jess." She touched his face in the darkness and felt his jaw go tense. "Oh, Jess, I'm so sorry. I don't know why I did that. I just . . . I . . ." She stopped when her stammering made no progress.

Jess moved away and sighed as his head fell back against the pillow. Alexa squeezed her eyes shut with a self-punishing grimace. How could she not think of the night she had done the same to Richard by crying out Jess's name? It had been for different reasons, but how could she explain that to Jess?

Just as when it had happened before, Alexa's humiliation tempted her to run away and be alone until the feelings cooled off. But she had learned that running didn't solve problems. It only complicated them.

She waited patiently for him to say something, wondering if he was hurt or angry—or both. When he finally spoke, his voice was simply sad. "I think I deserved that."

"No, Jess, you didn't."

"I don't know why you were thinking about him, and I don't want to know, but I think I'm glad it happened."

"Why on earth would you—"

"I believe Richard and I are somehow even now."

Alexa didn't understand why his words tempted her to cry. She wanted to try and explain, but feared betraying her emotion.

Jess sighed again, hating the way he felt inside. But he had to admit, "He was a better man than I am, Alexa."

"Why do you say that?" Her voice cracked only a little.

"If he was alive, I'd be tempted to do something rash."

"But you wouldn't, even if he was alive."

"No, I suppose I wouldn't. I respected him too much."

"Do you think he ever felt that way?"

Jess gave a humorless chuckle. "Alexa, I think I know exactly how he felt."

"Perhaps to a degree." She leaned on her elbow to gaze at him through the darkness. "But not entirely." His face turned toward her. "You said you didn't want to know, but I'm going to tell you anyway, because you *should* know. It was never spoken between us in so many words, Jess, but Richard knew that I loved you in a way I could never love him.

"I wasn't thinking about Richard because I was longing for something I couldn't have, Jess. In truth, I think of him very little. But it was different with Richard. I thought about you day and night. I ached for you, and he knew it. If it will make you feel any better, I believe there were times when he wanted to see you suffer. But one of his strongest traits was self-discipline. He never did or said what would have been justified. He did what he knew he had to in order to keep our marriage together. He loved both you and me, Jess. And that's why we loved him."

Nothing more was said as Jess pulled Alexa close to him, but in unified silence they felt gratitude for Richard's love. Destiny was a complicated thing, but they both suspected that without Richard, they might never have found happiness together.

❦   ❦   ❦

Jess left early to go into town, and Alexa lay in bed far past breakfast, trying to ignore the smoldering nausea. Again she pored over the poetry Emma had written, feeling a vague kinship with Jess's mother. But there were too many holes, too many things left unexplained.

It was a pleasant surprise when Mrs. Brown brought up a break-fast tray. "You're a mind reader," Alexa said. "If I don't eat soon I'll be doomed for the day, but I had no ambition to get up."

"I'm no mind reader," Mrs. Brown chortled. "Your husband suggested it before he left. You can thank him."

"I'll be sure and do that."

"And how are you feelin', Mrs. Davies?" she asked, setting the tray over Alexa's lap.

"Fine, most of the time."

"You enjoy your breakfast now," Mrs. Brown said and scurried out the door.

Alexa ate slowly, trying again to piece it all together in her mind. If only Emma or Ben were here to ask, but they weren't and it had to be accepted. Then a thought struck Alexa so obviously that she near-ly felt stupid for having overlooked it.

Quickly she tied a wrapper around her waist and carried her tray down to the kitchen, where Mrs. Brown was peeling vegetables to add to a simmering broth. She watched Alexa set the tray down and said kindly, "You didn't have t' do that."

"It's all right. I was coming down anyway." Alexa hesitated, won-dering how to start this conversation. "Mrs. Brown," she said cau-tiously, "you were here when Jess was born, weren't you?"

Mrs. Brown stopped peeling and eyed her warily. "Yes. It was me who first laid that baby in his mother's arms."

Alexa's heart pounded with hope, but she maintained a calm voice, trying to introduce her motives into the conversation. "You know, of course, that we will all likely have to leave soon."

"Yes, I know, but I was plannin' on goin' with you and Mr. Davies if—"

"We want you to; there's no question about that. But you see . . . Jess is having a difficult time with this."

"As any man would."

"Of course, but . . ." Alexa took a deep breath. Mrs. Brown was not known for being a conversationalist, but Alexa just had to broach this sensitive subject and learn all she could. "Mrs. Brown, Jess and I know that there were some unusual circumstances in the area, perhaps around the time Jess was born. Jess is in need of peace of mind, and I was hoping that if I could find the answers to some questions about his past, I might be able to help him. Is there anything—anything at all—you know that could shed some light on this?"

Mrs. Brown sighed and wiped her hands on her apron. Alexa felt hopeful when she sat near the big worktable and motioned for Alexa to sit beside her.

"My father was a merchant in town. Of course, back then it could hardly even be called a town. I worked helpin' my father, but I wanted t' do somethin' different. A fine-lookin' man came into the shop one day. He'd been askin' around and heard of me. He was lookin' for a young lady to care for his new bride. Mr. Davies was a kind man, and I eagerly took the position."

Alexa nearly held her breath, waiting for the story to go on. She tried to imagine Ben Davies in his youth and comprehend that he was her father.

Mrs. Brown continued with hardly a change in expression. "Of course the big house hadn't been built yet, but I was given a room in the old house and was left there t' care for Mrs. Davies while he saw to his business. Perhaps if I had known how difficult it would be, I would have declined the position. But then I often told myself that it was better t' know she was bein' treated with kindness than t' think of her in the care of someone who didn't understand such things."

"What do you mean?" Alexa had to ask.

"Why, she just stared at the wall, day in and day out. Gettin' her to eat was a constant battle, and sometimes, when she didn't know I was close by, she would just cry like I've never heard before or since."

Alexa put a hand to her mouth. An intense compassion rose within her on Emma's behalf. "Do you know why?" Alexa asked. Though she suspected the reasons, she hoped to glean all the information she could.

"Of course I asked Mr. Davies why. I couldn't understand why a man such as him would have married a woman in her condition. He was honest with me, and told me that she had . . . been . . ." Mrs. Brown cleared her throat then whispered, "Forced upon." Alexa nodded to indicate that she understood. "It was me that figured out she was goin' t' have a baby. At first Mr. Davies was devastated, but that child changed Emma. At least she was not so prone t' be obsessed with her pain. She adored little Jess, and Ben did too. Of course Ben loved

Emma, as well. He was kind t' her and did his best t' reach her, but one day he had t' accept that she would never recover."

"Then it's true," Alexa felt the need to confirm, "her mind was not whole."

Mrs. Brown looked so surprised that Alexa wondered if she had been that tactless.

"Oh, no," Mrs. Brown stated, "she wasn't crazy. I was with that woman day and night for years. Emma Davies knew her own mind as well as you or I. She suffered from the melancholia, that's all. And what woman wouldn't, who had been through what she had? I'd seen it before, and I've seen it since. She was hurtin' and didn't know how t' face it, so she found ways t' escape. She played the piano, she wrote her poems, and she painted. Often at night I would hear her cry, but there wasn't anything we could do about it."

Mrs. Brown sighed and resettled her hands on her lap. "He was a good man, Ben Davies. He did his best t' keep Emma and Jess secure in spite of it all."

"Then Jess never knew," Alexa said to reassure herself.

"Until I left t' get married, when Jess was fourteen or so, he had always believed Ben was his father."

"He knows now," Alexa said, and Mrs. Brown looked surprised. "Did anyone else know?"

"I thought I was the only one," Mrs. Brown said.

"My mother knew," Alexa said. The evidence was in her letters.

"Well, I should have guessed that, what with the way she and Ben were . . ." Alexa's eyes widened and Mrs. Brown stopped.

"You knew," Alexa said. "You knew that Ben Davies had an affair with my mother."

"I strongly suspected," she clarified.

"Did you know that I'm Ben's daughter?" Alexa asked.

"Not until I first saw you." She almost laughed. "You have a look of him. At first I was concerned about you bein' involved with Jess, then I realized that you didn't share any blood, and I just hoped things would work out. It was a strange situation," her eyes returned to the past, "but one couldn't judge too harshly considerin' the circumstances."

"What circumstances?" Alexa pressed, instinctively feeling close to something important.

"Why, that Emma was never really a wife t' him, and . . ." Mrs. Brown hesitated until she seemed to accept that Alexa already knew the worst of it. "And of course it was common knowledge that Mrs. Byrnehouse would have married Ben in the first place if she'd had her way."

"Why?" Alexa urged. "Tell me why."

"I would have thought you'd know all about that. She was your mother."

"My mother had many secrets, Mrs. Brown. She never even told me who my father was. Please, tell me what you know."

"The way I heard it, Faye was a ward t' the elder Mr. Byrnehouse. She'd come from Europe." Alexa nodded. She had known that. "She'd not been here long when she fell in love with a young man who had just claimed the neighborin' property." Alexa's eyes widened eagerly. "Mr. Byrnehouse would not allow her t' marry below herself, so Ben left for a time t' make his fortune. When he returned, Faye had been coerced int' marryin' Tyson Byrnehouse. I understand a healthy dowry had somethin' t' do with it."

Alexa leaned back in her chair. Things were starting to fall into place. But what Chad had to do with this was still a mystery. "So Ben married Emma, probably with the hope o' puttin' the past behind. But when circumstances turned bad, he went back to Faye." Mrs. Brown shrugged. "That's the way I understand it. I can't tell you no more than that."

"Thank you, Mrs. Brown." Alexa squeezed her hand. "You've been most helpful."

She went upstairs to read Emma's poetry again. True, much of it was trivial and pointless, but not necessarily the work of a mindless woman. There seemed to be some depth to it that Alexa found intriguing.

She thought so long and hard about Emma that her head began to ache. After enjoying a lunch of Mrs. Brown's soup, she wandered outside, searching for a distraction. She chatted with the boys a bit, then walked idly across the lawn, pausing to look at the old house and contemplate the portion of her life she had spent there. She thought of Emma giving birth to Jess there.

Perusing her surroundings, Alexa had to accept that it was likely they would be leaving. She told herself she could live with it, but everywhere she turned she found evidence that this was home. Everything was significant to Jess's past, and since Ben Davies was her father, this land was a part of her as well.

Alexa ambled to the little graveyard and contemplated the graves of Benjamin and Emma Davies. A turmoil filled her that increased as she knelt reverently by other graves nearby. She cried as she ran her hand over the names carved in stone. An ache filled her heart as she felt Richard's name beneath her fingers, but it deepened as she studied the words on a stone next to his: *Baby Wilhite*. How could she leave them behind? It tore at her, and she had to force herself away.

Instinctively groping for the answers, as if they might provide a way to allow them to stay, Alexa wandered into Emma's studio. She thought of the poem. What did she mean by her "source of pain"?

It all seemed futile as she leaned into the gable window and looked toward the trees. She thought of what Jess had said about the view, but something didn't seem right. "Of course," she said aloud. Jess had distinctly said the leaves had blocked the view. But these trees had yet to bud with the coming spring. Their branches were bare. Jess said he'd tried for weeks to figure it out, but had the changing of seasons been taken into consideration?

Alexa's heart quickened. She pulled the folded poem from her pocket and stared at it. Had it been written in winter? Alexa leaned toward the window pane and strained her eyes to see what might have come into view in the absence of the leaves. Something tugged at her to see a seemingly tiny structure against the far horizon, though she couldn't decipher what it was.

Impulsively she went outside and walked briskly toward the cluster of trees, wondering why Jess might have missed it before. But from this point of view, the slope of the land obscured whatever she had seen from the window. Alexa returned to the studio, where the elevation and added distance from the trees made it barely visible.

What could it mean? Could it be where Emma had been taken when the heinous act had been committed? Alexa was tempted to ride that direction until another idea occurred to her. She went into the house to find Jess's field glasses and returned with them to the studio. Carefully she put them to her eyes and focused. It took several attempts to get them aimed between the branches just so, and the picture before her was still blurred because of the distance. But then, as she realized what she was looking at, something crumbled inside of her. The dreadful thing was that it all made perfect sense.

Alexa was glad that Jess hadn't returned home yet. She needed time. If this was difficult for her to accept, what would it do to him? Thinking perhaps it could be a mistake, Alexa reread all of the letters and poetry with her discovery in mind. She didn't know if she was relieved or disappointed to realize that it was true.

Emotion filled and overwhelmed Alexa as she went again to the gable and looked eastward, wondering how she was going to tell Jess.

Thirty-one

THE SOURCE OF PAIN

"Hello, my love." Jess's voice startled Alexa, and she turned abruptly from the window.

"Hello." She moved across the room to kiss him.

"How long have you been up here?" He glanced wistfully around the studio.

"Too long, actually," she replied.

"Is something wrong?" He lifted her chin to look into her eyes as he realized she was especially distracted. She made no response and he said, "Still trying to figure it out?"

Alexa only closed her eyes.

"Forget about it," he insisted. "It makes no difference."

"Did you find anything out?" she asked, wondering if his appointments in town would have any bearing on her discovery.

"Only that no papers were found in Mr. Speer's possession. Either he didn't bring any or they are in Chad's hands. I talked to a solicitor. He told me straight out that I could oppose Chad, but it would cost me a great deal in legal fees, and there would be no guarantee that I'd win. Chad is very powerful around here, and too many people feel threatened by him.

"I don't know, Alexa." He pushed frustrated hands through his hair, then stuffed them into his pockets with a sigh of defeat. "I think it might be better if we just leave. I'm so weary of fighting. I wonder if it matters anymore."

"Oh, but it does," she said quietly.

Jess gazed at her severely. "You know something."

Alexa nodded and bit her lip.

"Tell me," he insisted.

"I spoke with Mrs. Brown this morning," she began. "She was here when you were born, Jess."

"I know, but I've talked to her before. Either she didn't know anything I didn't know, or she wouldn't admit to it."

"A little of both, perhaps. But I learned one thing from her that perhaps she overlooked telling you—or perhaps she just assumed you knew."

"What is that?"

"Your mother was not crazy, Jess. She suffered from severe melancholia."

His eyes narrowed. "I don't understand."

"She was depressed. What she had been through was devastating. But it did not ruin her mind, it only broke her spirit."

"Merciful heaven." Jess sat down and put a hand to his heart.

"She knew what was going on around her, and she knew the source of her pain."

Jess looked up sharply. While the wholeness of his mother's mind was something he wanted to absorb and deal with, it was evident Alexa knew more. "Do you know the source of her pain, Alexa?"

"I believe I do." She leaned on the window sill and fidgeted nervously with her hands.

"Tell me," he insisted when she seemed hesitant.

"Perhaps I should start at the beginning," she said. "From what I have gathered, when Ben Davies claimed this land, he also claimed the heart of a young woman who was a ward to my grandfather. He wanted to marry her, but he was told she could not marry a man with nothing. He went to seek his fortune and came back with it, only to find that she'd been manipulated into marrying Tyson Byrnehouse. Ben soon figured out that Faye was unhappy. They had a brief affair, but the guilt drove Ben temporarily away from the area. He returned with a woman he was going to marry, and told Faye it was over. He was going to put it behind him."

Alexa sighed wistfully. "But tragedy struck just prior to the wedding, when Tyson discovered his wife's secret. She swore to him that it was over, but he wanted vengeance for the affair."

Jess shifted uncomfortably, though he had no idea what was coming and how it tied together.

"Only hours after Ben Davies was married, his wife disappeared. She was returned to him with scars far deeper than her assailant could have ever imagined. But it backfired. When Ben had only a platonic marriage, he turned back to Faye for affection and the affair continued. I am the result." Alexa finished and stared at Jess, but he was bewildered.

"Don't you see?" she said.

"No," he said in exasperation, "I don't."

"Jess," she knelt before him and took his hands, "your father wasn't crazy. He might have been drunk. But you must understand that most of all he was hurt. It was an act of wounded pride, blanketed with anger. But I believe he came to regret it, Jess. In my heart, I would swear he had every intention of making right what he had wronged."

"What are you saying?" Jess asked hoarsely, coming to the edge of his seat. As much as he wanted to understand this, it was going right over his head.

Alexa swallowed hard and blinked several times. Her voice trembled as she spoke. "Jess. Listen to me. 'Through the gable facing east, I see my source of pain.'"

"I'm sorry, Alexa, but I don't grasp the connection."

"Only because it's so obvious you're not looking for it." He narrowed his eyes, and she motioned toward the gable with her hand. The dusky room added an eeriness to her words. "What is east of here, Jess?"

He thought a moment. "Byrnehouse." His eyes widened with a vague glimmer of perception.

"Jess," she whispered, "Tyson Byrnehouse is your father."

Jess held his breath. His hands tightened around Alexa's. "Are you sure?" he asked coarsely. He wasn't certain he liked this.

"It all makes sense," she replied gently.

Jess shook his head. He didn't want to believe it.

"How do you suppose Chad knew?" she asked.

"That's what I've always wondered," he said tersely.

"Tyson Byrnehouse did a lot of drinking, Jess. And when he did, his tongue always got loose. I'm guessing that he told Chad without intending to."

Alexa could think of nothing more to say that might ease the awkward silence while she waited for a reaction. She hadn't known what to expect, but she didn't like the tightness in his jaw and the hard look of his eyes.

"So," Jess leaned back and folded his arms over his chest, "you're trying to tell me that Chad Byrnehouse is my half-brother. And Tyson Byrnehouse . . . is my *father.*"

Alexa nodded hesitantly. Jess absorbed it a moment, then flew off his seat. Alexa winced as he groaned and kicked a chair so hard that it toppled and slid across the floor. "Damn him!" Jess shouted and hit his fist into the wall. "The bastard ruined my mother, all for the sake of his hurt pride. And he *knew!*" Jess clenched his teeth and tugged at his hair. "He *knew* I was his son, and he didn't have the guts to tell me himself. He had to tell Chad instead, and let him tear me to pieces." Jess kicked the chair again. "If he was alive now, I would—"

"Stop it, Jess," Alexa shouted. "You've got to face this realistically." She took both his arms into her hands with a firm grip. "You can't change the past, and even if he was here you'd never hurt him. You're too much of a man for that."

Jess squeezed his eyes shut as her words triggered a memory. Hadn't Tyson Byrnehouse once said the same thing to him? Perhaps he knew Jess would feel this way if he found out. Or had he hoped Jess would never find out? As if Alexa could read his mind, she said gently, "Jess, he couldn't have told you, at least not until you were older. He must have known Ben treated you as his own son. He wouldn't have wanted to shatter that."

"No, he told Chad and let *him* shatter it."

"Jess, listen to me. What he did was atrocious, but he changed in those later years. He stopped drinking. He spent less time with Chad and more time with me.

"Jess," she tightened her grip and leaned toward him, "he used to tell me to be careful what I did with my life, not to let my emotions rule my actions. He spoke of regrets and wanting to make amends that were impossible to make. I never understood until now."

Jess sighed and looked at the ceiling. "He could have made amends with me."

"Maybe he intended to but didn't get the chance. You told me once that you didn't believe he'd intended to disown me. He'd changed, Jess. And do you know what I believe changed him? One day he found himself alone with his guilt. In only a few years he saw Ben Davies die of illness, Emma Davies killed, and then his own wife was gone. Suddenly Tyson Byrnehouse had nothing to face but his regrets.

"Richard told me it takes circumstances to change a man. They changed him." She touched Jess's face. "They changed you. And I believe they changed Tyson Byrnehouse, too." She could still see a cold harshness in his eyes. "Jess, I know this is difficult for you, but—"

"I'm sorry, Alexa. I realize you loved him as a father, but I'm not certain I can accept him as *mine.*"

"Perhaps it will take time." She tried to remain empathetic and still give him an objective point of view. "I know there's a lot of pain involved, and—"

"A lot of pain?" He chuckled scornfully. "Alexa," he backed away and shouted, "do you realize what unspeakable things have occurred as a result of what he did? And telling Chad, now that *really* helped things along."

"He was drunk, Jess."

"Is that any excuse to—"

"Is that any excuse for a man to try to kill himself?" she shouted. Jess stopped with his mouth open. "When you sobered up, Jess Davies, you were certainly surprised to discover what you'd been doing with a gun."

"At least I was only hurting myself," he said more softly.

"Yourself?!" she shouted. "Do you have any idea what that would have done to me? I would have *never* gotten over it. Beyond that, a drunk man with a loaded gun in his hand could never be certain he would only hurt himself."

"What he did was unforgivable," Jess persisted. "Richard might still be alive if—"

"Now, wait a minute, Jess. Let's separate the issues here. True, he told Chad, but he can't be held responsible for everything Chad may or may not have done."

Jess stuffed his hands into his pockets. "It was still unforgivable."

"Can you judge him so harshly?" she retorted, and he glared at her. "I recall a time or two when you were just drunk enough to make a fool of yourself." His eyes blazed with defensive anger, but Alexa knew he needed to hear it. "Do you remember a particular night, Jess, in this very room? If you had succeeded with what you were attempting, I might have considered that forgivable. But Richard wouldn't have."

Jess squeezed his eyes shut. She was managing to make her point, and it struck deeply. Still, the anger boiled in his veins. He raised clenched fists and spoke in a coarse voice. "Do you know how many times I have imagined myself strangling the man who fathered me?"

Alexa bit her lip but she couldn't hold the tears back. "But you wouldn't," she stated, feeling somehow torn between her love of two men.

"No." Jess sat down weakly and watched his hands as he forced them to soften and open. "But I'd sure like to give him a bloody nose."

"And he'd probably be glad to let you do it if it would make everything right. But it wouldn't."

"I never liked Tyson Byrnehouse," Jess admitted quietly. "But I respected him. And as I got older, I almost believed that he respected me, too."

"I believe he did." Alexa sat on the floor beside Jess's leg and took his hand. "Jess, why do you think Chad has been trying so hard to destroy you? Is it possible he simply resented your being his brother, or could it be something more?" Jess looked at her sharply. "Analyze that question with what you know now." She waited a moment while he contemplated it. "Why do you suppose Tyson Byrnehouse's solicitor wanted to talk to you? Not me, but you. And he lost his life in the effort."

Jess's eyes widened as he began to grasp her implication, but he waited for her to explain. He hardly dared voice it himself.

"As I've been thinking about this, trying to fit all of it together, I recalled something I'd overheard. Not long before Father's death, I heard him and Chad arguing. Father told him if he didn't straighten up he was going to leave it all to someone who deserved it. I thought he meant me, but when Chad protested, Father referred to that someone as 'he.'"

"I doubt we could ever prove it," she said carefully, "but I believe that Tyson Byrnehouse was in the process of changing his will, and Chad knew it."

Jess's eyes widened, and again she read his mind. "Didn't the solicitor say he had a document that would be of interest to you?" Jess nodded feebly. "I hate to admit it," she continued, "but I believe now that

Chad must have . . ." Fresh tears brimmed in her eyes. "Jess, Tyson was such a good horseman. It never made sense to me that he would be killed in a riding accident." She bit her lip. "I wonder if Chad killed his own father."

Jess sighed and bowed his head as if he was too weary to hold it up. "And all along Chad has been playing this game with me. Doing just enough to keep me struggling and baffled." Jess wiped a sweating palm over his breeches, then slowly clenched his hand into a fist. "But I swear by heaven and earth, he's not going to get away with it."

Alexa's pulse quickened with a combination of hope and fear. "What are you going to do?"

"I don't know, but I'm going to do something. As long as I was ignorant I had no leverage, but the cards are in my hand now. I'm not leaving here without a fight—a fight that Chad Byrnehouse will never forget."

Even in the darkening room, Alexa saw the determination surge into his countenance. With all her heart she wanted to believe they could keep the land and stay here, but she knew all too well what Chad was capable of. A tangible fear took hold of her, and she gripped his thigh so tightly it startled him. "But Jess," she breathed intently, "what if he—"

He leaned forward and took hold of her shoulders. "I have to fight, Alexa. I *have* to!"

"But what if he—" she began again, but his emotions erupted.

"Don't you see, Alexa?" He stood abruptly and left her leaning against the chair. "Chad has dedicated his life to destroying me. Do you realize what he has taken from me?"

"Yes, I do." Alexa tried to remain in control despite the tears streaking her face and the knot forming somewhere between her heart and her throat. "Don't stand there and try to tell me that I don't know what you've been through, or what you're feeling. Do you think this hasn't affected me? Do you think I haven't felt the loss and the pain?"

"Then you should know why I can't stand by any longer and let him do whatever he pleases."

"Fine!" She gripped the chair at her side. "But don't go losing your head now and destroy what little we have left. Don't lower yourself to his level just because you've suddenly found out what you're fighting for."

Jess went to his knees and took her shoulders. "*You* are what I'm fighting for, Alexa." He pressed a firm hand down over her swollen belly. *"This,"* his voice lowered with a passion born of fury, "is what I'm fighting for. I want this child to grow up on the land Ben Davies intended for *us* to have. Can we live in peace, always wondering what Chad has done to desecrate all we hold dear? He's taken *everything* from me, Alexa, and I won't stand for it!"

"He'll not have everything unless you allow him to take your integrity." That muscle in his jaw twitched as she struck a nerve. Alexa lowered her voice to a coarse whisper. "As long as we have each other, we haven't truly lost. Fight if you must, Jess, but remember who you are. This is not a fight for vengeance, it's a fight for justice."

Jess inclined toward her, pressing closer to the child they'd created. "Is there justice in letting him get away with burning my home to the ground?" His teeth clenched as his grip on her shoulders tightened. "Is there justice in allowing him to murder and go on murdering?" Alexa sobbed and squeezed her eyes shut. "Look at me," he hissed. She opened her eyes and blinked the tears from her lashes. "He killed my mother, Alexandra." The rising pain made his voice rumble. "He probably killed that solicitor and Tyson Byrnehouse, as well." Jess leaned closer still. Alexa could hardly breathe. "I have every reason to believe he killed Richard," he nearly shouted. "How can you say there is justice in letting that go?"

The worst of Alexa's fears rushed forward, demanding to be acknowledged. "How can there be justice in letting him kill you, too?" She felt him soften, if only a little. "Jess," she cried, taking his face into her hands as if they might assist her words in reaching his conscience, "if I lost you, Jess, I fear it would leave me to suffer your mother's fate." She sobbed, and her chest heaved against his. "It would break my spirit, Jess. I would be nothing."

Jess thought he had felt it all. Grief and deceit had plagued him incessantly. Anguish and downfall were familiar companions. Fear and pain had once been a part of his daily breath. But not until this moment did Jess experience true heartache. The agony spurred by Alexa's confession struck the core of his determination. He *would* fight! But this fight was to preserve what he and Alexa had already fought so hard for: the right to be together and to be happy.

"I won't let that happen," he promised with a husky voice. A sob of relief erupted from Alexa's throat. "I *won't!*" he repeated through clenched teeth, and then he kissed her, attempting to express the full depth of all they shared. For one brief, inviolable moment, Jess could almost see her fears as clearly as if they were his own. She was his link to sanity, his reason in the midst of madness. Through Alexa, he had discovered the balance of his life. Sustained by her love, he had found the fortitude to fight for what he believed in without jeopardizing his integrity. Together they would survive this. Together they could win.

For timeless minutes they held to each other in desperate silence. Like dust in the wake of a violent wind, their fears slowly settled around them, mingling with every other emotion they had confronted within the walls of the gabled attic.

"Don't let him win, Jess." Her voice mirrored his inner determination, and he tightened his arms around her. How could he begin to express his love for her? In spite of her fears, she was willing to put her trust in him with full support.

Jess rummaged his hands through her hair and fondled her brow with his lips. "We'll do the best we can, Alexa. Whatever comes of it, we will be together."

Alexa tightened her embrace and wept silent tears. He truly did love her.

"Would you like to go to Brisbane, my love?"

"The solicitor's office?" she asked, and he nodded.

"It's a good place to start. I believe he has a partner. Perhaps he can tell us something."

Alexa agreed, and Jess's mind became distant. He was a Byrnehouse. He tried to recall every encounter he'd had with Tyson Byrnehouse, but the most prominent in his memory was the night he'd prevented Jess from strangling Chad after his mother had been killed. The words Tyson had spoken came back to him now with new meaning. *There is no good to be had in irrational vengeance, Jess. It will always come back to you, and there is no pain so great as living with the truth of your own mistakes.*

Something in Jess softened, and he looked to Alexa with emotion in his eyes. "You're right," he admitted. "Tyson Byrnehouse did change. I think he cared for me."

Alexa felt immense relief to see his acceptance. If he could learn to live with this, she believed he could face anything.

"There is a bright side to this, Alexa." He almost smiled. "My father was sane. If it's his blood flowing in me, then there is nothing to fear or hide from."

"And your mother, too, Jess. She was sane."

"My dear, sweet mother." Nostalgia filled his voice. "How she must have suffered."

"It's in the past, Jess. We must move forward."

"Yes," he said, smoothing a hand over her shoulder. "We'll leave early for the city and see if we can find a way to prove something—anything."

"Jess," she toyed with the curls against his neck, "isn't it ironic? I should have been born a Davies—and you a Byrnehouse."

Jess kissed her brow. "At least you're a Davies now."

"Which is by far the best thing that's ever happened to me."

"I love you, Alexandra," he whispered close to her ear, and she trembled in his arms.

❦ ❦ ❦

The night was still black when Jess lumbered out of bed without a moment's sleep behind him. He nudged Alexa's back. "I'm going to my office to take care of some paperwork. You'd best wake up. If we're going to leave at dawn, we need to be moving along."

"I'm coming," she said groggily, but Jess was already gone. Concerned for him, Alexa freshened up and dressed while she finished packing their things. Her mind wandered through the harrowing events of yesterday and a thought occurred to her. A short while later, she found Jess sitting at his desk, staring at the wall. She entered quietly and set a box in front of him.

"What is this?" he asked. It looked familiar.

Alexa opened the box and lifted out one of the two engraved silver goblets Chad had sent as a wedding gift. She handed him the enclosed card that now held new meaning. *From one Byrnehouse to another.*

"As I told you before, my grandfather gave them to my father, his eldest son, when he married. He wished for it to continue through the generations. The way I see it, Chad has been giving subtle hints for years."

Jess fondled the goblet in his hand, contemplating the name engraved there. It was difficult to comprehend that he was the eldest Byrnehouse by blood. "But he admitted that he didn't want me to know."

"Of course not," Alexa said. "He's a game player. He was doing it for sport—just to drive you crazy."

"It nearly worked." Jess handed the goblet to Alexa. "On the chance that we're staying, put them somewhere visible. I think I've earned the right to show them off."

Alexa nodded and placed the goblet reverently beside the other. "I believe," she said quietly, expressing another thought that had struck her coldly, "that Chad left the Byrnehouse calling card the night he burned the house down."

She tilted her head, and Jess caught the play on words. It left him feeling eerie, but all the more determined.

"Are you all right?" she asked when he got a faraway look.

"I'll be fine." He gave a stilted smile. "Let's just get out of here. I want to get to the bottom of this."

Alexa nodded and turned to leave just as Fiddler knocked at the open door.

Jess was surprised to see him. "Fiddler, is there a problem with the carriage or—"

"Oh, no. It's nearly ready to go, but . . ." He hesitated and glanced warily toward Alexa. "When I went into the carriage house earlier, I found a . . . ," he lowered his voice, "a young woman."

Alexa's interest was piqued as Jess retorted, "Well, who is she? What's she doing here?"

"She was asleep in the carriage; says she wants to see you. That's all she'll tell me."

Jess smirked toward Alexa. "She probably wants a job."

"Well, you'd best go talk to her," Alexa said. "But wait for me. It's quite an occasion to see another woman around here." She set the box aside and followed Jess and Fiddler outside.

Fiddler opened the bunkhouse door, and Jess stepped inside just in front of Alexa. Before she even got a glimpse of this woman, Jess said with a tone that bordered on guilt, "Lizzie. What on earth are you doing here?"

"You did say if I ever needed anything . . ."

Alexa stepped out from behind Jess, and Lizzie hesitated. The two women exchanged curious gazes before Jess cleared his throat. "Lizzie, this is my wife, Alexandra Davies."

Lizzie smiled, but Alexa caught the disappointment in her eyes.

"Alexandra, this is Lizzie, uh . . . I'm sorry, I don't remember your—"

"Stuart," she provided. Alexa wondered when and where Jess had met this woman, and what, if anything, had transpired between them. Though she was young, a wearied look aged her face. Her voluptuous figure was clad in a simple, low-cut dress that was dirty and worn. Alexa almost felt sorry for her. How far had she come, and how had she gotten here?

"It's a pleasure to meet you, Mrs. Davies," Lizzie said with a genuine smile. She unobtrusively eyed Alexa's breeches, then said to Jess, "Is she the jockey?"

Jess gave an embarrassed chuckle. "Yes, she is."

"Looks like everything worked out all right."

"Eventually," Jess stated, feeling terribly uncomfortable. Hoping to be free of Alexa's inquisitive glare, he tried to explain. "I met Lizzie in . . . was it Sydney?" Lizzie nodded and Jess smiled. "We . . . uh, had a little talk and . . . became fast friends . . . and . . . well, I told her if she—"

"I don't mean to cause you any trouble," Lizzie interrupted. "And I wouldn't have come if—"

"It's no trouble, Lizzie," Alexa interrupted kindly as this woman's distress increased.

Lizzie cleared her throat and seemed to relax slightly. "Well, I took your advice, Jess. I quit doin' what I was doin'." Jess's eyes widened. "But I couldn't find any respectable work that I could make it on, so I sold what little I had and started this direction."

"How long have you been traveling?" Alexa asked in concern.

"I lost track." Lizzie attempted a smile, but her eyes betrayed the worry and exhaustion that had accompanied her across the miles.

"I believe she walked from town," Fiddler said.

"Good heavens," Jess interjected, "if we had only known, we could have—"

"It's all right," Lizzie smiled. "I just hope I'm not imposin' by comin' here. I'm willin' to work. I can do about anything. I just had to get away from the city and . . ." She faltered uncomfortably.

"I told you to come, and I meant it," Jess quickly assured her. "I'm afraid you made it in the nick of time, however." Lizzie's eyes widened in alarm, and Alexa watched her husband with compassion. "Unless something changes," he continued, "we will all be leaving here next week." Jess paused before answering Lizzie's questioning gaze. "The land has been sold."

Jess's mind drifted into a helpless silence, and he was relieved when Alexa took over. "But we're all leaving together, and you're welcome to come with us, Lizzie."

"Thank you, Mrs. Davies," Lizzie said, and Alexa smiled.

Observing Alexa's acceptance of this woman made Jess's heart swell with a love that already overflowed. He suspected that many wives would be skeptical, even rude. But there she stood, managing to make an awkward situation seem easy. And despite the circumstances, he was glad Lizzie had come. Their brief encounter had brought together all the right elements to change his life. He only wished he could do more.

"In the meantime," Jess took over with an authoritative voice to ease the tense silence, "you can take one of the rooms above the carriage house. My wife and I are leaving this morning for the city, but Fiddler will make certain you have what you need." Fiddler nodded to indicate this was true. "Perhaps you could help out in the kitchen. Our cook is having trouble with his health. Fiddler can show you what to do as soon as he returns from taking us to the depot."

Fiddler smiled kindly in response to Lizzie's glance. He picked up Lizzie's bag, but Alexa took it from him. "You get the luggage loaded," she said. "I'll show Lizzie to her room. I'm quite familiar with the way." She turned to Jess and added, "Please tell Sarina to finish the packing. She'll know what to do. And have Mrs. Brown put our breakfast in a hamper. We'll eat on the way."

"Yes, dear," Jess grinned wryly as she walked past him and Lizzie followed.

"Thank you, Jess." Lizzie paused next to him and extended a hand. "I don't know where I would have gone."

Jess took her hand and squeezed it firmly. "I'm just glad you made it. We don't have much to offer, but we can give you a fresh start."

Lizzie nodded and followed Alexa into the predawn light. Just inside the carriage house door, Alexa handed the bag to Lizzie in order to find a lamp and light it. She wasn't prepared for the assault of memories as she started up the stairs. A thousand tiny incidents with Richard flitted through her mind in a matter of moments, then she thought of Lizzie and wondered again what had brought her and Jess together. For the first time in her life, Alexa felt jealousy. But rather than harboring it, she turned it to empathy. Perhaps she could find a glimmer of understanding for what both Jess and Richard had gone through.

Alexa paused at the top of the stairs and debated which room to give Lizzie. The thought of going into Richard's room made her somehow uneasy, so she opened the door to the other and motioned Lizzie inside. "The window overlooks the yard and has a beautiful view of the hills," she announced. "It's small, but it's clean and adequate. I think you'll like it here." She couldn't resist adding, "I did."

"You?" Lizzie interrupted her admiration of the room and raised curious blonde eyebrows.

"I came here to train Jess Davies' horses. This was my room for a long time."

"But he said you were a jockey."

"I did a little of that, too."

Lizzie gave an uncomfortable little laugh and set her bag on the bed. "I've seen lots of broken hearts, Mrs. Davies, but none like his."

As long as Lizzie had opened it up, Alexa couldn't resist asking, "Exactly how did you encounter . . . his broken heart?"

"I was workin' in a pub," she answered quickly. "He was drinkin' himself sick, and I . . ." Lizzie stopped so abruptly that Alexa was caught off guard by the logic. What had she said in the bunkhouse? *She'd quit doing what she'd been doing. She couldn't find any respectable work.* This woman was a prostitute.

Alexa tried not to betray her surprise, but Lizzie's expression faltered and she knew she'd failed. "It doesn't matter," Alexa insisted adamantly, while inside she found this hard to take.

With a defensive lift of her chin, Lizzie stated firmly, "I'm not askin' you to like me, Mrs. Davies; only to give me a chance. I know what it's like to be a woman and have to wonder, so I'll tell you straight out so you don't have to. Jess Davies is the only true gentleman I ever met. Even when he was drunk he was a gentleman. We talked. There was little more than that. He's a good man."

Alexa smiled genuinely. "Yes, Lizzie, I know." Their eyes met with mutual acceptance and Alexa added, "Whatever you were makes no difference to me. If you're honest and work hard, you'll always have a place with us."

Tears brimmed in Lizzie's eyes. "Thank you, Mrs. Davies."

"I'd best hurry along. I hear them loading up the luggage now. If you need any feminine respite, just hunt down Mrs. Brown or Sarina in the big house."

Lizzie nodded and Alexa hurried down the stairs. Jess was waiting by the carriage and extended a hand to help her inside.

The journey passed in silence until they were settled on the train to Brisbane. "Thank you," Jess finally said.

"For what?"

"For accepting her that way. You didn't have to."

"I told her if she's honest and works hard, she'll always have a place with us. That's all that matters to me, Jess."

Jess nodded with approval. He expected her to ask questions. When she didn't, he felt a need to justify. "I met her in a pub. I can't tell you exactly what had happened that day, but I remember feeling so much turmoil inside that I just wanted to die. She came along at the right moment and said the right things. I started home that night."

Alexa smiled and squeezed his hand, but Jess felt that he had to clarify an important point. "She was a prostitute."

"I know."

"How do you know?"

"It wasn't difficult to figure," she stated. Jess looked down guiltily until she touched his chin. "It doesn't matter, Jess. The past is behind us. Only the future matters now."

Jess smiled and kissed her. Whatever their future might be, they were together.

Thirty-two
VENGEANCE IN THE BLOOD

The journey to Brisbane was long and tedious for Jess. He knew Morgan Speer had a partner, but he could only hope there was something of worth to be discovered. Knowing now why Chad had felt threatened by his existence all these years, Jess found a growing determination to keep what was rightfully his, and swore he would not let it go. The problem was exactly how to go about it.

The hired carriage halted at the address Jess had given to the driver. He stepped down and Alexa waited for him to turn and help her, but he didn't.

"What's wrong?" she asked.

Jess moved aside and took Alexa's hand. She came to her feet beside him.

"Merciful heaven," she muttered. There was nothing before them but a heap of burned rubble.

"Do you know when this happened?" Jess called to the driver.

"There was a fire in this part o' town night before last. I assume this was it."

Jess sighed and helped Alexa back into the carriage. "It would appear," he observed as he seated himself across from her, "that your brother has left his calling card again."

"My brother?" Alexa laughed in a feeble attempt to lighten the mood. "He's as much your brother as he is mine."

"What a dreadful thought," Jess said too seriously.

"What do we do now?" Alexa asked.

"How about a prayer?" he said, and Alexa squeezed his hand.

A few hours later they had tracked down the residence of Ira Grant, Morgan Speer's partner. It was a conservative home on the edge of the city, with evidence of young children scattered in the fenced yard. Jess took a deep breath and knocked at the door. Alexa smiled with assurance just before it came open.

"Can I help you?" a handsome woman in her early thirties inquired.

"We're looking for Ira Grant," Jess stated. "I assume this is where we can find him?"

"Yes," she said hesitantly, "but I fear my husband isn't up to having visitors today."

Jess glanced warily toward Alexa. "Excuse me," he said before the woman could close the door. "We don't want to impose, but we have traveled far and . . ." The woman looked hesitant, and Jess sought quickly for something to say that would leave the right impression. "It's to do with Morgan Speer's death," he said quickly. "I believe I have some information that might shed some light on it." The woman's expression softened so abruptly that Jess felt goose bumps. Still, she hesitated until her eyes met Alexa's.

"Come in," she said, moving aside. Jess and Alexa stepped into the hall and she closed the door.

"I didn't get your names," she said, and Alexa noticed a young boy clinging to her skirts.

"Jess Davies," he stated, "and my wife, Alexa."

"Lucy Grant," she replied. "You must forgive my apprehension. My husband has been terribly upset since his partner was killed. It was such a shock, and then with the fire and all, well we just . . ."

She trailed off and Jess said, "I understand. Perhaps your husband and I will be able to help each other."

"Oh, I do hope so," she admitted, leading the way down the hall. "I've been praying we could find out what happened."

Alexa squeezed Jess's hand. Mrs. Grant knocked lightly at a door and peered inside. "Darling," she said quietly, "there are some people here to see you. They might be able to help. It's about Morgan."

"Bring them in," came an eager reply, and they were motioned into a dim office that felt close and stuffy.

"Mr. Grant," Jess held out his hand as the solicitor rose to greet him, "my name is Jess Davies, and this is my wife, Alexa. We are in a bit of a predicament that we were hoping you might help with, and perhaps the other way around as well."

"Please, sit down," he said, and they all did. Mrs. Grant left the room and closed the door.

"You knew Morgan?" Mr. Grant asked.

"I met him briefly just last week. He approached me at a race and told me there was a document he had that I might be interested in. He set an appointment to meet me two days later. I fear he was on his way to my home when he was . . . killed. Combined with other circumstances at this time, I had to wonder what that document might be. Forgive me if I'm stepping out of line to be so abrupt, but you might as well have it straight out. I have a hunch that Mr. Speer's death was not an accident, and neither was the fire that destroyed your office."

Mr. Grant absorbed Jess's statement. "Are you implying that they were connected?"

"It's just a guess, but in relation to other things that have been happening, I believe it's a good one. Though I have little evidence."

"Why don't you tell me what you do have," Mr. Grant leaned forward with interest, "and we'll go from there."

Jess briefly explained the situation, telling him a few of the incidents that he believed Chad was responsible for, and ending with the fact that his property had been purchased by Mr. Byrnehouse recently.

"And you say that Morgan told you this document had to do with Mr. Byrnehouse's late father?"

"Yes. That's what he said. Apparently Tyson Byrnehouse was a client of his."

"The name sounds familiar."

"We were hoping to find out what that document was, but I have to assume everything was lost in the fire. Still, we wanted to at least talk to you and see if—"

"I think I might be able to help you." Mr. Grant smiled slightly. "I would guess from knowing Morgan that he likely didn't have the document with him. He rarely carried important papers far from the office. He would have likely talked to you about it first. If the fire is connected, then we have two facts that tell us Mr. Byrnehouse doesn't have what you're looking for. Morgan also had a habit of keeping duplicates of important documents at home. We both did, actually. It always seemed a logical precaution."

"We tried to find his family, but—"

"Oh, you won't find them because he hasn't any. Morgan was a widower with no children. He's lived with us for the past few years."

Jess felt his heart pound. He met Alexa's eyes and knew that hers was pounding, too.

"If you'll wait here a few minutes, I will see what I can find. Byrnehouse, right?"

"That's right."

Mr. Grant left the room for what seemed an awfully long time. He returned carrying a large envelope with the name *Byrnehouse* scribbled carelessly on the outside.

"This is all I could find," he said. "Let's have a look at it." Mr. Grant put on glasses and broke the seal. He removed several pages folded in half together and read quietly for several minutes. The air hung heavy with expectancy while Jess glanced back and forth between the solicitor and the clock. Alexa began to feel a little queasy from the close quarters and the effect of her nerves. Jess tapped his fingers on his thigh and Alexa's hand sweat in his. Mr. Grant turned another page and continued reading. Suddenly his eyes darted up in surprise.

"You did say you're Jess Davies?"

"That's right."

"Forgive me, I'm not very good with names."

Mr. Grant continued to read, and Jess thought he would die of anxiety. "What is it?" he finally asked.

"It's a will," Mr. Grant replied blandly, but his concentration remained on the document. He finally removed his glasses and leaned back in his chair. He rubbed his eyes with his fingers and sighed audibly. "I've never seen anything quite like it," he stated. He cleared his throat and sat up straight. "Apparently Morgan was right in saying this would be of great interest to you. And it certainly answers some questions. I can see why Chad Byrnehouse wouldn't want you to know about this. Apparently it is of great interest to you and, uh . . ." He replaced his glasses and glanced through the papers quickly. "Ah, yes. Miss Alexandra Byrnehouse. That would be Chad's sister."

"That's me," Alexa said, and Mr. Grant's eyes widened.

"You're joking," he said.

"No, I'm quite serious."

Mr. Grant shook his head in apparent amazement. "It's too bad this will wasn't finalized." He gave an ironic chuckle. "The two of you together would have been very wealthy."

"What does it say?" Jess asked in exasperation.

Mr. Grant cleared his throat again and looked for a particular section. "'To Alexandra I leave fifty percent of all my financial assets and the whole of Byrnehouse racing facilities, including all equine and anything directly related.'"

Mr. Grant glanced up at Jess, then moved his eyes back quickly to the page in his hands. "'To my illegitimate son, Jess Davies, I leave the entirety of my belongings, properties, and assets, excluding only that specified for Alexandra Byrnehouse and the yearly allowance specified for Chad Byrnehouse.'" Mr. Grant waved his hand about carelessly. "There's a few odd things concerning some particular servants and friends that don't amount to much."

"I don't believe it," Jess muttered breathily.

"You did say that the two of you are married," Mr. Grant said carefully as he grasped the delicacy of their relationship.

"Yes," Alexa said, "but that's all right. Tyson Byrnehouse wasn't really my father. He disowned me in his first will. Actually, Jess's father was my father, and my father was Jess's."

Mr. Grant's eyes widened.

"Don't confuse the man, dear," Jess muttered.

"Then Chad is your half-brother," Mr. Grant said to Alexa.

"And Jess's, as well."

"As I said," Mr. Grant leaned back and drew a long breath, "I've never seen a will quite like this one."

"So, what is it worth?" Alexa asked.

"Absolutely nothing," he stated. "It was never finalized, and that makes it worthless—as far as Tyson Byrnehouse's wishes are concerned, that is."

"What do you mean?"

"I intend to use this to its full advantage. With your permission, Mr. Davies, I would like to call upon some friends of mine who are private investigators working closely with the law. This may not be worth much financially, but it will make a fine case of arson and murder."

Jess caught his breath, and Alexa squeezed his hand tightly.

"And as far as your property is concerned, Mr. Davies, my professional advice is that you fight to keep it. I would be more than willing to represent you. There will be no fee unless we win the case."

Mr. Grant stood and held out his hand. Jess rose and shook it firmly, unable to speak.

"Why don't the two of you stay for supper—in fact, you should stay the night. By tomorrow I'll be able to pull together some arrangements, and you can have some papers delivered to Mr. Byrnehouse when you return."

"Thank you, Mr. Grant." Jess chuckled breathily. "I don't know what to say. You've been so—"

"Call me Ira," he interrupted, slapping Jess on the shoulder and escorting him into the hall. "Let's go someplace more comfortable. You and I have a great deal to discuss. We must handle this very carefully."

Jess could do nothing but laugh as he put his arm around Alexa and followed their new friend toward the parlor.

❦   ❦   ❦

"I just don't believe it," Alexa whispered, lying close to Jess in the Grants' guest room. "It's as if everything is falling into place."

"It does seem we're being watched out for," Jess replied quietly. "I only hope our luck holds out. We're going to need it."

"How do you think you'd have felt to hear what that will said if we hadn't already figured it out?"

Jess was silent a long moment. "I can hardly imagine. It still leaves me stunned to think about it."

"How do you suppose Father intended to work leaving the racing facilities to me and the rest of the station to you? Doesn't it seem odd to divide it that way? They just seem to go together. You can't just lift the track out and put it someplace else."

"That's a good question. Maybe he wanted us to work it out for ourselves."

"It appears we would have crossed paths eventually, even if he had lived longer."

"That's a relief." Jess chuckled and pulled her close to him. "I'd like to think destiny had an alternate plan."

"I'm scared, Jess. Facing Chad in court isn't going to be easy."

"It's not facing him in court that frightens me," Jess said soberly. "But if Mr. Grant knows what he's doing, we might be all right."

"You will be careful?"

"Of course." He brushed his lips over her brow. "Everything will be all right, Mrs. Davies. I promise."

Alexa nuzzled closer to him and slept, concentrating on the peace of his promise and avoiding any thoughts of apprehension. But she knew Chad's fury had yet to be faced.

🐾 🐾 🐾

Chad Byrnehouse walked into his office and stopped cold to see a pair of fine riding boots planted in the center of the desk, with Jess Davies attached.

"What on earth are you doing here?" Chad asked sharply.

"Just thought I'd have a look," Jess said easily. He glanced around and added, "It's not such a bad place, I suppose."

"Who let you in?" Chad demanded.

"Nobody. I didn't see any point in knocking . . . under the circumstances."

"What circumstances?" Chad looked visibly unnerved, and Jess grinned.

"I won't bore you with trivialities," Jess retorted, bringing his feet to the floor. "Oh," he added as an apparent afterthought, "I did bring you this."

Jess threw an envelope on the desk and walked toward the door. "What is it?" Chad asked.

"I was going to let you open it and find out for yourself, but since you brought it up, it would be a pleasure to tell you. That envelope contains some legal papers. Just in case you have difficulty under-

standing them, I'll sum it up for you. You're not going to lay one finger on anything that is mine until it's settled in court."

"You'll regret it, Jess," Chad said, the edge of confidence returning
to his voice.

"Nah," Jess said casually, "I don't think so." He gave a complacent
smile. "Contrary to your beliefs, I've got the guts to win. Well, I'll be
on my way . . . old pal." Jess slapped his shoulder none too lightly and
chuckled. "It's good to see you," he stepped through the door then
leaned back briefly, "little brother."

Jess shut the door before Chad had a chance to absorb it. He had
to fight to keep from laughing aloud as he sauntered out of the house.

"Thank you, Lowery," Jess told the old stable hand as he retrieved
his horse. "You're a good man."

"Was my pleasure, Mr. Davies. Tell your lovely wife hello for me.
Things just haven't been the same without her."

"I can imagine," Jess chuckled as he mounted. "By the way,
Lowery, whatever became of Sam Tommey? Worked here on the
tracks, I believe."

"I know of him. Haven't seen him for quite some time. I assume
Byrnehouse sent him packing."

"Do you know where he went?"

"No, sir. I don't."

"If you ever see him again, tell him I could use him."

"I'll do that."

"Thank you, Lowery. With any luck, I'll be seeing you again soon."

❦   ❦   ❦

Jess was amazed at how quickly Ira Grant pulled everything
together. He felt sure Ira's personal motives helped. With complete
confidence in him to handle it all properly, Jess's fear of losing the station lessened as the court date drew closer.

Alexa feared what Chad might try to do when he realized it was closing in on him, but Jess felt certain Chad was being watched too closely.
Anything he attempted at this point would only strengthen Jess's case.

However, Jess had a hunch that he'd yet to contend with Chad
one-on-one. He was glad that he happened to have his feet on his desk

when Chad burst into his office. It added to the effect as Jess greeted him with a lazy smile. "You could at least knock," he said coolly.

"I want to know what's going on." Chad planted his palms on the desk and leaned over it. "And I want to know now!"

"I'm afraid you've got me baffled." Jess picked up his riding crop and twirled it carelessly.

"Don't play ignorant with me, Davies. You've got something up your sleeve, and I know it as well as I know I'm standing here."

"Of course I do," Jess grinned. "I'm taking you to court."

"Besides that."

"Besides that?" Jess looked completely innocent.

"All of a sudden I've got private investigators and the local constable breathing down my neck, and I want to know why."

"I don't know, why?"

"You're playing a game with me!" Chad slammed his fist on the desk.

"Isn't it fun?"

"No, it's not!"

"You've been playing games with me for better than a decade now, Byrnehouse. I figured it was about time I got in on the action."

"Then you *are* behind it." Chad stood up straight and folded his arms.

"You'll never prove it," Jess smirked.

"You'll never get away with it." Chad's expression turned threatening.

"I'm not trying to get away with anything but what is rightfully mine."

"Which is?" Chad asked testily.

"I want my land back—nothing more."

"I don't believe you."

"You can believe what you like." Jess brought his feet to the floor and leaned forward. "But it won't change the inevitable. A man can't do the things you've been doing forever and get away with it. I want my land back, and I want to live in peace."

"I don't believe you," he repeated.

"Why?"

"You know the truth of your paternity." Chad's voice was smug as he sauntered to a chair and sat down. Jess felt tension rising. "Though I have to wonder how you found out."

"I wonder the same about you."

Their eyes met, and Jess felt the reality sink in. Chad Byrnehouse was his half-brother.

"I know for a fact," Chad tapped his fingers together with confidence, "what kind of hell your mother went through because of our father, and I know how her circumstances affected you. Do you want to try and convince me that it hasn't left a mark on you?"

Jess said nothing, but he felt his cheek muscles twitch.

"You might believe that all you want is peace, but you have Tyson Byrnehouse in you, Jess. There is something in you that wants vengeance. You want to destroy me every bit as much as I want to destroy you. Just like he destroyed your mother."

"You're judging me by your standards, Byrnehouse. You have no idea what I want."

"Oh, but I can make a fair guess." Chad gave a demented laugh. "Admit it, Jess. You want vengeance."

"I want to know what makes you hate me so much. Is it simply that I had the audacity to have the same father? Or perhaps it's because I had the nerve to be conceived before you were? Or maybe," Jess's eyes became intent, "it's because you woke up one day and realized that Tyson Byrnehouse liked me."

Jess knew Chad was trying to remain expressionless, but his eyes told the truth. The statement got to the core of him.

"Face it, Chad," Jess went on, "the games are over. Anything you do to me now will come back to you. You'll destroy yourself."

"You see," Chad chuckled humorlessly, "you *are* out for vengeance."

"I'll never admit to it." Jess forced a smile in an effort to conceal that he, too, was being struck to the core.

Chad rose from his chair and put his hands casually behind his back. "Just remember, dear brother, that what you and I share is no small thing. If I go down, I'm taking you with me."

Chad left the office without closing the door. Jess had to fight back the evidence of the past that told him Chad was right. He lost track of hours as he sat pondering what had been said and how deeply it affected him. With his head pounding against the palms of his hands, Jess became engrossed with the severity of this conflict. This was no simple court battle. This was a feud as old as Cain and Abel, and Jess had to wonder if he had a little of Cain in himself.

Alexa's knock at the open door brought him abruptly back to the moment. "Are you all right?" she asked, sensing immediately that he was troubled.

"Your bro . . . our brother was here."

"Dare I ask what he wanted?"

"No." His tone was sharp, but Alexa seemed to understand.

"Will you tell me anyway?"

"He tried to get me to admit that I was out for vengeance."

Alexa sighed. It shouldn't surprise her that Chad would resort to mind games, but still it made her angry. "And did you?"

"No, I did not!"

"But are you?"

"I don't know." Jess stood and turned his back to her. "But I would be lying to myself if I didn't admit that it would give me pleasure to see him lose everything and rot in hell."

"And you would be no better than Chad if you believe that such an attitude will solve anything."

Jess turned to look at her sharply. Alexa wanted to apologize, but she believed he needed to hear it. The line between justice and vengeance was too fine.

"Am I a better man than he?" he asked with sincerity.

"Yes, you are." Alexa's reply was strong, but Jess didn't seem eager to believe her.

❦   ❦   ❦

Jess blessed the unseen hand that had led him to find Ira Grant. The man renewed Jess's trust in solicitors and their representation of the law. The more Jess got to know Ira, the more he had to admit that he trusted him with his life. And as the trial got underway, Jess realized he was doing just that.

Alexa, too, was left in awe as they observed Ira Grant take a series of facts, that in themselves seemed insignificant and without bearing, and weave them together with incredible skill. Without using any deception whatsoever, Ira Grant enchanted the judge and jury with a view of Chad Byrnehouse that Jess had thought no one else could ever see or understand.

At the trial's conclusion, the judge deemed that the bank had not been warranted to sell Jess Davies' property and the transaction had been illegal. The bank was ordered to return to Chad Byrnehouse what he had paid for the property, and to accept Jess Davies' final payment to free the mortgage.

Jess embraced Alexa and laughed as the verdict was announced. It then came as a surprise to everyone but Ira Grant as the judge added to his statement that in light of evidence brought forth during the course of the trial, he was ordering further investigation into the deaths of Morgan Speer, Richard Wilhite, and Tyson Byrnehouse. Chad turned visibly pale as it was mentioned that the validity of Tyson Byrnehouse's will was also a matter of importance to the case.

Jess's expression was genuine innocence when Chad turned cold, hard eyes upon him. Their last conversation came back freshly, and Jess couldn't suppress his fear over what chain reactions might result from this.

"Why didn't you tell me?" Jess demanded of Ira when the court was adjourned.

"I wasn't certain the judge would pursue it. I didn't want to get your hopes up."

"But I've got what I want," Jess stated firmly. "I want nothing to do with this."

"It's in the hands of the law now, Jess. You need not be involved if you don't wish to be. If you're worried about what insane thing Chad might do now that he's cornered, remember just that. He's cornered. Anything bizarre that happens now will only convict him further, and he has to know that."

Jess shook his head. "I'm sorry. I should be thanking you. You've saved me, and I owe you a great deal."

"Oh, you'll get the bill," Ira laughed. "But you don't need to apologize," he added more soberly. "I understand how you must be feeling, but nevertheless, justice must be met."

"I guess that's your business."

"It is indeed." Ira smiled proudly. "And I must say that I've never had such a gratifying case." His eyes narrowed, and Jess saw the loss of Ira's partner etched there as he added, "Chad Byrnehouse's days are numbered.

"By the way," his tone lightened as he reached into his pocket and pulled forth an envelope. "I finished going through all of Morgan's things recently, and I found this with another copy of the will among his personal papers. He must have been especially interested in the case to have left them there."

Ira shook Jess's hand again. "We'll keep in touch." Jess nodded and Ira left the courtroom.

Most of the way home, Jess gazed quietly at the envelope in his hands, wondering what it could be. "Why don't you just open it?" Alexa asked.

"I'm not sure I dare," he said lightly.

Alexa took it from him to read Jess's name and place of residence, with a notation that stated, *To accompany deliverance of Byrnehouse will, or to be delivered at request of client.*

"Do you want me to open it?" she asked.

"Not yet," he said and took it back, holding it quietly until they arrived home.

After they freshened up and had something to eat, Jess told Alexa he wanted to be alone, and she understood. Relieved over getting his land back, Jess concentrated more fully on the discovery of his paternity. His emotions were strung high as he walked to his mother's studio and made himself comfortable near a lamp. He pondered the circumstances a long while before he found the nerve to open the envelope at last.

Jess's fingers trembled slightly as he brought out the enclosed pages and unfolded them. His heart quickened when his suspicions were confirmed. It was not a legal document. It was a letter from his father, dated a short time before his death.

Jess glanced toward the gable window and swallowed hard, trying to perceive the full spectrum of what he had been born into. With courage he turned his eyes back to the page in his hand and read:

Dear Jess,

If things go as planned, this letter and its contents will come as no surprise to you. By the time you read this, I hope I have had the opportunity to tell you to your face that I am your father, and the plans I am making now for you will have come about. But tonight I feel the need to unburden myself for reasons I don't understand. I believe that by whatever means this letter comes into your hands, you will be accepting of it. I feel I know you well, Jess. I have watched you closely over the years and feel confident that the decisions I have made are right.

At this date, I am determined to find a way to be free of the guilt I have suffered concerning the means of your conception. I pray you will be willing to accept my attempts to rectify my mistakes of the past, and perhaps you can forgive me for the hell your mother went through. I don't know how or when you found out that Ben Davies wasn't your father, but I have a good idea. I have seen the changes in you and it fills me with regret. I only wish there was more I could do to soften the harshness of Chad's cynicism toward you. If nothing else, remember this, Jess: it was my fault, not yours. You were born guiltless into a situation you had no control over, and I regret the repercussions you have suffered.

Whether I am dead or alive at the time you read this, I hope you will appreciate what I am leaving to you. I realize all of it means little compared to the true elements of happiness, but accept it as an offering of something your father was proud of, knowing that you have earned the right to hold it.

I want to admonish you to be wary of Chad. Don't stand for his childish ploys. You are his elder brother, Jess, if only by months. I fear he got the worst of me, and it's my foolishness that put the wrong knowledge in the wrong hands. Of this too, I pray you will be forgiving.

My most important purpose behind this letter is something that at this moment fills me with happiness like I have never known. It concerns Alexandra.

Jess turned his face toward the ceiling and drew a deep breath. Already the things he'd read left him weak with emotion. But the deepening of ironies made him feel both at peace and in awe as he recalled words he'd spoken once to Alexa. It was nice to know that destiny had an alternate plan.

Shifting in his chair and breathing deeply, Jess turned his attention back to the letter, rereading the last phrase.

It concerns Alexandra. At this moment I'm not certain you know that I have a daughter. Though I confess she bears no blood of mine, I must consider her mine, for she is most precious to me above all else. It pleases me now to realize the two of you are not related by blood. An idea has come to me that thrills me in a way words could not explain. It seems pre-

posterous at the present, but I feel there is a good chance that by the time you read this the two of you will be married.

Jess had to stop and catch his breath. He could hardly believe it. But still it left him feeling the same thrill Tyson Byrnehouse must have felt when he wrote his ironic letter.

You see, Jess, it has just come to me. I had a dream about you, and with you was Alexandra. There was no more to it than that, but I feel I know you both well, and if I have my way, the two of you will see my reason. Of course I'm not about to force an arranged marriage on the two people I care for most, but it is worth considering from my point of view. If arranged marriages don't work, perhaps having to share my property with her will.

The prospect of being free of my past and seeing the two of you together makes an old man very happy, Jess. I hope I live long enough to see it come about. God bless you, son. From a distance you have been a treasure to me, and despite the circumstances, I am grateful for your existence.

Take special care of all that is mine, most especially Alexandra. I love her with all my soul, and I am grateful too for the blood that flows in her veins. She has softened me. I pray you will love her as I do.

With love, your father, Tyson Byrnehouse.

Jess leaned his head back and cried silent tears as the entire drama of the years behind him culminated with Tyson Byrnehouse's ability to perceive the future. Feeling completely happy and at peace, Jess rose from his chair and extinguished the lamp. He couldn't wait another minute to show this to Alexa. She wouldn't believe it.

Thirty-three
FIGHTING FIRE
WITH FIRE

The following day, Jess took care of his business at the bank and found Mr. Hemming especially cooperative. He returned home ready to celebrate, but Alexa met him with a sober expression.

"There's someone here to see you," she said.

"Who?" Jess questioned, but she only led him down the hall and stood aside for him to enter the parlor.

"Lowery." Jess was surprised to see the elderly man, who rose to greet him with a firm handshake.

"Mr. Davies," he said gravely, "I apologize for imposing on you like this, but I—"

"Nonsense." Alexa came beside Lowery and urged him to sit back down. "I've already told you that you did the right thing coming here. Where else could you have gone?"

"What's happened?" Jess asked carefully.

Lowery looked up at Jess with emotion filling his wise eyes. "I was hauling wood into the bunkhouse when I . . . well, I found Sam Tommey's body buried in the woodpile."

Jess sat down.

Lowery wrung his hands nervously. "You know he disappeared not more than a day or two after that last race. From the looks of him, he . . . he must o' been there since then."

The old man faltered, and Alexa put her arm around him. She met Jess's eyes with concern. "Lowery reported it to the constable right away," she reported. "You know, with the present circumstances it won't take them long to have Chad cornered."

Jess nodded numbly. He didn't want to acknowledge the instinctive uneasiness creeping over him.

"I told Lowery he must stay here. He can't possibly go back there considering that—"

"Alexa is right," Jess insisted. "You can use one of the rooms above the carriage house. Take your pick."

Alexa looked alarmed. "One of them is being used, Jess." He looked baffled and she reminded him, "Lizzie."

"Oh, of course." Jess had honestly forgotten. He'd seen Lizzie coming and going some, but he'd been far too preoccupied to give it much thought. He turned to Lowery. "You can take the room Lizzie isn't using. If you need anything at all, let us know and we'll do what we can. Consider yourself one of us."

Lowery's eyes showed warm appreciation.

"In the meantime," a positive note crept into Jess's voice, "we've got some celebrating to do." He nodded toward Lowery. "You must join us."

Jess reached into his pocket and pulled out some papers that he waved comically in front of Alexa's face. "In the mood for a fire, my dear?"

❦ ❦ ❦

Under Alexa's supervision, the boys and Lizzie all gathered around a fire in the yard just like old times. With a great deal of pomp, Jess burned the mortgage, and Alexa had never heard the boys whoop and holler so loudly. By the way Lizzie joined in, it was evident she was feeling at home among them. And Lowery, too, appeared to be enjoying himself.

Fiddler played with so much enthusiasm that they could hardly resist dancing, and Jess supplied champagne to their content. Occasionally Jess would throw his head back and laugh, or lift Alexa off the ground with a hearty twirl.

"I guess this means we're staying," Lizzie said to Jess after the music had stopped and they were all gathered quietly around the fire in varied states of exhaustion.

"We certainly are," Jess grinned.

"How do you like it here so far?" Alexa asked.

"I love it." She laughed, and a moment later Fiddler approached and put his arm around Lizzie's shoulders. Jess and Alexa exchanged an unobtrusive glance as Lizzie took Fiddler's hand where it rested on her shoulder.

"Lizzie's quite a cook," Fiddler announced.

"Yeah," Edward called with a grin, though he looked especially pale and weary. "Now I can die in peace, knowing you guys won't starve."

"I can cook," Fiddler protested.

"Not like Lizzie," Murphy added.

"Cooking or not," Alexa said emphatically to Edward, "you'd best be with us a long while yet."

"I'll try." Edward gave a wan smile.

Alexa leaned heavily against Jess, and he looked down in concern. "Tired?"

"Exhausted."

"Well, good night, boys," Jess called. He took a step toward the house, then paused. His eyes filled with emotion and a hush fell over the group. "Thank you," he said quietly, "all of you, for seeing us through this. We've had some tough years, and you've pulled me out many times. We can look forward to good times ahead."

The boys cheered. Alexa kissed Jess exuberantly, and together they went toward the house. Jess laughed as they came through the door and Alexa looked up at him in question.

"It's all ours, love. No more mortgage. No more debt. I feel like the world is in my hands."

"It is," she assured him, and he reacted by scooping her into his arms to carry her up the stairs. Once in the bedroom, he kicked the door shut and laughed as he nearly jumped into the center of the bed, Alexa still in his arms. Alexa pulled his face into her hands and kissed him vibrantly.

"Oooh, Mrs. Davies," he muttered, and she could hear him smile in the darkness, "I thought you were exhausted."

"Did I say I was exhausted?"

"You most certainly did." He rolled onto his back and brought her with him.

"I must have been mistaken." She laughed. "What I meant to say was that I wanted to have a private celebration with my husband."

"Aha," Jess kissed her throat repeatedly, "and what might that entail?"

"There's no need to talk." Alexa sighed and eased closer to him. "I think you've figured it out."

A sense of awe washed over Alexa as, once again, Jess proved just how wondrous their love could be. Somewhere in the midst of their lovemaking, she became distantly aware of thunder. But she didn't care if it poured all night. She laughed softly as Jess took notice of her belly where it swelled with pregnancy. "You really are going to have a baby," he declared.

"Yes, I am," she whispered, "and it's going to grow up on the same land you grew up on."

"You can't know what that means to me." He kissed her and continued to caress her belly as if he might touch the child within. "Is it supposed to be this big already?" he asked, trying not to recall the worries that had plagued him when she'd been pregnant before.

"Stop playing with your baby," she giggled to suppress her own concerns, "and kiss me, Jess Davies."

Jess laughed and kissed her with a hunger that had become a familiar part of her life. "I love you," he murmured with such strength that tears moistened her eyes.

In the peaceful aftermath, Alexa's mind wandered to the drama she had witnessed in the courtroom. She wondered what would become of Chad now. Would they prove that he was behind his father's death, and Mr. Speer's—and Richard's? As always, with thoughts of Richard a brief longing passed through her. Though she would not want her life to be any different, his death still remained a tragic loss, and it always would be.

Her thoughts passed over the letter Jess had received through Ira Grant's hands. She liked trying to imagine how it might have been to be introduced to Jess Davies with full knowledge that marriage was a possibility.

Jess remained still and silent beside her, but Alexa sensed his thoughts churning similarly. She knew that he was yet in awe of Tyson Byrnehouse's confessions, and he could hardly help wondering what would become of Chad as a result of this. She felt certain that Jess, too, held fears that they had not seen the last of his vengeance.

But Alexa was content to let her thoughts go unspoken. With Jess in her arms and the aura of celebration still hovering around them, she had no desire to shatter it with worries. Until footsteps bounding down the hallway suddenly made those worries tangible.

"What?" Jess's voice was sharp with fear as he pulled open the door and put on a shirt at the same time.

"Land fire to the west," Jimmy said breathlessly. "Wind's movin' this way."

"I'm coming," Jess said, but Jimmy was already down the hall. Jess sat to pull on his boots while Alexa hurried to gather her clothes. "I should have known better than to think he'd let me have it back in one piece. The man's a wretched pyromaniac."

"Be careful," Alexa called as he ran out of the room. "I'll be down as soon as I'm dressed."

Alexa put on a shirt and breeches and prayed aloud. She pulled on her boots and headed for the door, but stopped cold.

"Where you going, little sister?" Chad calmly filled the doorframe to prevent her from leaving. "To a fire?" he added with a smirk.

"I knew you had something to do with this," she spat. "How dare you show your face here when—"

"I appreciate the cordial welcome." He pushed past her into the bedroom, taking her arm to keep her with him. "But we haven't time right now for niceties."

"What are you doing?" She tried to keep her voice steady.

"I'm leaving a little note for your husband," he said as if it was funny. Alexa watched him set a piece of paper on the bed, but she didn't get a chance to read it. She cried out in protest when he tugged at her wedding ring. Despite her attempt to keep her hand in a fist, Chad tore it from her finger.

"How dare you!" she snarled, trying futilely to free herself from his grasp. "Give me back my ring. You can't—"

"I can and I will." He tightened his grip painfully as he set the ring with the note, then dragged her from the room. "But not to worry, Mrs. Davies. I'm certain your husband will make every effort to return it to you promptly."

"I don't know what kind of game you're playing, Chad, but it's not going to work."

"Oh, but it is," he sneered, "as long as you keep quiet."

Chad paused in his effort to leave the house and pushed her against the wall. He bound her wrists behind her back and tied a scarf around her mouth, laughing at her attempts to protest.

Fear consumed Alexa, unlike anything she'd ever experienced in her life. Chad dragged her out the front door, where a horse was waiting. He forced her into the saddle and mounted behind her. Alexa squeezed her eyes shut in fervent prayer as she was helplessly forced away from everything she loved, wondering if she would live to ever see it again.

❦ ❦ ❦

Jess was relieved to see that this fire wasn't as bad as he'd expected. But still he knew they couldn't take any chances in having it spread to more valuable land or any of the buildings. Murphy was barking orders at the boys who were moving efficiently, and Jess fell easily into helping them. The flames and smoke added fuel to his rage toward Chad Byrnehouse. He wanted to have his hands around Chad's throat, and it gave him peace to think that Tyson Byrnehouse would have felt the same way if he were still alive.

Lizzie's voice interrupted his heated thoughts just as he glanced around to wonder where Alexa was. He turned to Lizzie and wiped sweat from his brow with the back of his sleeve.

"Jess," she breathlessly held out a slip of paper, "I found this tacked to the main water pump."

Jess felt an odd quiver run through his arm as he reached out to take it. He stared dumbly at the words for what seemed a brief eternity. His mind flooded with horrid imaginings of the night he was conceived, meshed with the night his mother was killed.

Coming to his senses, Jess crumpled the paper into his fist. But the words echoed through his mind as if they had just been shouted. *Like father, like son. Vengeance is in the blood.*

"Alexa!" He breathed her name as his feet carried him toward the house. He already knew she wouldn't be there. "Have someone saddle Crazy for me," he called over his shoulder.

"Alexa!" he shouted as he came through the door and bounded up the stairs, taking three at a time. The bedroom was empty, as he had expected, but the lamp burning on the bedside table brought his eye quickly to the gold band lying on her pillow.

Again his hand quivered as he picked it up, then snatched the note beneath it to read: *If I can't have it, no man shall.*

"No!" he screamed, then added softly, "Please, no."

A fearful burning seized Jess's chest. He ran as fast as his legs could carry him down the stairs and to the stable.

"Where you going?" Fiddler demanded. Jess took the reins from him but said nothing. "What's wrong?"

"Chad's got Alexa," he finally muttered, swinging his leg over Crazy's back.

Jess was grateful for Fiddler's insight as he found himself seated in a racing saddle. With his feet high in the stirrups, Jess bent forward and pushed Crazy to her limit, whispering behind her ear, "Come on, girl. If you've ever needed to be fast, it's now."

Jess turned his conversation to verbal prayer as Crazy put furlongs behind her. Ahead in the distance, Jess could see a red glow against the black horizon. Tangible fear absorbed him painfully. Jess had been right when he'd said that Chad would destroy himself. But Chad had insisted he would take Jess down with him. And Chad knew that nothing meant more to Jess than Alexa.

The game had gone too far. If Jess found Alexa harmed in any way, Chad Byrnehouse would learn a new meaning for the word "vengeance."

❦   ❦   ❦

Alexa's mind raced in circles. What would her fate be? What kind of trap was Jess running into when he inevitably tried to find her? How long would it be before she was missed? She was more concerned than surprised when Chad took her to Byrnehouse Station and dismounted near the rear entrance of the house.

"How long has it been since you've seen the old place?" Chad asked cynically, forcing her ahead of him into the house. He lit a candle and urged her quickly from one room to the next on a silent tour of what had once been home to her. Furniture was overturned, drapes shredded, lamps and other odd things shattered over the floors.

"Seems awfully quiet, doesn't it," he said. "I let the servants go. All of them. No need for them to get hurt."

Alexa tried to protest, realizing more each moment that Chad's intentions were the worst. The scarf in her mouth prevented her words from being understood, but Chad laughed at her efforts. "Don't worry," he said, dragging her up the stairs, "you'll have a fair chance to speak your mind."

They came into Alexa's old bedroom, which appeared to have received the worst of his anger so far. "I know you're wondering what's going on." Chad forced Alexa to sit on what was left of the bed. He sat directly in front of her and placed his hand firmly on her shoulder.

"I'm certain that within a matter of hours I'm going to be arrested for the murder of Sam Tommey, if not more than that. Your husband has conveniently destroyed my life, and I'm beginning to see there isn't a thing I can do about it."

He smiled, and Alexa thought he looked terribly calm, considering what he was saying and the evidence all around her that he'd recently been otherwise.

"So I'm going to take the money and run. But before I leave you and your dear husband what Father intended for the two of you to have all along, I thought I'd play with it a little first. If you and Jess make it out of here alive, you'll have little left of mine to claim. With any luck, one or both of you won't make it, and you won't have to worry about assessing the damages."

Again Alexa attempted to protest, and Chad smirked at her indecipherable mumbling. "Now that you know the rules," he said coldly, "let's play the game. It's called fighting fire with fire."

Chad stood and pulled a cork from the barrel he'd been sitting on. Alexa smelled the kerosene before he tipped the barrel and the rank liquid spilled over the floor. Instinctively she tried to move toward the door, fighting to get out of the room. But Chad grabbed her arm and held it tightly as he pulled a piece of cloth from the shredded bed-hangings and touched it to the candle until it ignited.

Alexa's scream was muffled as Chad threw the burning cloth into the puddle and it began to burn. She was relieved when he dragged her out of the room with him, until he entered another in the opposite wing where the air was already tainted with the smell of kerosene. With that room in flames, she was forced to witness another dozen ignitings throughout the house.

Tears soaked the scarf tied about her head. Fear and sorrow consumed her entirely, and she was certain she would never live to see Jess again, or hold their child in her arms.

Relief gave her a glimmer of hope when Chad took her out of the house. They stood back a long while to watch the inward glow of the house gradually build into flames that showed outwardly. The different sources seemed to meet suddenly, and the house burst into unified flames. Alexa could feel the heat in spite of the distance.

"Quite a sight, don't you think, little sister?"

Alexa made no attempt to reply until Chad finally pulled the scarf from her mouth, leaving it to hang around her neck.

"You're mad!" she hissed.

"Nah," Chad laughed calmly, "I'm just sick to death of Jess Davies. Since Father told me what had resulted from his act of vengeance, I've known that I couldn't let Jess have what should have been mine. It's Father who was mad. When he told me if I didn't straighten up he was going to leave it all to Jess, I knew I had to take the matter seriously."

"You killed Father."

"I'll never admit to it." He laughed coldly, and Alexa closed her eyes in an effort to suppress the pain.

"You killed Richard, too, didn't you."

"Now that was something I hadn't contemplated, but when I saw Jess—or who I thought was Jess—riding toward me, the shot was just too much to resist."

Alexa cursed him and tried to push away, but with her hands tied it was futile.

"Enough sightseeing," Chad said and dragged her toward the stables. He ordered Alexa into a corner, and she gasped as he methodically poured kerosene from wall to wall in front of her.

Alexa's protests were answered with a demented laugh that sent chills through her. She screamed when Chad struck the match and flames began to build in front of her. She could see him ushering the

horses out, then he poured kerosene through the rest of the stable and
lit it in half a dozen places.

As the flames began to build, Chad called a dramatic farewell.
Alexa prayed aloud, preparing herself for certain death.

❦   ❦   ❦

Jess could only pray that Alexa was not in the house when he
arrived to see it consumed with roaring flames. Approaching the main
stable, he saw horses running out in enough order to know that someone was in there. He'd barely dismounted when a feminine cry struck
his ears. Alexa was alive. But could he make it to her in time?

Heat and smoke greeted Jess as he ran into the stable.

"Alexa!" he called.

"Jess!" she cried, relief matching her fear. "I'm here. Please help me."

"I'm coming," he assured her, but a fist came out of the smoke and
sent Jess reeling backward.

Alexa screamed. Through the flames she saw Chad's assault and
heard his vindictive words. "You bastard!" he hissed. Jess came carefully to his feet, but Chad hit him again.

"Don't be a fool." Jess coughed and came to his feet, wary enough
that he was able to duck and miss the next assault. "You'll kill us all."

"Sounds fun, doesn't it? I'd rather die in here with you than live to
see you with what should have been mine." Chad turned and swung
again. Jess blocked it with his arm and slugged Chad in the stomach.
His mind flew to Alexa, knowing he needed to get her out. But Chad
recovered quickly and hit him again.

"Stop it, Chad!" Jess shouted, struggling to come to his feet. "It
won't change anything. Do you want two more lives on your conscience—besides your own?"

"Yes!" he shouted malevolently and swung again.

"Don't be stupid!" Jess insisted, barely avoiding the blow aimed at
his jaw. "Let's get out of here and talk about it."

"There's nothing to talk about," Chad shouted. "It's too late."

Jess swung hard and carefully, sending Chad backward with a
hefty blow just as Alexa cried, "Jess! Help me!"

With no hesitation, Jess covered his head with his arms and rushed through the wall of fire. He found Alexa pressed into the corner, and they took hold of each other, making certain the other was all right. While Jess hurried to untie her wrists, the smell of singed hair permeated the smoke and kerosene. Jess took a deep breath and held Alexa tightly against him. He ran backward through the fire and felt the flames catch him. With Alexa in his arms, he fell backward onto the ground and rolled. They scrambled to their knees, frantically examining each other for signs of fire.

Together and safe, they laughed and cried, murmuring disjointed phrases of love and gratitude. Jess removed the scarf from around her neck and held her close. He reached into his pocket and pulled out her wedding ring. A happy sob erupted from her throat as he slid it into place then squeezed her hand. He pressed his mouth over hers and kissed her fervently until a blood-chilling scream brought them to reality. Chad was trapped inside the stable.

"No!" Alexa cried as Jess ran back inside, but he didn't even look back. Fighting the heat and smoke, he moved carefully toward where he knew Chad had landed after that last blow.

"Chad!" he called but got no response. "Chad! Where are you?" He heard violent coughing and inched toward the sound. "Chad!" he called again.

"Let me die in peace, Davies!" an angry voice shouted back.

Jess found him pinned beneath a fallen beam that was burning from the top down. Chad coughed helplessly as Jess tried to move it off him.

"Get out of here!" Chad barely managed to say between heaves. "Leave me in peace!"

"Don't be a fool!" Jess retorted, pushing against the beam with his shoulder. "If you had any brains, your life would be worth more than your pride and you'd let me help you."

"Why?" Chad managed to say.

"You're my brother, for heaven's sake," Jess heard himself say, and emotion quivered in his voice.

When the beam finally gave way, Chad cried out in pain and Jess could see that his leg was badly broken. Again Chad attempted to shout protests, but his coughing became incessant. Jess took hold beneath his arms and dragged him through the flames toward the door.

Jess dragged Chad away from the fire while he continued to cough relentlessly. Jess knelt beside him and put his arm beneath Chad's head to support it. He wondered what to do as he realized Chad was coughing blood. Before Jess could get hold of his senses, the coughing ceased.

Jess glanced helplessly at the two burning structures and Alexa standing nearby, as if his surroundings might answer the inevitable question. Reality settled in, and he carefully released his grip on Chad. Following a moment of stunned silence, Jess unwillingly clenched his fists and turned his face skyward, crying out in grief as he wondered why it hurt so badly to see his mortal enemy—his brother—die here in his arms.

As if to answer the wordless plea, the heavens opened up with sheeting rain. The fires sizzled and hissed in protest as water contested them. Jess removed what was left of his shirt and laid it over Chad's face. Alexa put a hand on his shoulder and he stood to pull her into his arms, pressing her face against his chest as they held each other and cried, mingling their tears with the bathing rain.

Thirty-four
WINNER TAKE ALL

Mrs. Brown scurried down the hall to answer the door. "Just what we need is more people in this house," she murmured to herself. "And of all times, why now?"

"What was that?" the gentleman on the porch asked as he caught the last of her utterance.

"What can I do for you?" she asked straightly, ignoring his question.

"I'd like to speak with Mr. Davies."

"Oh, he can't see anyone right now," she said in a near frenzy.

"But I have an appointment with him. Please tell him Ira Grant is here."

"It doesn't matter who you are, sir. Babies don't pay any mind to appointments."

"I beg your pardon?"

"Mrs. Davies is in labor," she said in exasperation, and Mr. Grant chuckled.

"Would it be all right if I wait?" he asked. "I'm not in any hurry."

"Oh, you might as well." She ushered him into the hall and closed the door. "Everyone else has made themselves a permanent fixture. I suppose nothin' will ever be the same again."

Mr. Grant chuckled again, finding the housekeeper's antics humorous.

"All the boys are in the dinin' room," she reported. "You can wait with them, or perhaps you'd find the library more relaxin'."

"I'll take the dining room," he replied, and Mrs. Brown led the way with an exasperated shrug.

"Ah," Murphy rose from the table when Mr. Grant entered, "it's the famous solicitor. Come in and have a seat. You're just in time."

"In time for what?" Ira pulled a chair up to the table and sat down.

"To place a bet, of course," Fiddler provided.

Ira watched in amusement as minute amounts of money were being passed back and forth with a great deal of bartering.

"What are we betting on?" he asked.

"Well," Lizzie spoke up before anyone else could, "if you're smart you'll bet on a girl. I know it's goin' to be a girl."

"Hogwash!" Lowery insisted. "It'll be a boy as sure as I'm sittin' here."

"I'm with Lizzie," Murphy growled. "It's got to be a girl."

Ira laughed and glanced around, noting by the looks of the room that they'd been here for hours.

"So, what do you think, Mr. Grant?" Edward asked. "We could use some professional advice."

"I'm not well-rehearsed at predictions, though I did get all but one of my own right. Where do the odds stand?"

Tod studied a paper briefly. "Odds favor you winning more if it's a boy."

"Well then," he reached into his pocket and brought out a five-pound note that he slapped in the middle of the table. All eyes widened. "I'll say it's going to be a boy."

"Smart man," Lowery muttered.

Jess Davies paraded into the dining room with no warning and announced, "It's posting time, boys." He looked weary but in good spirits, and they had to figure everything had gone well.

"You bet just in time." Jimmy nudged Mr. Grant.

"Is it here?" Murphy asked expectantly.

"It is," Jess laughed proudly.

"Well, what is it?" Edward insisted.

Jess said nothing. He just sauntered to the table and swept his arms across it to scoot all the money toward himself.

"What are you doin'?" Murphy protested.

"You all lose."

"Well, she had a baby, didn't she?" Jimmy asked in dismay.

"Of course she did."

"And everything's all right, isn't it?" Tod added.

"Yes, of course." Jess chuckled.

"Then how could we possibly all lose? It's got to be a boy or a girl." Murphy looked totally baffled. Jess only counted his money and smiled.

"Out with it!" Fiddler demanded, and Jess laughed.

"Very well. If you insist." He laughed again.

"Jess!" Lizzie shrieked when he held out another moment.

"Oh, all right." He grinned proudly. "It's one of each."

"Twins?!" Murphy's voice rose a pitch.

"Exactly."

The room went into peals of laughter, except for Ira, who leaned back in his chair and watched like a child at a circus.

"And I'm going to need this money," Jess stated, still counting. "It's not going to be cheap raising two babies." Seeing the five-pound note, he added, "Who was the brave one?"

"That would be me," Mr. Grant volunteered.

"Ira!" Jess laughed and held out his hand. "I didn't see you there with all the excitement."

Ira rose and shook Jess's hand firmly. "Congratulations. It appears I came just in time."

"You did indeed." Jess glanced to the boys, who were still laughing it up. "Perhaps we could go some place a little more quiet." They moved together toward the door, and Jess paused. "Hey, boys, I want that stable finished before Alexa gets out of bed. You can see the babies tomorrow." Jess chuckled from the reality of his own words and ushered Ira into the hall.

They went to the front parlor while Ira said, "I won't keep you long. I know you'll want to be with your wife, but I think you'll be pleased with the report."

"It's settled, then?" Jess asked as they were seated.

"I believe it is—finally," he added with a chuckle. "To get right to the point, Jess, I don't think you'll need to be concerned about providing for your children."

"What are you saying?" Jess held his breath.

"Well, it was amazing how many people were willing to come forth and testify once Chad Byrnehouse was dead. The evidence against him was staggering. Even though the second will was never finalized, the judge believed that Tyson Byrnehouse was murdered because of it. According to the evidence, and the fact that Mr. Byrnehouse had no remaining relatives in Australia beyond you and your wife, the judge ruled that the will be considered legitimate."

Jess was stunned. "I don't believe it," he finally said, then he laughed. "I don't believe it."

"It's true," Ira grinned. "It's all finalized and legal. As soon as you sign a few papers for me, you will officially own everything that belonged to Tyson Byrnehouse—which I would guess, combined with your own assets, makes you one of the wealthiest men in the country."

"Give me a pen," Jess laughed, then louder, "I don't believe it."

"So how does it feel?" Ira asked when it was done.

"No different," Jess stated easily. "I was already the wealthiest man in the country." He grinned broadly and patted Ira on the shoulder. "Stick around long enough to meet my children, and I'll prove it to you."

❦ ❦ ❦

Jess sat quietly in the bedroom, watching the last light of day cast shadows over the bed where Alexa lay sleeping. A day of miracles, he reminded himself yet again. It was all too incredible to be true. But it *was* true.

He moved closer to the bed and knelt beside it to marvel once more at the babies cuddling close to each other as they must have done in the womb. Jess touched a tiny fist and chuckled softly. They were both so tiny, and yet so strong, so alive. After what had happened to Alexa's first baby, neither of them had felt completely at ease. But it was over now, and everything was perfect.

One of the babies began to wiggle and make gurgling noises. Carefully Jess scooped it into his hands, hoping to console it before it woke Alexa. He'd like to know which one he was holding, but he didn't have a clue. They looked the same to him. The baby quieted as he bounced it gently. Again he marveled at the tiny miracle. His two hands together cradled it easily.

Jess watched the infant yawn and stretch, then attempt to peer up at him through dark eyes that barely opened. He contemplated all that had brought him and Alexa to this day, and speculated over what the future might hold.

"One day he'll be as tall as you," Alexa said. Jess looked up to see her watching him, a contented smile teasing the corners of her mouth.

"I must have Tyson." He turned his attention to the baby.

"You certainly do."

"How can you tell them apart?"

"When they've got their nappies on, you mean?" Jess nodded and chuckled. "Tyson has more hair than Emma."

Jess carefully set Tyson close to his sister and reached across them to kiss his wife. "How are you, my love?"

"Sore," she said with a smile, "but happy."

Jess touched her face with adoration, still marveling at all she'd been through to bring these babies into the world. "There's something I want to talk to you about, Alexa—about the babies' names."

"But we already decided." She touched her son's wispy hair. "Tyson Benjamin Davies and Emma Alexandra Davies."

"Byrnehouse-Davies," he corrected, and her eyes widened. "Yes," he clarified. "I want to make it official. I've been thinking about it for quite some time actually, and under the circumstances I think it would be appropriate. I already talked to Ira about legalizing it. What do you think?"

Alexa touched his face, warmed by his admiration for the man who had raised her. "I like it very much." She tilted her head. "When did you talk to Ira?"

"He came by earlier. I invited him to stay, but Lucy was expecting him back." Jess hesitated and tried to keep a straight face as Alexa's eyes questioned Ira's coming all the way out here. "He brought news that . . ."

"What?" she asked tensely, fearing something had gone wrong.

Jess did his best to show a grave expression, then he leaned forward to kiss her when he couldn't hold it any longer. In the midst of his kiss he began to chuckle, then he laughed.

"Jess?" Alexa pulled back with his face in her hands. "What is it?"

Jess kissed her again and hugged her tightly. "Alexandra, my love, Chad Byrnehouse has just turned over in his grave. I can feel him trying to fight his way out of hell right now."

"What on earth are you talking about?" she demanded.

"We're rich!" he whispered with a wry arch of that eyebrow. Alexa's eyes narrowed in question. "The will was declared legal, Alexa," he clarified. "You and I have just inherited a fortune."

Alexa leaned back against the headboard and put a hand over her heart. "I don't believe it."

"That's what I said," Jess laughed.

"I don't believe it," she repeated breathily.

"I said that, too." Jess laughed harder. He came around the bed to avoid disturbing the babies and pulled Alexa carefully into his arms.

"Oh, Jess!" Alexa laughed with him as she finally perceived it. "It's incredible. If I wasn't so sore, I'd jump up and down." She pulled back and touched his face. "You deserve it, Jess. You've earned it."

"*You* deserve it," he retorted, then his voice softened. "You deserve to live like a queen, Alexandra."

She kissed him with a familiar intimacy. "I already do, Jess Davies. I already do."

While Alexa attempted to nurse Tyson, Jess held Emma in the crook of his arm and played with her tiny toes. "This little girl is going to be a beautiful woman."

"Perhaps like her namesake?" Alexa said, and Jess smiled nostalgically.

"Between her mother and grandmother, she can't help but be beautiful."

"What are we going to do with it?" Alexa asked quietly.

"With the baby?"

"No," she laughed, "the money."

"I don't know," Jess said, concentrating on the infant nuzzling futilely against his hard chest, "but I do have one idea."

"What's that?"

"I told you once that if I had Chad's money, I would use it to help children like Sarina's Ben, who were born into difficult circumstances, whatever they might be. I don't know exactly how to go about it, but I intend to find a way to offer assistance and education for such children."

"You're a genius," Alexa proclaimed and kissed him vibrantly, momentarily ignoring the babies between them.

"No, my dear," he laughed, "you're the genius. I'd like to know how you made two babies at the same time. Is it anything like making apple pie out of peaches?"

"Not even close. Give me some time to recover, and I'll show you how it works."

"Promise?" he grinned.

"I promise. And as soon as Crazy has that foal, we'll have to get these children practicing so they can—"

"All in good time," Jess interrupted, chuckling.

Alexa kissed him again, then Jess methodically examined Tyson's tiny legs while the baby obliviously concentrated on his nourishment. "What do you think?" he asked. "Is he built like a jockey?"

"He'll do nicely until he gets too tall. But Emma . . ."

Jess chuckled and rubbed the tiny toes between his fingers. "I went to the studio while you were in labor." The tone of his voice turned distant. "Looking back, the whole thing still astounds me."

"That's understandable."

When Tyson was apparently finished, they exchanged babies and Jess watched in awe the ethereal picture before him. As Alexa struggled patiently to urge the baby to nurse, Jess's mind wandered through words and images. With Tyson snuggling against his shoulder and Emma content at Alexa's breast, he put his arm around his wife and spoke wistfully.

"Through the gable facing east I found my father's name. And with my children in my arms I give to them the same. A mother's gift of purest love, a father's gift of pride . . . have come to me and . . ."

"And what?" Alexa asked when he faltered.

"I can't think of an ending," he laughed.

"How about . . . on Crazy we will ride."

"That's terrible. Why don't you stick to racing and having babies."

"Well," she shrugged her shoulders, "you can't blame me for trying."

"I suppose not." Jess brushed his lips over her brow. "I guess we're all a little crazy."

ABOUT THE AUTHOR

Anita Stansfield has been writing for more than twenty years, and her best-selling novels have captivated and moved hundreds of thousands of readers with their deeply romantic stories and focus on important contemporary issues. Her interest in creating romantic fiction began in high school, and her work has appeared in *Cosmopolitan* and other publications. *The Gable Faces East* is her twelfth novel and first historical work to be published by Covenant.

Anita lives with her husband, Vince, and their five children and two cats in Alpine, Utah.